#1 *NEW YORK TIMES*
BESTSELLING AUTHOR

LISA JACKSON

NEW YORK TIMES BESTSELLING AUTHOR

RACHEL LEE

NOWHERE TO HIDE

Previously published as *Obsession* and
Cornered in Conard County

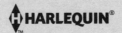

ISBN-13: 978-1-335-00888-6

Nowhere to Hide

Copyright © 2019 by Harlequin Books S.A.

First published as Obsession
by Harlequin Books in 1991
and Cornered in Conard County
by Harlequin Books in 2017.

Recycling programs
for this product may
not exist in your area.

The publisher acknowledges the copyright holders
of the individual works as follows:

Obsession
Copyright © 1991 by Lisa Jackson

Cornered in Conard County
Copyright © 2017 by Susan Civil Brown

Printed in U.S.A.

www.Harlequin.com

CONTENTS

Lisa Jackson is a #1 *New York Times* bestselling author of more than eighty-five books, including romantic suspense, thrillers and contemporary and historical romances. She is a recipient of the *RT Book Reviews* Reviewers' Choice Award and has also been honored with their Career Achievement Award for Romantic Suspense. Born in Oregon, she continues to make her home among family, friends and dogs in the Pacific Northwest. Visit her at lisajackson.com.

Books by Lisa Jackson

Illicit
Proof of Innocence
Memories
Suspicions
Disclosure: The McCaffertys
Confessions
Rumors: The McCaffertys
Secrets and Lies
Abandoned
Strangers
Sweet Revenge
Stormy Nights
Montana Fire
Risky Business
Missing
High Stakes

Visit the Author Profile page
at Harlequin.com for more titles.

OBSESSION

Lisa Jackson

Prologue

Whispering Hills Hospital

The patient rocked slowly back and forth in his chair. His eyes, deep-set and pale blue, stared at the television screen, and though he didn't speak, his lips moved, as if he were trying to say something to the woman on the small color screen, the cohost of *West Coast Morning*.

Kaylie, her name was. He had a picture of her. The one they hadn't found. The one the orderlies had overlooked. It was old and faded, the slickness nearly worn off, but every night he stared at that picture and pretended she was there, with him, in his hospital bed.

She was so beautiful. Her long blond hair shimmered in soft curls around her face, and her eyes were green-blue—like the ocean. He'd seen her once, touched her, felt her quiver against him.

He sucked in his breath at the familiar thought. He could almost smell her perfume.

"Hey! Lee, ol' buddy. How about some sound?" The orderly, the tall lanky one called Rick, walked to the television and fiddled with the controls. The volume roared, and the singsong jingle for cereal blared in a deafening roar to the patient's ears.

"Noooo!" the patient cried, clapping his hands to the sides of his head, trying to block out the sound. "No, no, no!"

"Okay, okay. Hey, man, don't get upset." Rick held his palms outward before quickly turning down the volume. "Hey, Lee, ya gotta learn to chill out a little. Relax."

"No noise!" the patient said with an effort, and Rick sighed loudly as he stripped the bed of soiled sheets.

"Yeah, I know, no noise. Just like every day at this time. I don't get it, you know. All day long you're fine, until the morning shows come on. Maybe you should watch something else—"

But the patient didn't hear. The program had resumed, and Kaylie—his Kaylie—was staring into the camera again, smiling. For him. He felt suddenly near tears as her green eyes locked with his and her perfect lips moved in silent words of love. It won't be long, he thought, his own lips twitching. Reaching deep into his pocket, he rubbed the worn picture between his thumb and forefinger.

Just wait for me. I'll come to you. Soon.

Chapter 1

"Who is this?" Zane Flannery demanded, his fingers clutching the phone's receiver in a death grip.

"Ted." The voice was barely audible; rough as a shark's skin. Zane couldn't identify the caller as a man or woman.

"Okay, Ted. So what is it?" Zane's mouth had turned to cotton, and the numbing fear that had gripped him ever since "Ted's" call the day before gnawed at his guts.

"It's Kaylie. She's not safe," the voice grated out.

Kaylie. Oh, God. A knot of painful memories twisted his stomach. "Why not?"

"I told you. Lee Johnston's about to be released."

Zane managed to keep his voice steady. "I went to the hospital. No one there is saying anything about letting him out." In fact, no one had said much of anything. Dr. Anthony Henshaw, Johnston's doctor, had been particularly tight-lipped about his patient. Phrases like patient confidentiality and maintaining patient equilibrium, had kept spouting from the doctor's mouth. He'd even had the gall to tell Zane point-blank that Zane wasn't Kaylie's husband any longer. That Zane had no *right* to be involved. Just because Zane was owner of the largest security firm on the West Coast didn't give him the authority to turn the hospital upside down or "persecute" one of his patients. Zane liked that. "Persecute." After what Johnston had attempted to do to Kaylie.

The man had nearly killed Kaylie, and now Zane was accused of "persecuting" the maniac. Figures.

In the well-modulated voice of one who weighs everything before he speaks, Henshaw had informed Zane that Johnston was still locked away and that Zane had nothing to worry about. As a patient of Whispering Hills hospital, Johnston was being observed constantly and there was nothing to fear. Though Lee was a model patient, Dr. Henshaw didn't *expect* Johnston to be released in the very near future. He *assumed* Johnston would remain a patient for "the time being."

Not good enough for Zane. He didn't work well with words like expect or assume.

Pacing between his desk and window, stretching the phone cord taut, Zane felt as helpless as he had seven years ago when Lee Johnston had nearly taken Kaylie's life.

"Why should I believe you?" Zane asked the caller, and there was a long silence. Ted was taking his time.

Zane waited him out.

"Because I care," the raspy voice stated. The phone went dead.

"Son of a bitch!" Zane slammed down the receiver and rewound the tape he'd made of the call.

Startled, the dog lying beneath Zane's desk barked, baring his teeth, dark eyes blinking open. Hairs bristled on the back of the brindled shepherd's neck.

"Relax, Franklin," Zane ordered, though his own skin prickled with dread and cold sweat collected on his forehead, underarms and hands. "Son of a damned—"

The door to his office burst open, and Brad Hastings, his second in command, strode in. A newspaper was tucked under his arm. "I called the police," he said, obviously aggravated. His dark eyes were barely slits, his nostrils flared. Not more than five-eight, but all muscle, Brad had once been a welterweight boxer and had been with Flannery Security since day one. Hastings was a force to be reckoned with. "There's nothing new on Johnston. He's locked up all right, just like Henshaw told you. As for the doctor, he seems to be on the level. He's been Johnston's shrink for five years."

And in those five years, Henshaw hadn't told Zane anything about his patient. Zane had checked in every six months or so and been told curtly that Mr. Johnston was still a patient and not much more.

When Dr. Loyola had been at Whispering Hills, things had been different. Loyola had been the admitting doctor. *He* understood the terror his patient inspired and *he'd* kept Zane informed of Johnston's progress or lack thereof. But Loyola was long gone, and no one now employed at the hospital considered Johnston a threat.

Except "Ted." Whoever the hell he was. Zane tried

to concentrate. "What about this Ted character?" Zane played back the tape, making a second copy as he did, and as Hastings listened, Zane tried to envision the man who was giving him the warning.

The tape ended. Zane rewound it again and took the copy from the recorder.

Hastings scratched the back of his balding head. "No Ted at Whispering Hills. No Ted listed as a friend or family member of Johnston."

"You checked all the workers at the hospital? Cafeteria employees, nurses, orderlies, janitors, gardeners?"

"No one with the name Theodore or Ted. The last guy to work there named Ted left two and a half years ago. He lives in Mississippi now, doesn't know a thing about what's happening at Whispering Hills these days. I talked to him myself."

Zane felt helpless, like a man struggling to desperately cling to a rope that was fraying bit by bit.

"What about a woman? Teddie, maybe," he said thoughtfully, "or Theresa, Thea, something like that?"

"You think that—" Hastings motioned skeptically toward the tape "—is a woman?"

"I couldn't tell, but I thought whoever called was disguising his or her voice…" He felt another wave of bone-chilling fear. What if the caller were Johnston himself? What if he'd had access to a phone and Bay Area phone book? What if that madman was calling Kaylie at the station?

Zane grabbed the phone again, punched out the number of the television station where she worked and drummed his fingers impatiently as the receptionist answered, then told him that Kaylie had left for the day.

Cursing under his breath, he hung up and dialed

her apartment. A recorder answered. He didn't bother to leave another message, but slammed the receiver down in frustration. *Get a grip, Flannery,* he ordered himself, but couldn't quell the fright.

Why hadn't Kaylie returned his calls? he wondered, panicking. Maybe it was already too late!

"Look, she's all right," Hastings said, as if reading his boss's thoughts. "Otherwise you would've heard. Besides, she was on the show this morning, and you know for a fact that Johnston's still at the hospital."

"For now."

Glancing surreptitiously at Zane, Hastings snorted. "I hate to bring up more bad news, but have you seen this?" He slapped the newspaper onto Zane's desk. The paper opened, and Zane realized that he was staring at page four of *The Insider,* a tabloid known for its gossip-riddled press. A grainy picture of Kaylie and the cohost of *West Coast Morning,* Alan Bently, stared up at him. They were seated at a table, laughing and talking, and Alan's arm was slung over Kaylie's shoulders. The bold headlines read: Wedding Bells For San Francisco's Number One Couple? And in smaller type: Is Kaylie Still His Number One OBSESSION?

"How can they print this stuff?" Zane growled, more irritated by the story than he had any right to be. Half of anything *The Insider* printed was purely sensationalism—nothing more than rumors. Yet Zane was infuriated by the picture of Alan and Kaylie together, and he was sickened at the hint of their marriage. It had to be a rumor just to boost ratings. He was certain Kaylie would never fall for a clown like Bently.

Worst of all was the reference to Kaylie's last movie, *Obsession,* a film that was, in Zane's estimation, the beginning of the end of his short-lived but passionate marriage to Kaylie.

Tossing the paper into the trash, Zane didn't comment, he just strode across the room and opened his closet door. He yanked his beat-up leather jacket from a hanger, and while shoving the copy of the anonymous caller's warning into the pocket of his jacket, he pushed aside any lingering jealousy he felt for Alan Bently. Zane didn't have time for emotion, especially not petty envy. Not until Kaylie was safe. A plan had been forming in his mind ever since the first chilling call from "Ted." It was time to put it into action.

Kaylie wouldn't like it. Hell, she'd fight him every step of the way. But that was just too damned bad. This time she was going to do things his way. He explained his plan to Hastings, instructed his right-hand man to take care of business and put Kaylie Melville's safety at the top of the list. "And give a copy of the tape to the police!"

Satisfied that Hastings could handle the business, he said, "I want every available man on the case. I don't give a damn about the costs. Just find out who this Ted is and what his connection is to Kaylie. And start tracing calls—calls that come in here, or to her house, or to the station where she works. I want to know where this nut case is!"

"Is that all?" Hastings mocked.

"It's all that matters," Zane muttered, shoving his fists into the pockets of his jacket. He whistled to the dog, and the sleek shepherd lifted one ear, then rose and padded after him.

Kaylie would kill him if she realized what he had

planned but he didn't care. He couldn't. Her life was more important than her damned pride.

Outside, the morning air was warm. Only a few clouds were scattered over the San Francisco sky. Zane unlocked the door of his Jeep, and the dog hopped into the back. He had one more phone call to make, he thought, pulling into the clog of traffic.

He made the call from his cellular phone.

Once his plan was set, he went about finding his headstrong ex-wife.

Hours later, Zane had tracked her down. She hadn't been at her apartment, nor had she gone back to the station, so he guessed she'd decided to spend the evening alone, at the house they'd shared in Carmel.

He parked in the familiar driveway and second-guessed himself. His plan was foolproof, but she would be furious. And she might end up hating him for the rest of her life.

But then, she didn't much like him now. She'd made it all too clear that she didn't want him in her life when she'd scribbled her signature across the divorce papers seven years before.

So why couldn't he forget her? Leave her alone? Let her fend for herself as she claimed she wanted to do?

Because she was in his blood. Always had been. Always would be. His personal curse. And he was scared.

He let the dog out of the Jeep, and the shepherd began investigating the small yard, scaring a gray tabby cat and sniffing at the shrubs.

"Stay, Franklin," Zane commanded when the dog attempted to wander too far.

Pressing on the doorbell, he waited, shifting from

one foot to the other. The house was silent. No footsteps padded to the door. Leaning on the bell again, he heard the peal of chimes within. Still no response.

Don't panic, he told himself, unnerved that he couldn't find her. Reaching into his pocket, he withdrew a set of keys he hadn't used in years and slid a key into the lock.

The lock clicked. The dead bolt slid easily.

So she hadn't bothered to change the locks. *Not smart, Kaylie.*

With a grimace, Zane pocketed his key and shoved on the familiar front door. It swung open without the slightest resistance, and he stood staring at the interior of the house that had once been his.

Swearing under his breath, he ignored the haunting memories—memories of Kaylie. Always Kaylie. God, how could one woman be imbedded so deeply in a man?

With another reminder to Franklin to stay, he closed the door behind him. Tossing his battle-worn leather jacket over the back of the couch, he surveyed the living room. Nothing much had changed. Except of course that he didn't live here, and he hadn't for a long, long time.

The same mauve carpet stretched through the house. The windows were spotless, the view of Carmel Bay as calming as he had always found it. And the furniture hadn't been moved or added to. Familiar pieces covered in white and gray were grouped around glass-topped tables. Even the artwork, framed watercolors of dolphins, sailing ships and sea gulls, provided the same splashes of blue, magenta and yellow as they had when he and Kaylie had shared this seaside cottage.

But all of the memorabilia from their marriage—
the pictures, tokens and mementos of their short life
together—were gone. Well, most of them, he thought
as he spied a single snapshot still sitting on the mantel.

The picture was of Kaylie and him, arms linked,
standing ankle-deep in white, hot sand on their honeymoon in Mazatlán. He picked up the snapshot and
scowled at the heady memories of hot sun, cold wine
and Kaylie's supple body yielding to his. The scent of
the ocean and perfume mingled with the perfume of
tropical flowers and a vision of a vast Mexican sky.

Dropping the photograph as if it suddenly seared his
fingers, he snorted in disgust. No time to think about
the past. It was over and done. Already, just being
near Kaylie was making him crazy. Well, he'd better
get used to it.

He crossed the room. Freshly cut flowers scented
the air and reminded him of Kaylie. Always Kaylie.
Despite the divorce and the past seven painful years
alone, he'd never truly forgotten her, never been able
to go to bed at night without feeling a hot pang of regret that she wasn't beside him, that he wasn't in her
life any longer.

Shoving the sleeves of his pullover up his forearms,
he walked to the recessed bar near a broad bank of windows. He leaned on one knee, dug through the cabinet
and smiled faintly when he found his favorite brand
of Scotch, the bottle dusty from neglect, the seal still
unbroken. With a flick of his wrist he opened the bottle, just as, by confronting her, he was reopening all
the old hurt and pain, the anger and fury, and the passion… As damning as it was exciting. Closing his eyes,
he reined in his runaway emotions—emotions over

which he usually had tight control. Except where Kaylie was concerned.

"Fool." Straightening, he poured himself a stiff shot. "Here's to old times," he muttered, then tossed back most of the drink, the warm, aged liquor hitting the back of his throat in a fiery splash.

Home at last, he thought ironically, topping off his glass again as he sauntered to the French doors.

Through the paned glass, he stared down the cliff to the beach below. Relief, in a wave, washed over him. There she was—safe! With no madman stalking her. She walked from the surf, wringing saltwater from her long, sun-streaked hair as if she hadn't a care in the world. If she only knew.

Wearing only a white one-piece swimming suit that molded to her body, sculpting her breasts and exposing the tanned length of her slim legs, she tossed her thick, curly mane over her shoulders.

His gut tightened as he watched her bend over and scoop up a towel from the white sand. The next couple of weeks were going to be hell.

Kaylie shook the sand from her towel, then looped the terry cloth around her neck. The last few rays of sun dried the water on her back and warmed her shoulders as she slipped into her thongs and cast one last longing glance at the sea. Sailboats skimmed the horizon, dark silhouettes against a blaze of magenta and gold. Gulls wheeled high overhead, filling the air with their lonely cries.

The beach was nearly deserted as she climbed up the weathered staircase to the house. Leaving her thongs on the deck, she pushed open the back door, then tossed her towel into the hamper in the laundry room. Maybe she'd pour herself a glass of wine. Pulling down the strap of her bathing suit, she headed for the bedroom. First a long, hot shower and then—

"How're you, Kaylie?" a familiar voice drawled.

Kaylie gasped, stopping dead in her tracks. The hairs on the back of her neck rose, and she spun around quickly, drops from her hair spraying against the wall. *Zane? Here? Now? Why?*

Draped over the couch, long jean-clad legs stretched out in front of him, he looked as damnably masculine as he ever had. His ankles were crossed, his expression bland, except for the lifting of one dark brow. However, she knew him too well and expected his pose of studied relaxation was all for show.

His steely gray gaze touched hers, and his lips quirked. For a few seconds she remembered how much she had loved him, how much she had wanted to spend the rest of her life with him. With an effort, she closed her mind to such traitorous thoughts. Her throat worked, and slowly she became conscious that one strap of her swimsuit dangled over her forearm, leaving the swell of her breast exposed.

"W-what the devil are you doing here—trying to scare me to death?" she finally spluttered, adjusting the strap back over her shoulder. But before he could respond, she changed her mind and shook her head. She wasn't up to talking to Zane—not now, probably not ever. "No, wait, don't answer that, I don't think I want to know."

He didn't budge, damn him, just lounged there, on *her* couch, drinking *her* Scotch, stretched out and making himself comfortable. His nerve was unbelievable, and yet there was something about him, something restless and dangerous that still touched a forbidden part of her heart. And she knew he wouldn't have shown up without a reason.

His scuffed running shoes dropped to the floor. "You didn't call me back."

She felt a jab of guilt. She'd gotten his messages, but hadn't worked up the courage to talk to him. "And that's why you're here?"

"I was worried about you."

"Oh, please, don't start with this," she said, reminded of the reasons she'd divorced him, his all-consuming need to protect her. "You don't have to worry about me or even be concerned that—"

"Lee Johnston's going to be released."

The words were like frigid water poured over her, stopping her cold. Zane's feigned casualness disappeared.

"He's *what?*" she whispered. In her mind's eye, she pictured Lee Johnston, a short, burly man with flaming red hair and lifeless blue eyes. And she remembered the knife—oh, God, the long-bladed knife that he'd pressed to her throat.

"Y-you're sure about this?" Oh, Lord, how could she keep her voice from quavering? The look on his face convinced her that he believed she was in grave danger, and yet she didn't want to believe it. Not entirely. There were too many dimensions to Zane to take anything he said at face value. Although she'd never known him to lie.

He hesitated, rubbing the back of his neck thoughtfully. "Someone called me."

"Who?"

"I don't know. Someone who called himself 'Ted.'"

"Ted? Ted who?" she asked.

"I wish I knew. I thought maybe you could help me figure it out," he admitted, launching into his short tale and starting with the first nerve-jangling call from "Ted," and ending with his gut feeling that Dr. Henshaw was holding out on him. "Do you have a recorder—a tape player?"

She nodded mutely, then retrieved the portable player from her bedroom. Zane picked up his jacket and took out a small tape, which he snapped into the machine. A few seconds later, "Ted's" warning echoed through the room.

"Oh, my God," Kaylie whispered, her hand to her mouth. She listened to the tape twice, her insides wrenching as the warning was repeated. Zane, though he attempted to appear calm, was coiled tightly, his features tense, his eyes flicking from her to the corners of the room, as if he half expected someone to jump out and attack her.

Why now? she wondered frantically. *Why ever?*

She bit her lower lip, then thinking it a sign of weakness, stopped just as the tape clicked off. "Why did this 'Ted' guy call you? Why not me?"

"Beats me," Zane admitted, sipping amber liquor from a short glass, his jaw sliding pensively to the side. "None of this is official. At least not yet." Zane's features were hard, and a quiet fury burned in his eyes. "So far we've only got this guy's—whoever he is— word for it. I talked with Johnston's psychiatrist and I didn't like what he said."

"But he didn't say Johnston would be released." She turned pleading eyes up at him.

"No, but I've got a gut feeling on this one. Henshaw was being too careful. My bet is that the man's going to walk, Kaylie. Whoever called me had a reason."

"Oh, God." Her whole body shook. Stark moments of terror returned—memories of a deranged man who'd sworn he'd kill for her. "They can't let him go. He's sick! Beyond sick!"

Zane lifted a shoulder. "He's been locked up a long time. Model patient. It wouldn't surprise me if the courts decide he got better."

Her world spun back to that horrible night when Johnston had threatened her, waved a knife in front of her eyes, his other arm hard against her stomach as he'd dragged her from the theater. He'd sworn then that he would kill for her and he wanted her to witness the sacrifice…

In her mind's eye, she could still see his crazed smile, feel him tremble excitedly against her, smell the scent of his stale breath.

She sagged against the wall and felt the rough texture of plaster against her bare back. *Think, Kaylie,* she told herself, refusing to appear weak. Swallowing back her fear, she straightened and squared her shoulders. She couldn't fall apart—she wouldn't! Forcing her gaze to Zane's, she silently prayed she didn't betray any of the panic surging through her veins. "I think I'd better talk to Henshaw myself."

"Be my guest."

On weak legs she walked into the kitchen, looked up the number of the mental hospital, and dialed with shaky fingers. A receptionist answered on the fourth ring. "Whispering Hills."

"Yes, oh, I'd like to talk to Dr. Henshaw, please. This is Kaylie Melville—I, um, I know one of his patients."

"Oh, Miss Melville! Of course. I see you on television every morning," the voice exclaimed excitedly. "But I'm sorry, Dr. Henshaw isn't in right now."

"Then maybe I could speak to someone else." Kaylie tried to explain her predicament, but she couldn't get past square one with the cheery voice on the other end of the line. No other doctor would talk to her, nor a nurse for that matter. On impulse she asked to talk to Ted and was informed that no one named Ted was employed by the hospital. Before the receptionist could hang up, Kaylie asked, "Please, just tell me, is Mr. Lee Johnston still a patient there?"

"Yes, he is," she said, whispering a little. "But I really can't tell you anything else. I'm sorry, but we have rules about discussing patients, you know. If you'll leave your number, I'll ask Dr. Henshaw to call you."

"Thanks," Kaylie whispered, replacing the receiver. She poured herself a glass of water and tried to quiet the raging fear. *Think, Kaylie, think! Don't fall apart!* She drank the water, then made fists of her hands, willing herself to be calm.

When she walked back into the living room, Zane still sat on the couch, his elbows propped on his knees, his silvery eyes dark with concern. A part of her loved him for the fact that he cared, another part despised him for shoving his way back into her life when she'd just about convinced herself that she was over him.

"Well?"

"I didn't get very far. Henshaw's out. He'll call back."

The furrow in Zane's brow deepened.

Kaylie, trying to take control of the situation, said, "I'll—I'll talk to my lawyer."

"I already did."

"You *what?*" she demanded, surprised that Zane would call *her* attorney, the very man who had drawn up the papers for their divorce.

"I called Blake. His hands are tied."

She was already ahead of him. "Then I'll talk to Detective Montello. He was the arresting officer. Surely he'd…" Her voice faded as she saw him shake his head, his dark hair rubbing across the back of his collar. "Unless you've already called him, too."

"Montello's not with the force any longer. The guy who took his place says he'll look into it."

"But you don't believe him," she said, guessing, her heart beginning to pound at the thought of Lee Johnston on the loose. Icy sweat collected between her shoulder blades.

"I just don't want to take any chances."

For the first time, she thought about him being in the house—waiting for her when she finished her swim. "Wait a minute, how did you get in here?"

Zane glanced away, avoiding her eyes. "I still have my keys."

"You *what?*" she demanded, astounded at his audacity. He hadn't seemed to age in the past seven years. His hair was still a rich, coffee brown, his features rough hewn and handsome. His eyes, erotic gray, were set deep behind thick black brows and long, spiky lashes. "But you gave them to me," she said.

He offered her that same, off-center smile she'd found so disconcerting and sexy in the past. "I had an extra set."

"And you kept them. So that seven years later you could break and enter? Of all the low, despicable… You have no right, *no right* to barge in here and make yourself at home—"

"I still care about you, Kaylie."

All further protests died on her lips. Emotions, long buried, enveloped her, blinded her. Love and hate, anger and fear, joy and sorrow all tore at her as she remembered how much he had meant to her. Her breath was suddenly trapped tight in her lungs, and she had to swallow before she could speak. She shook her head. "Don't, okay? Just…don't." She willfully controlled the traitorous part of her that wanted to trust him, to believe him, to love him again. Instead she concentrated on the truth. She couldn't allow herself to feel anything for him. What they'd shared was long over. And their marriage hadn't been a partnership. It had been a prison—a beautiful but painful fortress where their fragile love hadn't had a ghost of a chance.

"Look, Kaylie, I just thought you should know that Johnston's about to become a free man—"

"Oh, Lord." Her knees went weak again, and her insides turned cold.

Zane sighed, offering her a tender look that once would have soothed her. But he didn't cross the room, didn't hold her as he once would have. Instead he rubbed impatiently at the back of his neck and glanced at a picture on the mantel—the small snapshot of their honeymoon. "Johnston was obsessed with you before, and I doubt that's changed."

"I haven't heard from him in a long while."

"No letters?"

She shook her head, trying to convince herself that

Lee Johnston had forgotten her. After all, it had been years since that terrifying encounter, and the man had been in a mental hospital, receiving treatment. Maybe he'd changed...

"Don't even think it," Zane warned, as if reading the expressions on her face. "He's a maniac. A psycho. He always will be."

Deep down, Kaylie knew Zane was right. But what could she do? Live her life in terrified paranoia that Lee Johnston might come after her again? No way. She glanced down and noticed that she was wearing only her bathing suit still. "Your information could be wrong," she said, walking to the laundry room, where she snagged her cover-up off a brass hook near the door. Standing half-naked in front of him only made the situation worse. She struggled into the peach-colored oversize top and pulled her hair through the neck hole only to find that Zane had followed her and was standing in the arch between the kitchen and laundry room, one shoulder propped against the wall. His gaze flicked down her body to her thighs, where the hem of her cover-up brushed against her bare skin.

"And the call?"

"A crank call."

"You really think so?" he asked.

"I—I don't know." Kaylie cleared her throat and tried to concentrate on the conversation. "But I think you overreacted by driving all the way down here—"

"I called, damn it," he snapped, his patience obviously in shreds as his eyes flashed back to hers. "But you didn't bother to call me back."

She felt another guilty pang, but ignored it. She'd considered returning his call and had even reached for the phone once or twice, but each time she'd stopped, unsure that she could deal with him and unwilling to complicate her life again.

"You didn't say anything about Johnston—"

"Of course not! I didn't want to freak you out with a message on your recorder."

"Well, you're doing a damn good job of it now," she snapped, her own composure hanging by a thread. Just seeing Zane again sent all her emotions reeling, and now this…this talk about Johnston. It was just too much. Her nerves were stretched to the breaking point.

Zane's voice was softer. "Look, Kaylie, I think you should take some precautions—go low profile."

"Low profile?" she repeated, trying to get a grip on herself as she walked past him into the kitchen. She couldn't let him see her falling apart; she'd fought hard for her independence and she had to prove to him—and to herself—that she was able to take care of herself. She picked up a small pitcher and began watering the small pots of African violets behind her sink. But as she moved the glass pitcher from one small blossom to the next, the stream of water spilled on the blue tiles. She mopped up the mess with a towel and felt Zane's eyes watching her, taking stock of her nervousness. "And what do you think I should do?" she asked, glancing over her shoulder.

His gaze, so rock steady it was maddening, met hers. "First of all, install new locks—a couple of dead bolts and a security system. State-of-the-art equipment."

"With lasers and sirens and a secret code?" she mocked, trying to break the tension.

"With motion detectors and alarms. But that won't

be enough. If Johnston's released, you'll need me, Kaylie. It's as simple as that."

Desperate now, she tried to joke. "You? As what?
My bodyguard again?" She watched him flinch. "I
don't think so—"

His hand shot out and he caught her wrist, spinning
her around. She dropped her dish towel. "I'm serious,
Kaylie," he assured her, his voice low, nearly threatening. "This is nothing to joke about!"

Was he out of his mind? The inside of her wrist felt
hot, and she fought the urge to lick her lips.

"And I think it would be best if you took some time
off—"

"Now, wait a minute, I can't leave the station high
and dry!"

"Your career just about did you in before," he reminded her, then glanced down to where his fingers
were wrapped around her arm. Slowly he withdrew his
hand. "You need a less visible job." Then, as if realizing his request bordered on the ridiculous, he wiped
his palms on his jeans and added, "Why don't you just
ask for a leave of absence until this mess with Johnston
is straightened out?"

"No way. I'm not going to live the rest of my life
in high anxiety—especially over some stupid call."
Though she was afraid, she couldn't give in to the fear
that had numbed her after Johnston's last attack. And
the man *was* still locked away.

Tossing her damp curls over her shoulder, she
reached down and grabbed the towel from the floor.
Her wrist, where Zane had held it so possessively only
seconds before, still burned, but she ignored the sensa-

tion, refused to rub the sensitive spot where the pads of his fingers had left their impressions.

"Look, Kaylie," he said, his voice edged with exasperation. "I'm just trying to help you."

"And I appreciate it," she replied, though they both knew she was lying, that the question of her independence had been a determining factor in their divorce. "I—I'll take care of myself, Zane. Thanks for the warning," she heard herself say, though a part of her screamed that she was crazy to let him go—that she needed him to keep her safe. She extended her hand, palm up. "Now, I think you have something of mine?" When he didn't move, she prodded him again. "The keys?"

Zane's eyes darkened to the shade of storm clouds.

Her heart began to pound. He wasn't giving up. She could see his determination in the set of his jaw.

"How about a deal?" he suggested, not moving.

"Believe me, I'm not in the mood."

"The keys for a date."

"For a *date?* Get real—"

"I am, Kaylie. You go out with me, just for old times' sake, and I'll turn the keys over to you."

"And in the meantime you won't make an extra set?"

"We'll go tonight. I won't have time to do anything so devious."

Kaylie wasn't so sure. And she was tempted, far more than she wanted to be. Standing so close to Zane, seeing the shading of his eyes, feeling the raw masculinity that was so uniquely his, she was lured into the prospect of spending some time with him again. There had been a time in her life when he'd been everything. From bodyguard to lover to husband. Her life with him had seemed so natural, so right...until the horrid night when their safe little world was thrown upside down. All because of Lee Johnston.

Kaylie had fallen in love with Zane, trusted him, relied upon him. Now her throat grew dry, and she shook all the happy memories aside. She couldn't trust herself when she thought of the first magic moments they'd shared—when their love had been new and fresh, before Zane had become so intolerably overprotective and domineering. No. Her dependence on him was long over. Now she was older, and wiser, and on to his tricks. She wouldn't repeat past mistakes. "I don't think a date would be such a good idea."

"Come on, Kaylie, what've you got to lose?" he asked, his voice low and disturbingly familiar.

Everything she thought, her palms beginning to sweat.

"You've got other plans tonight?" he asked.

"No—"

"No date with Alan?" he mocked, obviously referring to the ridiculous article in *The Insider.* Her producer had left a copy of the rag on her desk as a joke. She wasn't engaged to Alan and never would be, but no amount of denial to the press had seemed to change the public's view that she and Alan, who had once been costars of *Obsession* and were now cohosts of a popular morning show, were not lovers.

"No date with Alan," she said dryly.

"Then there's no reason not to spend a little time with me. Come on," he insisted, his smile irresistible.

"But—" Why not? It's just a few hours, a voice inside her head teased. Wouldn't it be nice to rely on him just a little and find out what he really knows about Lee

Johnston? What could it hurt? She looked up at him and swallowed hard. There was a tiny part of her, a feminine part she tried to deny, that loved Zane's image of power and brooding masculinity, that being around him did make her feel warm inside. But being around Zane was unsafe—her emotions were still much too raw.

"Let's go. I know a great place in the mountains. You can tell me all about your career as a talk-show hostess and maybe you'll be able to convince me that you'll take all the precautions necessary to keep you safe from Johnston."

"Okay," she finally agreed, telling herself she *wasn't* excited about the prospect of spending time with him. "But I'll need time to change."

"I'll wait," he said amiably as he walked back to the bar. She watched him pour a drink, as she'd watched him a hundred times before. His shirt was a dark blue. His sleeves were pushed over his forearms to expose dark-skinned muscles that moved fluidly as he handled the bottle and glass. And his hands... She shouldn't even look at his long, sensual fingers and blunt-cut nails.

She swallowed hard against the memories—erotic memories that she'd hoped she'd forgotten. His gaze found hers in the mirror over the bar, and he smiled a little sexy smile. Her insides quivered.

Turning quickly, before she stared any longer, she headed for the bedroom and told herself that she was a fool, but now that she'd committed herself, somehow she'd get through the evening ahead.

Chapter 2

Zane tried to ignore the disturbing sensations—sensations that were way out of line. Kaylie was his ex-wife for crying out loud, and here he was, pouring himself another drink, feeling like a teenager in the throes of lust. Returning to this house—this cottage by the sea where he and Kaylie had spent hours making love—had probably been a mistake of colossal proportions, but he'd had no choice. Not if he wanted his plan to work. And he did. More than anything.

After the divorce he'd promised himself he'd give her room to grow. When he'd married her she'd been nineteen, and the most beautiful woman he'd ever met. Blond and tanned, slim and coy. Her laugh had been special, her touch divine.

Though he'd fought his attraction to her, he couldn't resist the wide innocence in her eyes, the genuine smile that curved her lips, her ingenious wit, though it was often used at his expense. His hands tightened around his glass as he remembered the scent of her perfume, the feel of her skin rubbing against his, the wonder of looking down into her eyes as he'd made love to her. And it had all changed the night a maniac had held a knife to her beautiful throat.

Now Kaylie was beautiful but mature, her humor sharper, her sarcasm biting. Yet he still wanted her— more than a man with any sense should want a woman.

And now her life was threatened.

Paralyzing fear gripped him. Living without her had been hell. He'd just have to convince her that they belonged together. Hearing the bedroom door open, he turned, and his throat went desert dry.

She was dressed in a white off-the-shoulder dress, her blond curls swept away from one side of her face, her eyes glinting with a gloriously seductive green light. "Okay, cowboy, this is your ride. Where're we going?"

The line was from one of her movies—she'd said it to him as well, late at night, when they had been alone in bed. Had she remembered? Undoubtedly. Zane's diaphragm pressed hard against his lungs. "It's a surprise."

She tilted her head at an angle. "Well, it had better be a short surprise. I have to get up at five tomorrow to tape the show."

"I'll have you back by ten," he lied, pretending ease as he snagged his scuffed jacket off the back of the couch and walked with her to the front door.

He reached for the knob, but she laid a hand across his. "This is all on the up and up, isn't it? One dinner and then you'll hand over the keys?"

His gut twisted. "That was the bargain."

"Then I'll trust you," she said, the corners of her beautiful mouth relaxing.

He felt a twinge of guilt at deceiving her, but shrugged it off as he opened the door and she swept outside ahead of him. He'd played by her rules long enough. Now it was time she played by his.

Kaylie was nervous as a cat when, as they walked outside, she discovered a large brown-and-black shepherd lying on the porch. "Who are *you?*"

"Man's best friend. Right, Franklin?" Zane said, whistling as he opened the back door of the Jeep and the dog leaped inside.

"You bring him on all your dates?" she teased.

He flicked her an interested glance. "My chaperon," he drawled. "Just to keep you in line."

"Me?" she replied, but grinned as she slid into the passenger side. Maybe this date wouldn't turn out to be the disaster she'd predicted.

Casting a glance in his direction as he climbed behind the wheel, she realized that he would never change. He'd always be strong, arrogant, determined, stubborn and self-righteous. But funny, she reminded herself. He had been blessed with a sense of humor.

Still, she was uneasy. She'd seen his mouth turn down when she'd quoted one of his favorite lines from an old movie. She'd done it on purpose, to check his reaction. He'd tried to hide his surprise, but she'd noticed the ghost of change in his eyes.

So why hadn't she refused to get into the Jeep with him?

Kaylie cast her eyes about, not wanting to confront

her actions. A part of her was still intrigued with him. And she'd been lonely in the past seven years. She'd missed him far more than she'd ever admit. Yes, she couldn't handle the way he'd overreacted and tried to treat her like some fragile possession, but she'd missed his smile. She recalled it now with bittersweet poignancy, how that lazy slash of white would gleam against a darkened jaw as she'd awakened in his arms.

Her heart pounded at the memory, and she silently cursed herself for being a nostalgic idiot. So she missed his sexy looks, his playful grin, his presence in her house.

He headed east, leaving the sun to cast a few dying rays over the darkening waters of the Pacific. The sky had turned a dusky shade of lavender, reflected in the restless sea.

Zane drove without saying much, but she could sense him watching her, smell the clean earthy scent of his after-shave. She'd been crazy to agree to this, she decided. She was much too aware of him.

"Why did we leave the city?" she asked, to break the awkward silence stretching between them.

"Because I discovered a place you'll like."

"In Kansas?"

His sensual lips twitched. "Not quite."

"So let me get this straight. You thought, 'Gee, Lee Johnston's about to be released from the hospital—this would be a great time to break into Kaylie's house and take her to dinner in some restaurant in Timbuktu.'"

He grinned. "You're astounding, Kaylie. The way you read me like a book," he said sarcastically. "You know, that's exactly what I thought!"

She rolled her eyes and held her tongue for the rest of the journey.

Two hours later, Kaylie's stomach rumbled as she stepped out of his Jeep and eyed the restaurant he'd chosen. She'd expected him to take her to one of their old haunts along the waterfront in Carmel where they could eat seafood and laugh, drink a little wine and remember the good times—the few carefree times they'd shared as man and wife. When he'd mentioned the mountains, her interest had been piqued.

This place, this ivy-covered, two-storied house that looked as if it had been built before the turn of the century, wasn't like Zane at all. Mystified, she walked up the worn steps to a wide plank porch. A few rockers moved with the wind, and leaves in the surrounding maple and ash trees rustled as they turned with the breeze. *Quaint,* she thought. And so unlike Zane.

She eyed him from beneath her lashes, but his strong features seemed relaxed, his face handsome and rakish, one thatch of dark hair falling over his eyes. He shoved the wayward lock from his forehead, but it fell back again, making him look less than perfect and all the more wonderful.

Get a grip, she reminded herself as they walked into the old house and Zane tied Franklin to a tree near the entrance.

"You sure he won't scare the guests?" Kaylie asked.

"This ol' boy? No way," Zane said, rubbing the dog behind his ears.

Inside, a maître d' escorted them to a small table in what once had been the parlor.

Zane ordered wine for them both, then after a waiter

had poured them each a glass of claret, Zane touched his glass to hers. "To old times," he said.

"And independence," she replied.

They dined on fresh oysters, grilled scallops, vegetables and crusty warm bread. Zane's features seemed sharper in the candlelight, his eyes a warmer shade of gray as he poured the last of the bottle into their glasses, then ordered another.

Conversation was difficult. Kaylie talked of work at the station; Zane listened, never contributing. As if in unspoken agreement, they didn't discuss Lee Johnston.

"So where'd you get the dog?" she asked as he topped off her glass. She was beginning to relax as the wine seeped into her blood.

"He used to work for the police."

"What happened—they fire him?"

"He retired."

Kaylie stifled a yawn and tried not to notice the play of candlelight in his hair. "And you ended up with him."

Zane shrugged. "We get along."

"Better than we did?" she asked, leaning back in her chair and sipping from her glass.

"Much."

"He must do just as you say."

Zane's teeth flashed in the soft light. "That's about the size of it."

Kaylie was caught up in the romantic mood of the old house with its wainscoted walls and flickering sconces. A fire glowed in the grate and no one else was seated in the small room, though there were four other tables near the windows.

"How'd you arrange this?" she asked, finishing her

second—or was it her third?—glass of wine. Pinpoints of light reflected against the crystal.

"Arrange what?"

She motioned to the empty room. "The privacy."

"Oh, connections," he said offhandedly, and she was reminded again of how powerful he'd become as his security business had taken off and his clientele had expanded to the rich and famous. He'd opened an office that catered to Beverly Hills, another to Hollywood, as well as San Francisco, Portland, Seattle and on and on. In seven years his business had prospered, as if he'd thrown himself body and soul into the company after their divorce.

He refilled her glass. "I thought we should be alone."

"What? No bodyguards? No private investigators?" she teased, then regretted her sarcasm when his eyes darkened.

"I think we should declare a truce."

"Is that possible for divorced people?" she asked, and watched as he twisted his wineglass in his fingers.

"Mature divorced people."

"Oh, well, we're that, aren't we? And I guess you're bodyguard enough, right?" She sipped the wine and felt a languid sleepiness run through her blood. Maybe she should slow down on the claret. It was just that she was so nervous around him. Her muscles relaxed, and she slumped lower in her chair, eyeing him over the rim of her glass. He was so handsome, so erotically male, so…dangerous to be around.

The waiter cleared their plates and brought coffee. He offered dessert, but both Zane and Kaylie declined.

"Well," she said as Zane reached into his wallet for his credit card, "don't forget the keys."

"The what?"

"Your end of the bargain. The keys to my house."

"Oh, right." He dropped his credit card on the tray, then reached into his pocket and withdrew a key ring from which he extracted two keys. He slid them across the table. "There you go. Front door and garage."

She could hardly believe it as she plopped the keys into her wallet. "No strings attached?"

Something flickered in his eyes, but quickly disappeared. "No strings."

Kaylie felt a twinge of remorse for thinking so little of him. Why couldn't she open her heart and trust him—just a little? Because she couldn't trust herself around him, she thought with realistic fatalism.

They walked outside and into a balmy night. The sky had darkened, and jewellike stars winked high over the mountains. Zane opened the Jeep door for Kaylie, and Franklin hopped onto the passenger seat, growling as Zane ordered him into the back.

"You're in his space," Zane explained. The dog jumped nimbly into the back seat, but his dark eyes followed Kaylie's every move as she climbed inside.

"I don't know if that's so safe."

"He's fine. He likes you."

"Oh, right."

Once back on the road, Zane switched on the radio, and the soft music, coupled with the drone of the engine and the security of being with Zane again made Kaylie feel a contentment she hadn't experienced in years.

Drowsy from the wine, she leaned her head against the window and glimpsed his profile through the sweep of her curling, dark lashes. His hair brushed his collar, his eyes squinted into the darkness as he drove, staring through the windshield.

The road serpentined through dark forests of pine. Every once in a while the trees receded enough to allow a low-hanging moon to splash a silvery glow over the mountainside.

Kaylie leaned back against the leather seat and closed her eyes. The notes of a familiar song, popular during the short span of their marriage, drifted through the speaker. She punched a button on the radio and classical music filled the interior of the Jeep. That was better. No memories here. She'd just let the music carry her away. Her muscles relaxed, and she sighed heavily, not intending to doze off.

But she did. On a cloud of wine and warmth she drifted out of consciousness.

Furtively, his palms sweating, Zane watched her from the corner of his eye. He noticed that her jaw and arms slackened and her breasts rose and fell in even, deep breaths.

Ten minutes passed. She didn't stir. *It's now or never,* he thought as he approached the intersection. Turning off the main road and heading into the mountains, he guided the car eastward.

There was a chance she'd end up hating him for his deception and high-handedness, but it was a chance he had to take. He frowned into the darkness, his eyes on the two-lane highway that cut through the dark stands of pine and redwood. *Don't wake up,* he thought as the seconds ticked by and the miles passed much too slowly.

It took nearly an hour to reach the old logging road,

but he slowed, rounded a sharp corner and shifted down. From here on in, the lane—barely more than two dirt ruts with a spray of gravel—was rough. It angled up the mountain in sharp switchbacks.

He drove slowly, but not slowly enough. Before he'd gone two miles, Kaylie stirred.

The Jeep hit a rock and shimmied and she started. Stretching and swallowing back a yawn, she blinked, her brows knit in concentration. "Where are we?"

"Not in Carmel yet."

"I guess not," she said, rotating the crick out of her shoulders and neck as her eyes adjusted to the darkness. "What is this—a park?"

"Nope."

"Zane?"

He heard her turn toward him. The air was suddenly charged. For a few seconds all he heard was the thrum of the engine and the strains of some familiar concerto on the radio.

Finally she whispered, "We're not going back to Carmel, are we?"

No reason to lie any longer. "No."

"No?"

When he didn't answer, pure anger sparkled in her eyes. "I knew it! I knew it!" she shouted. "I should have never trusted you!" She flopped back in the seat. "Kaylie, you idiot!" she ranted, outraged. "After all he's done to you, you trust him!"

Zane's heart twisted.

She skewered him with a furious glare. "Okay, Zane, just where are you taking me?"

"To my weekend place."

"In the boonies?"

"Right." He nodded crisply.

"But you don't have—"

"You don't know what I have now, do you?" he threw back at her. "In the past seven years I've acquired a few new things."

"A mountain cabin? It's hardly your style."

"Maybe you don't know what my style is anymore."

"Then I guess I'll find out, won't I? I can hardly wait," she muttered, her eyes thinning in fury. She tossed her hair over her shoulder and waited, then quietly, her voice trembling with rage, she asked, "Why?"

"Because you won't listen to reason."

"I don't understand."

"We're talking about your life, damn it. And you were going to go on as if nothing had happened, as if this—" he reached into his pocket and extracted the tape "—doesn't exist! Well, it does, damn it, and until I find out if there's any reason to believe 'Ted,' I'm going to make sure you're safe."

"You're what? How?" she asked, though she was beginning to understand. "I think you'd better stop this rig and turn it around, right now," she ground out.

"No way."

"I'm warning you, if you don't take me home, I'll file charges against you for kidnapping!"

"Go right ahead," he said with maddening calm. He cranked on the wheel to round another corner.

"You can't do this!" she cried. What was he thinking?

"I'm doing it, aren't I?"

"I mean it, Zane," she said, her voice low and threatening. "Take me back to Carmel right now, or I'll make your life miserable!"

"You already have," he said through tightly clenched teeth. "The day you walked out on me."

"I didn't—"

"Like hell!" he roared, and from the back seat Franklin growled. Zane flicked her a menacing glance. "You didn't give me—us—a chance."

"We were married a year!" Even to her own ears, it sounded as brief as it had been.

"Not long enough!"

"This is madness!"

"Probably," he responded with deceptive calm, wheeling around a final corner. The Jeep lurched to a stop in the middle of a clearing. "But, damn it, this time I'm not taking any chances with your life!"

Kaylie stared out the window at the massive log cabin. Even in the darkness, she could see that the house was huge, with a sloping roof, dormers and large windows reflecting the twin beams of the headlights. "Where are we?" she demanded.

"Heaven," he replied.

She didn't believe him. Her heart squeezed at the thought of being alone with him. How would she ever control the emotions that tore through her soul?

Oh, no, Kaylie thought, this giant log house wasn't heaven. To her, it looked like pure hell!

Chapter 3

"This will never work," Kaylie predicted as Zane cut the engine.

"It already has." He walked out to the back of the vehicle, opened the hatchback, unrolled a trap and yanked out two suitcases. Franklin scrambled over the back seat and bounded onto the gravel road.

Thunderstruck, Kaylie didn't move. *His suitcases,* for crying out loud! Her heart dropped to her knees. Zane had planned this kidnapping before they left Carmel. And she'd been played for a fool!

"Let's go inside," he said.

"You're not serious. This is a colossal joke, right?" But she knew from the rigid thrust of his chin that he wasn't joking.

To his credit, he did seem concerned. The lines around the edges of his mouth were harsh, and he actually looked disconcerted by her outrage. "Look," he finally said, glaring down at her. "Are you planning to stay out here and freeze?"

"No, I'm going to wait for common sense to strike you so that you'll drive me back home!"

"It's gonna be a long wait."

That did it. She hopped out of the Jeep. Her sandaled feet crunched in gravel as she marched up to him. "This is crazy, Zane, just plain crazy."

"Maybe." He strode up the plank steps, fumbled with a key in the dark and shoved hard on a heavy oak door.

"If you think I'm going in there with you, you've got another think coming!"

He ignored her outburst. A few seconds later, the house lights blazed cozily from paned windows. "Come on, Kaylie," he called from deep in the interior. "You're here now. You may as well make the best of it."

But she wasn't done fighting yet. Crossing her arms over her chest, she waited. She'd be damned if she'd walk into this…this prison for God's sake! She had no intention—

He clicked on the porch lights and stood on the threshold of the log house. Kaylie didn't budge. As if rooted to the gravel drive, she tried to ignore the fact that he nearly filled the doorway, his shoulders almost touching each side of the doorjamb. And she refused to be swayed by the handsome sight of his long, lean frame, thrown in relief by the interior light behind him. She was just too damned mad.

"It's gonna get cold out here."

"I'm not going inside."

"Oh, yes, you are."

"No way, Flannery," she argued, her head pounding from too much wine, her pride deflated. "What's going to happen is that you're going back into the house for your keys, then you're going to climb back into this damned Jeep and take me home. Maybe I'll forget about pressing charges for breaking and entering and kidnapping and you'll be a free man!"

He shook his head and rolled his eyes to the night-darkened heavens. "Don't you know you can't bully me, Kaylie?"

"And here I thought you were the one doing the bullying!" she snapped back. It didn't matter what his reasons for bringing her here were. Whether Lee Johnston was in the hospital or on the loose, Zane had no right, *no right,* to force his will on her. The fact that he'd purposely planned to shanghai her was more than she could take.

Slowly, his face knotted in frustration, he started back down the steps. His eyes were trained on her face. "Come on, Kaylie."

"Out of the question."

"Look, you're getting into that house if I have to carry you in there myself!"

"No way." Her throat went dry as he advanced on her. She had the urge to run as fast as her legs would carry her, but she didn't want to give him the satisfaction of seeing her flee. No, by God, she'd stand up to him. And hold her ground she did, not moving an inch when he strode up so close that his shoes nudged the toes of her sandals.

"We can do this the hard way, or you can make it easy."

"Take me home, Zane," she said more softly. In the

shadows she thought she saw him hesitate, and that flicker of doubt gave her hope. Maybe he'd change his mind. She touched his arm and watched his jaw clench. "This is insane. We both know it. Johnston's still under lock and key and I've got to get back. Come on, Zane, this…this…stunt of yours is just no good and I'm—I'm not moving until you assure me we're going back to Carmel!"

"Have it your way," he said softly. His hands circled her waist. "But don't say I didn't warn you."

"No, Zane, don't—" she cried, mortified, as he lifted her easily and her feet left the ground.

"I didn't bring you up here so that you could kill yourself by catching pneumonia." He swung her over his shoulder and hauled her, as a fireman would, toward the house. Her hair fell over her face. All the blood rushed to her pounding head.

"Zane, this is ridiculous!" she cried, clinging to his sweater, feeling his muscles ripple beneath the knit. "Let me down, damn you. Stop! Zane, please!"

Up the porch stairs and into the house. He kicked the door shut behind him and set her, sputtering and furious, on the floor. "You bastard!" she barked, throwing her hair out of her eyes and tugging at her dress.

"Kaylie—"

"This is America, Zane. You can't take the law into your own hands!"

He winced a little at that, and storm clouds gathered in his eyes.

"Just because you're a private detective you don't have the right to go around…around…abducting helpless women!"

"Helpless? You?" he flung back at her, shaking his

head as he strode through a pitch-ceilinged living room and beyond. "I'm the one taking my life in my hands by bringing you here!"

"Damn right," she agreed, right on his heels. "All I'll give you is grief."

"Amen." He flipped on the wall switch and walked briskly into the kitchen.

"So you may as well give me the keys—"

"Forget it!" He turned and clamped big, angry hands over her bare shoulders. "Now, listen, Kaylie, this is the way it is. I know what I've done by bringing you here. I don't need a lecture on kidnapping, abduction, the rights of the American people or women's lib! All I'm trying to do is make sure that you're safe."

"Spare me—"

"I have. For seven years." His fingers tightened over her shoulders and his eyes searched her face. She felt his anger, but in his eyes she saw deeper emotions brewing. "Just try to understand," he said quietly. "You've got this job where every morning anyone west of the Rockies can switch on his television and see you and Alan Bently on the tube."

"So?"

"So what's to prevent your personal nut case, Lee Johnston, from trying to do another number on you?"

"The law! The courts! Henshaw."

Zane snorted, then shoved a hand through his hair in frustration. "I deal with the law and the courts every day. Things don't always turn out like they're supposed to. As for Henshaw and Whispering Hills, I've got my doubts about that setup, too."

"Johnston's been there seven years."

"Then he's probably due for reevaluation," Zane said. "We'll know in a few days."

"A few days?" she echoed. He expected her to stay up here that long?

"That's how long it will take to check out the rumor. Maybe this Ted guy knows what he's talking about. Then again, maybe he doesn't. Believe it or not, I didn't bring you up here just to get you angry. I'm scared, damn it. Scared for you. When I think of what Johnston could have done to you—what he's still capable of..." Zane shuddered. Rubbing his arms, he strode to the window and, leaning his palms on the counter, stared through the glass to the black night beyond.

Kaylie's heart softened a little. Though she was furious with him for abducting her, she couldn't help but feel a kindness toward him, a thawing of that cold part of her heart where she'd kept her memories of their short marriage. She had loved him with all of her young, naive heart, and no other man had ever taken his place. No man could. But she forced all those long-buried thoughts of love aside.

"You have no right to do this," she said quietly.

"I have every right."

"Why?"

"Because I care, damn it." He whirled on her, and his gaze, flinty gray, drilled deep into hers. "I care more about you than anyone else on this planet—even more than your precious Alan Bently. If you haven't figured it out yet, that man's a leech. He only cares about you because he thinks a public romance with you will further his career."

"Oh, save me—"

"It's true."

"How do you know? Have you ever talked to Alan?"

He snorted derisively. "Of course not."

"Well, if you had, you might have found out that I've never been involved with him."

"That's not what the tabloids say."

"*You* read the tabloids?" she repeated, amused.

"No, but where there's smoke, there's fire."

"And you care?"

His lips twisted downward. "I told you—I care about you. As for Bently, the man's the worst kind of opportunist. All those rumors that link you to Alan, I can just imagine what they do to the ratings."

"Wh-what?" she demanded, getting a glimmer of what he was alluding to.

"It's a ratings thing, isn't it? Your morning talk show is pitted against a couple of other shows, isn't it? I'll bet your network thought it would boost viewership if you and Alan got married."

"That's absurd!" she gasped.

"Is it?" He opened a cupboard and found a brand-new bottle of Scotch. With a hard twist of his wrist, he snapped open the cap, breaking the label, and after locating a small glass, poured himself a stiff shot.

He took a slow swallow, and her gaze traveled from his firm chin to the silky way his Adam's apple moved in his neck. God, he could reach her as no other man could. There was an irresistible male force surrounding him, and she was oh, so susceptible. She dragged her gaze away.

"I know you never believed it, Kaylie, but I loved you. More than any man should love a woman. I was the one who was obsessed."

"And now?" she asked, her voice trembling. They

were wading in hazardous water. "Did you bring me up here because of Johnston? Or was there another reason?"

His gaze locked with hers for a second. Then he tossed back his drink. "And now I'm protecting you. Period. If you think this is some kind of exotic seduction, guess again. I don't have to go to so much trouble."

"I'd hope not," she said evenly, though emotions were tearing through her, "because if you did, you would've lived a very celibate life in the past seven years!"

"Maybe I have," he said, but he had to have been joking. Dear Lord, when she thought of his passion, his wild lovemaking, his wanton sense of adventure in the bedroom, delicious chills still skittered down her spine. No, Zane Flannery might have gone seven days without a woman, possibly even a month or two, but seven years—never! His sexual appetite was too primal, too instinctive. She studied the rock-hard jut of his chin, the angle of his cheeks, the authority in the curve of his thin lips.

He eyed her just as speculatively. "And what about you, Kaylie?" he asked suddenly, his eyes darkening to the color of a winter storm. "What about your sex life?"

She hadn't blushed in years, but now a red heat stole steadily up her neck and face, stinging her cheeks. "I don't think we should be discussing this!"

"It's just one question. A pretty straightforward question."

She swallowed back the urge to lie and tell him that she'd had a dozen or so lovers. "My work keeps me pretty busy," she hedged. "I haven't had time for too many relationships."

"Neither have I," he replied, his gaze finding hers. The silent seconds stretched between them. Kaylie heard only the rapid cadence of her heartbeat, the air whispering through his lungs. "I wasn't lying when I said I loved you, Kaylie," he added, staring into the amber depths of his glass. "You can deny it all you want, you can even pretend that you didn't love me, but there it is. I handled it badly, I admit. But I just loved you too much." Drawing in a deep breath, he finished his drink, dropped his empty glass into the sink, then started out of the room. "Your bedroom is upstairs to the right. I'm next door. But don't worry about your virtue tonight. I'm just too damned tired from arguing with you to do anything about it."

Her throat closed in on itself as she watched him saunter out of the room, the dog at his heels. The faded fabric of Zane's jeans clung to his hips, and his buttocks moved fluidly, though his shoulders and back were ramrod stiff.

"Good night, Kaylie," he called over his shoulder as he mounted the stairs. "Turn out the lights when you go to bed."

"And what makes you think I'll stay here?" she replied, following him to the stairs, but remaining at the bottom of the steps.

He paused at the landing, one hand resting on the banister. Turning, he towered over her, and again she noticed the torment in his eyes. "It's dark, and the nearest house is over ten miles away. The main road is even farther. Now, if you want to start making tracks through the wilderness, there's nothing I can do to stop you, but I will catch up to you."

"You have no right to do this! No right!" she screamed.

He suddenly looked tired. "That's a difference of opinion," he said, then mounted the rest of the steps, leaving her, fists clenched in fury, to stare after him. She felt a twinge of regret for the fleeting, giddy love they'd shared, but she shoved those old emotions into a shadowy corner of her heart. Loving Zane had been a mistake; marrying him had nearly stripped her of her own personality, and she wasn't about to fall into that trap again.

She glanced down at her hands and slowly uncoiled her fingers. Though she remembered her love with Zane as being unique, it was based on all the wrong emotions.

And now she was scared—frightened that the ominous warning on the tape was true. If only she could call someone—anyone—and find out the truth about Lee Johnston. Once she knew where she stood, she could face the rage of emotions Zane provoked in her.

Shivering, she walked outside and made her way to the Jeep. It was locked; the keys were not in the ignition and, of course, there was no mobile phone. Though she suspected he had a phone somewhere. But where? Miserably, she stared at the darkened dashboard. She didn't know the first thing about hot-wiring a Jeep— or any other car for that matter. Hot-wiring, as well as breaking into a car were among those valuable high school lessons she'd missed while growing up on a Hollywood back lot.

She kicked at the gravel in disgust and felt the breath of a mountain breeze touch her bare shoulders. Rubbing her arms, she stared dismally at the black woods looming all around her. If she left now, she wouldn't get far in sandals and a thin cotton dress. Nope. Zane had made sure escape was impossible. At least for tonight.

Turning on her heel, she started back up the steps. There had to be a way, she thought, refusing to give up. If she couldn't leave tonight, she'd find a way tomorrow.

Back in the house, she searched all the downstairs' rooms for a telephone, but though she found phone jacks, there wasn't one telephone in sight. She clenched her teeth in frustration. Damn the man. He'd made sure to thwart her. In the living room, hidden behind panels, she discovered a television, and she worried about her job. What would happen when she didn't show up tomorrow morning?

She turned on the power to the set but nothing happened. Then she noticed that the connecting cables swung free. Obviously the cable had been switched off.

She tried not to think of her position as cohostess of *West Coast Morning*. There was time enough to worry later. First she had to find a means of escape. And then, once back in the city, she'd check out Ted's warning personally, even drive to Whispering Hills to see Dr. Henshaw in person. With renewed purpose, she continued her quick search. In the pantry she found a flashlight and an old army jacket—not the most elegant or comfortable, but something to protect her from the elements, should she have to walk any distance. But taking off in the woods alone at night was too intimidating, even though it would serve Zane right to discover her gone come morning.

Leaving the jacket and flashlight untouched, she

padded upstairs and noted that the lamp in Zane's room was still burning—a sliver of light showed beneath his closed door. She didn't bother knocking, but twisted the knob and found Zane, wearing only the worn Levi's, leaning back on the bed, almost as if he were waiting for her.

His head was supported by two pillows, and his eyes were the color of slate. His chest was covered with a mat of dark, swirling hair that covered a tanned skin and a washboard of rigid abdominal muscles before disappearing enticingly beneath his waistband.

The back of Kaylie's throat went dry. She forced her gaze back to his face. His lazy smile flashed white against a day's growth of beard.

"You room's to the *right,* remember?" His lips curved speculatively. "Unless of course you want to stay with me."

The shepherd, lying on the floor near the foot of the bed, lifted his head and cocked it to one side, as if he were sizing up Kaylie.

Kaylie turned her attention back to Zane. "I just want control of my life again."

Reaching over to the lamp, his shoulder muscles gliding with easy, corded strength, he clicked off the light. "Your choice," he said in the darkness. "Here—" he thumped on the bed "—or down the hall."

"I have a job to get to—"

"Forget it."

"They'll miss me."

He chuckled, as if he knew something she didn't. "Alan will be thrilled to have a chance to show the whole world he doesn't need you."

"You'll regret this, Zane," she muttered as she fumbled in the dark, then finding the door, walked quickly out of the room, slamming the door behind her.

What had she been thinking of? She'd been out of her mind to walk into his room and see him half-naked on the bed. A warmth in the pit of her stomach curled invitingly, and she remembered how lying next to him had been safe, secure, loving. The scent of his body lingering on the bedsheets, the feel of a strong arm wrapped around her waist.

"Stop it," she told herself as she marched to the room designated as hers and closed the door behind her. She surveyed her surroundings with a critical eye. The bedside lamps were lit, and golden light glowed warmly against the pine-paneled walls. The hand-stitched quilt on the double bed had been turned down. "How thoughtful," she grumbled, as if he could hear her as she stared at the plumped pillows. "But you forgot the mints!" She kicked off her sandals and padded barefoot against the smooth floor. The room was inviting, in an elemental sort of way, but she couldn't forget that she had been shanghaied here against her will, even if, as Zane so emphatically insisted, her life were in danger.

She groaned at the thought of what would happen tomorrow morning when she didn't arrive on the set of *West Coast Morning*. There would be chaos; her boss would be furious, and the phones at her apartment in San Francisco as well as at the beach house, would be ringing off the hook. Someone would call her sister, and Margot would worry herself sick.

"Oh, Lord, what a mess!" She grabbed a handful of hair and flung it over her shoulders as she padded to the closet and, out of curiosity, opened the door.

An array of clothes—women's clothes—filled every available space. Skirts, sweaters, jeans and slacks were draped on hangers or folded neatly on the shelves. So she hadn't been the first, she thought cynically. Disappointment welled up in her, and she slammed the door shut. No time for sentimentality.

So Zane had a woman—or women. So what? She didn't really believe that he'd lived the life of a monk, did she? It was only surprising that he would expect her to buy that whacked-out story, what with this closet chock-full of women's things.

Flopping onto the mattress, she tossed one arm over her eyes, trying to relieve the headache that was pounding at her temples. Too much wine, too much fear and way too much Zane Flannery, she thought. But tomorrow she'd find a way to force him to take her back to Carmel or straight to San Francisco, back to her home, her job, her life without him.

She only had to get through one night of sleeping under the same roof with him. One night with him lying, stripped bare to the waist, on a king-size bed only a dozen feet away.

Stop it! she thought, squeezing her eyes shut against the pure, sensual vision of him sprawled lazily across the smooth eiderdown quilt.

She didn't want him! She didn't! And yet there was something so provocatively male and charming about him, that she wondered, just for a fleeting moment, what it would be like to love Zane again.

Tossing the quilt over her shoulders, she started counting slowly, hoping that sleep would envelop her and that by morning Zane would come to his senses!

* * *

Zane climbed out of bed and stared out the window. He wondered if he'd made a big mistake. He'd known she'd be angry, of course, even expected her temper to boil. But he hadn't been prepared for her accusations cutting so close to the bone. Nor had he expected to want her so badly. Already he ached for her, and the thought of a night alone in the bed, with Kaylie only a few steps down the hall, would be torture.

From the foot of the bed, Franklin whined.

"Shh." Zane patted the big dog's head, then resumed his stance at the window, his thoughts drawn, as ever, to the only woman he'd ever loved.

She'd changed in the past seven years, he realized, placing one hand high on the window casing and leaning the side of his head against his arm. She'd grown up.

Gone was any trace of the naive young woman he'd married—the teenager who had made a string of semisuccessful movies before *Obsession*.

No, this new woman was strong, forceful and well able to control her own life. He'd have to be on his toes, he thought as he stared moodily into the dense, inky forest, because if he let down his guard for a second, she'd find a way to escape and throw her life in jeopardy. She didn't really believe that Johnston would be set free soon.

But Zane did.

He knew what it was like to have death take those he loved, and he was bound and determined that this time he'd thwart the grim reaper. Even if he had to keep Kaylie locked away for the next six months!

Chapter 4

The first few streaks of dawn crept across the bed. Groaning, Kaylie roused herself.

She was in an isolated cabin. With Zane.

God, what a mess!

Climbing out of bed, she stretched and looked out the window. The sun was rising behind a wall of sharply spired mountains. Golden light shone through the stands of pine, glittering in the dewdrops. What was she doing here?

"Oh, Zane," she murmured, grabbing the quilt and wrapping it around her. What was she going to do? Zane had always been an enigma of sorts, and she'd never learned how to handle him—just, she supposed, as he thought he'd never learned to handle her.

Smiling at the thought, she sat on the window seat and drew her knees under her chin. She remembered the first time she'd seen Zane and the tiny knot of apprehension that had coiled in her stomach, the same warm knot she felt now as she thought about him in the next room. She should be angry with him and she was, but the morning took the edge off her anger.

Had it been ten years ago when she'd first laid eyes on Zane Flannery? She'd only been seventeen at the time, and yet, the first time she'd seen him seemed as though it had occurred only yesterday...

A bodyguard! She, Kaylie Melville, with a bodyguard! She almost laughed at the thought. Just because she'd made a couple of pictures and she'd been receiving fan mail—some of it not so nice—didn't mean she needed a bodyguard!

"It's a bodyguard or nothing," her father warned her. "We can't be following you off to God-only-knows where every time you make a movie. So, you tell that producer of yours that you get your own personal bodyguard or you won't be making any more films for him!"

Her father, a short, wiry man with a temper that could skyrocket, wasn't about to take no for an answer.

"That's right," her mother had agreed, as she did with any of Dad's rules. "You listen to your father." Her mother had winked broadly. "No reason to give up your career. Just have the studio hire a guard. I'll talk to them myself."

Kaylie didn't argue. She loved making films. Her first picture had been mildly successful—a teen horror flick that made the studio more money than had been expected. Her second film was meatier, as she played a teenager who fell for the boy from the wrong side of the tracks and had to deal with unsupportive parents and pregnancy. Her third movie, *Carefree,* was a teen comedy that surprised the critics and earned the director, as well as Kaylie, glowing reviews. The film had grossed over a hundred million. Triumph Studios was ecstatic. Barely sixteen, Kaylie had become a household word, a budding star who received fan mail and was asked to do interview upon interview to promote her forthcoming projects. She was compared to other young actresses of the time. People sought her autograph. And the fan mail kept pouring in. Letters of undying love, proposals of marriage, and a few not-so-kind missives from a few tortured fans.

Soon the powers-that-be at Triumph Studios agreed with her father and insisted she retain a bodyguard.

But, at seventeen, she hadn't expected anything like Zane Flannery to walk into the offices of Triumph Pictures and announce that he would be looking after her. Not by a long shot! She had thought she'd be protected by some husky ex-football player with a couple of teeth missing. Or by some man with a huge belly and unshaven jaw who had once been the bouncer at a bar. But oh, no, Flannery was nothing like either man she'd envisioned.

He was younger than she'd expected—in his early twenties, by the looks of him, and much cuter—well, more handsome than any of her costars. His hair was longer than stylish and sable brown, curling over his collar and falling over his forehead in shiny, wind-blown waves. His face, though rough-hewn, took on a boyish quality whenever he flashed a rakish, devil-may-care smile that turned her inside out.

"Miss Melville," he said, extending a work-roughened

palm. They were seated in the cluttered office of Martin York, the producer of her latest film, *Someone to Love*.

Flannery's large palm dwarfed hers as he shook her hand, then released her fingers. Wearing only a leather jacket, jeans and a T-shirt, he looked as if he were one of the stagehands or construction workers on the set, but his eyes gave him away. Gray and penetrating, they seemed to take in all of the office at once as he turned back to the producer.

Martin tossed his Dodgers baseball cap onto a chair behind him. Grinning beneath his beard, he reached over a desk piled high with scripts, reels of film and overflowing ashtrays, and clasped Zane's outstretched hand. "How the hell are you?"

"'Bout the same," Zane drawled, dropping into the chair next to hers and slouching low, his jean-encased legs stretched out in front of him.

"That bad, eh?"

Both men laughed, and Kaylie repressed the urge to giggle. Their easy camaraderie caused her to feel like an outsider, and when she was nervous, she often giggled. But she didn't want Zane to see her as the least bit girlish. He looked like the kind of person who wouldn't easily suffer fools, and she didn't want to get on his bad side.

"I've known Flannery here for more than a few years," Martin said, looking at her as if suddenly remembering she was in the room. "We knew each other in the navy. So don't let his appearance fool you. He's the best in the business."

Kaylie trained her gaze on the man who was to be her protector. The best in the business? So young?

"Zane's worked on some top-secret stuff for the

armed services, then he landed a job at Gemini Security. Now he's starting his own company—right?"

"That's the rumor," Zane replied lazily. He glanced at Kaylie again, and his smile faded. "I'll take care of you, Miss Melville. You can count on it."

"Kaylie," she replied with a shrug. "And I'll call you Zane. Okay?"

"If that's the way you want it."

She looked from Zane to Martin, but Martin, too, lifted a shoulder. "Whatever works."

Kaylie grinned and tried not to be lost in the power of Zane's gaze. But she felt giddy and conspicuous and—What was wrong with her? He was just her bodyguard. No big deal. Or was it? This man—well, he looked as if one hot look from him could melt a glacier.

"Okay, okay," Martin said, handing Zane an address book. "Now, here's Kaylie's address. She still lives with her folks and her sister, and she'll be working here as well as on location in Mexico and Australia. Her folks won't be going along, so Kaylie will be your responsibility. She's been getting a few crank letters…" He tossed a stack of mail, bound by a rubber band, to Flannery just as he finished copying her address into his own book. "I want you to check them all out—"

"Hey, wait a minute," Kaylie cut in, surprised. "That's my mail, right?"

Martin nodded, his expression growing peevish.

Objecting, Kaylie reached for the small bundle. "Don't I get to read it?"

Martin waved off her request. "Don't worry about it. The secretary will respond."

"No way. I always read—"

"You don't have time," Martin said, obviously irritated. "You've got a plane to catch in three days and—"

"And it's mine," Kaylie said, hoping not to sound too petulant. But she wasn't going to let this new guy think he could boss her around. She'd agreed to the bodyguard but that was all. To Zane, she said, "If there's something else you want to know about me, just ask."

He arched one dark brow, and a smile tugged at the corners of Flannery's lips, though he tried to keep his expression grave as he slapped the stack of envelopes into her hand. "When you're done with them, I'd like to see them again."

Martin was fit to be tied. "We don't have time—"

"It's cool," Kaylie assured him, and Martin rolled his eyes.

"Women," Martin muttered under his breath, but Kaylie, cheeks burning, jaw tight, refused to rise to the bait. She just wanted this bodyguard to understand that she wouldn't be treated like a little kid. As for Martin's bad mood, he'd get over it.

From that point on, Zane was all business. He was with her constantly, but never obtrusively, and she began to relax around him. He helped her with her studies and taught her card games and even ran through her lines with her. Once in a while he'd show her a different side to him—a side that proved he did have a sense of humor. While going over her lines, he'd ad-lib, all very seriously, and she'd foul up her lines and they'd both end up laughing. Once in a while she'd catch him looking at her intensely, his eyes darkening, and she'd feel a tightening in her stomach, a warmth that seeped through her whole body.

When they were together, she felt secure. Even when

they went out at night, he was cool and calm, almost relaxed. But at the slightest hint of danger, if any fan got too close and he sensed her unease, every muscle would flex and his eyes would glint with warning.

Being so close to him, closer than she was to any other male, she began to rely on him and fantasize about him. He was as handsome as any of her costars and seemed much more virile and worldly. He didn't party, nor try to impress the stars. He was just there—steady as a rock—with his sexy smile that turned her insides to jelly. They spent month after month together.

In Australia, after grueling hours on the set, he'd swim with her in the ocean, and walk with her as the warm sand squished between her toes. He never touched her, though she'd caught his gaze drifting over her body as the wind teased the hem of her dress or the drops of saltwater dried on her skin.

Once, she caught him staring at the dusky hollow between her breasts. She couldn't breathe for a second. Instinctively she placed her hand over the halter of her swimsuit and his gaze moved, but not before she saw the flame in his eyes. Without a word, he tossed her a beach towel and kept his distance from her for the rest of the day.

It wasn't until the next year, after the success of *Someone to Love,* when they were filming in Victoria, British Columbia, that their relationship changed. Her parents had stayed with her on the set for two weeks, then flown back to California.

Kaylie, feeling restless, paced in her room. From her window, she spied the storm clouds gathering to the west, reflecting her own mood as they shifted in dark patterns on the water. She opened the window, feeling a stiff breeze, smelling the heavy scent of rain. There was electricity in the air, currents as charged as her emotions, and she couldn't think of anything but Zane and what it would be like to kiss him.

She told herself she was crazy, that her mother would tell her she was in the throes of puppy love, that her feelings for Zane were nothing more than a schoolgirl crush.

Nonetheless, she was wild for him.

For the first time in her life she had sexual fantasies, and they always involved Zane. Sometimes she blushed just looking at him.

After filming, she and Zane decided to walk back to the hotel. The wind picked up and the clouds overhead opened. Huge raindrops peppered the ground, forming puddles. "Come on," Zane said, turning up his collar and grabbing her hand as he dashed across a street. "We'll catch a cab."

Laughing, she followed, raindrops catching in her hair and running down her cheeks. They hurried past other pedestrians fumbling with umbrellas, carriages pulled by huge horses and double-decker buses rumbling through the slick streets. But each cab that passed was full.

As a final cab roared past, Zane muttered an oath. Then, tugging at her hand, he said, "I think this is a shortcut." He pulled her through a park. They ran down gravel paths, their shoes crunching, their breath fogging in the air.

Kaylie's legs began to ache. "Hey, slow down," she said, gasping from his quick pace.

He slid her a disbelieving glance. "Out of shape?" he mocked, but tugged on her arm and pulled her beneath the leafy cover of a willow tree. The smell of damp earth and ferns filled the air. Magenta azaleas and pale lavender rhododendrons splashed color through the mist that seemed to rise from the loamy soil.

Zane threw his arm across her shoulders and wiped a drop from the tip of her nose. "I guess even I can't protect you from Mother Nature," he said with a crooked grin. His dark hair fell across his eyes, and raindrops glistened, jewellike, in the blackened strands.

His gaze touched hers, and in one breathless instant Kaylie knew he was going to kiss her. The arm around her shoulders tightened, his fingers wound in her hair, and, as she tilted her head back, his lips found hers in a kiss that was gentle and fierce.

She responded, opening her mouth to the tender insistence of his tongue. He moved closer to her, his suede jacket smelling of leather and rain, his after-shave tingling her nostrils.

She moaned his name and strained against him— intimately.

Zane stiffened as if he'd been hit by an electric current. Quickly he stepped backward until the heel of his boot scraped against the scarred trunk of the willow. "Damn." Running a shaking hand over his wet forehead, he stared past her, over her shoulder, to a point in the distance. "I can't let this... This just can't happen," he said raggedly, passion in his eyes as he attempted to fixate on anything but her.

"But—" She took a step closer.

"No!" Holding up his palm, he shook his head. "My job is to protect you, not seduce you." His gaze found hers. "Your parents—"

"Are in L.A.," she blurted out.

"—trust me."

He was right, of course, but she was too young and stubborn to admit it.

"Come on, let's get out of this downpour…"

Throwing caution to the wind, she flung her arms around his neck and pressed her anxious lips to his. She felt him shudder. From his shoulders to his knees a shiver of desire possessed him.

"No, we can't… Oh, God," And with that desperate prayer, he kissed her, long and hard, his arms surrounding her, his mouth exploring. Turning quickly, he pinned her against the rough bole of the tree, but she barely noticed as she kissed him with all the wild abandonment she'd dreamed of.

His hands moved upward until the weight of her breast filled his palm. His hips shoved tight against her, and she felt the rock-hard force of his desire creating an answering awakening in her. Warm and moist, like the spring shower, she experienced a want that was dark and dusky and so demanding she ached for him, wanting him as she had no other.

He kissed her eyes, her nose, her cheeks, her throat, his tongue licking away the raindrops as his hands found the zipper of her jacket. The bleached denim opened, and he lifted her blouse until his damp fingertip plundered beneath her bra, touching and delving, causing her nipples to crest into small, hard buds.

Desire crept up her spine, spilled into her blood, causing her to moan and kiss him feverishly.

Beneath the drooping branches of the willow tree, with the wind sighing and the rain creating a moist curtain, Kaylie wanted to be loved.

"Oh, I should be hanged for this."

"Don't stop—" she cried, feeling him pull away.

"You're barely eighteen," he whispered, once again moving away from her.

"But I love you."

The words seemed to sting. He stepped backward and sucked in a long, slow breath while Kaylie, her breasts still aching, her jacket draped off one shoulder, felt suddenly bereft and empty. Didn't he want her? She had only to look at him to know.

"Those are strong words," he said, his voice so low and rough she barely recognized it.

"But—"

"Shh!" Stepping forward, he placed a finger to her lips, and she kissed his knuckle, touching it with her tongue. He grabbed her roughly. "Stop it, damn you!" he growled. "Don't you know you're playing with fire?"

"I'm—"

"You're eighteen. Eighteen! And I'm being paid to keep you safe!" In frustration, he straightened her jacket. "Let's get out of here before we do something we'll both regret."

"This is what I want," she pleaded, as his fingers clamped around her wrist and he yanked her toward the path again.

"You're too young to know what you want."

"I'm not—"

"And you're too used to getting anything you desire. On a whim," he said with more than a trace of remorse. "I'm not a rich man, Kaylie. And I'm not going to blow this job by getting involved with you." Casting her a dark look over his shoulder he added, "And I'm not some toy that you'll experiment with, lose interest in, then discard when you're bored."

"What?" she cried, planting her feet and trying to pull free of his grasp.

He stopped and then, as if he were searching for a way to throw away her feelings, he said, "Grow up."

She slapped him. With all the force of offended youth, she hauled back and smacked him across his wet cheek.

"You spoiled brat," he muttered, and she couldn't tell if he were angry or relieved. Maybe he'd baited her on purpose. But this time, when he took hold of her wrist, his grip was punishing, almost brutal as he half dragged her through the park, mindless of the muddy puddles that splashed her boots. The path cut through a rose garden and a thicket of oaks before spilling onto the sidewalk that flanked the hotel. "Thank God."

Furious, she couldn't resist taunting him. "So what're you going to do with me, Zane?" she baited, still reeling from his assessment of her as a "brat."

"Turn me over your knee and spank me?"

He stopped dead in his tracks. His face went stark white. His fingers slackened, and he squeezed his eyes shut, pinching the bridge of his nose between thumb and forefinger, as if in so doing he could call up his fleeing patience. "No, Kaylie," he said, slowly opening eyes as hard as glass. "As soon as you're safely back at the hotel, I'm getting the hell out of here."

"Meaning?"

"That you'll just have to find yourself another body-guard."

No! Desperation tore at her. "But I don't want anyone else." She coiled her fingers around the lapels of his jacket and held on tightly, as if afraid he might run. "Don't you understand, Zane. I want you. *You.*"

Staring down at her upturned face, he let out a groan and dragged her closer still, kissing her over and over again. She felt him shudder against her, as if he were trying and failing to rein in impossible emotions.

Oblivious to the pedestrians hurrying, head and umbrellas tucked against the wind and rain, they held each other, she clinging to him as if to life itself, he embracing her as if she were a rare and fragile creature he was afraid to release for fear of never seeing again.

The wind and rain blew past, but they didn't care.

Finally he stepped away, his expression tortured and grim. He took both her chilled, wet hands in his. "This can't happen, you know."

"It already has."

He shook his head, though his eyes betrayed him. "Then it has to stop."

"No!" She knew what she wanted. Zane, Zane, Zane!

"Come on. You're getting drenched," he muttered, twining his fingers through hers as he pulled her up the steps to the glorious old hotel. Built to resemble an English castle, the hotel stretched a full city block. Gold brick, leaded glass and tall, narrow windows created seven stories. Lush gardens and brick courtyards surrounded the sprawling building.

Zane, propelling Kaylie by her elbow, hastened her through the lobby and into an elevator. Once on the seventh floor, he unlocked the door to her room and made a sweeping search of the suite.

"Take a hot shower and I'll meet you downstairs for dinner."

She wouldn't let him go. "Stay with me."

"Kaylie—"

"Please!"

He groaned and pulled his hand from hers. "I can't. You can't. *We can't!*"

"But—"

"Don't you know this is killing me?" he finally admitted, as she reached for him again, trying to kiss him, feeling tears fill her eyes.

"I love—"

"Oh, God, Kaylie, don't!" he whispered, his voice raw as he left her and closed the connecting door between their rooms.

Later, at dinner, he refused to talk about their relationship. Instead, he was all business, sitting stiffly across from her, his gaze moving restlessly over the other guests, looking, searching for danger that didn't exist.

The meal, in Kaylie's opinion, was a disaster, and upstairs in their suite again, things didn't improve. He closed the door between them and refused to kiss her.

"I don't understand," she cried against the door panels, slamming her fist against the wall in frustration, but she received no answer.

The next few days were torture. Zane acted like a complete stranger. He was distant and proper to the point that she thought she might scream. She tried to draw him into conversation, but his replies were quick monosyllabic answers. No more laughing. No more jokes. No more ad-libbing to her lines. Stiff and businesslike, he became the antithesis of the man with whom she'd fallen in love.

On the set three days later, she cracked. She blew her lines for the third time when the director waved everyone off the set and called for an hour break.

Kaylie, cheeks burning, walked straight to the docks. Zane was near her side, though, of course, he didn't say a word. Not one solitary word.

She clamped her hands over the rail and, without looking in his direction, shouted, "What's wrong with you?"

Zane leaned against the fender of a car as she pressed her nails into the painted railing and stared at the rippling blue waters reflecting against a clear, cerulean sky.

Gulls floated on the air currents near the docks, while sailboats and fishing trawlers skimmed across the horizon. Kaylie barely noticed, her concentration centered solely on Zane.

"Well?" she demanded, wanting to shake him.

"Nothing's wrong."

"Like hell! You've changed, Zane!"

"I'm just here to do a job."

"You care about me!"

"You're my client. My responsibility."

She flew at him. Emotionally strung out, she raised her fists as if to pummel his chest, but he captured her wrists and pinned them together over her head before she had a chance to strike. So close she could see her own reflection in his sunglasses, she felt helpless and tired. Tears welled in her eyes and she crumpled against him. "There's more—we both know it. Tell me there's more," she pleaded, her throat closing against the pain of his rejection.

"There can't be." But the corners of his lips turned down, and she knew he was fighting his own ragged emotions.

"I *love* you."

"Kaylie, no!" But his face was pained, and he sighed loudly...sadly. "God, help us," he whispered, releasing her and shoving one hand through his wind-ruffled hair. Looking toward the heavens, he swore. Was he angry? At her? Or himself?

"I do love you, damn it, and I always will." Sobs choked her. "I love you, Zane. Please, just love me back."

"It won't work."

"We'll make it work!" she cried, reaching up and lifting his sunglasses to see the agony in his eyes.

With a moan, he wrapped his arms around her and dropped his mouth on hers in a kiss that nearly strangled her with promised passion.

She closed her eyes to the storm of desire overtaking her. He did care! He did!

When he raised his head, she saw the torment on his face. "This *can't* happen. We can't let it."

But she kissed him again and again. Only when she knew the director would send someone looking for her did she pull back.

That night she expected Zane to come to her. She lay on her bed, wearing a soft pink nightgown, trembling at the thought of what she intended.

She watched the clock as the hours passed. Ten. Eleven. Midnight. Still the light beneath his door shone. At twelve-thirty, she could wait no longer and knocked softly. "Zane?"

The door opened. He stuck his head into her room. "What?"

She swallowed hard. Though she'd played the role before, she'd never seduced a man, never been in bed with a man. "I—I uh, thought, you might like to come in…" Oh, Lord, why did her voice sound so high-pitched and trembling—like a child's?

"Are you all right?"

"Yes, but—"

"Then let's just leave it, Kaylie," he said, his voice as rough as sandpaper.

"I can't."

"Go to sleep." He shut the door firmly, and she wanted to die of embarrassment.

She couldn't sleep that night, nor the next. She was a failure at rehearsals, and the director, running behind schedule, was in a foul mood.

Zane was adamant. Cool and distant again. And no amount of anger or pleading would change his mind.

Until the phone call.

It came through at eleven o'clock on a rainy Monday night. Kaylie, restless anyway, picked up the receiver only to hear Margot's frail voice on the other end. "Kaylie?" Margot cried, her voice breaking. "Oh, Kaylie…"

"What?" Kaylie's heart leaped to her throat. Fear engulfed her.

"Oh, God, Kaylie. It's Mom and Dad…" Margot wailed. Nearly incoherent and sobbing uncontrollably, Margot cried on and on. Kaylie's insides turned to ice as she understood part of what Margot was saying— something about an accident and Mom and Dad and another car.

Trevor, Margot's boyfriend, took control, and his voice was firm as he explained about the accident. As he spoke, Kaylie understood. The room went out of focus. The floor tilted. Blackness surrounded her as she realized both her parents were dead, killed in a hideous accident on a winding mountain road in northern California.

She wasn't aware that she'd screamed, didn't realize that she'd sunk to the floor, couldn't feel the tears drizzling down her face, but all at once Zane was there, holding her, cuddling her, calming her as he spoke to Trevor.

He hung up and tried to get her to talk, to drink some water, to do anything, but her grief eclipsed all else.

"Shh, baby, shh," he said rocking her, but she was inconsolable.

He must have called the producer, who sent over a doctor, because she was given something to help her sleep. Even in her drugged state, images of her mother and father and a fiery automobile fused in her mind.

When she finally roused twelve hours later, Zane was there, his flinty eyes regarding her carefully, his jaw unshaven, his clothes wrinkled from sitting in the chair near her bed.

"I—I can't believe it," she said. Her head thundered, and her eyes burned with new tears. Her throat was hot and swollen and she felt as if she'd aged twenty years.

He came to her then. Took her into his arms and stretched out on the rumpled bed with her. "Oh, Kaylie, I'm so sorry," he whispered, his voice cracking. "But I'll take care of you," he vowed, kissing her crown. "I promise."

And he had. From that moment on, he'd never left her side. Through the funeral and resulting media circus, Zane was there, protecting her, sheltering her, being her rock in her storm-tossed sea of grief.

When the pain had finally lessened and she was able

to put her life back together, Zane had come to her bed as a lover, not a protector. He held her and made love to her and became her reason for living. His caresses were divine, his lovemaking glorious, and she was certain she was in love.

They married in June, and for months Kaylie was in heaven. Living with and loving Zane was perfect. Their happiness knew no bounds, and though Zane sometimes seemed a little more concerned about her welfare than she thought was necessary, she loved him with all her heart.

Then the letters started arriving. Letters about love and lust and weird rituals. An anonymous person wrote her every day, pledging his love, promising that he would "perform an act of supreme sacrifice" for her. These letters were much more frightening than any others she'd received and the fact that the terrifying missives arrived daily put Zane on edge.

Kaylie wasn't concerned, and even thought Zane was overreacting. And he started calling her day and night when he wasn't with her, asking about her friends, checking into their backgrounds.

She began to feel smothered.

Terrified for her safety, he spent every waking hour trying to locate the man who was invading her life. He spent days with the police to no avail, and he transformed their home in Malibu, where they were living at the time, into a veritable fortress, with guard dogs, an electronic security system and remote-controlled gates.

Kaylie, always a free spirit, felt as if she were withering. Her home began to seem like a military compound.

Zane even tried to secure the cottage in Carmel, but

Kaylie put her foot down. They needed some normalcy in their lives, she reasoned, and against his better judgment, he'd acquiesced.

But they grew further and further apart. Hell-bent on protecting her, Zane refused to see that she was dying inside.

At nineteen she wanted an independence she'd never tasted, a freedom to make her own decisions, to live her own life, and all she wanted from him was his love.

They had worked on the marriage. Oh, Lord, she thought now, as she realized that they had both tried and fought to save their dying union. But they just hadn't tried hard enough.

Zane had become autocratic, and she'd become fiercely independent.

The letters had gotten worse, and when Lee Johnston, the anonymous person, finally accosted them at the premiere of *Obsession,* Zane had lost all control.

Now, seven years later, Kaylie swallowed the taste of fear that still touched the back of her throat as she remembered Johnston's blank face, his unseeing eyes, his hard body thrust up against hers. And the knife. God, she'd never forget the feel of polished steel against her throat.

If not for Zane, she might have died that night.

But Zane turned paranoid on her. Even though Johnston was locked up and the letters no longer made their way to her mailbox, Zane installed bigger and better security systems and used his best men to constantly patrol their home.

The marriage dissolved in its prison, and Kaylie had no option but to file for divorce.

At first he fought it. And he even tried to change. But he couldn't, and she doubted that he ever would. Even now, after seven years, he was still trying to run her life. Like Don Quixote fighting windmills, Zane was still grappling with the ghost of Lee Johnston.

And so was she.

Now, staring at the sunlight streaming over the mountains, Kaylie tossed off the old quilt. Today she'd talk some sense into him—today when she wasn't tipsy, when she was rational and calm.

She'd find a way to convince him that they couldn't stay up here alone together. Her heart couldn't take it.

Chapter 5

It was time to take the offensive, Kaylie decided when she heard him rattling around downstairs. With renewed determination, she swept down the stairs and into the kitchen to find him seated on a bar stool, one booted foot propped on the bracing of the matching stool as he lazily flipped through the pages of a magazine.

"'Morning," he drawled with maddening calm. "Sleep okay?"

"As a matter of fact I didn't sleep much at all," she said, irritated, struggling to remain calm and rational. "So you've enjoyed your little joke," she said, shivering in her wrinkled sundress. "Now, let's get back to the real world."

Motioning around him, he said, "This, Lady Melville, is the real world."

"I can't stay here, Zane, even if I wanted to," she said, hoping to sound logical. "What do you think is going to happen when I don't show up on the set?"

He shoved the magazine aside. "Not much."

"Not much?" she repeated, hardly believing her ears but his expression didn't change. She glanced pointedly at her watch. "We have exactly forty-five minutes to get to the city."

"We won't make it," he said, climbing off his stool long enough to pour two cups of coffee. "Even if we wanted to."

"We do want to."

"Correction. You want to." He handed her one of the cups and took an experimental sip from his. "Careful. It's hot."

Kaylie's temper soared. "And I have no say in the matter—right? All my citizen's rights have been stripped since you brought me here to this...this prison! Well, I'm warning you, when my producer figures out that I've been kidnapped, there'll be hell to pay!"

He looked maddeningly unconcerned. "Relax. He won't guess."

"But when he calls—"

"He'll get your answering machine."

"Not good enough, Zane," she said, crossing the room and glaring straight into his eyes. For an instant, a flicker of pain crossed those gray irises, and Kaylie thought there was hope. He wasn't as immune to her feelings as he'd like to pretend.

"Crowley won't call."

"Of course he'll ca—" she started to say, but stopped short. Obviously Zane had taken steps to prevent anything from going wrong with this ridiculous plan of his! Of course! Fury caused her heart to surge wildly. "What'd you do, Zane?" she demanded. "I mean besides becoming a major criminal now wanted by the FBI. What *else* did you do?"

"I made sure that you wouldn't be missed." He settled back on his bar stool and propped his elbows on the counter, eyeing her over the rim of his cup.

Now she was worried. "How?"

"By making the appropriate calls."

"What calls?"

"To the station."

"No—"

"And your sister." He took another long swallow from his coffee.

"You called Margot?" she whispered, disbelieving.

"No, but my secretary did."

She believed him, and her heart sank. Finally she realized that this was no joke. He was dead serious. He intended to keep her captive for God-only-knew how long! She slumped onto the nearest bar stool and wrapped her suddenly chilled fingers around the hot cup of coffee. Was he really that worried about Johnston? Licking dry lips, she tried to think and stay rational. "No matter what you think might happen to me," she said, her voice uneven, "you had no right to bring me up here against my will."

"I know."

"But you don't care," she said, seeing him wince. She took a gulp of her coffee. It was hot and burned a path to her stomach. Avoiding his gaze, she glanced around the room and noticed the phone jack. "You took out all the phones," she said. "Afraid I might call for help."

"Afraid you might do something stupid."

"Nothing could top this trick of yours," she said, and to her surprise he laughed.

"I need to make some calls."

He eyed her speculatively, then finished his coffee in one swallow and walked out of the room and headed upstairs. The floorboards creaked overhead. He was down in a few minutes, cellular phone in hand. "Okay. Who do you want to call?"

She couldn't believe her good luck. "First the station, then Margot—"

"How about the hospital again? Or Henshaw's home—I've got the number."

"But—"

"No one else," he said firmly, his gaze hard. "I brought you up here for your safety and we're not blowing it."

Angry, she watched as he dialed a number, then handed the phone to her. Henshaw's answering machine clicked on, and she left a message that she would call back. Zane connected with Whispering Hills Hospital again, but Henshaw wasn't available. Again, Kaylie was stymied in her requests about Johnston.

Then it was Zane's turn. As he drank a second cup of coffee, he called his office and received an update from Brad Hastings.

"Nothing new yet," Zane said, hanging up. "Look, I know you're furious with me for bringing you here, but it's for your own good." When she started to protest, he held up a palm. "And don't give me any grief about treating you like a child. I don't mean to. I—I just don't want to lose you."

The honesty in his eyes cut straight to her soul. Her

mouth worked, but no sound came out. *Don't,* she reminded herself, *don't trust him again. It's too easy to
get lost in him.* All too vividly she remembered just
how much she'd loved him; how she'd waken every
day looking forward to his kiss, his laugh, his touch…
She cleared her throat as well as her mind. She wanted
to tell him that he'd already lost her, but she held her
tongue because there always had been and always
would be a frail connection between them.

Phone in hand, he grabbed hold of the back door. "I
have to take care of the stock."

"The what?"

"Horses and cattle."

She glanced out the window to the hills. Blue-green
pine and spruce were interspersed with thickets of oak
and maple. Through a break in the trees she noticed
a weathered barn and split-rail fence. "What is this
place?"

"It was an old logging camp, then it was turned into
a ranch of sorts. I bought it a couple of years ago." He
glanced at her, and one side of his mouth lifted. "Kind
of a spur-of-the-moment thing. I decided I needed a
place to get away from it all. I knew the guy who
owned the property, and we struck a deal."

"This guy—your friend—did he abduct women
against their will and bring them here, too?" she baited,
unable to keep from smiling. There was a modicum of
humor in this situation, after all.

His grin was slightly off center. "Not that I know
of," he replied, "but you never can tell. Anyway, I sold
some of the timber rights, but I decided to keep this
house and a few acres for vacations."

"I didn't know you knew the meaning of the word."

"I'm learning," he drawled, "though no one ever accused me of being quick on the uptake."

Kaylie couldn't help but laugh. This was a new side to Zane, a side that was definitely appealing. She'd never thought of him as a person who was willing to kick back. That he, too, needed time to unwind and enjoy life touched her.

She eyed the big kitchen with its hanging copper pots, gleaming brass fittings and butcher-block counters. The room was airy and light, the windows sparkling clean. "So who keeps everything up when you're not here?"

"A retired couple—Max and Leona." Zane opened the door.

"And where are they?" Kaylie asked, hope springing in her heart. If she could just get the woman alone, explain her predicament, maybe Leona would understand and help her...

"Don't even consider it," Zane said, as if reading her mind. "I gave them an extended vacation and said I'd look after everything myself."

Kaylie's hopes crashed to the floor.

His gaze turned tender as he stared at her. What a sight she must be in her wrinkled dress, no makeup and tangled, unruly hair—a far cry from the famous teenager he'd once married, she thought ruefully.

"I'll be back in a minute." He walked through the door, leaving Kaylie alone. She took advantage of her short-lived freedom, hurrying from room to room, looking, with the help of daylight, for any means of escape. He took the phone with him and there was no CB radio! No living soul for miles!

She worked her way from the kitchen, dining room,

living room and ended up in the den. A huge river-rock fireplace dominated one wall, and a bank of windows opposite offered a view of the sloping hillside and valley far below. A river, silver-gray against the blue-green pines, glinted through the trees. Autumn had touched the maples and oaks, turning the leaves gold or fiery red. Wild flowers bloomed in vibrant yellow, pink and blue, providing splashes of color in the dark forest.

"Beautiful, isn't it?" Zane asked, lounging in the doorway.

Kaylie whirled to see him staring at her. Goose bumps appeared on her skin. "I suppose it could be, were the situation different."

"It can be different, Kaylie. All you have to do is accept the fact that you're here and enjoy it."

She hesitated. It sounded so perfect. And too good to be true. "I can't."

He shrugged. "Then you're probably going to have a miserable couple of weeks."

A couple of weeks! she thought in horror. She had to get back now, today, as soon as possible. She couldn't be gone for two days, much less two weeks, for God's sake! For the first time she noticed the duffel bag hanging from his fingers. Her bag! "What's in that?" she asked, dreading the answer.

"I thought you might need a change."

"But how—"

"While you were swimming," he said, then his smile twisted. "I didn't have much time, though, so I just threw some things into the bag. It was hidden beneath the tarp in the back of the Jeep."

"You went through my drawers?" she asked, furious

as she conjured up the image of him pawing through her clothes, her stockings, her lingerie…

"It wasn't anything I hadn't seen before," he reminded her softly, then cleared his throat. "I didn't think you'd wear anything I bought you."

"You bought me?" she queried.

"There are clothes in the closet upstairs. Surely you saw them—"

"They don't belong to some woman you're involved with?"

He smiled sadly. "They're yours."

"Mine?" Her heart stopped. "Then this was planned, right? For *days?*" So angry she was shaking, she started for the door.

Zane was quick. His hand shot out, and strong fingers wrapped around her wrist. "Kaylie," he said softly, "slow down a minute—don't go jumping to conclusions." His hands were gentle, his gaze fastened on hers. "Yes, this took a little time to arrange," he admitted. "About ten hours, give or take a few minutes. I found out about Johnston yesterday morning. I had my secretary run out and buy clothes—size six, right?— and ship them here via a company van. At the same time I called the Browns—Max and Leona—and offered them a dream vacation that they well deserved and told them to take the telephones with them."

"And what about me, Zane?" she asked, pressing her face closer to his, standing on tiptoe to stare at him. "Did you ever wonder how I'd react? Did you realize that there's a good chance that I'll never forgive you for hauling me up here against my will?"

His jaw slid to the side, and his eyes searched her face. "That would be a shame, Kaylie," he said, his voice husky, and she knew in an instant that he intended to kiss her. She tried to yank away from him, but his fingers tightened around her arm. "Whether you admit it or not, we're good together." In one swift motion, he tugged impatiently on her wrist, lowered his head and captured her lips with his.

Kaylie struggled, but his arms closed possessively around her and his mouth moved sensually against hers. No! No! Her mind screamed, though her body began to tingle and familiar emotions tore at her heart. With all her strength she pushed away from him, away from the seduction of his body against hers. But he held her tighter, kissing her and stealing the breath from her lungs. The harder she struggled, the stronger he became, his will as unbending as steel.

His hands were hot against her bare shoulders, his mouth demanding. His tongue pressed hard against her teeth and gained entrance to her mouth.

A thousand memories—glorious and loving—flitted through her mind.

He groaned softly, and her blood turned to fire. Heedless of the danger signals, she began to kiss him back, passion exploding from anger. He smelled and tasted and felt so right. His hard, anxious body, pressed tightly to hers, caused an ache to burn deep in the most feminine part of her. As if in a dream, she wondered how it would feel to make love to him again.

The thought hit her like a bucket of cold water. Realizing just how easily she could be seduced, she recoiled inside and shoved hard against his shoulders, struggling and breaking free.

"Don't—don't ever," she gasped, trying to think rationally and failing miserably, "do that again!"

"Why not?" he asked, his eyes gleaming, a satisfied smile plastered across his jaw. "Didn't you enjoy it?"

"No!"

"Kaylie, don't lie!"

She backed up, her cheeks flaming, her feet nearly stumbling over an ottoman. "You took me by surprise, that's all."

He cocked a disbelieving dark brow. "Maybe I should plan some more surprises."

"Maybe you should go out and feed the cows or horses or chickens or whatever it is you've got here and leave me alone!"

One dark brow arched in skepticism. "Leave you alone. That, I'm afraid, will be hard to do."

"Consider it a challenge!" she said, though she knew that being locked in close quarters with him would make it as difficult for her as it was for him.

He didn't leave. Instead he crossed his arms over his chest. To her consternation, he actually grinned—that boyish and adorable grin that wormed its way straight through her cold facade. "We *should* declare a truce. You know, wave the white flag—try to be civil to each other instead of always lunging for the jugular."

"In this situation?"

"It'll make things easier."

"For you!"

"For both of us," he said softly. "Come on, give it a rest. You might just find that you'll enjoy yourself."

She swallowed hard. That was exactly what she was afraid of—enjoying herself. Why couldn't she just hate him? It would be so much easier than fighting these lingering feelings that she couldn't quite forget. "I—I don't know."

"I'll be good," he promised, but a gleam sparked in his eyes.

What would it hurt? She was tired of the constant battle, though she still bristled at the thought of his high-handed technique of kidnapping her. She had rights, rights he had no business ignoring. "You know, Zane, I'd like to trust you—to get along with you, I really would," she admitted honestly, "but it'll be hard."

"Try," he suggested. "I'll be on my best behavior— charming and good-natured and...as fair as possible."

She blew her bangs out of her eyes in frustration. Fair? Impossible. But there was something beguiling about his smile, something she couldn't resist—something she had never been able to fight. "A truce, hmm?" she said, picking up a crystal paperweight and tossing it into the air only to catch it again. "Okay—on one condition."

"Name it."

"That as soon as we find out that Lee Johnston won't be allowed out of the mental hospital, you release me."

His mouth tightened imperceptibly, but he rounded the desk and extended his hand to her. "It's a deal," he said, wrapping strong fingers over hers.

"Deal," she agreed, shaking his hand, then trying to retrieve her palm from his grasp.

But he didn't let go. Instead he tugged slightly and, lowering his head, dropped a gentle kiss across her mouth. Soft as a whisper, his lips lingered against hers. Tenderness flooded her and she felt weak inside.

"I promise you," he reassured, lifting his head and staring into her eyes, "I won't let anything happen to you."

Her throat clogged. "I—I don't need a bodyguard."

One side of his mouth twisted wryly. "I hope you're right." He scooped a felt Stetson from the brass tree near the door and sauntered out of the room.

She touched her lips with her fingertips. Her pulse was thundering, her knees weak. She sagged against the desk and ran trembling fingers through her hair. *Oh, Kaylie, girl, you're in a mess this time! You thought he was out of your system for good, but just one kiss and you melted inside.*

She closed her eyes, squeezing them shut, forcing her breathing to slow, her heartbeat to quiet. This would never do. She had to think, be on her toes every minute. Or else she would end up falling in love with him again! "Oh, God," she whispered, afraid of the pain and heartache.

She heard the back door slam shut. Taking a deep breath, she moved to the window and saw Zane, his stride lazy and sensual, as he walked to the barns.

After watching him disappear into a weathered building, Kaylie pulled herself together. Hauling her bag with her, she climbed the stairs again. She needed to shower, change and think. But being around Zane made rational thought nearly an impossibility.

In her room, she opened the walk-in closet and studied the clothes neatly folded and stacked on the shelves. Once again, Zane had surprised her. Slacks, blouses, sweaters, shorts, skirts and dresses—all in her size! Now it was blindingly clear that the outfits, purchased from upscale department stores in San Francisco, were intended for her. How could she have thought otherwise?

As Kaylie gazed at the wardrobe, her heart sank. There was certainly more than two weeks of clothes here!

She intended to shower and change, then she'd put escape plan A into action.

"And what's that?" she asked herself as she stripped and stepped under the shower's steamy spray. But she had no answer. She just knew she couldn't let Zane dominate her again. She could handle her life by herself, but the thought of Lee Johnston turned her insides to ice.

Lolling her head back, she forced herself to relax. Warm rivulets of water ran down her shoulders and back. She closed her eyes and thought about Zane again, the power of his kiss flooding her senses.

Unconsciously she licked her lips and shivered deliciously at the memory of his mouth sliding seductively over hers.

Her eyes flew open, and she silently cursed her own weakness. Truce or no truce, she had to get out of here and fast. And it wasn't only because of the way in which he'd shoved himself back in her life. No, she realized fatalistically, she had to get away from him! Because, like it or not, he was right. It wouldn't take long before she might let herself fall in love with him all over again.

Chapter 6

Two can play at this game, Kaylie thought, buffing her body with a towel. If Zane intended to charm her to death, well, she'd just charm him right back, lead him to trust her enough to let down his guard.

And then she'd make good her escape, somehow leaving him high and dry, his plans foiled. A part of her yearned for that satisfaction; she was just plain tired of him trying to run her life, and yet she couldn't fault him completely. He was, or so he claimed, only looking out for her own good.

A breath of wind slipped through the window, and Kaylie shivered. Wrapping the towel around her body, she strode into the bedroom and surveyed it with new eyes. It was a prison, yes, but not a horrible place to stay. Zane could have made the accommodations much worse; as it was, she had a little freedom, which, she supposed, she should savor. He wasn't breathing down her neck twenty-four hours a day, and she wasn't sleeping with him. Opening the closet, she remembered how much she'd loved Zane in the past, how she'd trusted him with her life. In all truth, he'd saved her once before just as he thought he was saving her now.

Her eyes narrowed thoughtfully as she pulled a pair of stone-washed jeans and a peach-colored T-shirt from the shelf.

"Breakfast's ready," Zane whispered from behind her.

She nearly jumped out of her skin. Clutching the bath sheet around her, she turned to find him in the doorway. She'd been so lost in thought she hadn't heard him climb the stairs or push open the door. "Do you mind?" she asked, arching a lofty brow. "I'm trying to get dressed."

"Don't let me stop you," he drawled, an amused smile toying with the corners of his mouth.

"You're pushing it, Flannery," she warned.

He lifted his palms. "We agreed to a truce, remember?"

"Ahh. The truce. Don't you think we should set down some rules to this agreement? And I think the first should be that you quit sneaking up behind me and scaring the living daylights out of me." She tucked her towel more securely over her breasts. "I'll be down in a minute. And next time…knock, okay?"

He rubbed a hand around his neck and cast a devilish glance over his shoulder. "And miss seeing you like this?" He shook his head, and a lock of hair fell over his forehead. "No way. If you want privacy, next time lock your door."

She finished dressing and hurried downstairs where the scents of sausage and coffee wafted through the rooms. The kitchen table had been set for two, and a huge platter of eggs, sausage links and toast was steaming on the counter.

Zane waved her into a chair and poured black coffee into their cups. "I'll be right back."

"Where're you going...?" But he was already out the kitchen door.

A few minutes later he returned carrying a portable television. "Where'd you get that?" she demanded.

One side of his mouth lifted cynically. "There you go again, hoping to get me to divulge my darkest secrets."

"I thought we had a truce," she reminded him.

He plugged the TV into the counter outlet, snapped it on, then fiddled with the antenna. "We do. That's why I'm being so irresistible."

"So *that's* the reason," she remarked dryly.

"Aha!" he said, finally satisfied with the reception. Kaylie heard the familiar lead-in music to *West Coast Morning*.

"Oh, no," she said, her appetite nearly forgotten as the camera closed in on Alan Bently's handsome face.

"There he is—your fiancé," Zane said good-naturedly, though Kaylie thought she saw a muscle tighten in his jaw. "What a guy! Look at that! Even his makeup is perfect."

"He's not my fiancé." Kaylie shot Zane a warning glance, just as Alan made eye contact with the camera.

"Good morning!" Alan said. His brown eyes didn't blink, and his smile seemed a little forced. "You may have noticed that Kaylie Melville isn't with us today," he said half-apologetically. "She won't be with us for the rest of the week as she was called away from the city for personal reasons…"

"I was *what?*" Kaylie cried, astounded.

"Sick aunt," Zane explained, fiddling with the dials at the bottom of the set.

"What?"

"Your aunt. Very ill. Needs care."

"I don't like the sound of this," she said, pinning him with a glare that was meant to bore holes through solid steel. "I don't even have an aunt!" She reached for a piece of toast and thought aloud. "So you must've told Margot something else. She wouldn't buy into the sick-aunt scenario."

"Nope. But your sister thought it was romantic that I was whisking you away to a private hideaway."

"You *told* her?"

"Of course I told her."

"Just wait 'til I see her again," Kaylie muttered, feeling betrayed by her own flesh and blood. Margot might not know it yet, but when Kaylie saw her again, there was going to be trouble. Big trouble! She ripped off a piece of toast and popped it into her mouth.

"Margot will probably defend me," Zane predicted. "In fact, she said she wished some 'knight on a white steed would carry her away to some romantic hideaway.'"

"Oh, give me a break!" But Kaylie could almost hear Margot uttering those exact words. Whereas Kaylie had always been sensible when it came to men—well, men other than Zane—Margot had been the dreamer, the romantic.

"Besides, she's concerned about your safety and she let me know that she doesn't much like Alan."

"She *knows* how I feel about Alan. No two-bit scandal sheet would change her mind."

As Zane buttered toast and scooped eggs onto his plate, Kaylie turned her attention back to the set. Didn't Zane know that Alan wasn't her type? Even years ago, when they'd filmed *Obsession* together and Alan had shown some interest in her, Kaylie had told him in no uncertain terms to keep his distance. She had been married to Zanc at the time, and she wasn't interested in a steamy off-camera affair with Alan or anyone else for that matter. In fact, she had been so head over heels in love with Zane that she had actually laughed at Alan's sleazy attempts at seduction. Fortunately, Alan had taken the hint. Long ago.

"Old Alan looks pretty comfortable without you," Zane observed, taking a bite. "He kind of glossed over your absence, don't you think?"

"What was he going to say?" she countered. "He's not exactly dealing with all the facts, is he?"

Zane stopped chewing. "When you and Alan did your last picture together, he was the one ranting and raving for top billing, higher salaries, a bigger dressing room."

"A lot has changed since we filmed *Obsession*."

Zane's eyes darkened. "Amen." He shoved his plate aside, half his food uneaten, and touched the tips of her fingertips with his. "So if you're not involved with Bently, who is the man in your life?"

Her lungs grew tight, and she quickly pulled her hand away. "Why don't you tell me? You're the one who seems to know everything about my life." She wished he'd just drop the subject; she didn't want to admit that she wasn't romantically involved with anyone, nor had she been since Zane. The dates and publicized relationships over the past few years had never become serious. She hadn't let herself become involved with any one man. However, she wasn't about to tell Zane about her less-than-fulfilling love live. If Zane knew she was entirely unattached, the feelings hovering in the shadows would only intensify the emotions already charging the air between them. No, it was better if Zane thought she was involved with another man.

"There is something more I should tell you," he admitted, his finger slowly rimming his cup in suggestive circles.

Kaylie's throat went dry. "What?"

The honesty honing his features disarmed her, his fingers quit moving on the rim of his cup. "I've missed you, Kaylie. I've missed everything about you."

"Zane, please—"

"You wanted the truth, didn't you? Well, you're going to get it."

She watched as he shoved his chair back and walked to the window. Staring out, his rigid back to her, he said, "I missed coming home to you at night. I missed hearing you sing in the shower. I missed your lingerie draped in the bathroom, I missed your perfume on the pillows, the feel of your hair brushing my face at night, the way you kicked your shoes into the closet... I missed...." He turned and stared at her, his expression pensive and tormented. "I missed you, Kaylie. All of you."

Her throat tightened, and for a second she thought the tears burning behind her eyes might spill. He

sounded so sincere and a part of her longed to believe him.

"So...you've taken advantage of this...situation. Is
that what this is all about?" she whispered, her voice
shaky, her hands clenched so tightly around her napkin her fingers ached.

The muscles in the back of his neck tensed. "No."
Without another word, he walked out the door and it
slammed behind him with a bang.

Kaylie tried to eat but the food stuck in her throat.
Her appetite was gone. Angrily shoving her plate aside,
she attempted to think rationally, to tell herself not to
fall under Zane's spell again, but the simple truth was
that she still cared about him—maybe loved him.

"You're the worst kind of fool," she muttered, blinking back tears. She ran up to her room, snagged a jacket
from the closet and struggled into boots that were a
little too tight. Clomping back downstairs, she headed
out the front door and nearly ran over Franklin, who,
upon spying her, growled.

"I hope your bark is worse than your bite," she said,
sidestepping the dog.

The morning air was crisp. Drops of dew glistened
on the sun-bleached grass, and sunlight streamed
through the trees, warming the ground in dappled
patches. Craggy mountains towered over the forests,
and a few stray clouds drifted lazily in the blue sky.

This place was a touch of heaven, she thought reluctantly, remembering Zane's description last night as
he hauled her up here. And it did seem heavenly compared to her hectic pace in the city and the job she'd
left. "The job you were hijacked from," she corrected
herself. "Sick aunt, indeed!"

She stopped at the Jeep and checked to see if it was unlocked. But the shiny rig hadn't moved since Zane had parked it and the cellular phone was nowhere in sight. Every door, including the tailgate, was secured. The windows were rolled up and even the hood was latched. "Wonderful," she sighed, dusting her hands.

She headed around the corner of the house and down a gravel lane to several outbuildings. The first small building was locked, so she balanced on her tiptoes on a chunk of wood and brushed aside the dust which had collected on the windowpanes. Shading her eyes, she squinted into the darkened interior. This particular building was a storage shed of sorts. Bags of feed and drums of oil, wheelbarrows and rakes, chain saws and other tools were stacked against the walls. In her peripheral vision she saw movement—a shadow. She braced herself.

"Find what you're looking for?" Zane asked, propping one booted foot against the bottom rail of a fence. Franklin had linked up with him again and flopped down in the shade cast by the barn.

"Here, maybe this will help." He reached into his pocket, withdrew a key ring and tossed it to her.

Kaylie snatched the ring in midair. She couldn't believe he'd give her his keys. Now, if she could make it to the Jeep...

As if reading her thoughts, he extracted a second ring. "These are to the equipment," he said, jangling his keys in the air. Kaylie watched as sunlight glinted against the sharp piece of metal. "But those—" he motioned to the keys gripped tightly in her fingers "—will get you in and out of most of the buildings on the place. Just be sure to lock all the doors behind you."

The man was absolutely infuriating! "Oh, yes, *master*," she mocked. "And when I leave the room, I'll bow at your feet."

"That would be nice," he drawled, with the hint of a smile.

"You're insufferable and overbearing—and a bully to boot!"

Zane's smile disappeared. "Let's get out of here," he said, striding across the gravel that separated them and grabbing hold of her wrist.

"Sounds good to me. This wasn't my idea in the first place!"

"Then you won't object?"

"Me? Object to anything you say? Never!"

"That's more like it!"

Insufferable. That's what he was! But she didn't protest as he tugged on her arm. Though she had to half run to keep up with him, she let him pull her along the short lane to the barn she'd spied earlier from the den. The exterior of the old building was weathered, the metal roof rusted in places, but the fenced paddocks still held a few head of white-faced cattle.

Zane shoved on a huge door of the barn, and it creaked open. They stepped inside. The interior was dark. It smelled of horses and new hay, dust and cobwebs.

"Over there," he said, taking her arm and propelling her across the worn plank floor to the back of the barn where two horses, on the other side of the manger, stood, tails switching, bridled and saddled. "I thought we'd take a ride."

Kaylie cocked a brow. "And what makes you think I won't just take off?"

"On Dallas, here?" he asked, nodding toward a rangy bay gelding. "Not much chance. He knows when it's feeding time and no matter where he is, he high-tails it back here."

The horse looked docile enough. Big brown eyes blinked as the gelding studied her without much interest.

"Unless you've taken a few riding lessons in the past seven years, you won't get two miles from this place on Dallas." He grinned deviously in the half-light. "Besides, even if you try, this boy, here," he said, hooking a thumb at a muscular chestnut stallion, "will catch you. Meet His Majesty."

She looked pointedly at him and deadpanned, "I thought I already had."

Zane's lips twitched. "He's second in command."

"Oh." Kaylie looked thoughtful. "Let me get this straight. I'm riding a horse named Dallas and you're on His Majesty?"

"You got it." Zane opened the stalls and led both animals out of the barn.

"Figures," Kaylie muttered, blinking against the sudden brightness as Zane shouldered open the door.

They mounted the horses and rode through a series of paddocks holding several other horses and a few head of cattle. The grass was dry, the ground hard, but still the animals grazed, plucking at the few yellow blades, flicking flies with their tails, or standing in the shadows of the nearby forest.

A few spindly legged foals hid behind their mother's rumps and one feisty white-faced calf bellowed as they passed. Zane, surprisingly, seemed relaxed in the saddle and Kaylie, not much of a horsewoman, pretended that it was second nature to sit astride a huge animal with a mind of his own.

"Where're we going?" she asked, shading her eyes and wishing she had thought to bring along a pair of sunglasses.

"To the ridge."

"Why?"

He glanced over his shoulder, and his gray gaze touched hers. "For the view."

Zane was riding a horse up to a ridge in the mountains in order to show her a view? If anyone had told her two days ago this would be happening, she would have laughed in his face. And yet she found Zane's newfound laid-back, get-away-from-the-rat-race attitude appealing.

The ride took nearly two hours as the horses picked their way up an overgrown trail. Kaylie's legs began to ache, and her eyes burned from squinting against the sun. She took off her jacket and tied the sleeves around her waist as Dallas plodded after His Majesty.

As she swayed in the saddle, Kaylie tried to find interest in the wildflowers sprinkled among the trees, or in the flight of a hawk circling high overhead, but her gaze, as if controlled by an unnamed force, continually wandered back to Zane. His dark hair shimmered in the sunlight and curled seductively over his collar. His shoulders stretched wide, pulling at the seams of his shirt. His sleeves were pushed over his forearms, exposing tanned skin, a simple watchband and a dusting of dark hair.

There was something earthy and masculine that surrounded him, an aura she found captivating. She noticed how his shirt bunched over the waistband of his jeans, the way his belt dipped in back as he rode.

Right now all she could think about was one man— the one man who had once been her husband, the man who had loved her so thoroughly she'd been sure no other could take his place.

Maybe no one could.

That thought caused her to draw back on the reins. Dallas sidestepped, snorting and prancing, his ears flicking as Kaylie eased up on the bit. How easy it would be to fall in love with Zane again. *If you're not in love with him already.* "No!" she cried, and Dallas reared.

Zane yanked his horse around. His face was grim. "What?"

"Nothing," she said quickly, feeling her cheeks flame as she settled her horse. "I—I just lost control for a minute." She couldn't fall in love with him again! Wouldn't allow herself the painful luxury!

"You're okay?" He didn't seem convinced, and the concern in his eyes touched a forbidden part of her soul.

"Just fine," she answered with only a trace of sarcasm.

One side of his mouth lifted. "Good. We're almost there."

The path curved sharply north, and the tall pines gave way to a rolling meadow of dry grass. A creek cut into the dry earth as it raced downhill to pool in a lake that reflected the blue of the mountain sky.

Kaylie, as she slid from the saddle, couldn't help but be enchanted. "It's gorgeous," she murmured, looking past this little alpine valley and over the ridge, where mountains steepled and gray-green forests covered the lower slopes. Zane tethered the horses, and the two dusty beasts sipped from the stream.

"That's the house," he said, standing behind her and pointing over her shoulder. His sleeve barely touched hers, and yet she was all too aware of him, his earthy scent, the warmth of his skin, the clean, sharp angle of his jaw. He extended one long finger, and Kaylie was mesmerized by the tanned length of arm and hand stretched in front of her.

She followed his gaze and saw, far below, nearly obliterated by fir trees, the roof of the old log cabin.

"You know," she said, "I never saw you as someone who would retreat up here."

He glanced down at her, and his lips pressed tightly together. "I learned a few years ago that some things are more important than business."

Her heart nearly stopped beating. "Did you?"

"You taught me that lesson, Kaylie." The look in his eyes grew distant and guarded. Tension controlled his rugged features. "Seeing you with Johnston on the night of the premiere brought everything into sharp focus. Nothing mattered but your safety. But, of course, it was too late." She watched as his naked pain dissolved to a cynical expression. He swept his hair back with the flat of his hand. "But you've never understood that I only protected you because I loved you and I was afraid of losing you. And I drove you away—did the one thing I was afraid someone else would do."

The air between them hung heavy with silence. Only the lapping of the water, the twitter of birds in the surrounding pines and the painful cadence of her own heartbeat broke the stillness. Kaylie knew the devastating grief of losing people she loved. Hadn't she lost her parents when she was young? And Zane had been there to pick up the pieces.

He leaned closer, so close that she saw flecks of blue in his gray eyes. "Losing you was the hardest thing I've ever experienced."

Kaylie's eyes burned. When Zane's hand slid upward and strong fingers wrapped around the back of her neck, she didn't resist, but tilted her face upward.

His lips brushed intimately over hers, and she parted her mouth expectantly.

The wind swept through the trees, soughing through the scented pine boughs. Shadows shifted in the sunlight as Zane's arms wrapped tightly around her.

Kaylie closed her eyes and tried to think of all the reasons she should push him away. But the pressure of his mouth on hers, the intimate caress of his tongue, the feel of strong fingers splayed possessively along her back were too seductive to ignore. With the sun warm against her back, she succumbed, winding her arms around his neck.

Desire surged through her, and she moved closer to him, felt his anxious thighs against hers. The sweet pressure of his arms wrapped around her and held her so close that her breasts were crushed and she could barely breathe.

Her feet left the ground. He carried her to a thicket of pines and laid her on a bed of needles near the water. Then he stretched out beside her and his lips found hers in a kiss that was hot and wild and filled with emotion.

His hands moved downward, sculpting each of her ribs, his thumbs brushing the swell of her breasts.

Kaylie moaned softly as her nipples hardened and

a moist heat in the depths of her womanhood swirled. Lost in battling emotions, she clung to him, laid her head back and felt the warm moist trail of his tongue as he kissed her throat and tugged on her shirt, exposing more of her skin.

Her breasts ached for his touch, her body quivered in a need that was overpowering.

He rolled atop her, and the weight of his body was welcome, the feel of his skin against hers divine.

She ignored all the voices in her head that still whispered she was making an irrevocable mistake, and she wound her hands in his hair, then let her fingers trail down the strident muscles of his back and shoulders.

"Make love to me, Kaylie," he whispered against her ear, and she could barely think. Blood was pounding at her temples, desire creating an ache so intense, she only wanted release.

He stroked the front of her T-shirt, resting the flat of his hand over her pounding heart.

"You want me."

She stared up at him. His handsome face was strained, perspiration dotted his brow. Above him, branches shifted against the blue, blue sky.

"You want me," he said again.

"Y-yes." She couldn't deny what was so patently obvious. She ached for him, yearned for him, burned deep inside with a longing so intense, she could think of nothing but the feel of his sweat-soaked body claiming hers in lovemaking as savage as it was sweet.

"And I want you," he whispered hoarsely.

He wasn't lying. She could feel his hardness through his jeans, rubbing against her hips, causing a friction that seared to her very core. She moved with him and sighed when he pulled her T-shirt from the waistband of her jeans and reached upward, the tips of his fingers grazing her lace-encased nipples.

"Oh, Zane," she whispered, her mouth finding his as she arched closer, wanting more.

He kissed her again, then his tongue slid down the milk-white skin of her throat, past her breasts, to the sensitive flesh of her abdomen.

"Zane," she whispered, and he buried his face in her.

A strangled sound escaped his lips, his breath fanned against her skin, and when he dragged his head upward and met her gaze, his eyes were glazed and stormy, as if he were fighting an inner battle that tore at his soul.

She reached upward to clasp her arms around his neck and drag his lips to hers, but he grabbed her hands. "Don't," he said, clenching his eyes shut and sucking in a swift breath.

"Zane?"

"Just don't!" The skin across his cheeks was stretched taut, and he dropped her hands, pushing himself upright. He swore violently.

"Is something wrong?" she asked as he rolled away, sitting with his back to her as he drew in long, steadying breaths.

"Everything."

"I don't understand."

"Don't you?" He twisted around, facing her again. "I intended to seduce you, Kaylie. I've planned it ever since I knew we'd be together again."

She could barely keep her eyes raised to his.

"But it's not enough."

"What—?"

"Physical lust isn't enough," he explained, the brackets near the corners of his mouth showing white. "It has to be more!" His fist pounded the dusty ground and he swore at himself between clenched teeth.

"But—I mean, I thought—"

"I know what you thought. And you were right. I planned to have you—right here and now. But I need more than a quick, hot session in the forest, Kaylie!"

She gasped and blushed to the roots of her hair. "I don't understand—"

"Sure you do. I want it all." He pulled her close to him, roughly jerking her against the rock-hard wall of his chest. His face was warm and close, his breath scented with coffee. "Let's go—"

"But—"

He whistled for the dog and climbed onto his mount. Kaylie straightened her clothes, confused and bereft and feeling like a complete fool. Good Lord, she'd nearly made love to him and he'd rejected her!

She gathered up Dallas's reins, and slapping the leather against the gelding's withers, she wondered how she was ever going to survive the next few days being trapped up here alone with Zane.

Chapter 7

"It's just not like Kaylie to leave us in the lurch like this," Jim Crowley, producer of *West Coast Morning,* grumbled. He stepped over the thick camera cables as he made his way off the cozy set, which was designed to look like the living room in one of San Francisco's charming row houses.

He headed down a short hall to his office, with his assistant, Tracy Montclair, following one step behind.

"Even Kaylie Melville has a personal life, you know," she pointed out.

"All of a sudden? In the past six and a half years, Kaylie hasn't missed one show. Not one. This just isn't like her." He shoved open the glass door to his office and stalked to the desk.

The ashtray was overflowing, and he dumped the

contents into a wastebasket, then settled into his creaky leather chair.

"Call that sister of hers—Marge, isn't it?"

"Margot."

"Whatever." Jim winced as a nerve in his lower back twinged, the aftermath from a game of racquetball. "Phone Margot and see if there's a number where we can reach Kaylie."

"Oh, come on, Jim. You're not serious, are you? She's with her aunt in a hospital somewhere, for God's sake!"

"Well, even hospitals have phone numbers." Jim tried to ignore his craving for a cigarette and unwrapped a stick of gum. "I need to talk to her. We've got a helluva schedule next week and I don't think Alan can handle it alone."

"She may be back by then."

"Well, let's not leave it to chance, okay?" He wadded the gum into a small clump and tossed it into his mouth just as there was a quick rap on the door. Through the glass he spied Alan Bently.

"I swear that guy's got radar," Jim muttered under his breath. Alan had the annoying habit of showing up every time his name was mentioned. "What's up?" he asked, as Alan slid into the chair next to Tracy's.

Alan flashed his thousand-watt smile. Though no longer a leading man, he still had an on-camera charisma that attracted the female viewers. "I just thought we'd better discuss the next couple of shows. Unless Kaylie gets back soon, we've got to rethink the format. Starting with Monday."

Jim scowled. "Reformat? How?"

"Well, I assume I'll have to do all the interviews

as well as the news." Alan leaned forward, resting his elbows on his knees, looking earnest as he proceeded to explain to Jim that he could host the hour format of *West Coast Morning* all by himself.

For Kaylie, the next few days were torture. Torn between her life in San Francisco and the excitement of this adventure with Zane, she alternately formed plans of escape and talked herself out of them.

She felt as if she were on an emotional battlefield. One minute they were at each other's throats, the next, waving the white flag.

Zane's office hadn't come up with any new information on Lee Johnston. "Ted" hadn't called again. Dr. Henshaw was still out of town, though Brad Hastings promised to visit him at Whispering Hills the minute he returned. He also had an appointment scheduled with the administrator of the hospital.

Zane's nerves were strung tight. He admitted that he felt useless up here, that he should be in San Francisco checking things out for himself, but at the mention of returning to civilization, he blew up. Kaylie was safe here—at least temporarily.

It almost seemed as if they were married again, except of course, they didn't go to bed together. And, as in their marriage, Zane was dominating the relationship.

Half the time Kaylie was furious with him, and yet she could feel her emotions swaying and she was softening bit by bit. Often in the past seventy-two hours she'd caught him watching her when he'd thought she wasn't looking, and she had noticed how he'd avoided even the briefest physical contact. That was the hard part—being so close to him and yet not touching.

During the days, they took horseback rides, mended the fence, worked on the house, took care of the stock, and Kaylie found herself fantasizing about Zane—remembering the good part of their marriage, the love that had been so special. In the evenings they talked, watched television, played cribbage or petted the dog. Franklin still wasn't crazy about her, but he accepted her and even thumped his tail on the floor when she walked into a room. And that was progress.

To her surprise, she discovered Zane had changed, just as he'd said he had—he'd mellowed with the past seven years, and she couldn't help wondering what life would be like now, were she married to him.

But that was an entirely irrational thought.

Now, as he knelt at the fireplace and laid firewood in the grate, she watched the pull of his jeans at his hips, the slice of skin that was exposed as his sweater inched upward. He glanced over his shoulder and motioned to the empty wood basket. "You could help, you know."

"Could I?" She laughed. Seated on the couch and swirling a glass of wine, she added, "And here I thought you were going to treat me to a life of leisure—you know, pamper me to death."

"No way." He dusted his hands. "I thought you were a fiercely independent woman who wouldn't let any man treat you as less than an equal."

"Well, I am, but—"

"Then get some wood," he suggested, nudging the empty basket toward her with the toe of his boot.

"Slave driver," she whispered, taking a last swallow of wine. "You'll pay for this, Flannery." Smiling good-naturedly, she grabbed the basket and marched out the front door.

"I don't doubt it," he called after her.

Outside, a cool breeze swept over the mountainside and a thin stream of moonlight guided her. A few stars winked jewellike in the black sky and an owl hooted from a nearby stand of pine. The wind picked up, and the air was heavy with the promise of rain.

Kaylie walked past the Jeep and noticed that the interior light was on.

Her heart skipped a beat.

She reached for the door, and it opened.

She hesitated for a second. This was her chance, but did she really want to leave? She chewed on the inside of her lip and glanced at the house. Of course she had to leave—she had no choice! As long as Zane tried to control her, she had no will of her own. And she was falling for him again. That was dangerous.

Swallowing hard, she dropped the basket and slid into the interior, realizing that she didn't have his keys. Crossing her fingers, she silently prayed that he'd left the keys in the ignition. No such luck. Even though Zane had made several trips carrying grain from the storage shed to the barn in the Jeep, he hadn't forgotten his keys. Nor the phone. It, too, was missing.

"Damn!" she muttered, sneaking a glance at the house. Light spilled from the windows but she couldn't see Zane. It didn't matter. He was busy with the fire. He wouldn't miss her for a good five minutes. But how in the world did one go about hot-wiring a car?

"Think, Kaylie," she said, deciding that she had to look behind the ignition and try to find two wires that when touched, would create an electrical charge. Or at least that's what she guessed. It seemed logical. And she didn't have time for any other speculation. It was now or never. Do or die.

She lay on the driver's seat, her head under the dash, eyeing the wires that ran every which way. Biting her lip, she tugged gently on a tangled group that seemed to feed into the ignition switch. There was a red wire and a black one—if she pulled them out of the dash, unwrapped the plastic coating, then touched the wires…?

Hopefully she wouldn't detonate the engine or shoot herself into orbit, she thought ruefully.

She pulled on one of the black wires.

A low growl erupted from the woods.

Kaylie's heart leaped to her throat.

"Don't tell me. You've decided to take a crash course in auto mechanics," Zane guessed, his voice so soft she barcly heard him. But Franklin, lurking in the shadows, barked loudly.

She froze, dropping the wires as if they were indeed hot.

Feeling like a fool, she tilted her head so that she could see him, and took the offensive. "I think I've already mentioned your vile habit of sneaking up on people." She pinned the dog with her glare. "The same goes for you."

Franklin wagged his tail, proud of himself, and Zane threw back his head and laughed. "And you, Ms. Melville, have a *vile* habit of trying to run away." He eyed the interior of the Jeep, and his mouth quirked. "So you were trying to start the Jeep without the aid of a key. Well, don't let me stop you." Gesturing grandly to the dash, he swallowed an amused smile. "Go right ahead."

"And have you stop me the minute the engine turns over?"

"A risk you'll have to take."

Her temper started to soar. What she wouldn't do to start this damned Jeep and take off, leaving him in a spray of gravel.

Zane leaned his hip against the fender. "And of course, you could shock yourself while you're at it."

"I realize that!" Sitting upright, she slid out of the car. "If you're done belittling me—"

"And if you're done with this teenaged prank."

She shot him a withering glance. "Prank? After the stunt you pulled by kidnap—"

He held up a palm, and she clamped her mouth shut, determined not to break their fragile truce.

"I thought we'd gotten beyond that," he said, his brows beetling.

"I—we—I thought we had to," she said, knowing he didn't believe her. "But the opportunity to leave just presented itself. You can't blame me for—" She bit her tongue.

He grabbed her by the arm and propelled her toward the house. "Oh, no? Then who should I blame?"

"Yourself! For hauling me up here in the first place. It's been three days, Zane! Three days of being away from the real world!"

"And it's been great, hasn't it?" he said, pressing his face close to hers.

"Just spiffy," she shot back, not letting him know for even a second that he was right, that being here with him was a little touch of heaven.

He picked up her discarded basket and glanced up at the sky. "*I'll* go get the firewood. It's safer. You'd better go inside. It's gonna rain soon." Swinging the damned basket, he strode to the woodpile with Franklin trotting after him.

Later, once the fire was burning in yellow and orange flames, Zane left the room for a few minutes. When he returned, he was carrying a small tape player, a bottle of wine and two glasses.

"Okay, it's time to get serious," he said, uncorking the wine and pouring them each a glass.

"About what?"

"This." He punched a button, and the tape of his phone call with Ted started playing.

Kaylie couldn't take a sip.

"Does this sound like anyone you know, anyone you've ever met?"

"I—I don't think so," Kaylie replied, her skin crawling at the sound of the raspy warning.

"Think, Kaylie! This is important." Zane rewound the tape and played it again and again until Kaylie could repeat the conversation word for word.

"I don't know," she admitted, biting her lower lip.

Zane snapped the recorder off and plowed angry fingers through his hair. "Obviously Ted knows you and your connection with me. He also knows all about Whispering Hills and Lee Johnston. And he knows that you and I are together."

"He does?" she cried. "How?"

"You weren't on the show, but that doesn't necessarily mean that you were with me. However, the fact that Ted's quit calling makes me think he's got a line on us."

Kaylie's fingers slipped on her glass. She spilled wine on her pants, but quickly mopped it up. "A line—"

"Well, maybe that's a little drastic. Maybe he

would've quit calling anyway. He only called a couple of times. But it's a coincidence and I don't believe in coincidence."

"So, what—what does that mean?" she asked, not feeling safer knowing that some other nut case might guess where they were.

"It means we stay put until Hastings gets some more information."

"Don't you think this Ted, if he's so smart, might find us?"

Zane frowned into his wine, swirling the glass thoughtfully. "I don't think so. Only a few people know I own this place."

"But he could find out." Fear strangled her. "Do you think Ted is Johnston?" she asked, her thoughts racing ahead wildly. "And that he placed the call to you, knowing that you would drag me up here?"

Zane shook his head, but his expression remained grim. "I doubt it. You were too visible in San Francisco. He could find you more easily. If he's going to be released, he wouldn't want to tip you off." His gaze moved from his glass to search her face. "Don't worry, I'll take care of you."

Surprisingly, that thought was comforting.

"But it would help me a lot, if we could figure out who Ted really is."

He played the tape again, and a headache began to pound at Kaylie's temples. She finished her wine and, before she began feeling too cozy and safe with Zane, set her glass on the coffee table. "I think I'll turn in."

She started to stand, but Zane placed a restraining hand on her shoulder. "Just remember one thing," he said, his voice firm.

"What's that?"

"If you try to escape again, I'll have to make sure that it doesn't happen. And that means I'll stick to you like glue."

Shrugging off his hand, she couldn't help but rise to the bait. "You'll have to catch me first."

"I know." One side of his mouth lifted, and his eyes glowed in the firelight.

She knew then that she loved him with all of her foolish heart. And if she didn't leave him soon, she never would be able to. She would have to give up her freedom and independence for the sake of love.

She hurried upstairs to her room. "Oh, Zane," she whispered, her throat aching. She had no choice but to escape—for both their sakes.

Zane drained his glass and wondered how long he could keep up this charade. Soon he would have to go back to the city and he couldn't, even in his wildest fantasies, keep her locked away forever. Tomorrow morning she'd miss another taping of her program and sooner or later the producer would start checking. Margot wouldn't be able to keep Crowley at bay forever.

And he couldn't force Kaylie to love him.

That thought tore open old wounds. He'd lost her once, and the surest way to lose her again was to keep imposing his will on her.

Absently, he flicked on the tape again, and Ted's hoarse voice filled the room. "Who are you?" Zane said aloud. "Just who the hell are you?"

And what about Johnston?

An icy knot curled in his stomach. Maybe this Ted character was wrong. Surely the courts wouldn't set a psychotic like Johnston back on the streets. But it had happened time and time again. He shivered inside. He loved Kaylie; he'd never stopped. But he wasn't going to sacrifice her life for anything—not even for a reconciliation. So, if it meant Kaylie would hate him for the rest of her life, so be it. At least she would be safe.

Or would she?

Even here, Zane wasn't completely at ease.

He walked outside to a shed where he kept his phone and, despite the late hour, dialed Brad Hastings. Something had to happen soon. He couldn't keep Kaylie up here forever.

Kaylie didn't waste any time. The situation was intolerable. She was getting in much too deep with Zane, and she'd have to leave him soon, or she'd never find the willpower. As for Lee Johnston, she'd take care of herself—hire a bodyguard if necessary.

A bodyguard like Zane?

Her heart turned over and she had to fight the strong pull of emotions.

Upstairs she tossed a pair of jeans, her running shoes, a sweater and jacket over the end of the bed. She drew the covers to her neck and waited, listening to the sounds of the old house: timbers creaking, wind rattling windowpanes, clock ticking in the hall.

Go to bed, Zane, she silently prayed.

An hour passed before she heard his footsteps on the stairs. He paused at the landing, and she wondered if he'd check on her. How would she explain her clothes? The fact that she was still awake?

Chewing on her lip, her heart pumping crazily, she

heard his footsteps retreat and the door to his room open and close.

She let out her breath. Now she could get started. She gave him a half hour to get to sleep, then fifteen minutes more for good measure. At a quarter to one, she slid out of bed and dressed in the moonlight streaming through her window.

Tucking her shoes under her arm, she headed in stockinged feet through her door and into the hallway. Her footsteps didn't make a sound, but her pulse was thundering in her brain.

Slowly she started downstairs, wincing on the third step when it creaked beneath her weight.

She waited, holding her breath, but Zane's door didn't bang open, so she hurried down the rest of the flight, picked her way through the living room to the kitchen, then dug in the pantry where she had discovered the old jacket and flashlight. Carefully she switched on the portable light and was rewarded with a steady, if pale, beam.

Good enough, she thought, unlatching the back door and slipping outside. She closed the door behind her, slid into her Reebok tennis shoes and, using only the faint light from a cloud-covered moon as her guide, made her way to the barn.

Inside, the horses snorted and pawed at the stalls. "Shh," Kaylie whispered, flashing her light until she found His Majesty. "It's all right."

Dallas poked his silken nose over the stall door and Kaylie petted him fondly. "Not tonight," she whispered, feeling a little like a traitor. "Tonight I need speed. I can't take a chance that you-know-who will catch me."

With surprising quickness, she bridled and saddled

His Majesty, then led him from the barn. He danced and minced as the wind rushed through the trees, and Kaylie felt the first drop of rain fall from the sky. "Oh, great," she murmured. She tried hard to disregard the fact that she wasn't horsewoman enough for him if he were spooked.

His hoofbeats seemed to echo through the night as she unlatched the main gate and guided him through.

She had no idea where she was going, but intended to follow the long lane until daylight. Hopefully, by then, she'd find a crossroad or two and be able to lose Zane, because, if and when he caught up with her, all hell would break loose.

She didn't pause to consider the consequences of his wrath now. Instead she swung into the saddle and shoved her heels into His Majesty's sides. The horse picked up speed, trotting down the drive as the cold wind rushed against her face.

Kaylie squinted in the darkness, hoping beyond hope that His Majesty had some vague idea where civilization would lie, because she didn't.

The sky was dark—no bright lights over the hill-side guiding her. Nope, this time she'd have to let common sense and her mount's instincts lead the way. *And I need a little luck,* she thought with an inward smile as she shone her flashlight toward the sky and caught the reflection of heavy cable. She'd follow the electricity and telephone wires. Eventually, she reasoned, the cables would lead to civilization.

The road was steep, the switchbacks hairpin curves, but His Majesty picked his way along the gravel without faltering. Kaylie, tense, forever listening to the sounds of the night, prayed that Zane would sleep in and not wake until after nine. By that time she'd be well on her way to San Francisco. Clucking her tongue, she encouraged the stallion to pick up his pace as rain beat down in a steady drizzle.

She'd ridden for nearly an hour before she came to the first road of any significance. Her shoulders had already begun to ache, and her fingers and cheeks were slick with rain. "Okay, boy, what do you think?" she asked, patting the chestnut's sleek neck and frowning when she noticed the wires overhead were strung in both directions. One way would lead to a city, the other could lead to another isolated, and perhaps abandoned, house in the forest.

"Great," she mumbled to her disinterested horse. "Just fine and dandy!" No doubt Zane would expect her to head west, for that was the most likely way to reach civilization. And, blast it, she didn't have much choice as the mountains to the north and east were forbidding and there were no roads that led south.

"West it is," she ground out, refusing to think about the cold water seeping through her collar and running down her neck. She urged His Majesty forward, her ears straining for the sound of an engine behind them. But all she heard was the sigh of the wind, the steady drip of rain and the rhythmic plop of the stallion's hooves. Occasionally a rustle in the undergrowth would startle the horse as a hidden animal scurried through the woods flanking the gravel road. "Squirrels and raccoons and rabbits," she told herself. "Nothing bigger or creepy. No bats or snakes or cougars..."

As the night wore on, Kaylie shone her flashlight whenever there was a crossroads, but otherwise followed the road by using the thick power cables as her guide.

Lightning struck in jagged flashes that illuminated the distant hills for a few sizzling moments. His Majesty shied and reared at the eerie light and the growl of thunder as it echoed over the hills.

"Hold, on, boy." Kaylie's hands tightened over the reins. "Steady."

The night closed in around her, and she felt the silence of the woods, the breath of the wind against her fingers and bare neck, the cold damp touch of the rain. She considered turning back a couple of times, but pressed on. Being with Zane was just too dangerous. Some women were cursed to love the wrong men. She just happened to be one of them.

Eventually, the road grew less steep. Kaylie's heart soared. She closed her eyes and thought she heard the hum of traffic on a faraway interstate. Or was it the rattle of a train on distant tracks? No matter. It meant she was approaching some sort of civilization.

Suddenly His Majesty tossed back his head and snorted violently. Stopping short, he rolled wide, white-rimmed eyes backward. His nostrils distended, and his wet coat quivered under her hands.

"Hey, whoa—" The hairs on the back of Kaylie's neck rose as her mount minced and sidestepped. "What is it?" she whispered, hoping she didn't convey her fear to the horse.

She shone her flashlight ahead, and its tiny beam landed on Zane, half lying on the hood of his Jeep, soaked to the skin, his back propped by the windshield, his arms crossed over his chest, his expression positively murderous.

"Oh, God." Kaylie's heart plummeted.

Lightning flashed over the hills, and His Majesty reared, but at the sound of Zane's voice, the horse quieted, nickering softly.

"Well, well, Ms. Melville," Zane drawled in a tone so low and angry it rivaled the distant thunder, "I was wondering when you'd finally show up."

Chapter 8

"But how—" Kaylie sputtered, shivering as she stared past Zane to the road beyond. Maybe she could make a run for it—or maybe His Majesty could find a path through the woods, a path the Jeep couldn't follow...

"Don't do anything crazy," Zane warned, shoving himself upright and hopping to the wet ground. "And the way I found you is simple. Most of the side roads around here are old logging trails—roads that crisscross over the mountain but eventually end up here. I knew if I waited long enough, you'd turn up."

"You heard me leave?" she asked, swiping at a drip of rain on the tip of her nose.

"Take my advice—don't apply for a job with the CIA."

"You tricked me!"

"No, you tricked me." He strode over and reached for the bridle, but she pulled hard on the reins and His Majesty's broad head swung away from Zane. Kicking sharply into the stallion's sides, Kaylie tried to spur past Zane, but he was too quick.

With an oath, Zane sprang like a puma and grabbed hold of the reins, ripping the wet leather straps from Kaylie's chilled fingers. "That was a stupid thing to do! Even worse than trying to hot-wire the Jeep!"

A ragged streak of lightning scarred the sky.

The horse reared, and Kaylie, thrown off balance, grabbed wildly at the saddle horn and His Majesty's wet mane.

"Whoa—slow down." Zane soothed the stallion, murmuring softly until the anxious beast slowly relaxed. "That's it, boy." Zane patted the chestnut's shoulder.

Kaylie, her hair tossed around her face, accused, "You pretended to be asleep! You heard me leave and you followed me!"

"Of course I heard you leave. Do you think I'd trust you after I caught you tampering with my ignition?"

"Tampering?" she repeated, furious and cold and hurt. "I was just trying to regain my freedom—you know, one of the basic constitutional rights guaranteed to every citizen!"

"I've heard this all before."

"Well, you're going to hear it again!"

"Get down, Kaylie."

"No way."

"Get down. Now!" he roared.

"You have no right to order me around!" she yelled, tossing her head imperiously.

"Probably not," he admitted, "but it's late and I'm tired and wet. Now let's go home."

"That log monstrosity is *not* my home!" she shot back, frustrated and angry that he'd caught up with her twice. Why, when it was so hard to leave him, didn't he make it easy for her and just let her go?

"Not your permanent home maybe, but for now—"

"Don't you know I'll hate you forever for this?" she hurled down at him, glaring.

Moonlight washed his face, and a sliver of pain slashed through his silvery eyes. "So hate me," he replied, his mouth tightening at the corners. "But while you're hating me, get down." When she didn't budge, he glanced up. "Okay, have it your way. You can ride His Majesty all the way back in this damned rain while I lead him in the Jeep, or you can enjoy the relative comforts of a heater, radio and padded bucket seats. Your choice."

"Get in that Jeep with you?" she challenged, though it did sound inviting, and she wished for just a second that loving Zane were simple. "That's what got me into this mess in the first place!"

"Fine." He tugged on the reins, and His Majesty followed docilely.

"Traitor," Kaylie whispered to the horse, and Zane rolled down the driver's window, climbed into the Jeep and fired the ignition.

His Majesty sidestepped. Kaylie patted the stallion's sleek neck. "It's okay," she said, lying, as Zane rammed the vehicle into gear.

"Last chance," he called, and Kaylie, though she longed to climb down from the saddle and sit in the warm interior of the Jeep, didn't move. Zane shook his head in disgust as the rig crawled slowly forward.

Kaylie grabbed hold of the saddle horn as His Majesty started the long trek back at a fast trot. The brisk pace jarred her, and the cold, wet air seeped through her jacket, but she'd be damned if she'd complain! Gritting her teeth, she tried to keep her mind off her discomfort, though her muscles were already aching, her teeth chattering.

As the incline grew more steep, Zane slowed, letting the horse walk. Kaylie was chilled to the bone, and her arms and thighs burned mercilessly, but she refused to call out and ask Zane to stop. Rain dripped down her nose and neck. Clenching her teeth, she endured the painful journey, head high, jaw thrust forward.

After about twenty minutes, Zane muttered something unintelligible, then stood on the brakes. The Jeep ground to a halt in the gravel and mud. "This is insane," he growled, opening his door and splashing through the puddles to His Majesty's side. "Maybe you don't give a damn about yourself, but you could give the horse a break!"

He pulled her from the saddle, and she landed on the ground so hard, her knees nearly gave way. Zane kept a strong arm around her. "A little wobbly?" he mocked, but there was a kindness in his features as he helped her to the Jeep. And the rain seemed to soften the hard lines surrounding his mouth. He touched her forehead, shoving a wet strand of curling hair from her eyes. "Come on, Kaylie," he whispered, his voice so tender it nearly broke her heart, "give it up for the night."

"I—I can't," she stammered.

"Sure you can."

"But—"

"Please, love," he insisted gently, opening the door. "It isn't worth it."

"How would you know?"

He rolled his eyes, and a self-effacing smile tugged at the corners of his mouth. "When it comes to stubborn pride," he admitted, "I think I wrote the book."

His unexpected kindness pierced her pride. Tears filled her throat, and she had to grit her teeth to keep from crying as he gently lifted her into the Jeep. She sagged against him. The warmth of him, the fact that he so obviously still cared for her, perhaps loved her, caused more tears to burn in her eyes. She wanted to cling to him and never let go. Inside the Jeep, she could barely stretch out her cramped, cold muscles.

Before he slid behind the steering wheel again, Zane unsaddled the horse and tossed the saddle and blanket into the back. He found a clean, thick towel, and a worn sheepskin jacket. "Here, dry off a little," he said, handing her the jacket and towel and turning up the heat as he shoved the rig into first.

Kaylie glanced his way as the vehicle rolled forward. Blotting her face with the towel, she leaned her head back against the seat and tried to ignore the cramps in her shoulders and legs as she fought back tears and the overwhelming urge to fall against him and be held and comforted; to let him take control.

His narrowed eyes were trained on the winding gravel road. Every so often he would glance in the sideview mirror, checking his stallion. It was romantic, in a way, she thought, how he kept chasing her down, swearing to protect her, saying he loved her. If only she dared believe him…trust him a little…love him a lot.

"Did you really think you could get away with it?" Zane asked, as the silence grew thick around them and the gloom of the forest seeped into the interior.

Shivering, she rubbed her arms, trying to keep her teeth from chattering. "I thought it was worth a shot."

"You cold?" He worked with the knobs of the heater, then, still driving, eased out of his own jacket and laid it across the blanket. "I'll probably end up taking you to the hospital."

"I'll be fine," she replied, still chilled to the bone.

Zane sighed. "And what would you have done if you had, by some miracle, found the freeway? Ride the horse down four lanes?"

"No," she said, her spine stiffening involuntarily, "I intended to stop at the first house and call."

"Whom?" he asked.

"Jim maybe—or Alan. Not Margot since she's in cahoots with you."

"And what would Alan have done?"

"Rescued me!"

"Ha!" He barked out a laugh and twisted hard on the wheel. "So now you want to be rescued?"

"No, I just want my life back," she said, staring out the window and watching the wipers slap away the rain.

"A life without me."

She drew in a steadying breath and tried to lie, but couldn't. The words stuck in her throat. She didn't want him completely out of her life—not anymore. And that was the problem. There was no letting Zane in a little bit. With him it was all or nothing. "All" meant giving up her hard-fought independence. "Nothing" meant never seeing him again. Her heart squeezed painfully at the thought. These past few days had been exhilarating and romantic, and her life back in the city seemed colorless in comparison.

"I thought Alan didn't mean anything to you."

"He's a friend. A co-worker and a friend."

He snorted and fiddled with the heater as the windows began to fog. "So what about us?"

"I don't know what to do about us," she admitted, her emotions as raw as the dark night. "Part of me would like to see you burn in hell for what you've put me through."

"And the other part?"

She slid him a glance. "The other part tells me you're the best thing that ever happened to me."

Zane drew a slow breath, then smiled painfully. "I definitely think you should listen to part two."

"How can I," she asked, turning to face him, "when all you've done since you showed up at my house is bully me into doing things your way?"

The honesty in her eyes cut deep into his soul. He knew that he'd gone too far. But now there was no turning back. He'd considered letting her leave, pretending not to hear her sneak out of the house and into the barn. But what then? Let her show up in San Francisco with his horse and never see her again? The thought was unbearable. "I'll let you go, Kaylie," he promised, forcing the words through his teeth. "Once I'm assured that you'll be safe." He swallowed with difficulty and almost tripped over the lie. "That's all I really want for you."

As the rain stopped, he turned off the wipers and checked the side mirror. His Majesty was tiring. "I think we'd better pull over for a little while," he said, frowning. "Give the old guy a break. He's had a hard night."

"Haven't we all?" she said, but climbed out of the Jeep when it slowed to a halt. Both she and Zane checked the horse, who was sweating and starting to lather. Zane walked him slowly for a while, until the stallion's heavy breathing returned to normal. Zane slanted a glance at Kaylie, and his gut twisted.

She caught his gaze, and her lips moved a little so seductive and innocently erotic. He wondered how much more of this self-induced torment he could stand.

Time seemed to stand still as they stood, not touching, gazes locked, the earthy, rain-washed forest surrounding them.

"We'd better get going," he said, his voice gruff.

She glanced away, breaking the spell. Nodding, she replied, "I'll lead His Majesty."

Zane didn't argue. Once she was safely inside the Jeep, he handed her the reins, then climbed behind the wheel. The rest of the ride was tense and excruciatingly slow. Several times his fingers, gripping the gearshift, brushed against her knee, and she looked sharply up at him, but there weren't accusations in her gaze. If anything, there was an unspoken invitation.

Zane's fingers tightened over the wheel, and he thought he'd go out of his mind battling the urge to stop, take her into his arms and make love to her right then and there!

Finally, after agonizing minutes, he steered the vehicle around the final corner, and the log house loomed in the darkness ahead.

"I'll take care of the horse," he said as he parked the rig and looked long and hard at Kaylie. "And you should take a hot bath, drink something warm and then find the heaviest nightgown in the closet and wrap yourself up in about a thousand blankets." She reached for the door, and he couldn't let her escape. He grabbed her and pulled. She fell against him. As she did, he covered her mouth with his, pressing hard, insistent lips to hers and surrendering to the emotions that had warred with him ever since he'd seen her walking out of the water on the beach in Carmel.

His blood thundered, his body burned, and all those vows he'd sworn to himself—vows to stay away from her until she was ready—vanished.

She seemed to melt against him, her supple lips responding, a quiet moan escaping her throat. "Why?" he rasped, when he finally lifted his head from hers. "Why do you continue to fight me?"

"Because you fight me," she responded, eyes glazed as she slowly disentangled herself. "And that's what it is with us—a battlefield—your will against mine. It's always been that way, always will be."

She opened the door and stepped into the darkness, and Zane, wishing the throbbing in his loins would subside, struggled out of the Jeep. Pocketing his keys, he said, "I'll only be a few minutes."

She stared at him with wide, vulnerable eyes, then hurried into the house.

He should have just let her go back to the city, he realized, knowing that he couldn't hold out much longer. Sooner or later, he'd give in to the demands of his body, and then... Oh, God, then who knew what would happen?

There was a good chance that he'd lose her forever.

"If you haven't already," he reminded himself grimly. With a gentle tug, he led the tired stallion to the barn.

Kaylie kicked off her soiled clothes and made a bee-line for the shower. She let the hot spray soothe her throbbing muscles and loosen her sore joints, while the warm water restored feeling in her fingers and toes. She felt as if she'd been in the saddle for a millennium.

"As a pioneer woman you're a failure, Melville," she said, chiding herself as she squeezed water from a sponge and lathered her body. "And as a modern woman, you need some lessons on the male of the species." What was wrong with her? she wondered, twisting off the faucets and snatching a bath towel from the rack. Every time Zane touched her or kissed her or looked at her, she turned into jelly.

"Don't let him know that," she warned her reflection as she rubbed away the moisture from the mirror. "You're supposed to be strong, independent and in control!" But the green eyes staring back at her accused her of the lie. When it came to Zane, whether she wanted to admit it or not, she was in love. Always had been.

"And you're a fool," she whispered bitterly, toweling dry her hair.

She flung open the closet door and picked out a white cotton nightgown and a robe.

She'd go downstairs, get something to eat and then try to get to sleep. Right now, she knew that sleep was out of the question.

She started downstairs, only to stop short at the doorway to Zane's room. The door was open a crack, and she could see him, standing in front of the mirror, wearing only low-slung jeans.

His eyes caught hers in the reflection, and the look he sent her stopped her breath somewhere between her throat and lungs. "I thought you were going to rest," he said.

"I'm not tired."

He cocked a disdainful brow. "You should be dead on your feet."

"Nope," she replied, hoping to sound chipper, though she had to stifle a yawn.

Turning to face her, he smiled, a small, lazy grin. "So, how're you going to plan your next escape attempt?"

"Next time it won't just be an attempt," she replied, unable to resist teasing him.

"Oh?" One dark eyebrow cocked in interest. He crossed the room and held the door open. "So next time you'll dupe me."

"That's right."

"I can hardly wait," he drawled, baiting her.

"Oh, you won't have to wait long," she promised, though she had no idea how she'd ever pull it off.

"No?" His eyes narrowed speculatively, and Kaylie could feel the air charge between them. "You know, Kaylie, I wonder about all those reasons you concoct to go back to San Francisco." He studied his nails. "The job, the empty apartment, your co-worker, that all-fired important life."

"It is important."

"No doubt, but I think there's another reason you can't wait to make tracks out of here." He looked up at her and his gaze was so intense, she could barely breathe.

"And what's that?" she asked, swallowing hard.

"I think you're afraid of me—or at least of being alone with me."

"That's silly."

"Is it?" His gaze accused her of the lie. "I think you're less afraid of dealing with that madman who would like to slit your throat than you are of facing your real feelings for me."

"My feelings?" she asked, licking her lips in unwitting invitation.

"Right. I think you're afraid that if you stay here too long with me, you won't have the willpower to leave."

Though his guess was close to the truth, she laughed nervously. "You always did have an incredible ego."

His smoldering look accused her of the lie. She knew he was going to kiss her. In the intimate room, alone in the wilderness, he was going to take her into his arms and she wouldn't be able to resist. "Please, Zane, if you care about me—"

"I do. I told you that. I also told you that I love you."

"Then, if you love me, take me home."

He hesitated, pain shadowing his eyes. "This is home, Kaylie. You and me together—that's home."

"Not anymore, Zane," she said, forcing the words out. "And never again."

"You're kidding yourself."

"I—I think you're the one doing the kidding."

"Am I?" His expression darkened, and the lines around the corners of his mouth grew tight. He grabbed her wrist and slowly tugged, pulling her toward him. Deliberately he lowered his head, until his lips hovered over hers. "I can't leave you alone," he admitted hoarsely, his face only inches from her, his breath stirring the wet strands of her hair, his gaze moving to

the pout of her lips. "Damn it, I want to, but I...just...
can't." He tugged on her arm, and his mouth claimed
hers in a kiss that burned deep into her heart.

Though a thousand reasons to run flitted through
her mind, her love for him still lingered. His lips were
warm, his body, hard and long, his arms strong. Tilting her head upward, she wrapped her arms around his
neck and kissed him with all the pent-up desire she'd
tried so desperately to suppress. Lost in the wonder of
his male body pressed urgently against hers, she didn't
stop him when one hand tangled in her hair, the other
splaying possessively against her back. He kissed her
throat and eyes and cheeks, and she tingled everywhere, aching for him.

Slowly he lowered her onto the bed and she didn't
protest. His tongue slid between her teeth, flicking
against her tongue, causing thrills to chase up her
spine.

Her nipples grew hard, and dark peaks pressed
against the thin cotton of her gown. Her breasts ached
for his touch, and she moved intimately against him,
rewarded by the feel of his hands slipping past the cotton, sliding the nightgown over her shoulder, exposing
her white skin.

His thumb grazed her nipple, and she moaned. Zane
lowered his head, suckling on the tiny dark bud, flicking it with his tongue, igniting her blood. Wanting so
much more, Kaylie writhed against him. Impatiently
his hands slid the nightgown over her other shoulder,
baring both breasts.

With a primal groan he kissed both white mounds
and buried his head in the cleft between them, alternately suckling from one, then the other.

"Oh, Kaylie," he rasped, kneading one soft mound as he kissed the other. "Don't ever stop." Slowly his hand lowered to the hem of her nightgown, his fingers grazing her thigh, skimming her skin that already felt on fire.

"Please…" she whispered.

He groaned, ripping the nightgown from her body and dropping to his knees, his hands on her bare buttocks as he touched her heated flesh with his tongue, kissing her breasts and abdomen and lower. Sucking in her breath, she leaned against him, her hands tangling in his hair as he explored and probed until she could think of nothing but the swirling hot void, a vortex of want, an emptiness only he could fill.

"I love you," he vowed, his hands still massaging her buttocks as he stood.

Oh, God, if she could only believe him. The words rang in her ears. But did he know that love and possession weren't the same? Could he learn?

Unable to resist, she boldly touched the waistband of his jeans. He made a primal sound deep in his throat, then tilted her head up to his. "Yes, love," he whispered, eyes glazed with passion.

She slid his jeans over his legs and he kicked himself free of them and wrapped strong arms around her middle. In one swift motion, he whirled her onto the bed and was lying over her, his gaze locked with hers, his tongue rimming her lips. "Just love me," he whispered.

"Oh, Zane, I do."

Closing his eyes for a second, he parted her legs with his and entered her swiftly. She sucked in her breath as he began to move, slowly at first, then with an ever-increasing rhythm that drove all thoughts from her mind.

She was here with Zane, making love, and that was all that mattered. They moved together, fusing, loving, spiraling upward and soaring above the clouds. Heaven and earth seemed to splinter before her eyes and she cried his name as she tumbled on a slow, heated cloud back to earth. "Zane, oh, Zane!"

"I'm here, love," he murmured into her hair. "I always will be."

"I know," she whispered, more content than she'd ever been, snuggling deep in his arms, resting her head against the soft mat of hair on his chest, listening to the loud cadence of his heart. This seemed so right, so perfect.

As afterglow finally faded, his lips found hers again and they made love—more slowly this time—exploring and touching, rekindling old fires that flamed and sizzled, becoming intimate as naturally as if they'd never separated.

Afterward, Kaylie sighed contentedly against him as he drifted into a deep sleep. Closing her eyes, she knew that she loved him. It was that simple. And that complicated.

Moaning, he rolled away from her, then sighed, still sleeping. His face, in slumber, was carefree, his mouth a soft line, his lashes dark against his cheek.

Kaylie touched his hair, and her heart nearly broke. Why was she doomed to love a man who was so smothering? Pressing a soft kiss to his lips, she rolled over, intending to fall asleep and deal with her feelings in the morning with a clear head. Maybe she and Zane could work things out. He was a reasonable man, and she was now a mature woman. If she only explained...

She noticed a reflection of moonlight on the floor—a dazzling flash of silver in the dark pile of his clothes. Her heart stopped when she realized that she was staring at his keys as they poked from the pocket of his jeans.

She closed her eyes for a second, wishing the vision away, but when she lifted her lids, the keys still lay there. Beckoning. Offering escape and freedom.

Her mouth turned to cotton.

Oh, God, she thought, shaking inside. Could she leave him? She glanced at his peaceful, trusting profile, tanned skin in relief against the white pillow, and her heart felt as if it were tearing in two.

She had no choice. She had to control her own life. She couldn't allow him to manipulate her.

Holding her breath and fighting tears, she slipped slowly from the bedcovers and silently picked up his keys. As her fingers closed around the cool metal, she hardly dared breathe. They jangled softly, but Zane just snorted and turned over.

For a few precious seconds Kaylie stood silently in the room, staring longingly down at Zane. If only they could love each other again—if only...but it would never work. Wasn't the fact that he kidnapped her proof enough that he always intended to force her will to his?

She couldn't let him control her! Her heart in her throat, she grabbed her clothes and sneaked out of the room.

She dressed quickly on the landing and fought the overpowering urge to run back to him.

Instead she slipped silently downstairs and outside.

The air was fresh from the rain, and the first streaks of dawn illuminated the eastern sky.

Kaylie braced herself, then strode off the porch.

The Jeep waited for her.

Chapter 9

Rick Taylor jabbed at a broken piece of pottery with his broom. Rolling his eyes, he cocked his head toward the patient, "He's been this way ever since Friday."

Dr. Anthony Henshaw rubbed his chin as he surveyed the damage in the small room. Books were thrown haphazardly on the floor, the desk chair was overturned, a bulletin board ripped from the wall, papers scattered on the floor and the pieces of clay pottery and dirt smashed against one corner. "What's the matter, Lee?" Henshaw asked the patient with the flaming red hair.

"He won't talk about it," Rick said, tossing the trash into a plastic bag. "But it started the other day during that show he watches, *West Coast Morning*. The woman who usually does the interviews—Kaylie whatever-her-name-is—wasn't on that day; out for 'personal reasons' the other guy said, and ol' Lee, here—" he cocked his head toward the patient again "—went 'round the bend. I've been cleaning up this room once a day."

Henshaw frowned. This didn't sound good. He'd just returned from a symposium in Chicago and discovered from Dr. Jones that Lee Johnston had relapsed. "You miss Kaylie, Lee?" he asked, but the patient, sitting on the end of the unmade bed, didn't reply, just stared blankly ahead, hands clasped prayerlike on his lap.

Dr. Henshaw scratched his chin. Lee was a difficult case; always had been. He sat next to the patient. "Does it bother you when Kaylie isn't on the show?"

No reply, just a slight movement of Johnston's thin lips.

"Even people who work on television take vacations. They need time off, too."

"He's not talkin' today," Rick said, shaking his head as he restacked books and magazines in the bookcase. "Won't say a word. Not one. Not to me, nor to Jeff or Pam, either. If you ask me, he's waitin' for the show." Shoving the last book on the bottom shelf, he glanced over his shoulder at the doctor. "Let's just hope she's back. Then maybe Lee here will calm down."

Rick left the room, and Henshaw tried communicating with Lee, but to no avail. Quiet, but obviously still upset, Lee refused to acknowledge the doctor's presence. After ten minutes, Henshaw gave up. He had other patients to see and a staff meeting in half an hour.

Ramming his hands deep into his pockets, he walked down the long hallway, rounded a couple of corners to the administrative offices. His own cubicle was near the back, with one window and a view of the gardens.

Dropping into his chair, he scowled to himself. Johnston obviously still had problems. Henshaw doubted if the man would ever fit into society. Yet there was talk that he might be released soon. Aside from a few incidents like the trashing of the room, Lee had been a model patient.

Henshaw picked up a pen and clicked it several times. Then there was the matter of Johnston's privacy. Several people were interested in his case and wondered about his freedom. Henshaw had been called by Kaylie Melville's ex-husband often enough. The man was obviously still hung up on her. As, apparently, was Lee. And then there was Kaylie's costar, Alan Bently, a man who seemed always linked with her. There were even rumors of their engagement. Not that Henshaw cared. What she did with her life was her business— until it involved his patient.

Henshaw had met Kaylie a couple of times and even he, happily married for twenty-seven years, a proud father and grandfather twice over, understood a man's fascination with Ms. Melville. Whether she knew it or not, she had a way of stirring up a man.

The doctor shoved thin strands of hair from his face and set his glasses on the table. He rubbed his eyes and wondered how he could get through to Lee. With a long sigh, he decided convincing Johnston that his obsession was pure fantasy and in no way reciprocated would take a miracle. Lee had been obsessed with Kaylie for over seven years. Making Johnston believe that Kaylie had no interest in him would be no easier than walking on water.

* * *

Returning to San Francisco took hours. During the long drive through the mountains as the sun climbed higher in the sky, Kaylie felt more than one twinge of guilt. Gritting her teeth, she shoved the ridiculous feeling aside. She couldn't start second-guessing herself. Not now. Not after seven years of living without Zane.

Her throat grew tight at the thought of the love they'd shared, the passion that had rocked her to her very soul. She could still remember his whispered words of endearment, smell the scent of him clinging to her skin, see in her mind's eye his body lying across the bed.

Glancing into the rearview mirror, she noticed shadows in her eyes. "Oh, Kaylie," she said with a sigh, "forget him." Then, her lips twisting at the irony of it all, she murmured, "He asked to be left up there alone—he *deserves* it for barreling back into your life again!"

But she couldn't forget the fire of their lovemaking, the tenderness with which he kissed her, the passion he used to try and keep her safe.

He was wonderful and horrible, and she didn't want him out of her life. To forget about him, she flipped on the radio and tried to catch up on the news, yet she couldn't shrug off the guilt of leaving him high and dry. "Remember," she told herself, "*he* kidnapped you. You owe him nothing!" But the guilt remained.

She followed the highway signs west toward San Francisco. She'd have to return Zane's keys and Jeep to the headquarters of his security firm. When she squared off with Brad Hastings, Zane's right-hand man, she'd tell him where to look for his boss.

At that thought, she grinned sadly. Zane would be furious! But at least she'd finally gotten the better of him, even if her victory seemed somehow hollow.

Kaylie's fingers tightened around the steering wheel just as the deep green waters of the bay came into view. Sunlight spangled the surface, and the San Francisco skyline stretched to the sky.

Once in the city, traffic slowed and clogged the main arterials. Pedestrians crowded the sidewalk.

The Jeep climbed the city's hills easily, and she parked in the lot of her apartment building. She yanked on the emergency brake, then switched off the ignition. The parking lot was quiet save for the ticking of the engine as it cooled, and Kaylie was left with the empty feeling that she'd left something important— something vital—back at the log house in the forest.

"Don't be a fool," she snapped, locking Zane's Jeep and making her way to the elevator that would take her to her third-floor flat.

Inside, her apartment looked the same as it had when she'd left it last week, but the atmosphere in the rooms was different—cooler, somehow. Vacant. Though Zane had never lived here.

"You're imagining things," she chided herself, stripping off her clothes and heading for the shower. She needed to clear her mind, make a few calls, and then, when she was refreshed, tackle the issue of Zane again.

Smiling at the irony of it all, she imagined returning the Jeep and explaining to Brad Hastings that Zane was stranded. She stepped under the shower's steamy spray and relaxed. Yes, she decided, Zane, for his high-handedness, deserved everything she'd given him and more.

So why, as she washed, did she still feel regrets that their idyllic time together had come to an abrupt end?

As she dressed and dried her hair, images of Zane flitted through her mind. She listened to her answering machine. Several people had called including Alan, Tracy and Dr. Henshaw. Dialing Whispering Hills, she waited, her stomach knotting, for the receptionist to put her through to Lee Johnston's psychiatrist.

Eventually he picked up. "I'm sorry it took so long to get back to you," he said, explaining that he'd been out of town. Kaylie asked him point-blank about Johnston, and there was a pause on the other end of the line.

"You shouldn't have to worry about him for a long while," Henshaw said slowly.

The relief she should have felt didn't wash over her. In fact, Henshaw's pregnant pause caused her mind to race in a thousand questions. Zane was right—Henshaw seemed to be holding back. "How long?"

"That's for the courts to decide."

"Upon recommendation from you and the other doctors at the hospital."

"Don't worry, Ms. Melville. Lee's not going anywhere. Not for a long, long time, I'm afraid."

"Well, I think you should know someone is saying differently," she said, deciding that confiding in him wouldn't hurt. But he already knew about the two calls from Ted and he dismissed them as a "twisted petty prank."

By the time she replaced the receiver, she was reasonably certain that Johnston would remain at the hospital for a while, and yet she wasn't satisfied.

It's because Zane isn't here, a voice inside her head insisted as she punched out the number for the station.

The receptionist answered and put her through to the producer of *West Coast Morning*. "Kaylie!" Jim shouted, bringing a smile to her face, "about time we heard from you! How's that aunt of yours?"

Kaylie's face fell. How was she going to deal with Zane's intricate web of lies? "She's—uh, improving," Kaylie finally replied, deciding to keep Zane's kidnapping to herself—at least for a while. "Incredible recovery," Kaylie forced herself to say, inwardly cursing Zane. "I'm sorry I didn't call you myself—everything got really crazy..." At least *that* wasn't a lie.

"Not to worry. Margot explained everything."

Not quite everything. In Kaylie's estimation, Margot had a lot of questions to answer.

"We've missed you around here," Jim joked good-naturedly. "The show just hasn't been the same without you. And we've been getting a lot of calls. People wondering how you and your aunt are doing. You might have to bring it up on the show tomorrow. Viewers really get off on all that personal stuff."

The thought of lying on the air curled Kaylie's stomach. But Jim was right. "About those calls," Kaylie asked. "Did I get any from a guy named 'Ted'?"

"I don't think so. What is it with that guy? Someone else called about him. Tracy took the call." She heard a muffled noise as Jim placed his hand over the receiver and talked to his assistant. "She says that a guy named Hastings called—a guy who works for your ex. Is something going on?"

"Just a crank call," Kaylie said, quickly explaining to Jim about the threats, though he didn't seem overly concerned when she explained that Lee Johnston was still locked up.

"Another nut. I tell ya, this town is full of 'em," Jim said before the conversation ended.

She hung up the phone, grabbed her jacket and purse and headed out the door.

The offices of Flannery Security were located on the fifth floor of a building not far from the waterfront. Bracing herself, Kaylie pushed open glass doors and recognized the receptionist. Peggy Wagner was a plump woman, somewhere near fifty, with tight gray curls and wire-rimmed glasses. Peggy had worked for Zane forever.

"Mrs. Flannery!" Peggy cried, a smile gracing her soft features as she glanced up from her word processor. "Are you here to see Mr.—"

"Hastings. The executive vice president," Kaylie replied, hoping that the couple waiting on a low slung couch in the reception area hadn't overheard. Peggy never had been able to use Kaylie's maiden name. Apparently she still thought of Kaylie as Zane's wife.

"You're in luck. He's in," Peggy said, flipping a switch on an intercom and announcing Kaylie. "I'll walk you back." She ripped off her headgear and motioned to another woman at a nearby desk. "I'll be right back," she said, then guided Kaylie through a labyrinth of corridors.

At the end of one hall, Peggy knocked, then opened a door to a small office. The floor was hardwood, the desk oak and the rest of the furniture was expensive and neat, but far from opulent.

Peggy motioned to a pair of leather couches. "Just have a seat and he'll be with you in a moment. Would you like anything while you wait? Coffee or tea?"

"I'm fine," Kaylie replied, wishing Hastings would suddenly appear so she could explain how he could find Zane, then get out.

Peggy crossed the room again. "It'll just be a little while," she assured Kaylie as she closed the doors behind her.

Kaylie, rather than sit anxiously twiddling her thumbs, walked to the windows and stared through the glass to the city beyond. Skyscrapers knifed upward against a hazy blue sky, and a jet circled over the bay. Below, traffic twisted and pedestrians bustled along sidewalks.

The door clicked softly behind her.

Finally! Grinning to herself, Kaylie reached into her purse for Zane's keys. "I'm so glad you could see me," she said, turning, only to wish she could drop through the floor.

Zane was locking the door behind him.

Her heart slammed against her ribs as she stood face-to-face with him. The keys fell from her hand, and her mouth went suddenly bone-dry.

"Me, too," he replied with more than a trace of sarcasm. His expression was dark and murderous, and every exposed muscle contracted tightly. His eyes were the cold gray of the barrel of a gun, and his lips were razor thin. He looked dangerous and coiled—like a whip ready to crack.

Kaylie gulped, but stood her ground.

"Surprised?"

"I think the word is thunderstruck," she said, hoping to make light of the tension crackling through the room.

"Well, I've got to hand it to you, Kaylie. You fooled

me." His jaw slid to one side, and he shot her a glance from the corner of his eye. "I thought we were making progress, but you decided to take one last gamble. And it worked. Almost." He tossed his leather jacket into his chair and shoved the sleeves of his blue sweater up his forearms. His hair was still wind-tossed and wild, and his pallor had darkened with the quietly repressed fury burning in his gaze. "I guess I should offer you a job. You're the only person who's been able to pull one over on me in a long while."

Slowly he advanced upon her. "You lifted my keys, then stole my car—"

"I warned you, Zane," she said, refusing to back up, though she wanted to retreat desperately.

"Warned me?" He shook his head, and he was so close that the movement fanned her face. "That's a good one." The skin over the bridge of his nose was stretched taut, and his nostrils flared. Little white lines etched the corners of his mouth. He was furious—his eyes flared with savage fire, but she couldn't let him know that he frightened her at all.

"I trusted you," he said quietly.

"So that's why you had to keep me prisoner? Because of your 'trust'?" she tossed back at him.

His lips compressed. "We made love, damn it!"

"I—I know."

"And it meant nothing to you!" he charged, his rage exploding.

"No, Zane, I—"

"You slept with me, toyed with me, then the minute I let down my guard, you took off in the night, like some cheap…" He let the sentenced dangle between them—unspoken accusations cutting deep.

"Like some cheap what?" she threw back at him.

"Oh, the hell with it!" His arms surrounded her suddenly, crushing her against him as he kissed her angrily, passionately, desperately. When he lifted his head, some of the fury had faded from his gaze. "What kind of a game are you playing with me, Kaylie?"

"Me? Play a game with you?" she whispered as he searched her face.

"I thought last night meant something."

"It did."

"What?"

"That—that—there's still something between us," she admitted.

"And what's that?"

"I don't know, Zane!" she said in exasperation, her nerves stretched tighter than piano wires as he held her so close that she was all wrapped up in the warm feel and smell of him again.

"You deliberately tricked me!"

"And you deliberately seduced me!"

His lips twisted at that. "If I remember correctly, you seemed to enjoy yourself. And there might be some argument about who seduced whom?"

That much was true, she thought, wrenching herself free so that she could think clearly. Her heart was knocking painfully in her chest, her ears rang with the rush of her own blood. When she reached upward to push a strand of hair from her eyes, her fingers trembled so, that she balled her fist and crammed it into her pocket. "How did you get back here?"

His eyes narrowed. "A helicopter. Less than a mile from the cabin," he said, clipping his words. "I was back in the city hours ago!"

"I told you I'd escape—"

"Ahh! But you didn't warn me that you'd sleep with me to lull me into trusting you, did you?"

"You must have expected—Ohh!"

Snagging her wrist in his strong fingers, he pulled her roughly against him. "I didn't expect to be *used,* Kaylie. I didn't think you'd stoop so low as to go to bed with me just to get what you wanted."

"I didn't!" she declared furiously.

"You couldn't prove it by me."

She stared into his eyes and saw a flicker of pain, a shadow of just how deeply she had wounded him. Her heart wrenched painfully, and she wondered if all love were this agonizing.

"I trusted you," he whispered, his breath caressing her face.

"But I gave you ample warning, Zane," she said quietly. "I told you over and over again that I wouldn't be coerced, threatened, kidnapped or held hostage. But you didn't believe me, did you? You know, maybe if you'd just have asked me—invited me to spend a few days with you—things would have been different."

"You would have come with me?" he asked, one dark disbelieving brow arching skeptically. "Do you really expect me to believe that you'd give up your precious job, even for a week or two, to spend time with me?"

"Yes!" she cried. "If I would have thought there was any chance that we could have recaptured the good parts of our marriage. If I'd believed for an instant that we could create something wonderful again, I'd have come with you!"

"But you don't believe we can recreate that happiness, do you?"

She shook her head, her heart twisting. "You showed your true colors by kidnapping me, Zane. You'll never change. You'll always smother and overprotect and try to force me into doing everything you want."

"Like I forced you last night?" he whispered, and her gaze was drawn to his Adam's apple as he swallowed.

Mesmerized, Kaylie was vaguely aware that he smelled of soap and a cologne that brought back far too many memories of lying naked with him. She noticed the rise and fall of his chest. Only a few hours ago, she'd touched that chest, a chest that had been bare and taut, with strong, strident muscles and covered by a mat of dark, swirling hair.

When she glanced up, his features had softened. "Oh, Kaylie…" He sighed. "What am I going to do with you?"

"Nothing, Zane. *You* can't do anything with me. That's the whole point. It's not *your* choice. You don't own me!"

"I've never wanted to own you."

"That's not the way I remember it," she said, though she felt a flicker of doubt. For seven years she'd thought of her short marriage as a prison, but now she wondered if she had only been stronger during the time that she was Zane's wife, if she had stood up for her rights, would those prison walls have crumbled?

"You didn't stick around long enough to know, did you?" he flung back.

Stung, Kaylie said, "I think I'd better leave before we say things we'll regret."

"Leave. And what about Johnston?"

"I talked with Dr. Henshaw. Whoever this Ted character is, he's all wet. Henshaw assured me that Lee Johnston will be locked up for a long, long time."

"And you believe him?"

"The man has no reason to lie."

Zane's expression grew thoughtful. His fist clenched as he attempted to control himself. He didn't trust Henshaw. No, he put more stock in crank phone calls than medical opinion. "I should never have let you escape."

"*Let* me?" she mocked.

"I was crazy to trust you. To let down my guard." A muscle worked in his jaw. "You know," he said slowly, "I had the ridiculous idea that if you and I spent enough time alone together, we could work things out. No matter what it was, we could handle it."

"We didn't before," she reminded him.

"I know. But we're older—wiser, I'd hoped."

"More mature?" she pointed out sardonically. "Think about the past few days! Nothing we've done can qualify under the 'mature' category."

He shrugged. "I guess we haven't acted much like adults, have we?" Shoving his hands into the back pockets of his jeans, he added, "Maybe I was wrong. I thought there might still be a chance that you could love me."

Her throat closed. If only he knew. A tide of emotion swept over her, and she realized she had to get away from him and fast, while she still could. She picked up his keys from the carpet and dropped them onto the desk. "Goodbye, Zane," she said, and the words, as if barbed, stuck in her throat.

"Why are you always running from me?" he asked suddenly. "Do I scare you so much?"

She couldn't lie. "Yes," she said, her voice raw.

He closed the distance between them, and his lips crashed down on hers so swiftly, she gasped. Her breath was trapped in her lungs, and immediate traitorous heat fired her blood. He pressed her back against the door, and his thighs fit familiarly over hers, his chest crushing her breasts. Memories of the night before enveloped her, and desire swept through her bloodstream in wicked, wanton fury.

Her heart pumped gloriously, her blood rushed through her ears. She pressed her palms against his chest, intending to shove him away, but all her strength fled, and she found herself clinging to him instead.

When at last he lifted his head, his face was flushed, his eyes shining with a passion that seared right to his soul. "Dear God, why can't I get over you?" he rasped.

For the same reasons I can't forget you, she thought, but held her tongue. She tried to move, to slide away from him, but he trapped her.

His hands were pressed against the door, his arms blocking her escape. "Why, Kaylie?" he finally asked. "Why did you leave me?"

Feeling suffocated, she drew in a breath. "For all the old reasons."

His jaw grew tight, and any pain she'd seen earlier was quickly hidden. "Last night you weren't pretending," he said slowly, and one of his fingers traced the line of her jaw. "Last night you felt what I did. And yet you can ignore how good we are together, how we feel about each other and—" he touched her lips with one finger "—don't lie to me. I *know* you feel it, too. So how can you pretend that you don't care?"

"Because I can't care!" she said shakily, her hands scrabbling behind her for the handle of the door. Her fingers found cool metal and she shifted, tugging on the knob.

Zane didn't stop her. Instead he backed away. "Escaping again?" he mocked, bitterness tinging his words. "Maybe you should seduce me first so that I'll let down my guard."

"You bastard," she bit out, but shrank as if physically wounded.

"You certainly have grown up," he jeered.

"So have you," she replied, tugging on the door until it opened. Then she slid an icy glance his direction. "Goodbye, Zane," she said stiffly. Marching rigidly through the doorway, she told herself it didn't matter what he thought of her—she had a life of her own to worry about.

A life without Zane Flannery.

Chapter 10

Zane slammed his fist onto the desk in frustration. The lamp rattled, a coffee cup rolled onto the floor, and his picture of Kaylie, a promotion shot for her second movie, toppled with a crash. The glass cracked, destroying the image of a smiling seventeen-year-old.

Her hair had been longer then, hanging nearly to her waist in luxurious golden waves, and her face had been more rounded, her cheeks fuller with adolescence, her green eyes filled with energy and the innocent sparkle of youth.

He'd fallen for her so hard, he'd felt as if the air had been knocked from his lungs. She'd been so young, so damned young, and he'd been hired by her agent as her bodyguard.

Now, running his finger along the crack in the glass, he remembered all too vividly how he'd come to love her. At first he'd resisted, of course, and she hadn't been aware of his changing feelings. But he, too, had been young, and keeping rein on his emotional downfall and charging lust had been impossible. He'd been with her constantly, to protect her, when, in fact, he'd often felt that he was the predator. He'd wanted her as he'd wanted no other woman, burning for her at night, hungering for her by day.

And though he'd sworn never to touch her, never to let her know that she was forever burning brightly in his mind, he'd succumbed at last, body and soul, foregoing his usually clear thinking and deciding that he wouldn't rest until he made her fall in love with him.

It hadn't been easy. Kaylie had as many reasons for not wanting him as he had for keeping his distance from her. But in time, all the walls disintegrated and they were married. And their marriage had ironically become the beginning of the end.

He frowned darkly to himself. She was right, he realized now, as he twisted a pen in his fingers and stared out the window. Clouds were rolling in from the west, converging over the bay, turning the murky waters as gray as his mood. He had been overprotective, near paranoid in his need to protect her.

He'd lost so many before. Both parents and his older brother had died in a mountain-climbing accident when he was twelve. Only he had survived, with injuries that should have killed or crippled him for life. But his mother's sister, Aunt Hilary, had been patient and caring and, with the reluctant help of her second husband, George, tried her best to raise him. George had referred to him as a teenaged hellion on wheels.

Four years after the mountaineering accident, a hit-

and-run driver sideswiped Aunt Hilary's car, killing her instantly. At that point Zane dropped out of school, left home and joined the navy.

So when, years later, he'd fallen so hard for Kaylie, he'd been paranoid that he might lose her. In his efforts to keep her safe, he'd smothered her, and she'd demanded a divorce.

"Idiot," he ground out now, "damned bloody idiot." Shaking off his nostalgia, he reached for the phone, dialed the number of Whispering Hills Hospital and waited impatiently, drumming his fingers, for the receptionist to locate Johnston's psychiatrist.

Henshaw eventually answered, but the call was brief. Even though Zane was one of the biggest names in the security business and Kaylie's ex-husband, the doctor, as usual, was reluctant to give out any information on his patient.

"Damn patient confidentiality!" Zane growled, hanging up. Henshaw had been vague, as if he were holding something back, and the hairs on the back of Zane's neck bristled. Something wasn't right. Though Henshaw had assured Zane there were no plans for Johnston's "immediate" release, he hadn't ruled out that someday Lee Johnston might be stalking the streets again.

"Terrific! Just bloody terrific!" Zane's hands felt clammy, and he wished there were some way to get through to Kaylie. She was and always had been much too cavalier about her safety. Even after the horror of the opening of *Obsession.* Because Johnston was locked up, she had refused to worry, going about her life as if the terror hadn't existed, as if her life hadn't hung by a fragile thread that one man had nearly sliced.

He strode to the recessed bar and poured himself a stiff shot of Scotch. He'd bungled this and badly. Gambling that he could convince Kaylie to stay with him at the cabin, he'd thought he'd be able to protect her, if and when Johnston ever saw the outside of the hospital again. But now things were much worse. Kaylie wouldn't even talk to him.

A cold, tight knot of dread twisted in the pit of his stomach. He wasn't out of this yet. Come hell or high water, he intended to protect Kaylie, even if, in so doing, he might ram a wedge between them that could never be removed.

Her life was more valuable than his love. With that miserable thought, he drained his glass, pressed the intercom on his desk and told his secretary to arrange a meeting of his most trusted men.

On the darkened set of *West Coast Morning,* Kaylie guessed that Alan didn't like anything she was telling him. In fact, he was being bullheaded and stubborn about an issue that she considered very cut-and-dried.

Maybe, Kaylie thought wearily, Zane had been right about Alan all along.

"I don't get it," Alan complained, plucking a piece of lint from his jacket. His mouth pinched together into a contrite pout. His auburn hair was brushed neatly, and his suit didn't dare have a single wrinkle. He sat on a bar stool in the kitchen of the set, his notes spread on the tile countertop of the island bar, near the gas range where Chef Glenn cooked up his Friday-morning concoctions. "What's the big deal about a little publicity?"

"It's not publicity, Alan, and we both know it. Who started the rumor that we were getting married?"

"Who knows? And who cares?" He lifted his shoulders in an exaggerated shrug. "If you're in the business and you're popular enough, eventually you find your name and face on the front page of *Up Front* or *The Insider* or some other rag."

"So you think we should be flattered?" she accused.

Alan forced a smile, and seeing his reflection in the copper pots hanging near the stove, smoothed his hair with the flat of his hand. "Well, I think the least we can do is go with the flow. Next week someone else will make the headlines and we'll be old news."

"That's not the point."

"Hey—just chill out, okay?" he said, irritated as he noticed a mistake in his notes, clicked open a pen and made a quick slash on the neatly typed pages.

"I'll 'chill out' just as long as both you and I deny this whole engagement thing to the legitimate press."

He lifted his palms. "Suits me." Looking back to his notes for the next day's show, he asked, "So what happened? Does Brenda take some rag that got you all riled?"

"Brenda?" she repeated, not understanding.

"Your aunt. The one who was so sick." Alan glanced up sharply, and a tiny line appeared between his thick brows. "The one you were visiting in the hospital for the past few days?" he prodded, eyeing her suspiciously from behind the wire-rimmed glasses he never wore on camera.

"Oh—no!" So Zane had gone so far as to name her supposedly seriously ill aunt. Kaylie cleared her throat. "No, I just had a lot of time to do some thinking..." Well, at least that wasn't a lie. She'd spent the past four days thinking, thinking, thinking. And she'd gotten nowhere. Her thoughts kept turning back to Zane.

"So?"

"So I thought we should take a professional stand against all this tabloid gossip."

"Tell that to the station. It's my bet that our ratings went up while we were splashed across the headlines."

"Still—"

"So cool it," Alan cut in, chuckling. "No harm done. Right?"

She wasn't so sure. "I just like to keep my private life private, that's all."

Alan's eyes, behind the thick lenses, narrowed as he studied her. He shoved his notes together, straightening the pages on the shiny mauve-colored tiles. When he looked at her again, his expression had turned thoughtful. "Is something else going on with you?"

"Meaning?"

He rubbed his chin pensively. "Before you left to take care of your aunt, Flannery called here a couple of times."

Kaylie didn't flinch. "Right."

"So—does all this talk about privacy have something to do with him?"

"Of course not," she said, rubbing her palms down the sides of her skirt.

"You're sure? Because it seems like a big coincidence, you know, that Flannery calls a couple of times after leaving you alone for years. Then you don't show up for work the next day—and now that you're back, you're all worked up about your privacy."

"You're not making any sense," Kaylie countered.

"If you say so." He touched his pen to his lips. "You know what I think?"

"I'm not sure I want to."

"If you ask me, you never really got over him." Alan set his notes on the table and walked to the front of the cameras to the grouping of couches and chairs that created a cozy living room on the set of *West Coast Morning*. Hands deep in his pockets, he leaned a shoulder against the fake mantel on the brick fireplace.

"Zane has nothing to do with this."

"You always were a poor liar. And, unless I miss my guess, Zane has everything to do with it! Remember—I know you. I've known you as long as he has. I saw the hell you went through during your divorce."

"Let's not dredge all that up again—"

He ignored her. "The way I see it, you never were divorced from him—not emotionally. Oh, I know you went through all the legal hoops and you haven't seen him for a while. But it's glaringly obvious to anyone who knows you that you're still in love with him." He tugged on his tie and flicked open his collar button. She wanted to argue with him, but before she could say another word, Alan went on, "If Zane whistled, you'd go running. You might have wanted out of your marriage a few years ago, but that's changed."

"And how would you know?" she wondered aloud.

"Because I've worked with you, Kaylie—seen you grow. Don't forget, I was at the premiere of *Obsession*. I remember what happened when you were attacked, how Zane reacted. Can't say as I blame him, either. He was scared spitless—and he should have been. Johnston was a maniac."

Kaylie crossed the set and took a seat in one of the

rose-colored chairs that she'd sat in for hundreds of tapings. So it was that obvious, was it? Even Alan, self-centered as he was, knew how she felt.

"You know, Flannery was just trying to keep you safe," Alan said, then muttered something under his breath and kicked at one of the ottomans on the set. "I don't know why I'm defending the guy—I don't even like him. But he was right in worrying about Johnston attacking you again."

Kaylie's head snapped up. "What does that mean?" she asked suspiciously, nervous fear burrowing deep in her heart. "Is Lee Johnston going to be released soon?"

Alan, not really interested, lifted a shoulder. "If he is, it's a well-kept secret. But he'll be out someday."

With that chilling prediction, he glanced at his watch and shot to his feet. "Got to run," he explained, reaching for his briefcase and athletic bag he'd tucked near the island. "Got a tennis game with my agent. See ya later." With a wave, he was down the hall and out the door.

Kaylie spent the next couple of hours at the station, checking her messages, but there was no pink slip asking her to return a call to "Ted." She answered her mail, returned her calls and reviewed the shows she'd missed, talked with Jim and Tracy and got ready for the next morning.

Eventually Kaylie left the station in a car she'd rented for the week—until she could drive to Carmel and pick up her Audi. She had one last errand to run. One very important errand.

She drove over the Golden Gate Bridge, barely noticing that the steel-colored clouds were moving inland and that the sun was once again sprinkling the bay with golden light.

Driving by instinct, she was unaware of the traffic or the change in scenery as the highway was flanked by vineyards. In Sonoma, she guided the rented Mustang up a steep hillside and parked in her sister's driveway. She turned off the engine and listened to the radio as she waited for Margot to get home from work. The interior of the car was warm, so she cranked open the sunroof. At five-thirty, the garage door opened, and Margot's sporty little Toyota wheeled into the garage.

As Kaylie climbed out of her Mustang, Margot shoved open the door of her car and fairly ran down the drive to Kaylie's car. "Kaylie! You're back!" she cried, crossing the asphalt and throwing her arms around her younger sister. Margot's shining coppery-gold hair gleamed in the sunlight, and her sky-blue eyes danced. "So tell me all about your adventure with Zane!"

Kaylie rolled her eyes. "Adventure? Is that what you think it was? He literally kidnapped me and held me hostage for days—"

"Umm—sounds divine."

"That's crazy!"

"Is it?" Margot's eyes twinkled. "I can't wait to hear what happened and I want details, Kaylie. Very explicit details."

"You're an incurable romantic," Kaylie said, laughing nonetheless. Some of Margot's enthusiasm was infectious. "I came over here to do you bodily harm, you know."

"Why?"

Kaylie was speechless for a moment. "You know why! Because you were in on it with him."

"And proud of it," Margot teased. "And don't give me this offended victim routine. It doesn't wash. You're crazy about Zane. Always have been, always will be. I don't known why you just don't admit it and make things easier on everyone. Now, come on, help me carry these groceries into the house and we'll have a glass of wine to celebrate."

"Celebrate what?"

"That you're back in the city. Or back with Zane. Whichever you choose." She glanced over her shoulder, and a dimple creased her cheek.

"I'm *not* involved with Zane."

"Sure you are. You're just too bullheaded to admit it." Opening the hatchback, she eyed her sacks of groceries, chose one and stuffed the ungainly bag into Kaylie's arms. "There you go." Balancing a second sack, she led the way to the house, unlocked the door and was greeted by several yowling cats. "Miss me?" she asked the felines as she deposited the groceries on the kitchen counter.

She was rewarded with a chorus of loud mewing, which didn't stop until she petted three furry heads.

Kaylie set her sack on the counter. Margot's house, which she'd built with her husband, Trevor, clung to the side of a steep canyon overlooking the rolling hills and valley floor of the wine country. Margot loved this house, and though Trevor had lost his life in a boating accident nearly two years before, she'd never moved. The good memories outweigh the bad, she'd always say, when the subject of selling the house would come up.

"You know," Margot said now, pouring dry cat food

into three separate bowls, "you're lucky Zane still cares enough to try to win you back."

"You think so?"

"Umm." Margot finished with the cats, washed her hands, then pulled a bottle of zinfandel from the refrigerator. Splashing some of the liquid into two glasses, she said sadly, "I just wish I had the chance to start over with Trevor." A tiny crease marred her forehead.

Kaylie felt a jab of remorse. "But Trevor was different from Zane."

"Not so much," Margot said, shaking her head. "He was stubborn, arrogant, prideful and—" her voice cracked "—loving and wonderful."

Wishing she could help Margot quit grieving for a man who'd never return, Kaylie said, "I miss Trevor, too. He was a great guy."

"The best." Margot's voice turned husky, and she blinked rapidly against gathering tears. She took a sip of wine and sniffed. "I guess that's why it's just so hard for me to understand why you're willing to throw away something so precious as Zane's love when he so obviously still wants to work things out."

"I just need to be independent."

"Oh, that's a cop-out and you know it. Let's take these drinks and go outside onto the deck." Margot opened the sliding door with her back. "Grab that bag of chips," she said, motioning to a sack of tortilla chips. "And there's homemade salsa, Chef Glenn's best recipe, in the fridge."

Kaylie poured the chips into a bowl and found the salsa. On the deck, she dropped the snack onto the round table and took a seat under the shade of the green-and-white umbrella. Margot was propped on the chaise longue, rolling her wineglass between her palms.

Kaylie dunked a chip in the salsa and took a bite.

"Believe me, I've had it with independence." Margot gazed dreamily over the rail to the sunset blazing in the west. "If I could have just one more day with Trevor..." She frowned and shoved her hair from her eyes. "You know, the night he left, we fought." Her teeth sank into her lower lip. "I never had a chance to take back all the horrid things we said to each other. But you—" she glanced over at her sister and arched a fine, dark brow "—you have the chance to make things right with Zane."

"It's not that easy," Kaylie admitted. "He kidnapped me, remember? Took me away against my will. Thrust his will on me without the least little concern for me."

"Well, this might sound strange, but I'd give anything for Trevor to come back and try to protect me..." she whispered wistfully. Then, as if realizing she'd said too much, she cleared her throat and took a quick sip of wine. "Well, I guess that's not going to happen, is it?"

"I don't think so." Trevor's body had never been found. For months Margot had believed he was alive and would eventually show up, healthy and robust, but time and reality had finally convinced her that he had been killed.

They sat in silence for a while, listening to insects hum in the trees and watching the sun sink lower in the sky.

"Maybe you're too hard on him," Margot finally said, reaching into the bowl of chips and thinking aloud.

"No way. He lied to me, Margot. And that cock-and-bull story about Lee Johnston—"

"That wasn't a lie." Margot shook her head, and a tiny furrow creased her brow. "You and I both know they won't keep Johnston locked up forever. Zane's just being careful."

"Oh, save me."

"I mean it, Kaylie. So Johnston's not on the loose right now. He may be soon. According to Zane, there's been talk. Now, come on…" The sparkle returned to Margot's blue eyes. "Let's hear it, Kaylie. What was it like being whisked to some romantic hideaway with Zane?"

Kaylie's lips twitched. "I don't know," she said sincerely. "I can't decide. I felt like I was caught somewhere between heaven and hell."

Margot dunked another chip. "Uh-oh, that's passion talking."

"Maybe," Kaylie admitted, wrinkling her nose. "And I haven't forgiven you for your part in this, you know. You sold me out."

"I only tried to help."

"I don't think I need it, thank you very much."

"Oh, get off it, Kay." Margot grinned and leaned closer. "Let's hear all about it, and don't you dare leave out one tiny detail!"

It was after eight when Kaylie finally parked in her own garage. She and Margot had gone out for Chinese food, and after Kaylie had told Margot everything about her stay with Zane—well, almost everything—she'd returned to the city. Margot would never understand leaving a man after making love to him, and Kaylie wasn't sure she did herself.

She noticed Zane immediately. Leaning against his Jeep, his arms crossed over his chest, he was waiting for her, and from the looks of him, had been for some time.

"What're you doing here?" she demanded, ignoring the tug on her heart at the sight of him.

"Waiting for you."

"Why?"

"I just wanted to know how things went today at the station."

"Sure." She didn't believe him for a minute. He didn't give a damn about her job. "What is it you really want, Zane?"

"You did go to see Margot, didn't you?"

"How'd you know that?" Kaylie cried, and then a fresh sense of betrayal washed over her. "No, don't tell me, my sister called you!"

"The minute you left her house."

"Why?" Kaylie whispered, wanting to throttle her meddling sister.

"She's a romantic," Zane said, cutting her off. "She seems to think we're destined to be together." He started forward, advancing on her, and Kaylie didn't know whether to throw her arms around him or run for cover. Instead she unlocked the door. "Why did she call you?"

"She seems to think there's still a chance for us."

Oh, Margot, how could you? "She didn't hear our argument this afternoon."

"Look, Kaylie, I'm sorry," he said suddenly. "I went

off the deep end today at the office. I said some things I didn't mean, and I... I don't want to leave it like that."

"I don't think there's any other way."

"Sure there is," he cajoled, cocking his head toward his Jeep. "How about a drive?"

She laughed. "We tried that once before," she said, shaking her head. "I'm not going to make the same mistake twice."

With a flip of the wrist, he tossed her the keys. "You drive. I'll let you take me anywhere you want to go."

Her fingers surrounded the cold bits of steel.

"Come on, Kaylie. It'll be fun."

"No tricks?" she asked.

He lifted one hand. "On my honor."

"Now we are in trouble," she said, but couldn't resist. "I must be out of my mind. We'll take my car. That way there's no mix-up with the keys. You seem to have a problem with that." He laughed and caught the keys she tossed back to him.

She climbed behind the wheel of her rented Mustang, and Zane folded himself into the passenger seat. "Anywhere I want to go?" she repeated, ramming the car into gear.

"Anywhere."

From the minute the car's wheels hit the pavement, she knew where she'd take him—a remote stretch of beach that she'd discovered on the other side of the peninsula.

Zane didn't say a word as she parked the car near the sea. He'd driven to her apartment on impulse, unable to let her go. Now, as she tucked her keys in her pocket, he knew he'd made the right decision.

The night-darkened ocean stretched for miles, disappearing into an inky horizon. Kaylie climbed out of the car. Rushing off the ocean, a breeze danced through the beach grass and trees, swirling and rustling leaves overhead. A pale moon, guarded by flimsy clouds, offered soft illumination and cast Kaylie's blond hair in silver light.

The scent of the sea mingled with Kaylie's perfume as they walked toward the frothy waves. They passed a few people, an elderly couple walking their dog and a group of teenagers bopping to the music cast from their radios.

As they neared the surf, Kaylie kicked off her sandals, cast an impish glance in his direction and taunted, "Bet you can't catch me."

Then she took off. Bare feet pounding on the sand, she laughed and headed for the pounding surf.

Zane grinned at the chance of a challenge. He struggled out of his shoes and socks, and though she had a huge head start, tore off after her, determined to catch her as he watched the wind stream through her hair and heard the soft tinkle of her laughter over the roar of the surf.

"You'd better run, Melville," he yelled, exhilarated as the distance between them shortened.

Kaylie felt the wet sand beneath her feet, smelled the briny scent of the sea and heard the slap of Zane's feet against wet sand as he shortened the distance between them. His breathing was loud, his footsteps pounding a quick, even rhythm.

Don't let him catch you, she thought, wondering why she'd started this stupid game. She should have known that Zane would rise to the challenge!

Hazarding one glance over her shoulder, she saw

him bearing down on her. In the moonlight his features appeared more harsh, and the gleam in his eye made her already thudding heart slam against her ribs. She pushed herself farther, the air burning in her lungs, her legs beginning to protest. Several large rocks loomed ahead. If she could just make it past them...

With a laugh, he caught up to her, grabbed her around the waist and spun her around, toppling them both in one quick movement.

He landed on the wet sand with one shoulder and dragged her on top of him, twining his fingers through her hair. He kissed her lightly on the lips. "Did you really think you could outrun me?"

"I hoped."

"Foolish girl."

"Woman," she corrected, and he laughed again, his teeth flashing white in the black night. Screened by the boulders from the rest of the beach, they were aware only of each other and the night surrounding them.

"Woman," he replied just before his lips claimed hers in a kiss as wild as the violent sea. Kaylie could do nothing but kiss him back as he shifted, rolling over so that he was above her.

Any thoughts of denial receded with the tide, and she wound her arms around his neck and curved her body to his. Why was it always like this with him? she wondered as his mouth moved from hers. Softly he kissed her eyes and cheeks before his lips returned to the corner of her mouth again and his tongue delved and tasted, rimming her parted lips and touching her teeth.

Vaguely she was aware of the foam that touched her bare legs and toes, the cool sea against her skin.

They were alone on this part of the beach, hidden by the rocks and the blackness of the night, as if they were the only two people on earth.

She shivered, but not from the water, as he slowly discovered the hem of her cotton sweater and his fingertips brushed the bare skin of her abdomen. His weight pinned her to the sand while his lips and tongue explored her mouth and neck, playing havoc with her senses.

Moaning softly, she kissed him back, her fingers coiling in the thick hair at his nape, her body arching to his. She didn't stop him when he lifted her sweater and dampened the lacy edge of her bra with his lips. Nor did she protest when his tongue dipped beneath the delicate fabric, gently prodding and wetting the edge of her nipple until her breast swelled and ached.

"Tell me you want me," he persuaded. His breath whispered across the wet lace, tantalizing her with its warmth.

"I—I want you."

"Forever?" he questioned, and in the moonlight she saw one of his dark brows cock.

He's playing with me, she realized, but couldn't control her body as he bent over her breast again and began, through the now-wet fabric, to suckle, gently tugging at her nipple with his teeth and lips. "Hmm, Kaylie?" he said huskily. "Forever?"

"Y-yes," she whispered, a familiar ache beginning to burn deep and hot.

He groaned and rubbed against her, suckling and petting, his breath hot and wet, his body lean and hard. She felt the grit of sand against her bare back, but she didn't care.

He shoved her strap over her shoulder, and her breast spilled out of her bra, translucent and veined in the moon glow, her nipple dark and standing proudly erect.

"You are beautiful," he murmured, reverently touching the hard bud before laving it again with his wet, hot mouth.

Kaylie closed her eyes and cradled his head against her, wanting more, feeling the hot ache of a void only he could fill. Anxiously she moved against him, and her fingers fumbled with the buttons of his shirt. With a growl, he ripped the offensive garment off, then returned his attention to her pants. Groaning, he yanked her skirt away and kicked off his trousers.

"Love me, Kaylie," he whispered, his hands on her shoulders, his gaze delving deep into hers and burning with a primal fire.

But before she could say anything, he moved over her, his perfect, sleek body poised above her, his knees parting her legs. "I can't help myself," he cried as he entered her and she arched upward to meet him.

Her fingers clung to the hard, strident muscles of his back as he moved, thrusting inside her with a passion so fierce she could barely breathe.

She met each of his impassioned lunges with her own. Time and space ceased to exist, and her mind spun out of control. The sound of the sea receded, and all she could hear was her own throbbing heartbeat and Zane's ragged breathing.

Staring up at him, watching the play of emotions across his strong features, she let her body control her until there was nothing in the universe save Zane and her. Hot and wild, she felt him stiffen, and a wondrous release caused her to cry out. "Zane—Oh, Zane!"

Her world tilted out of control as spasm after glorious spasm enveloped her.

"I'm here, love," he answered, before falling in exhaustion into her waiting arms.

Chapter 11

She let him stay. Telling herself she was every kind of fool, Kaylie let Zane spend the night. She was allowing herself one more night of pleasure without thinking of the consequences, and they spent the early hours of the morning making love.

At five, she reluctantly rolled out of bed. Zane turned over and groaned but didn't wake up. She showered quickly. As she dressed, she glanced at him still sprawled across her peach-colored quilt and blankets.

Her stomach twisted painfully when she thought that this might be the last time they would ever be together. She couldn't afford to become emotionally tangled up with him again, but a part of her longed for the marriage they had once shared, the happiness they'd held for so brief a moment.

She loved him still. As much, if not more, than on

the day they married. Now, as she gazed at his sleeping form, all tangled in her sheets, she felt a rush of hot tears in her throat. If only things had worked out differently...

"Stop it," she muttered, clasping a gold necklace around her neck and swiping at her eyes. She wouldn't cry now. Nostalgia would serve no purpose.

"What?" Zane growled, opening a sleepy eye. "Stop what?" His jaw darkened with the stubble of a beard, his eyelids drooping seductively, his bare muscles moving fluidly as he adjusted the covers. He looked so virile and male, she had to glance back to her reflection before she did or said anything stupid. "Were you talking to me?" he asked with a yawn.

She brushed her hair until it crackled. "No, I was talking to myself, but since you're awake, remember to lock the door when you leave." She adjusted her turquoise-colored skirt and slid her arms through a matching jacket. "And leave the extra set of keys on the table."

"You're throwing me out?" he asked, disbelieving. He stretched lazily, his skin dark against the sheets. His sable-brown hair fell rakishly over his eyes, and his lips twisted into a thin, sensual smile.

"I think it would be safer that way."

"For whom?"

"You," she quipped, seeing her eyes twinkle in the reflection as she added earrings and a dab of perfume. "You just never know when I might decide to have my way with you."

"So have it!" He tossed back the covers to display all too vividly his well-muscled body, his mat of dark curling chest hair, his firm legs and much, much more.

Kaylie's breath caught in her throat, and she had to swallow in order to speak. "It's, uh, tempting—very tempting, but really, I've got to go—"

"Call in sick," he suggested.

"Not on your life!" She slipped into bone-colored heels. "After already being gone while 'Aunt Brenda' was taken so ill, I don't think calling in sick would go over so well."

Zane grinned devilishly. "I could arrange it so that your aunt had a relapse."

"You're impossible!" Kaylie threw her brush at him, then strutted down the hall.

Zane scrambled off the bed, the glint in his eye unmistakable. Kaylie giggled as she half ran to the kitchen. Stark naked, he tore after her through the house and caught up with her at the back door.

"Zane, don't," she protested, fighting more laughter as his arms surrounded her and he kissed her passionately, holding her hostage against the back door. She squirmed and wriggled, but his kiss was warm and wet and reminded her of the way he'd felt the night before.

"Don't what?" he whispered, his tongue flicking sensually between her teeth.

She couldn't speak until he lifted his head.

"Don't muss my hair or clothes or…" The words faded away as he kissed her again, his tongue darting between her teeth, claiming her mouth, his hands moving downward to cup her buttocks and bring her hips hard against his.

"Or what?" he prodded, not abandoning his assault on her senses.

Kaylie's knees turned to jelly, and though she

knew she should shove him away, she couldn't find the strength. "Or I might just—"

"Have your way with me?" he mocked, his eyes dancing with gray light as he lifted his head and stared at her.

"Or worse!" she tossed back.

"Worse?" A wicked grin slashed across his jaw. "Believe me, I'm ready."

"I can tell," she teased. Glancing over his shoulder, he noticed the time on the wall clock and groaned. She was already late! "You wouldn't want me to lose my job, would you?"

He growled and kissed her again. "Yeah, that would be a real pity!"

"I'd never forgive you!"

"No?" He lifted a disbelieving brow, and his eyes were alight with challenge.

"I mean it!" She reached behind him until she found the door knob, then sidestepped him and hurried onto the covered porch leading to the parking lot. "I don't expect you to be here when I get home."

"Not even if I make your favorite dinner?" he asked in a high, falsetto voice.

"Oh, you're impossible!"

She climbed into the Mustang. But as she adjusted her side-view mirror, she caught a glimpse of Zane, naked as the day he was born, standing in the open doorway, arms crossed over his chest, one shoulder propped against the frame, not in the least concerned that the neighbors might see him.

"It would serve you right if you get arrested!" she yelled through the window, missing his response as she slammed the car into reverse.

Zane laughed, and the rich sound lingered in her thoughts as she drove toward the heart of the city.

"Lee?" Dr. Henshaw took a seat in the chair next to his patient. But Johnston didn't look up. As if he were rooted to the cushions of the old couch facing the television in the recreation room, Lee Johnston sat, waiting, the blank screen reflected in his icy eyes.

"Lee, can you hear me?"

Johnston scratched at a scab on the back of his right hand. But still he stared at the TV.

"No use trying to talk to him," Rick said, walking in and switching on the set. Music blared. Rick adjusted the volume with the remote control. A children's cartoon show was in progress. Johnston didn't move. "Until *West Coast Morning* comes on, he won't say a word."

Henshaw exchanged glances with the orderly, and he thought about the messages he'd received and had to return. Flannery had called again, as had Kaylie Melville herself. He'd have to talk to them both, which didn't present any particular problems.

It was the other call that bothered him, a call he didn't want to return. But, of course, he had no choice.

Rick, still cleaning off a table in the corner that had recently been used for arts and crafts, shook his head at the doctor. "Let's just hope you-know-who is on the show today," he said, placing the palates, brushes, paints and other tools onto a cart. He wheeled the cart next to Lee's chair just as a heavyset orderly named Pam rushed into the room. "Dr. Henshaw? There's a problem in 301," she said breathlessly, her pudgy face red. "Norman is upset—I mean really upset. He threw his breakfast all over the room and…and…" Seeing Lee for the first time, she gained control of herself. "Maybe you'd better come, too," she said to Rick.

Rick mumbled something inaudible under his breath, but gave the cart a shove. The corner caught on the edge of the couch, and several paint mixing tools and palates clattered to the floor.

"Son of a—" Rick caught himself and reached down, grabbing the paint-spattered knives and brushes. The floor was smudged with yellow ocher, Christmas green and scarlet. "Great—just great!"

Henshaw was already following Pam out of the room. Rick, in a foul mood, snarled at Lee, "Maybe you'd just better go back to your room until I clean this up. I don't want you messin' this up any more than it already is! Come on, get going! You'll be back for your stupid program!"

Rick prodded Lee on the shoulder. Johnston jerked away, his nostrils flared slightly. He didn't like to be touched. Not by Dr. Henshaw and especially not by Rick, the know-it-all with the smug smirk. Rick really thought he was crazy and he looked down on Lee, but Lee intended to show Rick and Henshaw and all the others just what he was made of. Reluctantly, he got to his feet.

"Hurry up, I don't got all day," Rick growled, looking around for a towel or mop.

Lee, spying a knife that had slid just under the couch, hazarded a sly look at Rick, whose back was turned as he unlocked a closet. Quick as a cat, Lee grabbed the dull knife, stuck it into the side of his shoe and pretended to be tying his laces.

"You still here?" Rick asked, facing him again.

"Well, come on, come on." He touched Lee again, and Lee recoiled, his stomach turning over.

Only one person had the right to touch his body. And that person was Kaylie…sweet, sweet Kaylie. He licked his lips and scratched absently at the itch on his hand as he stepped into the hallway. He'd missed Kaylie the last few days, but her absence from the program had brought one thing into perfect focus. He had to see her again, touch her, smell her, taste her. Soon.

His bloodless lips curved into the faintest of smiles as he felt the knife, wedged tightly between sock and leather, rubbing against the side of his foot.

Kaylie's first full day back at work started the minute she shoved open the glass doors of the building. She waved to the receptionist and made her way through the series of hallways toward her office. On the way, Tracy flagged her down with a sheaf of papers.

"Today's guests?" Kaylie asked.

Tracy nodded and slapped the papers into Kaylie's outstretched hand. "Yep. Just a little more information that came in late. Isn't that always the way?" She lifted her slim shoulders and turned her palms toward the ceiling.

"Always." Kaylie laughed, glad to be back in her normal routine. She didn't even think about Zane standing naked in her driveway—well, she didn't *dwell* on the vivid image she'd seen in her side-view mirror.

She stopped by the tiny cafeteria and saw a couple of technicians and cameramen.

"Great to have you back, Kay," Hal said as he grabbed a doughnut from the box of pastries lying

open on the glossy Formica table. Hal, thin and balding, was in charge of the sound booth.

"We missed you around here," his partner, Marvin, agreed.

"It didn't look like it," Kaylie replied, picking up
a cinnamon twist and a napkin. "I saw the program."

Hal snorted. "Old Alan was in his element; no doubt
about it. He was snapping orders around here like he
owned the place."

Marvin, his slight paunch jiggling, chuckled. "The
funny part was, no one paid him much mind."

"I bet that went over like the proverbial lead balloon."

"More like a lead zeppelin," Marvin said. "Hey,
how's that aunt of yours anyway? What was wrong
with her? Heart problems?" He dusted the sugar from
his fingers.

Hal, wiping the last crumb of a jelly doughnut from
his mouth, said, "I heard she was in an accident of some
sort—ended up in a coma."

"She's fine. Her heart did act up after the accident,
and she was in and out of consciousness, but she's fine
now, out of ICU," Kaylie replied, improvising, mentally
cursing Zane for his lies. She breezed out of the cafeteria, balancing a coffee cup, her pastry and napkin in
one hand, her briefcase swinging from the other and
the notes Tracy had handed her tucked under her arm.

"Welcome back to the rat race," she told herself as
she dropped into the chair behind her desk. Sipping her
coffee, she retrieved her notes from her briefcase. As
she added in the information Tracy had handed her, she
jotted down a few new questions and underlined background information she considered important.

She finished with the notes and her pastry just as the door of her office flew open and Audra, the hairdresser and makeup artist, scurried breathlessly inside. "Lord, what a day! Sorry I'm late. Alan's toupee, you know. He's never satisfied with that damned rug, and there's only so much I can do with it. If he hates it so much he should break down and buy a new one. Or go without. Hell, I think a man is much sexier in nothing than something, and that goes for hairpieces as well as clothes." She laughed at her own joke and unzipped her oversize makeup bag. "Well, anyway, I didn't mean to rush you."

"No problem," Kaylie said around a smile. Audra, with her fast tongue, stiletto heels and bloodred lipstick, was always a breath of fresh air in this conservative old building.

Audra eyed her critically. "Nope. You look none the worse for wear," she agreed, rifling in her bag with her red-tipped nails. "In fact, you look pretty damned good for hanging around a hospital for four or five days." She frowned thoughtfully as she pulled out a comb and swirled it in some cleanser. "How's that aunt of yours? Heard she had a gallstone operation."

"Uh, it was her heart—no operation," Kaylie replied. Thanks a lot, Zane, she thought as Audra smoothed a few errant strands of her hair into place.

"Well, at least you got away for a few days," Audra said, pointing an aerosol can in her direction and spraying a cloud of mist over her locks. "And don't be worrying about this—ozone friendly. See, right here on the can." She pointed to a symbol Kaylie couldn't read through the mist. "I'm an environmentalist now."

"Good," Kaylie said, coughing as she reached for her coffee.

Audra snatched the cup away, sloshing a few drops of brown liquid onto Kaylie's notes. "Oh, no, you don't. No, sirree! Your lipstick's perfect. Let's not be messing it up by leaving it on this here cup."

"Aye-aye, Captain," Kaylie teased, saluting Audra as the makeup artist picked up her gear, zipped her case closed and exited.

There was a rap on her door and the familiar sound of Tracy's voice. "Ten minutes, Kaylie!"

She scanned her notes one last time, then dashed to the set. Alan was already waiting. As Kaylie's microphone was pinned onto her jacket, she caught his glance and smile. He seemed genuinely glad to see her.

"Don't worry about a thing," he said, as she settled into her chair. He patted her hand affectionately. "I've got everything covered today. All you have to do is sit there and smile and be your gorgeous self."

"You're kidding," she replied. "Besides, I'm all set."

On the floor in front of camera three, Tracy was motioning for all quiet on the set.

At a silent signal to the sound box, the lead-in music filled the small auditorium. Kaylie took a deep breath, smiled and wondered if Zane was watching. Giving herself a mental slap, she forced thoughts of him aside.

The show went well. She interviewed a rock star named Death, a woman who grew an entirely organic garden, as well as the snake handler from the zoo, along with his favorite python and boa constrictor. She held the snakes and let them crawl across her shoulders as she spoke to their handler.

Alan handled the national news and talked with

Hugh Grimwold, a pitcher for one of the bay area teams.

After the local news, and another sports update, both Alan and Kaylie spoke with two high school seniors who had started their own recycling business.

In the final segment, Alan announced the guests for the next show and reminded the viewers that on Friday, Chef Glenn was going to create his famous Cajun breakfast. The credits began to roll as music once again drifted from the speakers positioned around the set.

"Good job, Kaylie," Jim said, clapping her on the back and smiling broadly. "You know, the show just didn't feel right without you." He waved and sauntered toward the reception area while Kaylie headed toward her office.

From the corner of her eye she noticed the dark look that Alan passed her way, but she ignored Alan's foul mood and bathed in Jim's compliments. Jim Crowley didn't hand out praise often.

At her desk, she pulled the cap off her underlining pen with her teeth and started reading the bio information on the guests for the next day.

The door to her office opened and slammed against the wall.

Alan, face scarlet, eyes blazing, stormed into the room. "You don't even have an Aunt Brenda!" he charged, crossing his arms indignantly over his chest.

"What?" she asked, nearly dropping her pen.

"Don't lie to me, Kaylie. I checked."

"You did *what?*"

"I called around, checked with some of your friends. Eventually I even talked to Margot. *She* told me the truth. She didn't want to—at least not at first—but she came clean. Jeez, Kaylie, I think she gained some perverse pleasure in telling me that you'd lied." His red face turned almost purple.

"Oh."

"'Oh' is right! You let me and everyone else here think you were on some mission of mercy when all the time you were shacking up with Flannery!"

"Now, wait a minute—" Kaylie's voice rose indignantly. Slowly getting to her feet, she wished she could throttle her meddling sister as well as Alan.

Alan made an impatient motion with one hand. "Oh, Margot didn't exactly fill me in, but she made enough broad hints that I figured it out. You were with Flannery last week, weren't you?"

This couldn't happen! Kaylie planted her palms on the top of her desk and tried her best to remain calm. "What I did or didn't do isn't really any of your business."

"You left us in the lurch, Kaylie!"

"You seemed to handle everything well enough without me. And if I remember correctly, I covered for you a couple of years ago—when you bruised your backside and your ego while snow-boarding."

Alan's face went white. "But I couldn't tell Jim or the rest of the crew that I'd…" His voice dropped off, and he swallowed hard.

"That you ended up with a broken tailbone trying some silly teenaged stunt with a ski bunny who'd been busted for drugs?"

"Oh, God." The wind disappeared from his sails. "You know about all that?" He ran a shaking hand across his hair, and his toupee slid a little. Kaylie almost felt sorry for him. Almost.

"So what happened?" he asked, his face puddling into a pout as he slid into a chair near her desk. "I thought it was over between you and Flannery."

"It was."

"But…?"

She was through lying. In fact, as soon as she was finished talking to Alan, she'd go and explain everything to Jim. If the powers-that-be in the station decided to fire her, so be it. At least she wouldn't have to walk this tightrope of lies any longer. "Zane stopped by the other night and we went to dinner. He persuaded me to go to the mountains with him for a few days."

"Just like that?" Alan snapped his fingers.

"Oh, no, it took a lot of convincing," she said, swallowing a smile as she remembered how Zane had fireman-carried her into the lodge. "A *lot* of convincing."

"For God's sake, why did you agree to have dinner with him in the first place?"

"It was part of the deal."

"The deal?" he repeated, shaking his head. He rolled his eyes and tossed his hands up. "So now she's making deals with her ex-husband! Kaylie, do you know that the press has us practically married?"

"We discussed this. It's a dead issue."

"I know, I know. But…well, I thought we could let it ride awhile. What could it hurt? But you running off with Flannery, well, that about kills it."

"Good!"

Alan left a few minutes later, and Kaylie marched into Jim Crowley's office to tell him the abbreviated truth. Jim took the news in stride. He wasn't happy, of course, and he warned her to "call next time—about ten days *before* you plan to leave." But she left his office with her pride and her job intact.

Hours later, she returned to her apartment. Zane was long gone, but the scent of him still lingered in the air. The bed was made, but she couldn't resist taking a pillow and breathing deeply. The feathers still smelled of his after-shave. "Oh, Melville, you've got it bad," she chided, still clutching the pillow as she fell back on her bed and stared up at the ceiling. "Real bad!"

Realizing that she sounded like an adolescent in the throes of puppy love, she tossed the pillow aside and walked into the kitchen.

The red light on the answering machine was blinking, and she played back the messages only to hear Zane's voice, as if he were there.

"I guess I'm hung up here at the office awhile," he said with a sigh. "So I won't be over."

"Too bad," she murmured, though she did feel a jab of disappointment.

"But I'll call you later and I'll see you soon."

He hung up, and she listened to a couple more messages—one from Margot begging her to call and another from an insurance salesman.

After popping a dinner into the microwave, she dialed Margot's number.

"Hello?"

"I should tar and feather you," Kaylie announced.

"I guess you talked to Alan."

"Screamed would be the appropriate word."

"I know I shouldn't have said a word to him, but he had the nerve to call here asking about you, and I just had to set him in his place. If you ask me, that guy's got a screw loose."

"Alan?" Kaylie laughed.

"I'm not kidding. I bet he's the one that gave all those papers the idea you two were engaged. Anyway, I couldn't resist hinting around about Zane. He deserved it."

Kaylie couldn't stay angry with Margot for long. "It's okay, I guess. I was tired of talking about this fictitious Aunt Brenda and I told Jim the whole story—well, most of it. Fortunately I still have my job."

The microwave beeped, and as they talked, Kaylie pulled out her dinner—a pathetic-looking concoction of chicken, peas and potatoes—while Margot asked about Zane.

"He's not here," Kaylie said, nearly burning her fingers as she opened the plastic cover.

"No?" Margot sounded worried.

"He does have his own life."

"I know but—"

"Look, Margot, I know you think that Zane and I should reconcile and live this storybook existence, but it's not going to happen."

"Why not?"

Exasperated, Kaylie replied, "For one reason, he's not Prince Charming and I'm not Snow White or Cinderella or whoever it was Prince Charming was linked up with."

"Oh, Kaylie," Margot said cryptically, "if you only knew."

At eleven-thirty, Zane was finally caught up. His work, while he'd been off in the mountains with Kaylie, had piled up. He'd had to deal with a complaint about one of his men in the Beverly Hills office, double-check two new security systems in offices downtown, hire three more men as well as go over the books quickly to keep his accountant appeased.

And through it all, he'd thought of Kaylie, worried about her, wished to God that she was with him.

He reached for the phone, but decided not to call her. It was too late. She'd be exhausted. And he'd promised himself to let her live her own life.

Lifting his arms over his head, he felt his spine pop from hours of restless sitting. He stood, walked to the window, and stretching the muscles of his back and shoulders, caught a glimpse of the city at night. Cars rushed by, their headlights cutting into the semidarkness, their taillights small red beacons. A few pedestrians scurried along the sidewalks, black forms visible in the lamplight.

He'd called Whispering Hills earlier in the day and been assured by Dr. Henshaw that Johnston was going to stay locked up for a while. But, though the good doctor had been forthcoming, Zane had a feeling Henshaw wasn't telling him everything.

It wasn't anything Henshaw had said; it was the hesitation in his voice that had caused the hairs on the back of Zane's neck to rise—it was as if the doctor were trying to hide information.

"But why?" Zane wondered aloud, rubbing the day's growth of beard on his chin. Maybe Kaylie was right. Maybe, where her safety was concerned, he was paranoid.

Even the tape from Ted could be a hoax. But why? *Why?*

He'd had gut feelings before and he never second-guessed his instincts. Right or wrong, he had to be careful. This was Kaylie's life—her *life,* damn it. He wasn't about to fool around.

He rotated his neck, closing his eyes. She would be furious if she even guessed that he'd sent someone to watch her apartment, to follow her, to protect her when he wasn't with her.

"You're getting in deep, Flannery," he told himself as he grabbed his keys and snapped off the lights. No, that was wrong. Where Kaylie was concerned, he'd always been in deep, so deep that he felt that sometimes he was drowning.

He wanted nothing more than to drive to her apartment and stay the night, make love to her and awake with her wrapped around him. But he couldn't.

"Breathing room," he muttered as he locked the door of the building behind him. "She wants breathing room."

Alan Bently swirled his onion in his glass and stared broodingly at his drink. Seated at a private table in an expensive restaurant, he was alone with his own bleak thoughts. He was past forty—pushing forty-five—and his hair was little more than a memory. Though he worked out every day, his physique was suffering and his career looked as if it was on hold. Or worse.

For a while, with all the hype and speculation about Kaylie and him being romantically involved, things had started to look up. His agent had talked about a possible part in a movie, and there was even a rumor that a big-name producer was interested in putting Kaylie and Alan back on the silver screen together—to do a sequel to *Obsession.* True it had been over seven years since the original movie had been released, but that didn't matter. Sequels were the thing now.

But Zane Flannery seemed hell-bent on ruining everything. It didn't matter that he and Kaylie had disappeared for a while, though Alan would have liked to milk that disappearance for a little publicity, and he'd enjoyed being the star of the show. Now she was back and definitely not interested in anything but Flannery. Again.

So all his dreams seemed to be slipping away. Like a ghost from his past, fame eluded him. Alan Bently wanted the big time and he'd tasted a little of it once. Not that his job with the station was anything to sneeze at. *West Coast Morning* was big—at least on the West Coast. But it wasn't as glamorous as a successful movie. He wanted his name in the credits. He was still young enough to be a leading man, but he couldn't wait much longer.

Alan tossed back his drink. He knew that his career was teetering on the brink. One wrong move and the fickle public would forget him. But, with the right amount of publicity and interest, he could reach the big time again.

Smiling as the liquor slid through his system, sending a cozy warmth through his bloodstream, he motioned to the mâitre d' for a telephone and made the call that would ensure his fame again.

Chapter 12

The next morning Kaylie felt a pang of loneliness. Zane wasn't lying in the sheets, nor was he winking at her, nor making jokes with her, nor, as she headed for the door, tossing off the blankets and, without a stitch on, chasing her down the hall.

"This is what you wanted," she told herself as she grabbed a piece of toast, slapped some butter on it and munched as she locked the door behind her.

She felt restless and anxious. For seven years she'd lived without Zane, and now, she told herself as she drove toward the station, she couldn't stand one night away from him.

Her thoughts still clouded by Zane, she flipped on the radio, hoping to hear the news, and tried to concentrate on what was happening in the world—to no avail.

At the station's lot, she parked her rental, snatched

her briefcase and climbed out of the car. In her peripheral vision, as she locked the car door, she noticed a
silver Ford Taurus parked on the other side of the short
hedge that separated the station's lot from the street.
The driver didn't get out of his car, but pulled a newspaper from the seat beside him and began scanning it
as if he were waiting for someone.

A car pool?

Had she seen the car before—yesterday morning?
She couldn't remember, and deciding the man had
every right to read his paper in the car, walked briskly
to the station doors.

Inside, she poured herself a cup of coffee, and after
talking with a few co-workers, none of whom asked
about Aunt Brenda, fortunately, she made her way to
her office where she sequestered herself with the intention to go over her notes on today's guests: a heart
surgeon from Moscow, a woman who wrote a diet book
for people who love chocolate, and a new young actor
promoting his latest movie.

She'd no more than sat down when there was a tap
on the door, and Alan, already in makeup, poked his
head inside. "I'd like to talk to you after the show," he
said, as Audra rushed by him with her huge case and
a quick "'Scuse me."

"Sure. What about?"

He glanced at Audra then shook his head. "It'll
wait."

"Good, because I can't!" Audra said, unzipping her
case and eyeing Kaylie. "Now, you don't look as good
as you did yesterday."

"Thanks a lot," Kaylie teased, but she knew the hairdresser was right. Two nights ago she'd slept soundly

in Zane's arms, only to be awakened to make love to him. Last night she'd tossed and turned, angry with him one minute, missing him the next. She hadn't gotten much sleep.

"A few eye drops—a little blush, and you'll be good as new," Audra announced, but Kaylie wasn't convinced.

However, Audra worked her magic and Kaylie felt better. The show went well, and aside from Alan sending her silent messages she didn't understand, the segments passed without a hitch.

Afterward she had lunch in the deli across the street, then spent the rest of the afternoon in her office, reviewing the tape of the day's show and making preparations for the next program.

There was a quick knock on the door, and Alan once again poked his head inside. "Got a minute?"

"Sure. What's up?" She tossed her pencil onto the desk as Alan closed the door behind him.

"There's talk about a sequel to *Obsession*."

"I've heard."

"The producer's talking with the writer of the original script as well as to Cameron." Cameron James had been the director of *Obsession*.

Alan's face was split with a huge grin. "This could revive both our careers," Alan went on, pacing on the other side of Kaylie's desk.

"No one's approached me yet," she said.

"And if they do?"

"I—I don't know." A shiver of fear slid down her spine as she remembered the premiere.

"'Don't know'?" he repeated, aghast. "Kaylie, just think of it. You never had a chance to prove yourself as anything but a child star, but now you could show how you've grown up, how your character has matured!" He was excited. His eyes practically glowed, and his hands became expressive. "This is an opportunity we can't pass up."

"No one's shown me a script yet."

"It'll happen," Alan predicted, buoyed. "I spoke with my agent last night and again this morning. Sequels are all the rage. Look at *Back to the Future,* the *Rocky* films. Not every one is a blockbuster, but some are. And they don't have to be action films. There's *Texasville.*"

Kaylie considered the idea. She'd been approached to do small parts in several movies over the years, but had always declined. "I'm happy here—doing what we do, Alan."

"Well," he said, rubbing his hands nervously, "it hasn't happened yet, but when it does, just promise me you'll keep an open mind. I know that the *Obsession* premiere was a real bummer, but it was a once-in-a-lifetime thing, and look at it this way, the publicity didn't hurt the ticket sales."

"Alan!"

He grinned as he reached for the door handle. "Just a little joke. You know, you're too serious, Kaylie. Much too serious. You need to lighten up."

"I'll keep that in mind."

He left, and Kaylie, a headache beginning to pound behind her eyes, decided to call it a day. She was tired of Alan and his schemes. How could he talk about the premiere of *Obsession* as if the entire horrifying experience were nothing more than a publicity stunt?

If only it had been...

But the memory was too vivid, the images too terrifying and real. Frowning darkly, trying not to dwell on the brutal image of that night, she shivered and told herself to shake off the lingering fears.

She didn't see him, so much as feel his presence.

"Kaylie?" Zane's voice drifted to her as if in a dream. Standing in the doorway, filling it with his broad shoulders and narrow hips, Zane was watching her. His hair was mussed, and Kaylie guessed he'd sprinted across the parking lot.

"Is something wrong?" His features were taut with concern.

"Oh—no, nothing." She decided there was no reason to worry him just because Alan had mentioned the premiere of *Obsession*.

"Nothing?" He closed the door behind him and crossed the room. "Something's bothering you," he challenged, hooking one leg over the corner of her desk. "What happened?" Concern etched the lines of his face, and she thought guiltily that she should be thankful that he cared.

She couldn't lie. "Well, for starters, Alan seems to think I should jump-start my movie career by agreeing to costar in *Obsession II* or whatever it may be called."

Zane didn't move.

"Never mind that there's no script or director, yet."

"You couldn't—"

"And that was on top of a pretty bad week to begin with."

"Bad?" he said, a small smile tugging at the corners of his lips.

"Well, you see, I have this ex-husband, who has been ramrodding his way back into my life." She crossed her arms over her chest. "You probably know the type—pushy, arrogant, opinionated."

"But handsome, sexy and intelligent."

"That's the one," she said, her bad mood beginning to evaporate.

"And you don't like him pushing you around, right?"

She avoided his eyes for a second and fingered the strand of pearls at her throat. "Well, the problem is, I do like him—a lot. More than I think I should. But I don't appreciate him trying to dominate me. But he knows that—"

Zane reached across the desk and took her hand in his. "Kaylie, I love you." The words hung in the air suspended by unseen emotional threads.

Her mouth went dry, and she had trouble finding her voice. As she stared into his eyes, she whispered, "Love isn't based on possession, Zane, and you've tried to possess me for as long as I can remember."

"Hey, Kaylie, about tomorrow's show—" Alan said, opening the door without knocking. With one glance at Zane, he froze.

To Kaylie's surprise, Zane actually smiled, releasing Kaylie's hand and facing Alan. "Bently," he drawled, as if seeing a long-lost friend. "I was just asking Kaylie if she's seen the front page of *The Insider*."

"You what...?" Kaylie asked, feeling a cold lump form in her stomach. Alan licked his lips.

Zane reached into the inner pocket of his jacket and withdrew a folded piece of newsprint. He smoothed it on her desk, and she read the bold, two-inch high headlines: Lover's Spat Forces Kaylie Off Morning Show.

"What is this?" she demanded, skimming the article that insinuated that she and Alan, still planning marriage, had been involved in an argument that sent her running away, seeking solace for her wounded heart. "This is absurd. I did no such thing!" she said, glaring first at Alan, then at Zane. "You're the reason I left. You kidnapped me!"

"Kidnapped?" Alan repeated, his mouth falling open, his gaze moving from Kaylie to Zane and back again. "Wait a minute. Let me get this straight. He *kidnapped* you?"

Zane shot her a look that cut to the bone.

Alan lounged one shoulder against the wall. "Is that what you call *persuading* you to go to the mountains?"

Zane pushed himself to his feet and said quietly, "Kaylie and I need to talk. Alone." He grabbed her jacket from a hook near the door. "Let's go."

Alan was amused and couldn't help the grin that toyed with his lips. "Well, Kaylie, what happened to all that independence you were so hell-bent to earn, hmm?"

"Oh, give it a rest, Alan," she snapped as she and Zane walked out of the building. Still stung by Alan's remark, she said, "I'll drive."

To her surprise, Zane didn't argue, just slid his long body into the small interior of the Mustang. As she cocked her wrist to twist the key in the ignition, he slanted a sexy, knowing smile in her direction. "I suppose it would be too much to expect you to kidnap me to a private lodge in the mountains."

"Way too much," she said as the engine started. But she laughed. "Okay," she said, and eased out of the parking lot and into the late-afternoon traffic, "talk."

Sighing, he stared out the window. Evening shadows stretched across the town as traffic moved sluggishly along the hilly streets. "Well, I've spent the last—" he checked his watch "—thirty-six hours staying away from you, giving you some space, and it's been hell. I just wanted to be alone with you again."

Kaylie's heart turned over.

"I'm trying to give you space—breathing room— all those things you figure are so important, but, if you want to know the truth, I don't like it much."

"Neither do I," she admitted, trying to concentrate on traffic as she switched lanes and stopped for a red light. As the light changed, she tromped on the accelerator and the car sped forward again.

"Then let's change things," he said quietly.

"How?"

"Pull over—"

"What?"

"Over there." He pointed to a side street near a park. Kaylie found a parking spot and turned off the car. Zane climbed out of the Mustang, and she followed, not sure what he was going to say.

The sun, partially obscured by a few flimsy clouds, was low in the sky and shadows lengthened over the ground. Leaves danced across the grass, pushed by a cool breeze. In the distance, children played football while dogs bounded in the thickets of trees nearby. Women pushed strollers, and squirrels chattered in the high branches of the oaks and maple trees.

Kaylie's heels scraped against the path. Zane took her hand, his warm fingers linking through hers. "I think we should try again," he said quietly, his voice rough with emotion as he looked down at her.

"Try?" she repeated, but she knew what he meant, and happiness and fear surged through her.

He brushed a strand of hair from her forehead, his fingers warm and gentle. "Marriage. I want you to be my wife again. Marry me, Kaylie."

She wanted to say yes, to throw her arms around his neck and kiss him and tell him that they could live together happily ever after. Tears sprang to her eyes, and she bit her lip. "I—I don't know," she whispered, blinking rapidly.

"Why not?"

"We tried marriage once before—"

"And we were young and immature. Both of us. This time it would be different. Come on, Kaylie." He drew her into the protective circle of his arms, and his lips brushed gently over her forehead.

God, how she loved him! Her arms wrapped around his back, and she laid her head against his chest, hearing the steady beat of his heart. She closed her eyes for a second. Living with Zane would either be ecstasy or torture—heaven or hell.

When her eyes opened, she focused on the street, where the cars whipped by, wheels spinning, horns blaring.

"Well?" he asked, holding her at arm's length.

Say yes! Don't be a fool! This is your one chance at happiness! "I just don't know," she admitted, and the pain that surfaced in his eyes cut through her heart. "I love you, Zane," she confessed. "I always have." His arms tightened around her.

"So what's the problem?"

"I just don't want to fail again."

"We won't," he promised, kissing her crown.

"Then... I... I need a few days to think it over."

Zane sighed, his breath ruffling her hair. "Why? So you can analyze our chances?"

"Last time we rushed things—ran on pure emotion. This time—if there is a this time—I want to make the right decision."

For a second she thought he'd be angry. His face clouded, and he dropped his hands. "Okay," he finally said, shoving a hand through his hair in frustration. "You have time to think it over, but don't take too long, okay?" He strode back to the car and climbed inside. She followed and slid behind the wheel.

"Why don't you take me to dinner?" he remarked as she checked her side-view mirror and tried to pull into traffic.

"I have a better idea—you take me."

"Only if I can persuade you to marry me."

She grinned inwardly. At least he wasn't furious with her. Signaling, she eased the car into the right-hand lane and noticed that a silver car about a block behind her followed suit. She frowned as she realized the car was a Taurus, but so what? The city was crawling with them.

Zane placed a hand on her knee. "How about someplace elegant—French dining overlooking the bay."

"How about pizza?" she countered, and he laughed.

"You're the driver, Kaylie. You can take me anywhere you want."

"You did *what?*" Margot nearly dropped her glass of Chablis as Kaylie finished her story about her relationship with Zane.

Margot had driven Kaylie to the house in Carmel so that she could turn in the rental and pick up her car.

"I told Zane that I'd consider it. Then we went out for pizza and I took him back to his car."

"Oh, boy, are you crazy." Margot took a long sip of wine and shook her head. Seated at a round umbrella table on the back deck of Kaylie's house in Carmel, she eyed her sister as if she had truly lost her mind. "Some women spend their entire lifetimes looking for a man like Zane Flannery. And you know what?"

"What?" Kaylie asked, not really interested in Margot's big-sister wisdom, but knowing she was going to hear it one way or another.

"They never find him, that's what! Men like Zane Flannery don't exactly grow on trees, you know!"

"Thanks for the advice."

Margot smiled. She was on a roll. "And you got lucky and found him twice! If I were you, I'd march right into the house and call him right now."

"And say what?" Kaylie teased.

"That you've already found the preacher, for crying out loud!"

Kaylie twisted the stem of her wineglass. She'd thought the very same thing and had even made it as far as the telephone a couple of times, but in the end she'd backed down. "I don't want to make the same mistake we did before."

"You won't. You're older now. And, most importantly, the man loves you, with a capital *L*. So why are you fighting it?"

Kaylie let her gaze wander out to sea. Margot had a point, she admitted to herself.

"And you miss him, don't you?"

Kaylie sighed and shrugged. "Yeah," she admitted, trying to sound indifferent when deep inside she missed him every minute of every day. She hadn't stopped thinking about him, couldn't sleep, plotted ways of bumping into him.

"Look, if it's a matter of pride—"

"It's more than that," Kaylie admitted, remembering the way Zane kidnapped her—just hauled her into the woods without even asking her first. "I can't accept a man who insists on dominating and pampering me."

"You did once."

"That was before."

"Right," Margot said, as if she'd just made her point. "Before that damned premiere of *Obsession!* Until then, you and Zane were comfortably ensconced in marital bliss. To tell you the truth, I was envious."

"You?" Kaylie's eyes rounded on her sister. "But you and Trevor—"

Margot waved impatiently, and sadness stole over her features. "I know, I know. But the truth of the matter was, my marriage wasn't perfect."

This was news to Kaylie. For as long as she could remember, Margot had been in love with Trevor Holloway.

"Oh, don't get me wrong. I loved Trevor more than I should have and I know that he loved me. But—" she lifted a shoulder "—we had our problems, just like anyone else."

"What kinds of problems?" Kaylie asked.

"It doesn't matter—they seem stupid now and petty. I'd gladly take all our problems back if Trevor were still alive." Margot sighed and squinted out to sea, watching the sun lower in a blaze of brilliant gold that scorched the sky and reflected on the water. She seemed to focus on a solitary sailboat that skimmed across the horizon—a sailboat not unlike the one on which Trevor had lost his life.

Kaylie thought she was finished, but Margot settled deeper into her deck chair and continued, "No marriage is perfect, but some are better than others and some are the best. I have a feeling that you and Zane had one of the best—at least until that creep Lee Johnston decided to mess things up." Margot shuddered.

"Even before the premiere, Zane was...autocratic."

"He was scared. You'd been getting those letters and he was terrified that something might happen to you—which it did." Margot leaned across the table, her gaze touching her sister's. "Give the guy a break, Kaylie. All he's ever done is love you too much. Is that such a crime?"

"I guess not."

"I know not!" Margot finished her glass of wine. "The point is that Zane's crazy about you. Also, he's handsome, successful, caring, dependable, honest, intelligent and has a great sense of humor. What more do you want?"

"Someone who'll let me make my own decisions," Kaylie replied before smiling and adding, "but of course he'll have to be handsome, successful, caring, dependable—and all the rest of those qualities you reeled off."

"Then if I were you, I wouldn't look any farther than your ex-husband," Margot said as she climbed out of her chair and stretched. "Mark my words, Kaylie, you'll never find a man who loves you more than Zane does. And, if you'll stop long enough to be honest with yourself, you'll realize that you'll never love a man the way you love him." She reached for her purse and concluded, "You just have to ask yourself what you really want in life—to be lonely and independent or to take a chance on love—real love. I'll see you later. Think about what I said."

Kaylie figured she didn't have much choice. She watched Margot leave and knew her older sister was right. She'd never love a man as she loved Zane.

Zane paced around his office. He'd spent the better part of the afternoon listening to his accountant argue that another office, located in Denver or Phoenix, was just what the company needed. Zane wasn't interested. Expanding the business suddenly seemed trivial.

For the past week he'd tried to stay away from Kaylie. He hadn't called her, he hadn't visited her, he hadn't even shown up on the set of *West Coast Morning,* though he had tuned in every day and had sworn under his breath whenever Kaylie and Alan shared a smile or a joke.

"It's just her job," he told himself, but he couldn't stem the stream of jealousy that swept through his blood. More than once, he had snapped off the TV in disgust, only to click it on again.

But he was giving her time to come to a decision— the most important decision of his life!

He slumped back into his chair, picked up the accountant's proposal, then tossed it into his wastebasket. He didn't need another office to stretch the corporate tentacles of Flannery Security. He didn't really care if he never made another dollar. He just wanted Kaylie.

"You're obsessed," he told himself, not for the first time, as he strode to the bar, found a bottle of Scotch and poured three fingers into his glass. Then he checked his watch. Barely one-thirty in the afternoon. Disgusted with himself, he tossed the drink into the sink, strode back to his desk and fished the figures for the new office from his wastebasket.

"Concentrate, Flannery," he ordered himself as he picked up a pencil to jot notes. But the letters and numbers on the pages jumbled before his eyes, and Kaylie's face, fresh and smiling, framed in a cloud of golden hair, swam in his mind.

His pencil snapped.

Muttering an oath aimed at himself, he grabbed his jacket and marched out of the office. "Cancel all my appointments this afternoon," he told Peggy as he headed toward the elevator.

"And where can I reach you?"

"I wish I knew," he replied. The elevator doors whispered open, and he climbed inside. He thought of a dozen schemes to contact Kaylie again, but dismissed them all. He'd just have to wait.

The following few days Kaylie was nervous as a cat. Margot's advice kept running through her mind. She half expected Zane to fall back into his old pattern—and she suspected that he might have her under surveillance.

But he never showed up at her apartment or the beach house again. Nor did he call or leave a message on her machine.

It was as if she'd finally gotten through to him and he was going to leave her alone.

"That's what you wanted, wasn't it?" she asked herself one evening. It was Friday and had been raining all day. Alan had been in a bad mood on the set, and the taping hadn't gone well. By the time Kaylie reached the beach house, she'd acquired a thundering head-ache and her shoes were soaked from her walk across the television station parking lot. All she could think about was a hot shower, a cup of tea and a good book.

And Zane of course. She let herself in with her key and smiled sadly. She never had bothered to change the locks; she hadn't had the heart to lock Zane out. And yet he'd never so much as tried any of her doors since the night he'd spirited her away.

And now he wanted to marry her. She was warmed by the thought. Her only hesitation was the thought of failing again, of the pain of divorce. She would never put herself, nor Zane for that matter, through all that pain again. Stripping off her clothes, she continued toward the bathroom.

The phone rang and she grabbed the bedroom extension, half expecting the caller to be Zane. "Hello?" she answered, smiling.

No answer.

"Hello?" she asked again, and there was still silence on the line. "Zane—is that you?" She waited, but heard nothing, and her nerves stretched taut. "Is anyone there? Look, I can't hear you. Why don't you try again?" She hung up slowly and waited, staring at the rain sheeting against her bedroom window and the dark, threatening clouds rolling in from the sea.

The only sounds were the distant rumble of thunder, the rain peppering the roof and the sound of her own heartbeat. The minutes ticked slowly by. "It was probably just a wrong number," she thought aloud, then continued toward the bathroom. She'd hoped the caller had been Zane, and her heart tripped at the thought that he'd tried to reach her.

Maybe Margot had been right, she finally decided, maybe it was her turn to reach out to Zane. Maybe there was a chance that they might start over again. If given the chance, surely Zane would treat her as an intelligent, mature woman.

He had to.

Because she loved him. With all her heart, she loved him and always would. There was no other man for her—no white knight lurking in the wings ready to dash up and carry her away. Zane was the only man in her life—always had been, always would be and she'd been a fool not to realize it before.

Wrenching off the faucets, she heard the phone ring again. She barely took the time to wrap a bath sheet around her before she dashed into the bedroom, leaving a trail of water behind her.

"Hello?" she called into the phone, her voice breathless, just as the caller hung up. "No! I'm here!" she yelled, feeling in her bones that the caller had been Zane. "Well, there's only one way to find out," she decided, throwing open her dresser drawers and yanking on her underwear. Tonight she was going to drive all the way back to the city, back to Zane's apartment and tell him she loved him. They'd have a chance to start over again.

Rick Taylor groaned. His hand went to his head and he felt something sticky and wet on the floor where he lay. Blinking hard, he forced his eyelids open only to close them again at the glare from the single shaft of light near the floor. He slipped back out of consciousness before jerking awake. His skull pounded, the pain creating orbs of light behind his closed lids.

"Wha-what the hell?" he muttered, licking his lips. He remembered walking into that loony patient Johnston's room. But Johnston had not been in his bed. Turning to sound an alarm, Rick had felt the hot flash of pain in his abdomen and, doubling over, the crash of something against the back of his head.

Now he propped himself on one elbow, feeling the wound in his side tearing open. "Help," he tried to cry, but the sound was barely a rattling whisper. How long had he been here? Seconds? Minutes? Hours?

But surely he'd be missed. Trying to push himself upright, he fell back and attempted to call for help again. The narrow sliver of light, coming from the hall outside the door, wavered in front of his eyes.

"Help me! Please!"

Using all his strength, he pulled himself toward the door and the hallway. Pain ripped through his body, pounding at his temple. The room, barely ten foot square, seemed to stretch on forever as he inched his way to the door.

With each agonizing tug, his muscles shuddered and sweat poured over his bleeding head. "Somebody help me!" he said again and again until he reached the door. His bloody fingers surrounded the knob and he tugged. But the door didn't budge. He tried again, then realized that the door was locked from the outside.

Swearing, Rick fumbled on his belt for his keys only to discover that his entire key ring—the keys to the hospital, his apartment and his car—was missing.

"Oh, God," he cried, using his last ounce of strength to pound on the door before slipping into unconsciousness again.

* * *

"Answer, Kaylie, answer!" Zane whispered, before giving up. "Damn it all to hell!" He swore violently as he slammed the receiver into the phone cradle. His heart was thudding, his palms sweating as he stared at the phone message stating that Lee Johnston had escaped from Whispering Hills Psychiatric Hospital.

Zanc's hands wcre shaking as he walked into the reception area where Peggy was bent over her word processor. "Dial 911. Ask for the police. Tell them that a patient who escaped from Whispering Hills threatened Kaylie once before and give them Kaylie's address— her apartment in the city as well as the house in Carmel." Uncapping his pen with his teeth, he scribbled out the information for her. "But first order the company helicopter to stand by," he commanded. "Tell Dave I want him to take me to Carmel and drop me off at the Buxton building."

"He's already waiting," Peggy said. "He was going to fly Hastings to—"

"Cancel that and have him wait for me."

"Will do." Peggy turned to the telephone and Zane raced out of the office. Heart thumping with fear, he took the stairs two at a time.

On the roof the helicopter was waiting, its gigantic blades churning in the night. Rain and wind lashed at Zane's face as he dashed across the wet concrete to the pad where Brad Hastings was climbing out of the passenger seat.

Covering his head with his briefcase Hastings yelled over the whir of the helicopter blades, "You just about missed us!"

"Emergency," Zane yelled back as he climbed into

the copter and Dave dashed for cover. Glancing at the pilot, he said, "Carmel, on the double. Radio ahead for a company car—a fast one. And get me a backup."

"You got it," Dave replied, talking into his headset as Zane strapped himself in. The helicopter lifted off and Zane sent up a silent prayer. Fear tore at his guts as his worst nightmare played through his mind. He only hoped they weren't too late.

Kaylie grabbed her purse and squared her shoulders. She wasn't very good at eating humble pie, but Zane was worth it. This time, she decided, her pride wouldn't get in her way. Snatching a raincoat and umbrella from the hall closet, she headed through the kitchen and slung the strap of her purse over her shoulder.

She punched the answer button on her answering machine and locked the door behind her. In the garage, she heard the phone ring, but ignored the call. Even if the caller were Zane, she found the idea of surprising him in person appealing. If only she had a set of keys to his apartment, she'd turn the tables on him and wait for him in the dark…maybe in his bed with champagne?

She smiled to herself and reached for the button to open the garage door when she heard the sound—a small sound—like the scrape of leather on concrete.

Kaylie froze. Her skin crawled. Telling herself the noise was only her imagination, she strained to listen. Maybe she heard the scurry of a mouse or the neighbor's tabby cat. He was always hanging around when she stayed here. He could have been locked in the garage.

She punched the button but the door didn't open.

Nothing happened. When she flicked on the light switch next to the opener, the garage remained dark.

Fear cut a swath into her heart, and she fumbled in her purse for her keys. She glanced nervously around the garage, to the shadowed corners. "Who's there?" she called, but heard nothing. "It's just your nerves," she told herself. Something moved in her peripheral vision.

Kaylie didn't wait. She shoved open the door to the house, letting the interior lights illuminate the darkened garage. Two steps inside a cold hand grabbed hold of her arm. Kaylie screamed.

Lee Johnston, his icy blue eyes blank, stared straight through her.

"Kaylie." His voice was rough and gritty. His flame-red hair was plastered to his head and the drip of rain ran down his neck and beneath the wet collar of his blue shirt.

Her knees went weak, but she pulled hard, intending to escape.

"Leave me alone," she screamed, but the words were only in her mind. Her throat was frozen. Light from the kitchen refracted off the knife in his hand.

Dizziness overwhelmed her. The premiere of *Obsession.* Her life flashed to a series of stills. Zane, oh, Zane, I'm so sorry, she thought.

"Kay-lee," her assailant mumbled and she tried vainly to wrench herself free. But he was strong and compact and determined. Thoughts ran through her mind. She needed a weapon. Tools in the garage. Knives in the kitchen. Anything!

"Kay-lee," he said again, his voice as chilling as the howl of a wolf. She backed up, stumbling over the edge

of rakes and shovels. Lee kept up with her, his fingers biting into her arm, the knife's blade somewhere in the dark beside her.

"Let—let me go," she demanded, trying to stay calm, to hold at bay the panic that surged through her brain. Maybe she could talk him out of this! He'd never hurt anyone before—not really. But then, as he passed by the window, she saw the dark smudges on his shirt and knew the stains were blood. Not his, certainly. But whose?

Zane's? Her thoughts rambled crazily, and she thought for a blinding moment that Johnston might have sought his revenge on the man who had captured him years before. The only man she'd ever loved. *Oh, Zane. No, please, God, let him be alive.* Why hadn't she listened to him? Why?

Her knees threatened to buckle. If Zane were dead or lying hurt and wounded…

"No!" she wailed, throwing her body hard against Johnston. He tripped on a rake or shovel, and his fingers slackened. She leaped forward, and he lost his balance. The kitchen! If she could just get into the kitchen and run outside.

"Help!" she screamed, and scrambled past her car.

She rounded the trunk, moving slowly backward, listening to Johnston's movements in the dim light. Was he following her or trying to cut her off by rounding the front of the car? If only the garage door weren't locked! *Think, Kaylie, think!* There was an ax—Oh, God, where was it? Or a crowbar. Anything to protect herself. And the garage door opener—by the back door.

Heart pounding, she inched toward the door.

She heard voices—or was it her imagination? No,

there were voices. Johnston heard them, too. He quit moving, though his breathing sounded close—between her and the kitchen. But where?

She stopped, listening, trying to focus. Moments passed. Tense, terrible moments.

Footsteps outside. "Kaylie! Kaylie!" Zane's voice rang through the house. "Oh, God, where are you?" He was alive! Kaylie's heart soared.

From a shadowy corner, Johnston lunged at her.

She screamed. "Zane! Don't come in here!" she cried. "He's got a knife—" But Zane came flying through the door, and in one quick motion, he threw himself into the darkness.

"Oh, please, no!" Kaylie cried as Zane propelled himself through the air and landed on Johnston and his raised knife. The blade flashed up, then swiftly down, landing with a thud in Zane's back before being torn out with a hideous sucking sound.

The two men struggled, and Johnston freed himself, struggling to his feet. Zane pulled himself upright, but swayed.

Kaylie thought she'd be sick. "No!" she screamed as Johnston raised his bloody knife again. She fell back against a shovel. Without thinking, she picked up the rusted tool and using all her strength, swung it, catching Johnston's knees. He dropped like a stone.

Zane sprang, quick as a cat. Blood oozed from the sleeve of his shirt. He rolled on top of the flailing man.

"Freeze!" A strong male voice yelled from the doorway, and Kaylie looked up to see a man in jeans and a sweater training a gun on Zane and Johnston.

"No!"

"Kay-lee, Kay-lee!" Johnston cried.

Kaylie shuddered.

"Back off!" the man in the doorway ordered, his face contorted in rage, his revolver aimed at Johnston's chest. "You okay?" he asked Zane.

"I thought you'd never get here."

"I radioed the police. Now, come on, let's get this lowlife out of here."

Sirens screamed outside. As Zane struggled to restrain Johnston, two policemen ran through the house and, pistols drawn, charged into the garage.

"Police! Everybody hold it!" the taller man said, his gun trained on Johnston and Zane.

"Call for an ambulance!" Kaylie cried, watching in horror as a scarlet stain spread across the back of Zane's shirt.

"Already done. Okay, someone called in about an escapee from Whispering Hills. What's going on here?"

Zane, his face white and drained, tried to explain, but Kaylie, frantic for his life, told the police that she'd answer all their questions once Zane was in the hospital. She wouldn't listen to the officers when they demanded answers. Instead she climbed into the back of the ambulance and held Zane's hand all the way to the hospital. He tried to smile, but failed, and his eyes closed wearily.

"You're okay," she said, her voice trembling as she assured herself more than him.

But he didn't respond, and she knew that he'd lost consciousness.

"Don't die, Zane," she whispered, clinging to his fingers as if she could will the life to remain in his body. She heard the whine of ambulance tires spinning against the rain-washed streets. She only wished she'd told him how much she loved him—how much he meant to her.

Lord, she'd been stupid; she knew now. Because of her stubbornness, Zane had nearly been killed. If only she'd listened to him, trusted him, relied upon him, *leaned* on him! If only she'd loved him enough to work with him to save their marriage. Oh, Lord, she'd been such a fool, she thought, tears tracking down her cheeks.

Now it was too late. Too late. Maybe much too late...

Chapter 13

Kaylie didn't leave Zane's bedside. The doctors assured her that Zane was fine, that the wound was shallow. The blade of Johnston's knife had only penetrated Zane's shoulder muscle. Though he would be sore for a while, the team of experts at Bayside Hospital were convinced that Zane would be "good as new" in no time. Nonetheless, she camped out at the hospital that night.

"He's sedated. He won't wake up for hours," Dr. Ripley predicted. "You can't do anything for him now. Tomorrow, unless he takes a turn for the worse, I'll release him."

"I want to be here when he wakes up."

"I'll have the nurse call you." Ripley was a thin man in his early fifties with freckles splashed all over his face, neck and arms. His once-red hair was turning to gray, but he seemed as fit as most thirty-year-olds.

"I'd rather wait. It's important," Kaylie insisted.

The doctor slanted a brow. Motioning toward Zane, he said, "He might not be in the greatest mood when he wakes up."

"I don't care."

"Well, okay. Have it your way," the doctor finally agreed, instructing the nurse that Kaylie was to spend the night.

She spent the night in a chair, alternately dozing and waking with a start, her muscles cramping. The small room was never dark. Light from the parking lot street lamps filtered through the blinds, and illumination from the hall made the shapes in the room visible.

In her fitful hours of sleep, she relived, over and over again, the horrible moments in the garage. The knife. The blade plunging into Zane's shoulder. Blood pooling on the floor. Johnston, dead-blue eyes staring at her, laughing maniacally as she threw herself on Zane's unmoving body. Tears choked her throat. She couldn't lose him…she couldn't…

"Zane! No! Please, no!" She woke to find herself in the hospital room, Zane sleeping on the bed, the worst over.

Relief brought tears to her eyes.

Zane blinked twice, shifted and felt a brutal pain rip through his shoulder. He sucked in a swift breath. Shadowy images flitted through the mists in his mind—terrifying visions of the madman and his knife. Kaylie—where was she? His eyes blinked against an intense light.

"Zane?"

Kaylie's voice was like a balm to the pain. Thank

God she was alive! Relief flooded through him. Those last frightening minutes in the inky garage, the maniac with his weapon...

Through the fog of his memory, Zane recalled leaping into the dark garage, flying at Johnston and struggling for the knife.

Now he focused with difficulty and discovered Kaylie standing on the other side of the bars of his bed, her hands white as she gripped the rails, her eyes clouded with worry. Her hair was tangled and mussed, her makeup long washed away, her clothes, the same as she'd been wearing the night before, wrinkled and smudged with blood—his blood. Her eyes were red-rimmed and cloudy green and her eyebrows pulled together with worry.

And she was gorgeous. He managed a smile. "You look like I feel."

Letting out her breath, she blinked against a sudden bout of tears. "So you're going to rejoin the living after all?"

"The jury's still out on that one," he grumbled, realizing he was in a hospital bed, bandaged and swathed, an IV dripping fluid into his wrist. Wincing, he attempted to sit up, but Kaylie's hands, cool and soft, restrained him.

"Slow down, cowboy," she said, and he noticed the tremor in her voice and saw the tracks of recent tears on her cheeks. "We've got all the time in the world."

"Do we?" he asked, his gaze locking with hers.

She sniffed loudly. "The rest of our lives."

"Why, Ms. Melville," he drawled, suddenly feeling no pain, "is this a proposal?"

She laughed, though her eyes were wet. Sniffing

loudly, she brushed her tears aside with the back of her hand. "You bet it is. And I don't expect to end up a widow before I'm a bride, so you just take care of yourself."

"So now you're giving orders."

"And you're taking them," she announced firmly, though she swallowed hard. "After all, someone's got to protect you."

He laughed at that. "So what're you? My personal bodyguard."

"No, Zane. Just your wife."

He reached up, and pain seared through his shoulder. Emotions clogged his throat. "You don't know how long I've waited to hear you say those words," he admitted, then with his free hand, playfully grabbed her. "I wish I had a tape recorder, because, no matter what, I'm holding you to it."

Her fingers linked through his. "I wouldn't have it any other way."

"Breakfast time." A nurse, pushing a rattling tray, shoved open the door. "But first I need to take your temperature and pulse and…"

Zane groaned, and the nurse winked at Kaylie. "Looks like he's out of the woods. Why don't you run down to the cafeteria and get yourself something to eat and a cup of coffee."

"Sounds like heaven," Kaylie admitted.

While the nurse tended to Zane, Kaylie made her way to the ladies' room where she washed her face as best she could, repaired her makeup and ran a comb through her wild hair. Glancing in the mirror, she snorted. "Not exactly the glamorous talk-show hostess today, Melville."

For the first time, she thought about her job, and tucking her comb and brush into her purse, she walked toward the lobby. Spying a pay phone near the admitting area, she dredged up a quarter and dialed the station. The receptionist answered on the second ring.

"Hi, Becky, it's Kaylie."

"Oh! Kaylie, let me put you through. Jim's been trying to get hold of you."

"I'll bet," Kaylie remarked as the phone clicked several times and Jim Crowley finally answered.

"You made the front page," Jim announced. "And not of *The Insider* for once. You're in the *Times*."

"I'm not surprised," she drawled.

"You okay?"

Kaylie wondered. She was still shaken by the incident, no doubt about it. Her skin prickled at the horrific memory, and yet she felt better than she had in years. She loved Zane, and planned to be with him for the rest of her life. "I'm fine," she assured Jim.

A pause. "You sure?"

"Absolutely."

"It's pretty late. I don't suppose you'll be in." He sounded hopeful.

She laughed without much mirth. "Not today."

"That's okay. Alan already said he'd fill in, though he'd like to interview you about last night."

"No way."

"I told him that's what you'd say. Anyway, since it's Friday, I'm asking Chef Glenn to add a couple of appetizers to go with whatever today's concoction is."

"Hot and Spicy Chicken Linguine," Tracy said in the background.

Jim snorted. "Yeah, some Italian thing. I'll see you Monday."

She rang off and took the stairs to the cafeteria. There she ate alone, devouring a bagel and cream cheese and fresh fruit along with two cups of coffee. She felt more than one curious look cast in her direction and heard a few whispered comments.

"Kaylie Melville...yes, channel fifteen...a crazed mental patient went after her... Yeah, maybe it was the same guy...the guy she was with is up on the second floor...no, not Bently... some other guy...you know those Hollywood types... Her husband? *Ex*-husband, you mean...are you sure...? Well, what's she doing with him?"

Ignoring the wagging tongues, Kaylie cleared her tray and picked up a newspaper near the lobby. Page one was splashed with the story. Pictures of her house in Carmel, photos of the retreating ambulance, and older shots of Zane and Johnston and her at the premiere of *Obsession* years before graced section two under local news. "Terrific," she muttered under her breath. "Just great."

Perusing the paper quickly, she decided Zane wasn't up to reading all about the "drama in Carmel" and stuffed the paper into the trash on her way back to his room.

The nurse had left. His breakfast, uneaten, had been pushed aside. Zane was propped up in bed, staring at the television, where a newscaster was reporting Johnston's escape and the attempt on Kaylie's life.

"Well, your name's on the tip of everyone's tongue today," he drawled.

"So's yours."

Zane rolled his eyes. "This is no good," he said. "The problem with all these reports is that it sensationalizes the crime. Who knows what nut is watching and thinking he'd like to get his name and picture on the television by imitating that maniac?" Scowling darkly, he scratched at the back of his hand. A bandage covered the spot where the IV needle had recently been attached to his skin.

"I think I'm safe," Kaylie replied. "Johnston's locked up."

"But how many more like him are out there?"

"It's the price of fame," she said, then nearly bit her tongue. Here it was. The same old argument. And she'd just inadvertently offered him a perfect opportunity to exploit his position. Still frowning, he clicked the remote control, and the lead-in music for *West Coast Morning* filled the room.

"Let's see what *your guys* say about it," Zane said, and Kaylie held her tongue, not wanting to let him know that Jim had already mentioned an interview to her.

Alan's face, gravely serious, was centered on the screen. "I'll be hosting the show alone today," he told the viewers, "because last night Kaylie Melville was viciously attacked by a knife-wielding assailant. The suspect is in custody, his alleged crime nearly identical to his assault on Kaylie seven years ago."

To Kaylie's horror, she watched old footage of the premiere of *Obsession*. Of course the cameramen had been there for quick peeks of the rich and famous. Those cameramen, who had been interested in showing who was dating whom and what dress Kaylie wore to the first showing, hadn't expected to capture a madman lunging at her on film. Nor had they intended for the terrifying drama to unfold in front of their lenses. But it had happened, and every heart-numbing second had been captured on film—from Kaylie's bloodless face, to Zane's heroic act that saved her life.

"Yes, history repeated itself last night at Kaylie Melville's beachside home in Carmel. Fortunately, once again her ex-husband, Zane Flannery, was on the scene to save her from a man who has been obsessed with her for years..."

Alan went on and on, recalling the details of last night's attack as well as bringing up the premier of *Obsession* again. He even publicly admitted that he and Kaylie were just friends, but very special friends, and he looked earnestly into the camera to wish her well.

"I think I'm gonna be sick." Zane clicked off the set.

"It's just his way," Kaylie said lamely, but she could hardly defend Alan. For, though he appeared concerned for her well-being, the entire segment reeked of publicity seeking and she couldn't help but think that all his references to *Obsession* were to drum up public interest in the old film in the hopes that the viewers and fans, as well as the studio heads, would demand a sequel.

"Well, for all his supposed friendship, he sure doesn't give a damn about exploiting you."

She couldn't argue with him and didn't. The less she thought about last night's attack, the better. She and Zane were together. Johnston was locked away. They were safe and in love. Nothing else mattered.

Zane was released just after noon, with strict orders to take care of himself and not strain the wound. "You've lost a lot of blood and you're carrying around fifteen stitches, so don't do anything foolish," Dr. Ripley told Zane as he signed the release forms.

To Zane's ultimate humiliation, Kaylie pushed him out of the hospital in a wheelchair and helped him into the passenger seat of his Jeep. Then she settled behind the steering wheel. The look she cast him should have tipped him off. Her green eyes danced with mischief as she headed east.

"Where're we going?"

"Can't you guess?"

He eyed her thoughtfully. "Don't tell me, you're kidnapping me to a certain mountain retreat..."

She laughed gaily. "I thought about it, but no, I've got something else in mind."

"What?"

"Lake Tahoe," she replied with an impish grin. "I know this great little place there. It's called the 'Chapel of No Return.'"

"No!"

"Scout's honor." She lifted one hand as if to pledge.

"So where's Franklin?"

"Your neighbor—Mrs. Howatch—called while you were sleeping and offered to watch him for the weekend." She grinned. "I hope she knows what she's getting into."

"Franklin likes her," Zane replied.

"Oh, it's just me he has problems with?" she teased.

"He'll get used to you. I did. Now, lead on, Ms. Melville," he suggested, settling back in his seat and staring at her as if he thought she might vanish and this entire fantasy give way to cruel reality.

Kaylie beamed. She felt as if she'd finally grown up enough to accept Zane as her husband. Yes, he'd been dominating and overzealous in his protection of her, but now she understood him better. She knew how frightened he must have been for her safety.

The few hours he'd been unconscious had been hell. She finally understood just what losing him would cost her. She didn't doubt that she loved him, always had loved him and always would. She didn't see that love as a curse any longer, but as a blessing. She wanted to spend the rest of her life with him, as his wife, as the mother of his children, as the lifelong partner with whom he would grow old.

And now, at twenty-seven, she felt secure and mature enough to handle him. No more temper tantrums—well, not too many. From here on in, they were partners.

She drove straight to Lakeside Chapel, and when Zane climbed out of the Jeep, stretched and grumbled that he wouldn't be married in anything less than the "Chapel of No Return," she offered to take him straight back to the city.

"I guess we'll just have to forget this whole marriage thing," she told him blithely.

At that he grabbed her roughly, spun her to him and growled in her ear, "Not on your life. I've waited too long for this."

She lifted her shoulders and rounded her eyes innocently. "Whatever you say, honey."

For that she was rewarded with a swat on the bottom. "Come on. No reason to keep the minister waiting."

Within thirty minutes they were married. The ceremony was simple. The preacher was a lively man who was pushing eighty, and his wife, a sparrow of a woman, served as pianist and witness. Another woman, heavyset and beaming, was the second witness, and at the end of the short ceremony, Kaylie and Zane were presented with a marriage certificate, a bouquet of roses, a brochure for Love Nest Cabins and a bottle of champagne.

"Not quite as elaborate as the first ceremony," Zane drawled, once they were back in the Jeep.

"But more lasting," Kaylie predicted.

"You think so?" His dark brow cocked insolently, but his gray eyes were flecked with humor.

"I'm sure!"

"So where to now?"

"Well, we could either go gambling…or…"

"Or what?"

"Or I could take you to the hotel and—" she lowered her voice suggestively and touched his thigh "—we could start the honeymoon."

He placed his warm palm over the top of her hand. "I'm definitely in favor of option two."

"Me, too." Her spirits soaring, she wheeled the Jeep into the parking lot of the hotel. Blue-green pines softened the lines of a rambling, three-storied lodge. With peaked dormers poking out of a sharply gabled roof and a covered porch that skirted the main floor, the rambling building rested on the shores of the vibrant blue lake.

"This is as close to 'heaven'—isn't that what you called your place in the mountains?—that I could find."

"I guess it'll just have to do," Zane drawled, as if he gave a damn about the hotel. All he wanted was Kaylie.

It took twenty minutes to register and have their bags carried to their third-floor suite. Impatiently Zane slapped a tip into the bellman's palm, then, when the young man left, locked the door behind him.

"Now, Mrs. Flannery, what was that you were saying about starting the honeymoon early?"

She laughed, the sound melodious as he wrapped his arms around her and lowered hungry lips to hers. Though his shoulder ached, he ignored the painful throb and got lost in the wonder of his wife.

Kissing her, holding her close, undressing her and feeling her clothes drop from her supple body, Zane felt a desperation that ripped through his soul.

Only hours before her life had been threatened by a knife-wielding madman intent on killing her.

The image was vivid and excruciating. What if he had lost her? What if Johnston's blade had found its mark? His heart nearly stopped at the thought, and he pulled her roughly against him, intent on washing away the horrid images in the smell and feel of her.

The nightmare was over. They could celebrate their lives and love.

Her body was warm and soft, yielding as he caressed her bare shoulder with the rough pad of his finger. She quivered at his touch, and her mouth opened easily at the gentle prod of his tongue. Her fingers were everywhere, as if she, too, felt the urgency of their union.

Life was so fleeting, so very precious, there was no time to waste. Her fingers pushed his shirt over his shoulders, and he flinched as she tugged on his sleeves and the wound in his upper back stung.

"Love me, Zane," she whispered, kissing the hairs on his chest, fanning the fire deep in his loins as her tongue touched his skin, rimming his nipples, lapping at his breastbone, tasting of him and causing wave after tormented wave of pure lust to wash through him.

With a groan he shifted his weight, shoving her slowly back against the down coverlet on the bed. He touched the outline of her bra with his fingers and mouth, kissing the soft curves of her breasts, kneading the white mounds until dark, petulant nipples peaked beneath the white lace. He teased those rosy buds with mouth and fingers as Kaylie writhed beneath him, arching anxiously, bucking her hips against his, silently begging for release.

Slow down, a voice in his mind protested. *Take your time.* But his body, and his desperation to love her, to prove that they had survived the terror of a madman's knife, wouldn't listen. His hands moved anxiously over her, tearing off her bra, stripping her of her underwear.

And she was just as desperate. Her hands worked at the waistband of his slacks, sliding them off his legs and kicking them aside as he mounted her.

With the first thrust, pain shot down his arm, ripping through him with a blinding agony that was matched only by the exquisite torture of her body moving in tandem with his. But he couldn't stop, and soon, as their tempo increased and their sweat-soaked bodies fused, he felt nothing but the sheer ecstasy of her body sliding against his.

"Kaylie, love," he cried, his voice as raw as a December night. He tried to hold back, resist, but the feel of her fingers digging into the muscles of his good shoulder and the deep-throated sound of her moans of pleasure brought him to quick and immediate release. He plunged into her with a primal cry that echoed through the room, and she shuddered against him, clawing and clinging, her face upturned in rapture, her low moan rippling through her body.

Collapsing against her, he held her tight, afraid that if he let go, he'd lose her. Rationally he knew that she was here, with him, and had pledged her life to him, but for so many years she'd been lost to him so that he clung to her as if to life itself. "I love you," he murmured into the sweat-darkened strands of her hair.

Propping up on one elbow, she gazed down on him with eyes that shifted from green to blue. "I thought the doctor said to take things easy," she teased.

"With you, nothing's easy."

Tilting her head back, she laughed, and the sound drifted to the rafters, high overhead. "I promise not to try to be impossible."

He slid her a knowing glance. "Don't make any rash statements."

"You're asking for it, Flannery."

His eyes sparked. "You bet I am." And with that, he grabbed her again, ignoring his doctor's instructions completely.

On Sunday morning Kaylie dragged herself out of bed, showered and dressed in clean jeans and a rose-colored sweater.

"What're you doing?" Zane asked, opening one sleepy eye and groaning as he watched her gather her hair into a ponytail and run a tube of lipstick over her lips.

"Duty calls," she replied, tilting her head to loop a gold earring through her earlobe. "I'm still a working woman, you know. I've got a million and one things to do before the show tomorrow."

He grunted, and Kaylie sensed the first argument of their short marriage. "You can call in and explain to Jim—"

"No."

"But wouldn't you love to prolong the honeymoon?"

"Absolutely. But I can't. I've already missed more than my share of work lately." She caught his reflection in the oval mirror above an antique dresser. Draped across the sheets, wearing only his bandage and a day's growth of beard, he grinned that sexy grin that caused her heart to trip.

Still, she couldn't let him push her around and try to dominate her life. They had to start off on the right foot.

"You don't have to work, you know. I can take care of us."

"It's my job, Zane. A job I happen to love. I'm not going to give it up."

"Not ever?"

Turning, she said, "Ever's a long time. But certainly not in the foreseeable future."

"So how long do you *plan* to be hostess of *West Coast Morning?*"

"How about for as long as I want to? Or as long as the station wants me? You know, this job won't be indefinite. Whether the producer admits it or not, there is some age prejudice involved." She expected him to object, to give her reason upon reason why she shouldn't continue with her career, but he only lifted a shoulder.

"Whatever you want," he muttered.

She could have been knocked over with a feather. "Wait a minute," she said. "Whatever *I* want?"

"Umm. Long as you take care of yourself."

"And you trust mc?"

"I'm trying," he said, his smile fading. "It's not easy."

Surprised at his turnabout, she snagged a pair of his jeans from the floor of the cabin and tossed them at him. "Come on, get dressed."

"I could use a little help," he suggested, one brow lifting craftily.

"Could you?" She couldn't help but play along with his game.

"Well, I am an invalid."

She laughed out loud. "That'll be the day. You didn't seem likc much of an invalid last night!"

To her surprise, he leaped off the bed and, catching her with his good arm, jerked her up against him. His lips came crashing down on hers with a savagery that stole her breath. "I lied about the invalid bit," he admitted, dragging her back to the bed and burying his face in the lush thickness of her hair.

"I know."

"I thought maybe I needed an excuse to get you back into bed."

"Never," she whispered against his lips. They tumbled onto the rumpled sheets together.

"You're married?" Alan's chin nearly dropped to his knees. "To Flannery?" Disbelief nearly choked him. "But you can't be... He—he—"

"He's my husband," she replied. Polishing an apple with a paper towel in the station's cafeteria, she ignored the opened box of pastries and settled for a cup of coffee instead.

Alan tried desperately to recover. "Well, I read all

about Johnston's escape," he said, "and I know that you must have been terrified. I mean, talk about nightmare déjà vu! But marriage? My God, Kaylie, what were you thinking?"

"That I loved him," she said, offering him a bright smile as she poured a thin stream of decaf coffee into her cup.

"You thought that once before."

"And I was right," she said, refusing to argue with him. She set the glass carafe onto the warming tray. "We—uh, just took a wrong turn." She took a sip from her cup and stared at him over the rim. "We won't make that mistake again."

Alan looked about to argue further, but snapped his mouth shut instead. Throwing his hands into the air, he shook his head. "Well, I guess there's nothing left but to congratulate you." To Kaylie's amazement, he hugged her. "Good luck, Kaylie. You know I've only wanted what was best for you. I hope this time you're happy." She almost sloshed coffee all over him.

"I am," she assured him. "And thanks."

Margot was ecstatic. Kaylie and Zane arrived on her doorstep with a bottle of champagne and celebrated. "I'm so happy for you!" she said, tears streaming from her eyes. "I'm just sorry it took that awful Johnston to get you two together."

"At least that's behind us now," Kaylie said. "He won't be released for years—maybe ever."

"You hope," Zane replied, his expression guarded.

Kaylie wanted to ask him more, but Margot changed the subject and she forgot about the maniac for a while. After all, Lee Johnston was out of their lives forever!

* * *

The next two weeks sped past in a blur. Kaylie moved into Zane's apartment in the evenings after work, and Zane, still recuperating, divided his time between the office and home. They talked, laughed and made plans for the future, and slowly Franklin accepted her. At first the dog lay next to Zane, never leaving his side, but as the days passed and Kaylie became a permanent fixture in the apartment, Franklin relaxed, even following Kaylie after mealtimes.

Occasionally Zane and Kaylie argued, but Kaylie tried to keep her temper in check and Zane did a decent job of letting her maintain a certain level of independence.

All in all, the marriage seemed to work, though sometimes, if Kaylie's name or picture appeared in the tabloids, Zane would explode about "invasion of privacy, libel, and yellow journalism," and threaten to "sue the living hell out of those bastards," but once he was assured that Lee Johnston was locked up for a long time, Zane took everything in stride.

A model husband, she thought as she pulled into her parking space at the station one morning. Fog had blanketed the city, lingering in a chill mist that seeped into Kaylie's bones.

Unconsciously, she glanced over her shoulder, to see if the car that often stopped at the curb when she arrived at the station was in tow. But no silver Taurus emerged from the fog and she told herself to stop worrying; Johnston had been apprehended—no one else would follow her. Besides, she'd only spotted a car a couple of times. Once in a while a blue station wagon would occupy the same spot. Obviously the drivers were just another couple of early-morning commuters. Maybe they even carpooled together.

She locked her car and walked briskly into the studio where Tracy met her in the reception area. "Here are the updates for today's show and you're supposed to join an emergency meeting with Jim and Alan in Jim's office."

"Emergency?" Kaylie repeated. "What happened?"

"There's a problem with scheduling, I think. One of Friday's guests is backing out."

"And that calls for an 'emergency meeting'?"

"Go figure," Tracy said, rolling her eyes. "Alan is into high drama these days."

Well, that much was true, Kaylie thought as she tapped on the glass door of Jim's office and entered when he waved her in. Alan, already seated near Jim's desk, flashed her a smile.

"Problems?" Kaylie asked as Jim motioned her into the vacant chair next to Alan.

"Two cancellations on Friday's show," Jim explained, reaching into his drawer for a pack of cigarettes. "First the author who wrote the self-analysis book calls and explains that he can't make it for, quote, 'personal reasons' and would we be so kind as to reschedule him? Then we get a call from Jennifer Abbott's agent and Jennifer won't do the show."

"Why not?" Kaylie asked. Jennifer was one of the most controversial actresses on daytime television. Though always in the running for an Emmy, she was notorious for her contract disputes.

"Seems as if Jennifer is keeping mum until after the final round of her contract negotiations, whenever that may be. So for now we're out of luck."

"I thought Tracy had a list of local people who were willing to pinch-hit."

"We've been through it," Alan interjected. "And we've got a couple of 'maybes'..." He cast a quick glance in Jim Crowley's direction, and Kaylie had the distinct impression that they were holding back on her.

"So?" she prodded, uneasy.

Alan leaned forward, as if to confide in her. "So, I called Dr. Henshaw—you know, Johnston's psychiatrist—"

"I know who he is," she said tightly.

"And I asked him to appear."

"You did *what?*" She couldn't believe her ears. No way. *No damned way!*

"Well, face it, Kaylie. The public would like to know more about the man who attacked you. And since you're the cohostess, what better medium than our program to give the viewers a little insight into the complexity of the man?"

"And the police will allow this?" she asked, turning stricken eyes on Jim. "Won't it interfere with Johnston's trial? And what about patient confidentiality?"

Jim reached for a cigarette, then tossed the pack in the drawer and wadded up a stick of gum. "You don't understand. You wouldn't be asking him questions about Johnston...at least not directly. Actually, he'd be on the hot seat. We'd ask him to talk about an ordinary day at Whispering Hills, the makeup of the patients, that sort of thing, and then question him on Johnston's escape."

"I don't believe this," she replied, shocked. "I don't know why he'd agree."

Again the two men exchanged glances. Jim said,

"Well, Henshaw does have something to gain from it all."

"What?"

"A little glory for himself," Alan explained. "He's been writing a book for years."

"What kind of a book?" Kaylie asked, dreading the answer.

Jim stepped in. "Apparently he's been working on psychological profiles of star stalkers for a few years. Must've started it before he got the job at Whispering Hills."

"Don't tell me," she said, "Lee Johnston is one of the cases in the book."

Alan grinned. "You got it. Anyway, the book is about done, and suddenly a few publishers are interested. His agent is pushing for big bucks."

"And the publishers are interested because of Johnston's escape and all the press recently," Kaylie suggested.

"Bingo." Alan practically beamed. "Of course, after Johnston's trial, Henshaw can add a final chapter."

"Of course," Kaylie said dryly.

"How'd you find out about it?" she asked.

"I called." Alan's face turned crafty. "I figured there was a lot of public interest right now. I would have liked to have that orderly who was hurt in the escape, but the hospital won't allow it—nor will the police."

"But it's all right for Henshaw."

"As long as we zero in on the book and the escape. But we can't talk about the attack on you."

Kaylie, who had tried to keep as calm as possible during the whole discussion, shook her head. "I can't do this," she said, her stomach churning at the thought of reliving the horrible ordeal again. She looked over at Jim. "You can understand, can't you, why I can't do this? I was attacked—by a madman. And Zane could've been killed."

"Oh, Kaylie—" Alan interjected. "This isn't personal. It's just business."

She took a deep breath. Facing Johnston's psychiatrist, talking about the attack of seven years ago, reliving all the hellish details again. For what? To satisfy America's curiosity? To gain viewers? To sell Henshaw's book? To further Alan's career? To further hers?

It all seemed so petty. A headache erupted behind her eyes. She closed her lids and rubbed her temples. In her mind's eye she saw Johnston's knife thrust into Zane's back. She opened her eyes and shook her head. "I—I don't think I can separate personal from professional on this one."

"You got a better idea?" Jim asked, popping the gum into his mouth.

"A dozen of them," she said, her mind spinning to any other possibility. "There's the leader of the senior citizens' rights group, Molly McGintry. She's in town. Or Consuela Martinez, the woman who came into the country illegally, had her baby so that he could be an American citizen, then went public with the fact to fight our immigration laws. Or how about Charles Brickworth, the guy who's tearing down one of the most historic buildings in the Bay area?" she asked, but she could have been talking to walls for all the good it did her.

By the time the meeting was over, Dr. Anthony Henshaw had agreed to be Friday's guest, and Kaylie, along with Alan, would get the grand privilege of interviewing him.

The thought turned her insides to jelly.

And she couldn't complain to Zane. What could he say except, "I told you so"?

No, all she could do was find a way to get through the interview.

"Don't worry about it," Alan said, clapping her on the back as she reached for her purse. "If we work things right, we could generate enough interest not only for a sequel to *Obsession,* but there might be enough of a story in Henshaw's book for a made-for-television movie or documentary."

"Oh, Alan, forget it," she snapped, angry at the situation.

"Loosen up, Kaylie," he replied. "You may not know it yet, but this is the best publicity we've ever had. And, face it, sure you were scared—hell, you went through a lot of pain and agony—but no one was really hurt, were they?"

"No one but Zane and an orderly at the hospital," she replied dryly, "but maybe they can cut movie deals of their own."

"There's no talking to you!" Alan muttered, grabbing his briefcase and athletic bag and storming out of the building.

Kaylie hiked the strap of her purse over her shoulder. How was she going to break the news to Zane?

Chapter 14

Zane kicked at his wastebasket, sending it rolling to the other side of his office. He'd wrestled with his conscience for weeks.

He strode down the hall. Wincing as his wound stretched, he rapped sharply on the door of Brad Hastings's office.

Brad was behind his desk. Tie askew, thin hair standing straight up from being repeatedly run through with his fingers, Hastings stared into the glowing screen of a computer terminal. He glimpsed Zane from the corner of his eye, typed a few quick commands and swiveled in his chair. "What can I do for you?"

"I think it's time to take Rafferty off the case."

"You sure?" Hastings had never before questioned Zane's judgment. But this was a difficult situation. "I thought you were still concerned for Kaylie's welfare."

"I am. But if she found out I was having her tailed, she'd hit the roof."

Hastings chanced a grin. "So who wears the pants in your family, eh?" He ribbed his boss, hazarding Zane's considerable wrath for a chance to needle him.

"Kaylie's big on independence."

"Whatever you say." Hastings shrugged and bit on his lower lip. "I could use Rafferty over on the McKay building."

"Trouble?"

"Looks that way. There's a glitch in the security system, probably a short or something and McKay wants to post a few extra guards. He's got some big client coming in with a truckload of jewels." Hastings consulted his screen again, and Zane looked over his shoulder, trying to show some interest in Frank McKay's import/export business. But all the while he talked with Hastings, he had the gnawing feeling that he was making a mistake—that Kaylie wasn't safe, that she needed his protection.

Paranoid, that's what he was, he decided.

Later, as he walked back to his office, he still wasn't convinced he'd made the right decision. But he had no choice. This was the way she wanted it, and he'd be damned if he was going to blow this marriage.

"Here are your messages, Mr. Flannery," Peggy said, waving the pink slips of paper as he started for his office.

"Oh, thanks."

"And your wife called."

His wife. It sounded so lasting. Grinning, Zane leaned across Peggy's desk. "I don't think I ever thanked you for getting through to the police so quickly. They were at the house in Carmel practically as soon as I was." Reading the messages, he started back to his office.

Peggy adjusted her headset. "I don't think you should thank me. By the time I got through, they'd already been called."

Zane stopped dead in his tracks, then turned on his heel. "They'd already been called?" he repeated slowly, his mind spinning ahead. "By whom? Someone at Whispering Falls?"

"I—I don't know," Peggy stammered. "I didn't think to ask. It took quite a while to connect with the right number in Carmel because I called the San Francisco Police Department first—you know, to check out her apartment here in the city. When I finally got through to the police in Carmel, I'm sure the dispatcher said something about already sending a unit over to her house. I—I guess I should have told you sooner, but everything turned out okay, and as soon as you were out of the hospital you took off to get married in Lake Tahoe...and..." She lifted her palms and blushed to the roots of her hair. Peggy prided herself on her work. "I didn't think it was that big of a deal."

From Peggy's reaction, Zane assumed the look on his face must be murderous. A hundred questions raced through his mind, but not one single answer filled the worrisome gaps. Who had called? How would that person know that Kaylie was in Carmel?

"Mr. Flannery...?" Peggy asked, apparently still shivering in her boots.

"Don't worry about it," he said, trying to keep his expression calm while inside he was tormented. He'd thought that having Lee Johnston readmitted to the hospital would solve the problem, but there were still some loose ends. It took all of his willpower not to march back to Hastings's office and order not only Rafferty, but six extra men to watch Kaylie every waking hour that Zane wasn't with her. "Call the police, get all the information you can... Never mind, I think I'd better do it myself."

Back in his office, he shoved aside the desire to pour himself a stiff shot. He knew several detectives on the force, men he'd worked with at Gemini Security ages ago, before he'd started his own company. Now, because of his position as owner of a private detective/security firm, he shouldn't have to wade through a lot of red tape to get the information he wanted. He picked up the phone and rested his hips against the desk. "Come on, come on," he muttered as the call was finally routed to Detective Mike Saragossa.

"Hey, ol' buddy!" Mike drawled lazily from somewhere deep in the bowels of the SFPD. "'Bout time I heard from you. What can I do for ya?"

Kaylie's day had gone from bad to worse. After the meeting with Jim and Alan, she'd muffed the introduction of a newspaper reporter who was investigating crime within the city government, and Alan had rescued her. Then during an interview with a woman running for mayor, there was trouble with her microphone and, once again, Alan had to take over until the station break. The defective microphone was whisked away and a new one clipped quickly onto her lapel. Meanwhile, the candidate, Kathleen McKenney, was more than a little miffed at the inconvenience, and pointedly ignored Kaylie from that point on.

The last half of the show ran more smoothly, but by the end of the program, Kaylie couldn't wait to climb off her chair, wipe off her smile and relax. She headed straight to the cafeteria, drowned herself in a diet soda, then, after going over the problems with Jim, grabbed her notes for the next day and left the station. All she wanted to do was go straight home and curl up with a good book and spend the rest of the evening with her new husband.

But first, she thought as she climbed into her car and flicked on the ignition, she'd surprise Zane. Rather than wait for him at home, she'd catch him at work. She guided her car out of the lot and merged into traffic. Adjusting her rearview mirror, she spotted a car, not a silver Taurus, but a blue wagon, roll into traffic behind her. No big deal, she decided, but she'd spied that wagon before—on days when the Taurus hadn't been around the parking lot.

So what? Lots of people go to the same place every day. The driver was probably someone who works around here. She drove a couple of blocks, turned right twice, doubling back, and couldn't help but check the rearview mirror. Sure enough, about four cars behind, the wagon tailed her.

Fear jarred her. *Oh, Lord, not again!* She nearly rear-ended the car in front of her. *Stay cool, Kaylie. Get a grip on yourself!* But her heart slammed against her rib cage, and a cold sweat broke out over her skin. Her fingers clamped the wheel in a death grip.

At the next stoplight she slowed, checking the mirror every five seconds.

The light turned green, and she tromped on the gas, her concentration split between the road ahead and the mirror. The blue wagon followed three cars behind. Kaylie shifted down. Timing the next light, she sailed through a yellow and the wagon got hung up on a red.

Her hands were sweating, the steering wheel felt slick as she drove ten blocks out of her way before turning again and heading for Zane's office. She felt numb inside. No one would be following her. Johnston was locked up.

But Zane's words, spoken in an angry blurt at the last mention of Johnston in *The Insider,* came back to haunt her. "The more the press makes of this, the more likely some other wacko is going to try to duplicate the same sick crime. If not with you then with someone else—no one who's famous is safe!" He'd slapped the paper onto the table in front of her to make his point, and she'd pointedly picked it up with two fingers, rotated in her chair and dropped the entire paper into the trash.

"I didn't know you subscribed," she'd mocked, though part of his anger had been conveyed to her.

He'd scowled at her and motioned impatiently toward the trash. "Articles like that only cause trouble. Believe me, I know." And he did. One part of his business, especially in his office near Hollywood, had grown by leaps and bounds, patronized by stars who needed protection from overly zealous or crazed fans. Any one of those "fans" could potentially endanger the star's life or the lives of members of his or her family.

Kaylie shivered. Her heart knocking crazily, she drove into the parking lot, slid into an open space, then turned off the engine and, with a shuddering sigh, leaned her head against the steering wheel. "You're okay," she told herself, and slowly her pulse decelerated. Should she tell Zane about the cars—the Taurus and the wagon? Would he think she was imagining things, or worse yet, would it send him into the same paranoid need to protect her that had destroyed their marriage once before?

She wanted to be honest with him. Good marriages were based on honesty and yet, just this once, she might let the truth slip.

And what if you're followed again?

Oh, Lord, what a mess! She grabbed a handful of hair and tossed it over her shoulder. Climbing out of her Audi, she stood on slightly unsteady legs just as another car eased into the garage. Glancing over her shoulder, she gasped. Fear petrified her. The car cruising into the lot of Flannery Security was the same wagon that had followed her. The tail she'd thought she'd lost. Oh, God! How could he have known?

The blond man behind the wheel stared straight at her and she saw his face—young and hard, flat nose, cold eyes and straight hair—stare back at her. He opened the car door, and Kaylie didn't wait. Closer to the elevator, she sprinted across the cement and pounded on the button. The doors opened as the taste of fear settled in the back of her throat.

Zane! she thought desperately. She had to get to Zane! Inside the elevator she slapped the door panel. The doors swept shut, blocking out the blond man, and Kaylie sagged against the metal rail as the car moved upward with a lurch. Now, if only the man didn't run up the stairs faster than the elevator... Again, fear tore at her.

"Zane, oh, God, Zane," she whispered, trying not to fall apart. When the doors opened, she half expected the man to be waiting, aiming a gun at her chest, but she found herself in the reception area of Flannery Security. She flew down the hall, past Peggy's desk and bolted into Zane's office.

"Kaylie?" He was standing at the windows, a dark expression on his face. She threw herself at him and clung to him, refusing to sob. "What the devil's going on?"

Trembling, she knew she was scaring him and wished she could calm down. "Call the police," she cried, "or send out your best man."

"Wh—"

"There's a man following me!" she cried, and Zane drew her closer to him, his muscles strong and hard.

"You're okay," he said, reaching behind him and pushing the button of the intercom, "Peggy, call Brad. Have him seal the building and send out a search team—an armed search team. There's a suspect somewhere in the building."

"The parking lot—" Kaylie clarified, glad for the feel of Zane's arms around her. Still holding her, Zane reached into the top drawer of his desk and pulled out his revolver.

"What's up?" Brad Hastings's voice boomed through the speaker.

"Someone followed Kaylie here. Check the exterior lot and the basement lot, all the staircases."

"You got it!" Hastings replied.

Zane checked his gun for ammunition.

Within seconds, the door to his office opened. "Is everything all right?" Peggy asked.

"Y-yes, fine," Kaylie stammered.

"Could I get you a cup of coffee?"

Kaylie shook her head, and Peggy, with a quick glance at Zane, stepped into the hallway and closed the door behind her.

"Oh, God, I didn't mean—I'm sorry."

Zane held her close and kissed her forehead. "Sorry for what?"

She had to tell him. She'd be foolish to keep information like this inside. Trying to calm down, she let him lead her to the couch.

Peggy knocked quietly, then left a tray of coffee for two on Zane's desk. When Kaylie tried to protest, the secretary held up a hand. "I know you said you didn't want anything, but frankly, you look like you could use a cup of coffee and a shot of bourbon." With those words of advice, she left the room again and locked the door behind her.

"Okay, so what happened?" Zane demanded, his lips a thin, dangerous line as he handed her one of the steaming cups.

Kaylie found strength in the warmth of the cup cradled between her palms. She hadn't known she felt cold, but now that the fear had subsided, she felt chilled to the bone. Haltingly, between sips, she found the words. "This isn't the first time," she admitted.

"What?" he nearly screamed. "What the hell do you mean 'isn't the first time'?"

"Just don't get mad…okay? I had this…feeling…for a few weeks now, but I told myself I was just overreacting to Johnston's attack. You know, seeing ghosts in every corner."

Zane became very still, every muscle in his body rigid and hard. "You should've told me."

"I know, but I didn't want to scare you."

"You just did."

"Maybe it was all in my mind," she said, then shook her head. "There are lots of Taurus cars on the road, and blue wagons are a dime a dozen."

Zane sucked a breath between his teeth. "You were followed here by a Taurus?" he asked, laying his gun on the table.

"No—it was the blue wagon." She explained about losing the car that had been chasing her only to run into it again in the parking garage.

She thought Zane would call additional men to seal off the garage, but instead he walked to the desk and punched the intercom. "Peggy, send Tim Rafferty in, if he's here."

A few seconds later a blond man of about twenty— the very man who had been behind the wheel of the blue station wagon—walked into Zane's office. Kaylie nearly screamed.

Zane dragged a hand through his hair. "Is this the guy?"

"Yes, but—" Cold realization started in the pit of her stomach and crawled up her spine.

"Tim works for me," Zane admitted, his face ashen. "Tim, this is my wife, Kaylie Melville. Kaylie… Tim."

"But—"

"I told him to follow you," Zane clarified.

"But why—Oh, God, no, don't tell me," she said, her heart dropping to her knees in disappointment. "You've already started it again, haven't you?" she whispered, her voice ragged.

"I had some of my men assigned to follow you for a few weeks—ever since I got the phone calls from Ted."

He motioned for Tim to leave the room, and the blond slipped out, shutting the door behind him.

Kaylie was furious. Her heart pounded in her ears as she realized they were replaying the same mistakes all over again. Her voice so low she could barely hear her own words, she said, "How could you?"

"Because I love you, damn it. And I wasn't going to lose you again."

Her throat worked, but no words came. Strangled with disappointment, she stared at her hands.

"I told Brad just this morning to take all the men off the case."

"All the men? You mean there were more than one?"

"Six men rotated."

"Six? Tim must've missed the message."

"Don't make this any harder than it is, Kaylie," he said, returning the revolver to his desk drawer.

"Oh, Lord, Zane, you don't trust me at all, do you?"

He snorted. "I just don't trust the public."

Closing her eyes against the tears that threatened, she shook her head slowly from side to side. "I should have known you wouldn't change," she said, dying a little when she noticed the band of gold and diamonds on her left ring finger.

"I have changed."

"Not enough." Why had she been so foolish? A tear slid from the corner of her eye, and she dashed it away. "I—I wanted this to work."

"It will, Kaylie. We'll make it work."

"Will we?" She sniffed loudly, then squared her shoulders. She'd been played for a fool, a childish, simpleminded fool for the last time. "And how will you handle the fact that one of the next guests on *West Coast Morning* might be Dr. Anthony Henshaw?"

Zane's eyes narrowed. "Johnston's doctor? Is this some kind of morbid joke?"

"I wish," she said with a sigh. She rubbed her arms as if suddenly chilled and explained her conversation with Jim and Alan.

"And you agreed to this?" Zane charged.

"I didn't have any choice. The decision had already been made."

"But that's crazy," Zane said, pacing between the desk and the window. "It just promotes—" He clamped his mouth shut and, though still tense, leaned his hips against the windowsill. His eyes, when he stared at her, still burned, but his expression was soft. "You look like you've had a rough day. How about I take you home and cook you dinner?"

She rolled her eyes and struggled out of her chair. "You don't have to—"

"I want to," he said, trying to break the tension, though apprehension grappled with his forced calmness. What the hell was going on at *West Coast Morning?* Didn't they know that they were potentially setting up Kaylie as a target for the next publicity-hungry nut?

And what about "Ted"? Who was he?

Alan's name kept popping into his mind, but the voice on the tape didn't sound like Alan at all. And he didn't suspect Jim Crowley. So who? *Who?* Someone at the television station? One of Kaylie's friends? Or someone at the hospital who had invented a fictitious name?

They drove separately back to the apartment, and

Franklin, the traitorous beast, padded after Kaylie when they walked inside.

Zane, true to his promise, poured them each a glass of wine, then began fixing dinner. But as he broiled steaks on the grill and steamed potatoes in the microwave, he thought about the upcoming show.

All his instincts told him the program was a big mistake. But his hands were tied. Kaylie had about come unglued when she'd found out he'd had men watching her, and, he supposed, glancing over his shoulder to the counter where she was chopping vegetables for a salad, he didn't blame her. He hadn't played fair.

And now he had to.

"Hey—watch out!" Kaylie cried. "Medium-rare, remember? I'm not into 'burned beyond recognition.'" She grabbed a long-handled fork from the drawer in the cooking island and flipped the steaks on the interior grill. Without asking, she dashed a shot of lemon pepper over the two T-bones.

"You're fouling up my recipe," he said with a good-natured gleam in his eye.

"Recipe?"

"I watch Chef Glenn on Friday mornings."

"Oh, give me a break," she said. "This is all well and good, Zane, but you don't know a curry sauce from a fruit compote—"

He whirled, grabbed her and swept her off her feet. One of her shoes dropped to the floor. "Watch it, lady," he growled in her ear, "or I might have to take my spatula to you."

"Promises, promises." She giggled as he carried her into the bedroom. "Hey, wait. Zane," she cried, laughing. "You can't—" He tossed her onto the bed and, while standing over her, ripped off his shirt in one swift motion.

"But the steaks," she protested, forcing her eyes away from the wide expanse of his chest.

"I've decided 'burned beyond recognition' is the best way to serve T-bones."

"But—"

He dropped onto the bed and covered her mouth with his. She was still laughing, but as his kiss deepened, her giggles gave way to moans. "Zane, please," she whispered, still thinking of the steaks sizzling into charred bones.

The smoke detector started beeping loudly.

"Saved by the bell," she said with a giggle. For that remark, she was rewarded with a pillow in the face. Zane, muttering under his breath, jumped off the bed and hurried into the kitchen. In a state of dishabille, she followed, laughing when she saw the T-bones— small, black replicas of steak.

Zane turned off the grill and opened the windows to air out the kitchen. "How about take-out Chinese, Mrs. Flannery?" he asked, a slightly off-center smile curving his lips as he tossed the burned meat into the sink. The smoke slowly dissipated, and the smoke alarm quit bleating.

"Anything's fine with me."

"But first we have some unfinished business," he said, thinking aloud, a menacing glint in his eye. He grabbed her again, and this time they weren't interrupted.

On Friday morning, Kaylie was nervous as a cat. She and Zane hadn't discussed the show again, and she'd finally forgiven him for having her followed. *It's going to take time,* she reminded herself. Zane was used to being in command, and slowly, with visible effort, he was allowing her to make her own decisions. Though, she suspected with a smile, it was killing him.

For the past few days there had been no silver Taurus, no blue wagon, no car or man following her. She couldn't help looking over her shoulder occasionally and checking her rearview mirror more often than usual, but she was convinced that Zane had kept to his word.

And she'd kept hers. She was more careful than she'd ever been and more in love.

She had great faith that this time, no matter what fate threw their way, she and Zane would make it. Together.

Zane couldn't get his mind off of today's program. He itched to go to the station, to watch Kaylie, to make sure that she was all right. Rationally, he knew that nothing would happen to her. Johnston's psychiatrist wasn't a madman; Henshaw couldn't hurt Kaylie.

But some other fruitcake could. He drove to work and dropped by Hastings's office. Brad, as usual, had been working for hours, though it was barely eight o'clock. He glanced up from his computer terminal when Zane walked in.

"Got a minute?" Zane asked.

"Sure. What's up?"

"This." Reaching into his jacket pocket, Zane withdrew the tape of his last conversation with Ted. "Did you find anyone who could have made this call?"

"Nope." Brad shook his head slowly. "But several

of the guys here are convinced the voice is that of a woman."

"A woman." That didn't make things any easier. Zane stuffed the tape back into his pocket.

"You want us to keep working on it?"

"As long as you've got leads."

"Well, we're about dried-up. As for the tracer, most of the calls that we can't identify came in from booths—different booths located usually in the financial district."

"Well, that's something," Zane said, thinking aloud. "I don't suppose anyone we suspect lives or works there."

Hastings shook his head. "No one we've scared up so far."

"What about Alan Bently?"

"He'd be my guess as suspect number one," Hastings agreed. "He seems to have the most to gain by all this publicity. Want a printout on the guy?"

"Sure."

Hastings turned back to his computer, and his nimble fingers flew over the keys. A printer whirred to life, and soon a four-paged single-spaced report was lying in the tray. Brad handed the pages to Zane. "Here you go. Everything you always wanted to know about Alan Bently but were afraid to ask."

Zane's mouth stretched into a grin. "That's what I keep you around here for, Brad, that lousy sense of humor of yours."

"Nope, boss. You keep me 'cause I'm the best."

Zane laughed. "Well, that might be part of it," he agreed, sauntering down the hall. He grabbed a cup of coffee, settled into his desk chair and began perusing the report, line by revealing line. Most of the information, he'd read before. The names, the places, the people who were associated with Alan Bently.

"Maybe you're barking up the wrong tree," he told himself as he leaned back and propped his feet on the desk. He dialed the police department in Carmel, hoping someone there could tell him who the anonymous caller was. Someone had called the police, and if he guessed right, that someone had called long distance.

When the police couldn't help him, he dialed the phone company. He had a friend in administration who owed him a favor. Maybe he could finally get some answers—answers his own phone surveillance hadn't uncovered.

While waiting to be connected to his friend, he pushed a button on the remote control for the television and waited for Kaylie's show to begin.

Dr. Henshaw was the guest scheduled for the first segment of the show. Kaylie, more nervous than she'd been while interviewing the president's wife, flipped through her notes one last time.

"Fifteen minutes," Tracy called through the door, and Kaylie let out her breath. She straightened her skirt and made her way to the set, where she and Alan were introduced to Dr. Henshaw by the assistant producer.

A small man with a beard that rimmed his chin and no mustache, he seemed as anxious about the interview as she was.

"Ms. Melville," he said, clasping her hand and forcing a thin smile.

"Mrs. Flannery now," she replied, "but, please, just call me Kaylie."

Tracy cut in. "Okay, now look Kaylie or Alan in the eye when they talk to you. Forget about the cameras. When I give you this signal…"

Kaylie had heard the spiel a hundred times before.

"Places, everyone!" Jim said loudly, and people scurried. Tracy led Dr. Henshaw to his spot on the end of the couch, Alan perched in his usual chair and Kaylie sat in her usual chair.

"Quiet, please, and five…four…three…"

The lead-in music filtered through the speakers, and Kaylie forced herself to smile calmly, as if every day she interviewed the man who was her attacker's doctor.

"Good morning," Alan said, grinning confidently into the cameras, and the show was off.

Kaylie worked on automatic. They talked about the doctor's forthcoming book, which he'd sold just the day before to a major publisher, and they discussed psychosis in broad terms. Alan brought up Johnston's name, but only in regard to the premiere of *Obsession*. Not only were clips from the film shown, but also footage of the original attack. It took all of Kaylie's professional acting skills to appear calm and detached when inside, her heart was thumping and sweat was beading along her spine.

Just let me get through this, she prayed inwardly as she turned to Dr. Henshaw and asked him about security at the hospital. The doctor became slightly defensive, but soon the interview and the ordeal were over.

Later, after the final segment where Chef Glenn whipped up his favorite apple torte, Kaylie left the set on unsteady legs. This has to be the worst, she thought, content to stay in her office for the rest of the day. She flipped on the radio, answered her mail and gathered some ideas for future shows. She wasn't going to be caught in a lurch again!

At three o'clock, Alan knocked on the door and stepped into her office. "Well," he said, smiling broadly. "Did you hear? The phones haven't stopped ringing. Today's show was a bona fide success! From the response, Jim thinks it may be in the top ten for the year."

Great. "It must've been the apple torte," Kaylie said, and Alan rolled his eyes.

"You should've seen the switchboard! Becky was going crazy out there. And that's not the best news."

"No?" Kaylie tried to sound interested, but her heart wasn't in it.

Alan didn't seem to notice. "I've had a million calls but only two that really count. One from my agent, the other from Cameron James. He's agreed to direct again, and he's got a screenwriter lined up to work out a sequel to *Obsession!* Triumph Pictures is interested in producing, and one of the major studios—probably Zeus—is backing the film. It's only a matter of time!"

Kaylie didn't know what to say. Alan was flying so high, he was so exhilarated that she didn't want to burst his bubble by saying she wasn't interested. "What about *West Coast Morning?* she asked quietly."

"Oh, who knows! It would only be for a few months... Jim would understand."

"I don't know," Kaylie began.

"You don't know? *You don't know?* What's to know? This is the opportunity of a lifetime and *you don't know?* What is this? Are you already trying to squeeze a little more money—"

"Of course not."

"Then you're afraid, right? Afraid of failure? Or afraid of some loony taking after you again? Or is it something else?" he said, thinking aloud as he closed the distance to her desk. "Don't tell me, it's Flannery, isn't it? You're afraid of him—of what he'll say, aren't you?"

Kaylie's temper got the better of her tongue. "I don't think it's even worth discussing. I haven't heard anything concrete yet. No one's offered me a part and so, as far as I can see, it's a moot point."

Alan threw his hands into the air. "God, Kaylie! We are talking major motion picture here! And you're not even willing to pursue it? What's gotten into you?"

"Maybe she's just using her head." Zane was standing in the doorway, and his face was a mask of slow-burning fury. Something was wrong. Kaylie could read it in the set of his jaw. Slowly, he reached into his jacket pocket, withdrew a tape and flipped the tape onto Kaylie's desk. "How about explaining this?" he suggested to Alan.

"What—a tape? Music? Rap? What?" Alan shrugged and lifted his palms. "What's going on, Flannery?"

But Kaylie knew. On the tape was the voice of "Ted." The warning. But Alan? No way. Her gaze flew to Zane's, but he was concentrating on Alan.

"Nope. Just a conversation with a friend of mine. His name's Ted," Zane said, crossing his arms over his chest.

"Ted who?" Alan asked, sending Kaylie a glance that insinuated Zane was walking around with more than one screw loose.

"I don't know his last name. Maybe you can fill that part in."

"Me?"

Zane slipped the tape into the radio/cassette player on Kaylie's credenza.

"Zane, I don't think…" Kaylie began, but the tape started to play and the conversation between Zane and Ted filled the room.

Alan stared at the tape player as if he couldn't believe what he was hearing. Zane swung one leg over the corner of Kaylie's desk and leaned closer to the other man. "The voice on this tape is that of a woman—I don't know her real name—but I think you do."

"A woman? But—"

"It's disguised of course, but it's probably someone you know—maybe someone you date. And no, I'm not talking about Kaylie, because you've never dated her, but have led all the tabloids to believe it."

"Are you out of your mind?"

"I don't think so." Zane let the words sink in, then once he was certain he had Alan's undivided attention, continued, "I talked to the phone company, and it seems there are several long-distance phone calls on your bill. Calls to the Carmel Police Department on the night that Kaylie was attacked by Johnston and calls to reporters for *The Insider* and a couple of other tabloids. Unfortunately there aren't any calls from your phone to my agency when 'Ted' rang me up. But we have the general vicinity in which the calls were made. My guess is that one of your girlfriends made the call. My men are checking into that right now."

"That's ridiculous," Alan said, but the lines around the corners of his mouth were tightening, and the glare he sent Zane was pure hatred.

Kaylie couldn't believe her ears. Not Alan. He couldn't, *wouldn't* put her life in danger!

"It only makes sense, Bently," Zane continued, rewinding the tape and playing it again, letting Ted's warning bounce off the corners of the room. Sweat dotted Alan's upper lip.

Zane motioned toward the recorder. "You've been pushing for more publicity for the past year and a half. You've moved behind the scenes to make people aware of you—and my wife."

"You're wrong, Flannery."

"Am I?" Zane clucked his tongue, and his foot swung slowly as he turned to Kaylie. "You know why Henshaw agreed to come onto this program, don't you?"

"Because of his book," Kaylie said.

Zane nodded. "And the movie rights tied into that book—rights dealing with Lee Johnston, rights to your story, our story and Alan's story."

Alan's face drained of color. "You're jumping to conclusions."

"Am I?" Zane demanded, his eyes narrowing on the shorter man. "I don't think so. In fact, I've already had a conversation with the good doctor. He seems to remember placing a call on the night of Johnston's escape attempt, and not just a call to the police. He called you, Alan. So that you could milk this for all it was worth."

"That's ridiculous!"

"At first I thought Henshaw might have been in on Johnston's escape—helped him along a little. But he convinced me and—" he stared pointedly at his watch "—right now he's convincing the police that you and he only took advantage of a situation that had already occurred. So, when Johnston escaped, he called you and you eventually called the Carmel police. Why?"

"I didn't—"

"There are telephone records, Bently."

Kaylie's stomach lurched. Surely Alan wouldn't have done anything to hurt her—to put her life in danger.

Alan turned to Kaylie, and all of his bravado escaped in a defeated rush. He fell into a chair and buried his face in his hands. "I didn't mean to hurt anyone," he whispered, his voice muffled.

"Oh, Alan, no!" Kaylie cried, tears of anger building behind her eyes. "You couldn't have!"

"You got it backward," Alan admitted, his voice barely a whisper as he looked up, his eyes filled with regret. "That night—the night he escaped. Johnston called here, asking for Kaylie. I didn't know who he was...but by the tone of his voice I guessed. And later, Henshaw called with the news."

"Oh, God," Kaylie whispered.

"So you gave him her address in Carmel," Zane said, not letting up for a second.

"But I called the police—almost immediately! I—I..." The look he sent Kaylie was pathetic. "I just didn't know that he was already over halfway there, that he'd been hitchhiking and so... I called Henshaw back and told him I'd already taken care of everything and that Kaylie was all right and that I thought he and I should do some business together. I'd talked to him before—about a movie on Johnston's life and now, together, I thought we could put something together. Viewer interest would already be high," he said, as if the American public's wishes erased all of his mistakes.

"And that's why he agreed to appear on your show?" Zane persisted.

"Yes—to promote his book and to get people interested in Lee Johnston's story."

"You'd better call an attorney, Bently," Zane suggested, his voice filled with loathing. "A good one. You're up to your neck in this, and the police are bound to show up any minute. I gave them a full report." He reached across the desk and grabbed Kaylie's hand. "Let's get out of here."

She picked up her purse from habit, but her entire world seemed to be turned upside down. Alan? A man she'd worked with forever had used her, betrayed her, felt so little concern for her life? Lord, how had she been so blind?

"Kaylie," Alan said, his features set and grim. His voice broke. "I—I'm sorry. I never—"

"So am I," she managed to say as she let Zane guide her out of the television station. The police were already in the reception area, two squad cars parked outside, four officers charging through the connecting room.

News cameras, some from the station itself, others from rivals, whirred, and reporters were already gathering information for their nightly reports. Microphones were thrust at Kaylie, and cameras chased them as Zane and Kaylie, arms linked, dashed across the parking lot.

"Ms. Melville—can you give us some insight on the reports that Alan Bently was involved in Lee Johnston's escape?"

Kaylie refused to answer that one.

"How do you feel—"

Zane spun around. "No comment," he growled, glaring at the reporters.

"Mr. Flannery—you're Ms. Melville's husband and—"

"Right now I'm her bodyguard," he clarified, his face thrust within bare inches of the slim man who was wielding his microphone like some jousting lance. "And, if you don't want me to get physical, you'd better back off!"

With that, he turned, helped Kaylie into the Jeep and climbed behind the wheel. He roared off, leaving the cameras still whirring.

"My bodyguard?" Kaylie repeated, sagging against the seat and lolling her head back as she looked at her husband. "Oh, boy, I can hardly wait. 'Talk-show hostess demotes husband to bodyguard. Film at eleven.'"

"That little jerk deserved it," Zane insisted, cranking on the wheel hard to round a corner.

"I work with that 'little jerk.'"

"You have my sympathy."

"My *bodyguard?*" she asked again, chuckling at the ludicrous title.

"That's right. Your bodyguard, your husband, your lover, your spouse, your fantasy and hopefully the father of your unborn children!"

He touched her hand, and tears blurred her vision. Yes, Zane was all of the above, and much, much more. He was her life. "I should wring your neck," she whispered without much conviction.

"I think you can be more imaginative than that," he said, slanting her a sexy grin. "My body parts are willingly at your disposal…"

"You know what I mean," she replied, unable to

smother a smile. "You're supposed to be letting me live my life."

"I just don't like to leave any loose ends dangling." Downshifting, he wheeled into the parking lot of their apartment building. "'Ted' was a loose end. The call to the police was a loose end. Those *Insider* lies about your relationship with Alan were loose ends!"

They rode up the elevator together, and Franklin, whining, greeted them. While Zane took the shepherd for a short walk, Kaylie dug through the pantry and found a bottle of champagne they'd never opened— the bottle from the chapel where they were married.

She should be furious with him, she supposed, but she wasn't. In fact, she liked the fact that he'd wrapped up all the loose ends. He hadn't stopped her from working, hadn't even objected when she'd mentioned that she might consider another movie. He was trying... and so was she.

She popped open the champagne and poured two glasses. Then, on a whim, she poured a little bit into a bowl. When Zane and Franklin returned, she set the bowl on the floor for the dog and handed Zane a glass.

"What's this?" he asked, but his gray eyes glinted.

"A celebration."

"Of what?"

"Kaylie Flannery's new independence." Without any more ado, Franklin began lapping from his bowl.

"This is sounding dangerous," he said, but he wrapped one arm around her waist, and she giggled, as they both sipped from their glasses.

"Well, I've become so independent, you see, that my husband's meddling in my life doesn't even bother me."

"I never meddle," Zane argued.

Franklin sneezed.

Kaylie laughed and, while balancing her glass, wrapped her arms around Zane's neck. "Don't ever stop caring, Zane Flannery," she said, her eyes crinkling at the corners.

"I never did," he vowed, and pressed champagne-laced kisses upon her waiting lips. "And I never will."

* * * * *

Rachel Lee was hooked on writing by the age of twelve and practiced her craft as she moved from place to place all over the United States. This *New York Times* bestselling author now resides in Florida and has the joy of writing full-time.

Books by Rachel Lee

Harlequin Romantic Suspense

Conard County: The Next Generation

Conard County Watch
Conard County Revenge
Undercover in Conard County
Conard County Marine
A Conard County Spy
A Secret in Conard County
Conard County Witness
Playing with Fire
Undercover Hunter
Snowstorm Confessions
Deadly Hunter
Killer's Prey
Rocky Mountain Lawman
What She Saw
Rancher's Deadly Risk
The Widow's Protector
Guardian in Disguise

Visit the Author Profile page
at Harlequin.com for more titles.

CORNERED IN
CONARD COUNTY

Rachel Lee

Prologue

Dory stirred from sleep and tried to cover her ears. Daddy was fighting with her big brother, George, again. But later she realized it sounded different. Voices shouted, but was Mommy laughing? It didn't sound like Mommy's fun laugh.

Curious, Dory climbed out of bed, picked up her favorite bunny and stood at the head of the stairs. Daddy was still shouting. Sticking her thumb in her mouth, she stared at the pool of light pouring out of the kitchen downstairs. Mommy made a strange sound, and curiosity pushed Dory to descend.

Before she was halfway down, things got very quiet and she stopped. She wondered if she'd get into trouble for being out of bed. Daddy and Mommy were very strict about that. Once in bed, stay in bed until morning. George laughed about it, but he said Mommy and

Daddy needed grown-up time. But George was mostly grown-up and he got to go out at night. That was probably why they were yelling. Dory hesitated. The yelling was gone.

But then she heard a strange sound and came downstairs the rest of the way. Bunny tucked under her arm, thumb in her mouth, she turned toward the light spilling from the kitchen.

Everything was red. Like paint. It was everywhere and Mommy and Daddy were on the floor covered in the paint. George stood there, his face all tight and funny as he looked at her.

"It's okay, Dory. I made the bad man run away." He squatted and held out his arms to her.

Usually Dory ran straight toward him, but George was covered with the red paint, too, and she didn't like that.

"Dory? Come here, pumpkin."

She saw what was in his hand. A knife. It was all red, too. Why was everything so red?

Some instinct pierced her, and terror shook her out of her confusion. She didn't know what was going on, but she ceased to think. Something deep within her reacted, and she ran out the front door onto the street and started screaming...screaming...screaming.

Chapter 1

*S*creaming.

Dory Lake awoke with her own screams ringing in her ears. The minute her eyes popped open, blessed lamplight greeted her, and for a moment, just a moment, she felt safe.

She remembered what she had seen, but over twenty-five years the nightmares had grown less frequent. Now they were coming back again, every night or several times a night.

Because her brother was about to be released from prison.

She sat up quickly, and was relieved when she didn't grow light-headed. She had low blood pressure, and sometimes it took her by surprise, causing her to faint briefly. A minor thing, a mere nuisance most of the time.

Drenched with sweat, she climbed from bed and

walked into the small bathroom to shower. He wasn't out yet. Not yet. She was okay.

But the dream had brought that terrifying night back. All the intervening years hadn't expunged the memory, although it had been troubling her less and less. But ever since she had learned George was about to complete his sentence, the nightmares had returned. Every single night. No escape.

There was no reason to think George would have any interest in her when she'd never spoken about any of it, and he couldn't be convicted of the murder again anyway, she told herself repeatedly as the cold water pounded her. As she'd been telling herself ever since she got the news. He couldn't even be interested in her inheritance which was locked up in an unbreakable trust, a trust his lawyer had told him about.

Hell, he probably wouldn't even be able to find her. The last name Lake was an extremely common one.

At last she toweled off, climbed into a fresh nightgown and robe, and started downstairs. No more sleep tonight. Too bad, she was moving into her own place tomorrow…or was it today?

Downstairs the kitchen light was on. Her friend Betty made sure the house stayed reasonably well lit at night. For Dory, who couldn't stand waking in the dark.

But when she stepped into the gaily colored kitchen, she found Betty was already there with a fresh pot of coffee. Betty sat at the table, mugs, spoons and sugar at the ready, along with a plate of cookies. Her short graying hair looked tousled and, true to her taste, she wore a zip-up robe that was nearly psychedelic with cat faces. Betty was determined to become the cat lady.

So far she'd acquired only three, all of whom were now swirling, wondering if it was time for breakfast.

"I heard the shower," Betty said. "Again?"

"Again. I'm sorry I woke you."

"What kind of friend would I be if I got annoyed by that? I don't have nightmares like yours, but I've had them. Nice to have someone near when they wake you." Betty bit her lower lip. "Are you *sure* you should move out? I can't stand thinking of you all alone."

Dory slid into one of the chairs. "I've been living on my own since college. I can't let George's release take my independence from me. Anyway, there's absolutely no reason he should want to find me. He served his time and I'm no threat. After all this time, we're strangers. And, as you know, I need to get back to my job."

Of course, those brave words ignored the fact that she'd run all the way to Conard County, Wyoming, from Kansas at Betty's invitation, when she'd learned her brother would soon be released and the nightmares had returned. Packed up and fled, if she was honest about it. Saying George wouldn't want to find her felt like whistling past the graveyard.

Betty, even back in the days when she taught Dory's high school English class, had been blunt, not one to pull her punches. So it bothered Dory that Betty had felt she should come here.

Apparently Betty didn't quite believe George wouldn't come looking for Dory. Or maybe she had just believed the move would ease Dory's nightmares. So much for that.

The coffee went down well, as did a cookie, and soon her fears eased enough that one of the cats, a ginger tabby called simply Ginger, was willing to leap on her lap and beg for pets.

Such a soothing scene, Dory thought as she rubbed the ginger cat's cheeks and elicited a surprisingly loud purr. Her relaxation deepened, and she thought that maybe she'd better get a cat herself.

"So therapy's out?" Betty asked quietly.

"I've been through years of it. I doubt they can do any more."

"Maybe not, but you're older now." Then Betty hesitated. "I have a friend I want you to meet this morning."

Dory stiffened a bit. She'd been here a week, and so far she'd avoided getting drawn into a social circle. She didn't know if she was ready for that, and anyway, she'd never been good at it.

"Oh, relax," Betty said, reading her reaction correctly. "Someday you'll want out of that shell, but I doubt it's going to be right away. You've been in it for too many years. No, this is a special kind of friend. He's the K-9 officer for the sheriff. He trains the dogs and other officers. Anyway, I want you to meet him."

"Why?"

"Well, apart from the fact that he's got two nasty ostriches he never wanted and can't get rid of, which I find hysterically funny and interesting, he has lots of dogs. I think you need a dog to keep you company."

Dory stared at her. "Why? I was thinking about a cat."

Betty smiled. "Think about it, Dory. What's going to make you feel safer? A guard dog or a guard cat?"

Almost in spite of herself, Dory laughed. "You make a point."

"I always have," Betty said.

Back in those long-ago days when Betty had been her sophomore English teacher, Betty alone had showed the infinite patience Dory needed to let someone become close to her. Betty's campaign had lasted well beyond high school until, finally, surprise of surprises, Dory realized she had a true friend.

No one else had come so close to her.

"Oh, and you're not moving today," Betty said, reaching for a cookie.

Dory preferred deciding things for herself. "Why?" she asked, a bit sharply.

Betty ignored her tone. "Because there was a voice mail message this morning. It'll be two more days before your high-speed internet is wired in. You need that to work, don't you?"

"They promised to do it today," she answered, but realized getting upset about it wouldn't help anything. Since she got here, Betty had offered to take her out to the community college to use the internet there. At home, Betty had little need for a high-speed connection. But her connection was good enough to pick up email, so Dory hadn't taken Betty up on her offer to go to the college. Anyway, the college didn't have what she needed.

But she couldn't stop working indefinitely and it had been too long already. Email sufficed for a short time only. "I need my connection," she said presently. "Two more days, huh?"

"What exactly do you do that keeps you online most of the day?" Betty asked. "I get the souped-up computer with all the whiz-bang gizmos, multiple monitors, a graphics card that would break anyone's bank account...but you can get your email here, right?"

Dory smiled faintly and poured herself a little more coffee. "I don't do graphic art all by myself. I work with a team most of the time. Being able to chat back and forth and share files is essential."

"I see." Betty furrowed her brow. "Well, I can call the company again and see if they can hop to it. I know Wil Gladston, and he should be able to pull a string or two."

Dory reached out to touch Betty's arm. "A couple of days more won't make or break my situation. Everyone knew I'd be off grid for a while. And everyone knows I'm moving. At least we're not under a tight deadline pressure right now."

"If you're sure," Betty said. "Things happen so differently in a small town, you know. Nobody's in a rush without a reason. I'm sure if I explained about your job…"

Dory shook her head. "It's all right," she insisted. "I've got more than enough to keep me busy, and I can check email on your connection, as you said."

She decided it was time to change the subject. She didn't want Betty worrying about her. "So this guy with the dogs? You said he has ostriches? Really?"

Betty's face smoothed, and a grin was born. "Two of 'em. Nasty critters."

"Then why does he have them?"

"He doesn't know." Betty laughed. "It's such a funny story. Cadell's dad died unexpectedly. When Cadell came home for the funeral, he found he'd not only inherited the ranch, but those damn ostriches, as well. No clue why or how they got there." She leaned forward a bit, still grinning. "Now I gotta tell you, that man is patient beyond belief and seldom cusses. But those birds can wind him up enough to cuss a blue streak. A very inventive blue streak. A show well worth watching."

Dory was smiling herself, verging on a laugh. "Why doesn't he get rid of them?"

"You think he hasn't tried? Oh, my." Betty threw her head back and laughed. "I'll let him tell you. It's a story and a half."

Several hours later as she dressed to go meet this K-9 guy with Betty, Dory wondered why she should need protection. Her brother always had been good to Dory before that night. More tolerant than most brothers that age with a girl of seven. Their relationship had been warm and loving.

Until that night. Every time she remembered him standing there drenched in blood, holding out his hand, holding a bloody knife, she wondered what his intentions had been. Would he have killed her, too? She still didn't understand why he'd killed her parents. Or how it was he hadn't gotten a life sentence.

But all those unanswered questions ate at her, and the nightmares proved that she was afraid of him to this day. Maybe that fear was groundless, but he *had* killed their parents and offered no good explanation for any of it that she had ever heard, not even much later when she was old enough to ask the questions.

Impatient with herself, she yanked on a polo shirt to go with her jeans and tried to look forward to seeing the nasty ostriches. And the dogs. She'd always liked dogs.

Just one step at a time, one day at a time, until her emotional upset settled once again. She'd be fine.

Cadell Marcus stood near the ostrich pen, eyeing his pair of nemeses with restrained dislike. Except for some pretty feathers, these were the ugliest-looking birds he'd ever seen. He was a tall man, but they towered over him, a fact they never seemed to let him forget. Dinosaurs. Why weren't they extinct?

But there they stood, edged into the small pen he sometimes needed to use because, occasionally, despite ostrich demands, he needed his corral for things besides them.

Nor did he ever let himself forget those birds could kick him to death with a few blows. Not that they tried, but they'd sure given him the evil eye often enough, and when they stopped being scared of him and quit hunkering down, they had discovered great delight in pecking at his cowboy hats. Two expensive ones had bitten the dust before he'd realized what he really needed was a football helmet when he came within six feet.

He'd rounded them up into the small pen today, because Betty Cassell was bringing that friend of hers out to see about a guard dog. Betty had given him only the sketchiest of accounts as to why she felt it necessary, so he hoped he'd get more of the story when they arrived.

In the meantime…those damn ostriches would have to behave whether they liked it or not. At least the electrified fencing contained them. He couldn't imagine trying to catch them if they ever got out. He'd need Mike Windwalker, the veterinarian, with his magic dart gun.

They were glaring at him now. He glared back. "You two don't know how lucky you are that I don't send you to a boot factory."

He finally heard a motor approaching and the sound of tires on the gravel. Both birds redirected their attention and backed up, settling low to the ground in a protective posture. "Stay that way," he suggested, then went to greet his guests.

A smile lit his face the instant he saw Betty. Something about her always made him smile. But the woman who climbed out the other side of the car made him catch his breath. He wouldn't have thought a living woman could have the face of a Botticelli angel, complete with long blond hair, but this one did. She caught and held his gaze until he realized he was being rude.

Then he saw the rest of her. Oh, man, no angel could have a body like that. Or at least shouldn't, because it caused an immediate firestorm in him, jeans and loose blue polo shirt notwithstanding.

"Hey, Cadell," Betty called with a wave.

Cadell gathered himself with effort, mentally whipped himself back into line and focused on her. He approached with outstretched hand. "Good to see you, Betty."

"Same here," she said, shaking his hand. "And this is my friend Dory Lake."

He turned and could no longer avoid looking at her. Simply breathtaking. With blue eyes the color of a summer sky. At one glance she made him feel dusty, unkempt and out of his league.

But she smiled warmly and extended her hand. When he reached for it, the touch was electric. "I heard about your ostriches."

"Not everything, I'm sure." Well, at least he could still talk, and the ostriches provided a bridge over his reaction to her. Never had a woman left him feeling so...well, hell, he was a cop. No one, male or female, ever left him gobsmacked.

Until now.

"Betty said you inherited the birds with the ranch?"

His grin returned. "Yup. I have no idea where they came from, just that apparently my dad had been taking care of them. Long enough to put in electrified fencing so they can't escape. So there they are." He turned and pointed to the pen. "Don't get too close—they peck."

She smiled, a beautiful expression. "Betty says you want to get rid of them?"

"To a good home somewhere the climate will suit them better. So far, no takers."

"I have to confess I had no idea how big they are," Dory said.

"Eight feet or so at maturity. Say, let's go look at the dogs. They make much better company."

He could feel the evil eyes following him as he led the ladies around his two-story ranch house to the dog run and kennels out back. At the moment he had six in various stages of training, mostly Belgian Malinois, but a German shepherd had joined the mix. In all he had ten kennels with access to fenced areas behind. It would have been unkind to expect them to live on concrete with their messes.

The dogs stood immediately, curious, ears pricked attentively. No barking, no crazy antics. Training showed.

He waited while the ladies looked them over, then Dory surprised him, pointing at the shepherd. "That's a different breed."

"Most people don't even notice," he answered. "Yeah, he's a German shepherd. The others are Belgian Malinois, sometimes called Belgian shepherds."

She looked at him with those blue eyes. "Do they behave differently?"

"A bit. The Malinois can be stubborn. He needs a good handler, but he's also more powerful than he looks. A great police dog. But the shepherd is more obedient, so…" He shrugged. "I've worked with both breeds over the last decade or so, and I love them both. Either breed would make you a good guard dog, but they're energetic. I hope you like to jog."

Her smiled dawned, and he felt his heart skip. Too much perfection?

"As it happens, I jog every day. Two or three miles. Would that be enough?"

"Like anything else, the faster you go, the faster they tire. They've got a lot of endurance, though, which is why they're such good working dogs. Both are also courageous to a fault."

He watched her look from dog to dog almost pensively. He pointed to two on the right end of the kennels. "Those two are almost ready to join the force as K-9s. Their handlers are about to finish training with them. But the other four are at various points in training, and any would make a good guard dog quite quickly."

She nodded. "Which would you recommend for a computer geek who can forget the time of day half the time?"

Cadell couldn't suppress a laugh. "The shepherd would lie at your feet and give you soulful looks. The Malinois might poke you with his nose to get your attention. But…they can all be mischievous. No guarantees on that."

He didn't expect her to decide just by looking, so he

opened two of the kennels, freeing the shepherd and one Malinois. Far from racing away along the dog run, they stepped out, surveyed the newcomers, then politely sniffed both Betty and Dory. Once their immediate curiosity was satisfied, both sat on their haunches and waited expectantly.

"I've never seen dogs so well trained," Dory exclaimed.

"Most people don't want to be jumped on," Cadell replied. "They will if you want them to, but I don't recommend it. Hold out your hand palm up. Once they've sniffed it, you should be able to pet them."

Dory loved the look of both dogs. Something about their eyes, at once alert and...empathetic? Did dogs feel empathy? She had no idea, but she was drawn to squat down so they were at eye level. Both dogs met her gaze steadily, which surprised her. She held out both hands, one to each dog, and as promised got nosed. Only then did she reach out to bury her fingers in their thick coats.

She'd never had a pet, she knew next to nothing about what she was getting into, but she knew in that instant that she very much wanted one of these dogs. She had the worst urge to wrap her arms around both their necks and hug them.

Amazed by her own response, one she almost never felt with people, she sat back on her heels and tried to regain her composure. "They're both beautiful. I have to decide right now?"

"Of course not," Cadell answered. "But it might help if we went out in the paddock and played a bit with them. They have different personalities, just like people do. One of them will catch your eye more than the other."

So, for a little while, Dory forgot everything else as they played fetch with tennis balls and tug with a twisted rope. In the end she settled on the Malinois. Yeah, she could see the mischief in him, but she loved his coloration, a dark muzzle and legs that looked like they were cased in dark socks. There was something else, too, something that happened when their eyes met. It was almost as if the dog were saying, "I'm yours."

Crazy, she thought, but she announced her decision. A Malinois it would be. As she turned toward Cadell to tell him, a smile on her lips, she saw the heat in his gaze. Quickly shuttered, but not so quickly she didn't feel a responsive heat in herself.

She swiftly looked to the dog that had stapled itself to the side of her leg. Cadell Marcus was a very attractive man. Well built, a strong face and a great smile. He stood there in his sweatshirt, hands on narrow jean-clad hips, waiting, and she didn't dare look at him again.

These kinds of feelings frightened her almost as much as her nightmares. She was broken, she thought as she stroked the dog's head. Broken in so many ways, and all those ways led back to George. A spark of anger stiffened her spine.

"This one," she said to Cadell.

He smiled. "You're already a pair. He really likes you. Great choice. We can start training you right now, if you like."

"Training me?" she asked, surprised.

"Training you," he repeated. "All we're going to do is ask him to use his native personality and skills for your benefit. But you need to know how to bring that out of him."

Looking down at the dog, she felt a real eagerness to get started, to develop a relationship with him. "Sure. What's his name?"

"Flash. But you can call him something else if you want."

She smiled again. "Flash is a good name, especially since I'm a geek."

He laughed and turned toward Betty. "It'll be a couple of hours. If you want to stay, there's coffee and snacks in the kitchen."

Betty glanced at her watch. "I'll be back about twelve thirty, okay? You two have fun."

Cadell waved and returned his attention to Dory, leaving her inexplicably breathless. "Let's go," he said.

Nearly a thousand miles away in a Missouri state prison, George Lake sat in the yard enjoying the taste of sun. Two more days and he'd be out of here. He had to school himself to patience.

At least no one bothered him anymore. He'd grown strong and tough here, and he intended to take both away with him. He would also take distrust. He knew better than to tell even his friends here what he had in mind. Any one of them could blab, and this time no one was going to be able to link him to what he had planned.

So he sat there smiling, turning his face up to the welcome sun. Life was about to become so good. Just one little hitch ahead of him.

"Say, man," said a familiar voice. Ed Krank sat beside him.

"Hey," George answered, opening his eyes just briefly to assess the yard for building trouble. There were no warnings.

"So whatcha gonna do? Man, I can't believe you're getting out in two days. How can you stand waiting?"

"I've been waiting for twenty-five years. Two days look short." Which was a lie. Right now they looked endlessly long.

"They don't give you much when you leave here," Ed remarked. "You got something lined up?"

"Sure do."

"Good for you. Somebody said you had some money."

George managed not to stiffen. He knew where that came from. Even the oldest news got passed around here relentlessly, because there was so little new to talk about. Money had been mentioned in the papers long ago. "Anything I inherited they took away from me when I was convicted. No, man, nothing like that."

"Too bad."

Except that he'd been using the computers at the prison library when he could and had been tracking his little sister's life. She still had most of the life insurance, because she'd gotten money for the house, too. And she apparently had a tidy little business going.

If something happened to her, say, something deadly, he'd be her only heir. This time he'd get it, because this time he was determined that they weren't going to link him to any of it.

Oh, he'd learned a lot of lessons here, just listening, occasionally acting.

Dory might have disappeared a couple of weeks ago, but he'd find her. She had to surface online again, and he'd spent some time in classes learning how to use those skills, as well.

He'd find her. Then he just had to make it look like an accident.

"I'll be fine," he told Ed, not that he cared what Ed thought about it one way or another. "I made some plans."

Ed laughed. "Got plenty of time in here to make plans."

"No kidding," George answered, smiling. "There's work waiting for me." He just wasn't going to say what kind.

"Good for you," Ed said approvingly. "I'm getting out in eight months. Maybe you can set up a job for me."

"I'll see what I can do." But he had no intention of that. Remove Dory, get his inheritance and then get the hell out of this country.

Closing his eyes, he imagined himself sitting on a beach, with plenty of beautiful women wandering around.

Oh, yeah. Not much longer.

But between here and there lay Dory. Such a shame, he thought. If she'd just stayed in bed like she was supposed to, he could have slipped away and covered his tracks. Neither of them would have had to endure this hell.

But she had disobeyed a strict rule, had come down those stairs and walked in on him. She wouldn't even listen when he tried to tell her he'd gotten rid of the bad man.

Instead she had run screaming into the streets, and soon the night had been filled with lights spilling from houses, people running to help her, and cop cars. He'd tried to run, but it was too late to cover his tracks. She was to blame for that. Her and no one else.

So, she'd get what was coming to her. He'd paid for his crimes, and now he deserved the life he should have had all along. Instead she owned it all.

Well, he was just going to have to change that. Given the group she worked for, it wouldn't be long before he located her.

Then he'd have to figure out how to cause her a fatal accident.

He almost felt a twinge for the little girl she used to be, but the intervening years had hardened any softness that might have been left in him, and she was no longer a little girl who sat on his lap for a bedtime story. No, she was grown now, and not once had she written or tried to visit him.

It was all over between them. Well, except for ending her existence the way he'd ended their parents'. Only much more cleanly, making sure it didn't look like murder.

His smile widened a bit. He'd bet she thought he'd forgotten all about her. Stupid woman. She'd cost him everything.

Chapter 2

Two hours later, Dory sat in the middle of the dog run, laughing while Flash licked her face. "He doesn't wear out!"

"Not easily," Cadell agreed. "I guess he's chosen you, too. He needs a little more training with you to cement his role, but if you want you can take him back to Betty's with you."

"She has three cats!"

"They might not like it, but Flash will leave them alone. Okay, I'll keep him here for now. I wouldn't mind tightening up his training some more." He dropped down onto the ground beside her, knees up slightly, arms hanging loosely over them. "Betty told me a bit about what's going on. Want to talk a little?"

She tensed. Here she'd been having such a good time, and now this popped up. She wanted to resent him for it but could understand his curiosity. After all, he was training a guard dog for her. "Will it help?"

He caught her gaze and held it, an electric moment that conveyed compassion, as well. "Up to you, but I usually like to know what kind of threats my dogs will be working on. It allows me to hone their training. A bomb-sniffing dog doesn't always make a good attack dog."

She nodded slowly, looking down at her crossed legs and Flash's head, now settled comfortably on her lap. Her fingers were buried in his scruff, the massaging movement comforting him as well as her. Dang dog was magical, she thought.

Finally she sighed. "Betty probably told you the important parts. My older brother killed our parents. I was seven and I walked in on it. Anyway, somehow he only got twenty-five years, not life, and he's getting out soon."

She turned to look at him again, her voice becoming earnest. "I have no reason to think he'll be the least interested in finding me. I haven't seen or talked to him since that night. He never even wrote me from prison. But… I'm having a lot of nightmares at night, and no matter how much I tell myself…"

"You still can't quite believe he's not a threat to you," he completed. "Hardly surprising, given what you saw him do." He paused. "So he never once tried to get in touch with you all these years?"

She couldn't understand why that appeared to bother him. "No. Which means he isn't interested in me at all. He's probably all but forgotten me."

"Maybe so, but I guess your subconscious isn't buying it."

In spite of herself, she emitted a short laugh. "Apparently not. I feel so silly sometimes. Nightmares every night? And now a guard dog. That's over-the-top."

He shook his head a little. "I don't think it's over-the-top. Nothing wrong with having a guard dog around, not for anyone. At the very least, Flash will be good company."

She looked down at the dog she was petting. "He sure will be. He's wonderful. Petting him feels good."

"It feels good to him, too. But you'll have to work him every day so he doesn't turn couch potato on you."

Astonishment filled her. "Couch potato? Him?"

"Well, I don't mean he's going to get lazy. But he needs to remain sharp, so every day you're going to have to work with him for at least a half hour. Can you do that?"

"Sure. It'll be fun for both of us."

He smiled. "Good. You'll be a great handler for him. He likes the work, you know. For him it's a fun game. Now let's get busy on the attack training. I'm going to put on my padded suit, and you're going to make him attack me."

She felt perplexed. "But he knows you and likes you! Why would he attack you?"

"Because it doesn't matter that he knows me. Protecting you is all that's going to matter. When you tell him to attack, he'll attack. It's not his job to make decisions like that, but to take care of you. You'll see."

She still hesitated, concerned. "Does he know how to attack?"

"We've been practicing. Now it's time to get serious."

He rose in a single easy movement and went down

the run to a shed at the end, disappearing inside. When he returned he wore thick padding on both arms.

Even so, that didn't seem like a whole lot of padding. Flash recognized it immediately and rose to his feet, tail wagging. Dory stood, too.

"He's been practicing on a dummy," Cadell said. "Now he gets the real thing."

They left the run and went out to a paddock, where the two ostriches stared at them over a fence. "Tell him what to do right now," Cadell said mildly.

Dory hesitated, then remembered. "Flash, heel."

The dog immediately came to stand alertly beside her. In all her life, she was sure she had never seen such an incredibly well-behaved dog. He was now still, watchful and right where she wanted him.

"Now you're not going to tell him to attack," Cadell said. "For that I don't like to use such an obvious word, one that he could hear in ordinary speech. It's not only tone that matters. They can pick words right out of a conversation. Now, some dog trainers don't worry about that, but I do. I don't want officers getting in trouble because someone is claiming to have been attacked and the dog reacts somehow."

She nodded, her heart beating nervously. "I understand." But she wasn't at all sure she wanted to command this dog to attack.

"The word I use is *fuss*. Long *u* sound. Like *foos*."

Her sense of humor poked its head up. "I hope I remember that when I need it."

"Well…" His eyes crinkled at the corners. "We'll practice until it becomes natural. But since you're going to start with a very simple command every night when you go to bed, or when you take him out, he'll know what to do even if he doesn't hear the word."

"Meaning?" She began to feel confused.

"If you tell him to guard, he will. And he won't always need an attack command to protect you. He's capable of evaluating a threat that gets too close. This is for when something is a little farther away and he might not see it as a threat to you immediately."

"Ah, okay." Now she was beginning to understand.

He patted her shoulder with his padded mitt. "It's about to all come together. I'm going to walk away about twenty feet. You're going to give the guard command. Then I'm going to turn around and point a toy gun at you. Pay attention to what happens as I approach you."

Okay, she thought. She could do this. "Flash, guard," she said. She felt the dog shift a little beside her but didn't look down at him.

About twenty paces away, Cadell turned around. He held a gun in right hand, but it was pointed down. Flash didn't stir a muscle. Step by step Cadell approached. At ten feet he raised the gun and pointed it at her. Flash didn't need another command. He took off like a shot and bit into the padding on Cadell's right forearm.

"My God," Dory whispered. She'd had no idea. The dog clung to that threatening arm and wouldn't let go even as Cadell tried to shake him off and whirled in circles, lifting Flash's feet from the ground.

"Stop him," Cadell finally said.

"Flash, release," Dory ordered, remembering the command he had taught her to make the dog drop his toy. Flash obeyed immediately, looking at her. "Heel."

He trotted over to her, looking quite pleased with himself.

"Now the reward," Cadell said.

Which was the yellow tennis ball. She told him he was a good boy as she gave him the ball. Flash chewed on it a few times, then dropped it at her feet, begging for her to throw it, so she did. He raced happily after it.

"It's just that simple," Cadell said, watching her as much as he watched the dog. "A few more steps, a couple of days of practice and he'll do anything for you."

She squatted, encouraging Flash to come back to her. "How do I let him know it's okay not to be on guard?"

"Throw his ball. That means playtime."

So simple, she thought. And so amazingly complex all at the same time. Beautiful, too, she thought as she hugged the Malinois. The dog already made her feel safer. What's more, he made her feel as if she weren't quite as alone.

After Dory left with Betty, Cadell spent the afternoon working with two more officers who were training to become handlers. What they needed was more complex than what Dory needed, and the training was going to take a little longer. Simple fact was, while a civilian could get in some trouble for a misbehaving dog, a cop could have his career ruined. Or the department could be sued. Plus, these guys went into a wider variety of situations, situations that required tracking, rescuing and so on. Dory wouldn't need all those skills.

When he finished that up, he ate a quick dinner, then headed into the sheriff's office to do his shortened shift. On training days, he worked as a deputy for no more than four hours.

Before he left, he took time to feed the ostriches their very expensive feed and open up their pen so they had more room for roaming. Neither of them appeared appreciative.

He and his dog Dasher, also a Malinois, drove into town in his official vehicle and parked near the office. Inside, they found the place quietly humming. Another placid night in Conard County, evidently. He was surprised sometimes how much he enjoyed the relief from the much higher activity level of Seattle. Must be getting old, he thought with an inward smile. Yeah, like thirty-five was ancient.

Dasher settled beside his desk, tucked his nose between his paws and just watched. Since nothing seemed to be happening, he used the computer on his desk to look up the story of Dory Lake and her brother. He felt no qualms about discovering what he could from public records about that incident. He wasn't snooping, but he'd be learning what she had faced and would get a much better threat assessment than Dory's, which seemed to be somewhere between terror and dismissal.

He wasn't surprised to find a twenty-five-year-old case still accessible. The basic police report would be available for many years to come in case George Lake ever got into trouble again. It *was* nice, however, to find it had all been digitized. Newspaper archives were also ready and waiting.

So Dory, just turned seven, had been found screaming in the middle of the street at nearly 2:00 a.m. Neighbors had come running and called the police, who arrived in time to catch George Lake trying to flee

the scene. Open-and-shut as far as George was concerned. He'd wiped the murder weapon, but he was far
too drenched in blood to claim innocence. For some
reason, not clearly explained, he'd been offered a plea
bargain for twenty-five years. Drugs appeared to be
involved, and the father had been abusive. He guessed
the prosecutor couldn't pull together enough to uphold
a first-degree murder charge, so George had accepted a
bargain down to twenty-five. Without a trial, there was
very little in the record to explain any of this.

But what stuck with him was a newspaper account.
Apparently, when Dory had stopped screaming, the
only words she had said for nearly a year were *red
paint.*

God. He sat back in his chair and closed his eyes,
seeing it all too clearly. The child had been well and
truly traumatized. There was even a mention of hys-
terical blindness, a conversion disorder, but that hadn't
lasted as long as her refusal to speak.

She'd been taken in by her godparents and raised
by them, so no additional trauma from foster care, but
what difference did that make after what she'd seen?
No one, at least in these files, knew exactly how much
she had seen, but it was clearly enough to be shriek-
ing in the middle of the road and rendered dumb for
nearly a year.

Except for *red paint.*

He'd seen a lot of bad stuff during his career, but
the thought of little Dory in the middle of the street…
well, the story was enough to break his heart.

As for her mixture of feelings about George…well,
that was settled in his mind when he read that Dory
had received the entire—very large—insurance payout

and all the rest of the property. George might be feeling cheated. In fact, Cadell was inclined to believe he was. He'd lost his entire inheritance because he'd been convicted of killing his parents. He might be thinking he could get some of that back. Make Dory pay him to leave her alone.

Or maybe worse. Because it occurred to him that if Dory died, her only heir would be her brother...and if he weren't linked to her death...

Hell. He switched over to the reports menu and tried to shake the ugly feelings.

Being a cop had made him a much more suspicious man by nature. Sometimes he had to pull himself back and take a colder view, stifle his feelings and use his brain.

But his gut was telling him this wasn't good at all.

Dory was all excited about Flash when she saw Betty again that afternoon. "I feel like a kid at Christmas," she confided. "That dog is wonderful. I fell in love instantly."

Betty laughed and poured the coffee. "I knew a dog was a good idea. He'll brighten your days even if you never need him."

"I need him already," Dory admitted. "I'm so used to living in a world that exists only on my computer I'd forgotten a few other things might be nice. A friend like you, a dog like Flash."

"A man like Cadell," Betty remarked casually.

It took a second for Dory to catch on. "Betty! Are you trying to matchmake?"

"Never." Betty grinned at her. "I just meant you should give him a chance to be a friend. He's been in town for a year now, and I haven't heard anything but kind words about him. So I'm fairly certain you can trust him…as a friend. But I ought to warn you— grapevine has it that he had a messy divorce and he doesn't even date."

Dory shifted uncomfortably. She was well aware that Betty felt she cut herself off too much from the real world. And not just because of her job.

But trust didn't come easily to her. It hadn't since that night. It had even taken her godparents a while to get past the barriers that had slammed in place back then. If she hadn't already known and loved them, it might never have happened. Betty was the unique exception, worming her way past ice and stone and into Dory's heart.

"I'll try, Betty," she said eventually. "But I tend to get stubborn if I feel pushed." And anyway, she hadn't missed Betty's warning about Cadell's aversion to women. Which suited her fine.

"Tell me about it, girl." Then Betty laughed. "No pushing. Just saying Cadell's a nice guy and you can trust him. I'd never advise you to reach for more than that. Anyway, I've got some women friends you'd probably like, too, but you notice I haven't invited them over since you arrived."

Instantly Dory felt ashamed. "I'm sorry. I don't want to disrupt your life. You should just keep living the way you always do. If I get uncomfortable, I can take a walk. And I'll be in my new place soon. I can go tonight if you want."

Betty sat straight up. "What makes you think I want you to go? Cut it out. I love having you here. Anyway, you're not moving until Cadell gives you a dog." Pause. "When is George getting out?"

"Tomorrow, I think. Or maybe the next day." She looked down. "You'd think the date would be engraved in my memory, considering what it's doing to me."

Betty's face tightened. "Then you're definitely staying with me. You need someone around when the nightmares disturb you. Maybe the dog will help once you have him. I hope so. But in the meantime, you're not going anywhere."

"They're just dreams," Dory protested, although neither her heart nor her gut entirely believed it. Her brother was a living, breathing monster, not some fantasy creature. She might never see him again. In fact, she hoped she never did. But as long as she was alive, he rode in the cold seas of her memory, a very real threat.

Later, as she helped Betty make dinner, she made up her mind. She was moving tomorrow. She'd dealt with the nightmares all her life. Maybe not as bad as they were right now, but she'd dealt with them. She could continue to deal with them.

But she wasn't going to turn Betty into some kind of shut-in for her own benefit. No way. The woman had a life here and deserved to enjoy it. As for herself, well, even though George might be released tomorrow, there was no possible way for him to get here tomorrow. Or even the next day.

And she still couldn't imagine any reason why he'd ever want to see her again. They'd been close when she was little. He'd held her on his lap and read to her to distract her from their parents' fighting. But that had been a very long time ago. After twenty-five years, there was nothing left to put back together. Nothing.

Besides, whoever she had thought her brother was when she was little, he'd shattered all that one night in the kitchen. No way those shards would ever fit together again.

In the morning she drove herself out to Cadell's ranch for another training session. Betty had a meeting to attend, but having been to the ranch once, Dory didn't have any trouble finding the place. She loved driving down the battered county roads in the open places, looking at the mountains that appeared to jut up suddenly from nowhere. The land rolled, hinting at foothills, but these mountains looked as if they had been dropped there, not developed slowly over eons. Maybe that was just perspective, but she stored it in her mind for use someday in her art.

Cadell was waiting for her when she pulled up. He sat in a rocker on his wide front porch and stood immediately. The day was exquisite, Dory thought as she climbed out of her car. Warm but not hot, tickled by a gentle breeze. The kind of day where it was possible just to feel good to be alive.

"Howdy," he said from the top of the steps. Today he wore a long-sleeved tan work shirt, sleeves rolled up, and jeans. "You want to get straight to work or do you have time for some coffee first?"

He probably wanted coffee himself, and while she *was* in a hurry, wanting to get her move taken care of during the afternoon, she decided to be polite. The man was doing her a big favor, after all.

Inside, his house was welcoming, showing signs that he was doing some renovation.

"Excuse my mess," he said as they went to the kitchen. "My dad kind of let things go the last few years, and I couldn't get away for long enough to really take this place in hand."

"I don't mind. So you grew up here?"

"Yup. Left when I was twenty for the law enforcement academy, then I took a job in Seattle."

She sat at the table and watched him as he moved around digging out mugs and pouring coffee. Man, was he built. She wished he'd just sit down so her eyes wouldn't be drawn like a magnet.

"This must seem awfully tame after Seattle."

"I like that part." Smiling, he brought her coffee. Sugar and milk were already on the table. "I get to spend more time with the dogs."

"And ostriches," she dared to tease.

He laughed and sat across from her. "And ostriches," he agreed.

"So no idea how they came to be here?"

He shook his head. "Dad had enough time to set up the electrified fencing, but the vet, Mike Windwalker, tells me he only had them a couple of months before he passed. Mike had no idea where they came from, either—Dad just asked for his advice on keeping them healthy. Once. I wish he'd mentioned them when we talked on the phone, but he never did."

"Maybe he thought he wouldn't have them for long."

He shook his head a little. "Possible, I suppose, but that fencing...well, yeah, he'd have needed to do something quick to keep them from escaping. I'd love to know where they came from, but when I ask around, nobody seems to know a thing."

A smile suddenly split his face. "In a way it was funny. I got the call that Dad had passed, and as I was packing to get out here, I got a second call that left me floored. It was from Mike, the vet. He said he'd take care of the ostriches for a few days so not to worry. I'm standing there holding the phone with my jaw dropped. Ostriches?"

A giggle escaped Dory. "That'd be a shocker."

"Believe it. And I was no less shocked when I got here and found out how ornery they are." He paused. "Okay, maybe that's just my feeling and I ought to give them more of a chance. But they've already killed two of my favorite hats, and I don't much like being pecked whenever they feel like it. I'm hoping we can eventually reach a truce."

She glanced out his window and saw the two ostriches in the small pen not far away. They weren't especially cuddly looking, even now when they were just looking around. "Are they hard to care for?"

"I have to special-order feed for them. One of the big pet food companies also makes food for zoos, so that helps. Special ostrich blend. And in the winter when it gets too cold, I need to keep them in the barn."

"So they don't have to be in a warm climate all the time?"

"Evidently not." He sighed, half smiling, an attractive man comfortable in his own skin. She envied him that. Had she ever felt comfortable within herself, apart from her work? "I really would like to give them to someone who actually wants them."

"Wants them as pets?"

"Not likely. As far as I can tell, they weren't hand raised as babies. Or maybe they just don't like me." He shrugged. "But I won't sell them for meat or leather. Betty keeps reminding me that ostriches are worth thousands of dollars, but I'm not looking for that. There's a market for their eggs, though, a very expensive market, so I'm just trying to find someone who wants them for that, or for breeding. Although some days I think they'd make fine boots."

She laughed, delighted by his self-deprecating humor. "Are they really troublesome?"

He leaned back, turning his coffee cup slowly on the table with one hand. "In all fairness, no. If they were parakeet-sized, they'd be cool. They're not doing a darn thing birds don't do. They're just doing it in a *much* bigger way."

She laughed again. "I had a parakeet when I was ten. You have my sympathy. My bird liked to peck."

"These like to peck, too. It can be painful."

"And costly in terms of hats, you said?"

"Two of my favorites, gone." He suddenly grinned. "Come on, let's go work with Flash."

Her own eagerness surprised her, but it shouldn't have. Since she awoke this morning, she'd been impatient to see Flash again. She was already coming to love that dog, she realized. She hoped Cadell judged her ready to take him with her soon.

Then it struck her: she had no way yet to care for Flash. No food, no bowls, no bed, no leash...wow. She needed to take care of that fast.

She mentioned that to Cadell as they stepped out back through his mudroom. "I feel silly for not taking care of it yesterday."

He shook his head. "Every dog here has his own bowls and leashes, and they go with him. Same with his favorite toy. As for a bed…he'll sleep just about anywhere you let him, but I'm warning you, if you invite him onto the bed, he may claim possession."

That elicited another laugh from her, and amazement wafted through her again. She hadn't felt this good since she got the news about George. Her spirits were up, her confidence was high—all because of one dog trainer and a dog named Flash.

She wondered how long that would last.

He paused halfway to the dog run and faced her. "You can love him, Dory. Just don't spoil him. Remember, he's a working dog, and working makes him happy. Keep his training fresh and establish your boundaries. Then you'll have a great relationship."

She nodded and followed him, thinking that was probably good advice for people, too.

Flash's tail wagged fast, and she could have sworn he grinned at her as they approached. Excited or not, however, he didn't misbehave, and when released from his kennel, he merely nosed her hand in greeting. Dory, however, was a little more exuberant, squatting to rub his neck and sides. "You're a beautiful boy," she heard herself saying. Talking to a dog?

But as she looked into Flash's warm brown eyes, it suddenly felt right. She suspected this dog understood more than she would ever know.

She looked up at Cadell and found him smiling affectionately down at her and the dog. "Okay," he said, "let's go. Maybe you can take him home with you today."

* * *

Cadell realized he was developing a problem. His attraction to Dory wouldn't quit. Yes, she'd caught his eye with her almost ethereal beauty, but that should have worn off quickly. It wasn't as if she was the only beautiful woman he had ever seen.

No, something about her was reaching deeper than mere superficial attraction, and that wasn't good. He had years of experience in a lousy marriage to teach him that even cop groupies didn't necessarily like being married to a cop. The endless complaints that had assaulted him after the first six months of marriage should have been lesson enough. If something kept him late and he missed dinner, an explosion would result. If he had to break a date because of his job, he found no understanding. Sometimes he'd wondered if the woman would be glad if he never came home from one of his shifts.

It wasn't his safety that had worried her. No, she was annoyed that his job interfered with her life, and that was not a happy way to live, for either of them.

In the process he'd learned that love could die fast with the wrong person, and that was painful all by itself. Since his divorce, finally agreed to when the fighting became almost constant after a few years, he'd avoided entanglements. He didn't know whether he was guilty of lousy judgment—although as a cop his judgment was usually pretty good—or whether he was just poison. Brenda had turned into a woman he didn't recognize, and he wondered if that was his doing.

Anyway, even in his new job the unexpected happened. A search for a missing person could keep him from home for days, often without warning. And that was only one example. So…he judged it best to avoid long-term affairs. Maybe later in life, he told himself. Maybe when he retired from being a cop and devoted himself to the dog-training school he was slowly starting. Maybe after he got rid of those dang ostriches.

He enjoyed helping Dory run Flash through his paces, though. As the sun rose higher, with frequent breaks for Flash to lap water, he watched the woman and dog bond more securely. From his perspective, Flash had totally given his loyalty to Dory. He was already crazy about her.

There was no better protection than that. But there was still her brother. Unease niggled at Cadell. While a trained dog was great, it wasn't a perfect solution. There were always ways around a dog if you thought about it—usually a bullet.

When they were done with training and Dory sat on the hard ground to play tug with Flash for a little while, Cadell dropped beside her and stretched out, propping himself on an elbow.

"You ever marry?" he asked, mainly because if she told him she'd had a lousy marriage he could hope she'd have as many reasons to avoid involvement as he had. One thing for sure—with this woman he was going to need a lot of protection for himself. Everything about her appealed to him.

"No," she answered as she threw the knotted rope and Flash leaped into the air to catch it. Her reply was remarkable in its brevity. Interestingly, she didn't ask him, which would have been the usual conversational flow.

He decided to plunge in anyway. An understated warning to both of them. "I was," he said.

Her attention returned to him as Flash brought the rope back to her and dropped it in her lap. "Flash, down," she said. All of this was coming naturally to her, and he smiled. Flash obeyed immediately, head still high and curious. "Not good?" she asked.

"Awful," he said frankly.

"I'm sorry."

He wondered if he should tell her more, then decided to go for it. She'd gotten his attention enough in so many ways that he was going to be checking up on her frequently. Officer Friendly, as long as George might be a threat.

"My wife, Brenda, was a cop groupie." He watched her eyes widen. "Now, a smart cop knows that's dangerous, that most of those women just want a notch on the headboard. But Brenda seemed different. Maybe she was. I never heard of her sleeping with any of the other guys. But she used to sit there in the bar with big eyes, encouraging us to talk, basking in as much of the camaraderie as we were willing to share with her."

Dory nodded slowly. "I'm picturing it, but probably all wrong."

"Probably not. Some women love the uniform, not what's inside it. And some cops want brief affairs and one-night stands, just like the women. Consenting adults and all that. But Brenda seemed different. Unfortunately, she was."

Dory looked down and scratched Flash behind one ear. "How so?"

"I felt drawn to her, so I started sitting with her more and more often. As we got to know each other better, I decided she was genuine and I liked her. So we started dating. Long story short, I fell in love, we got married, and six months later I started to learn how wrong I was."

He plucked a blade of dried grass, shaking his head, then stared away from her out over the pasture to the nearby mountains. He'd had mountains in Seattle, but here…these were already special to him somehow.

"Anyway, it turned out she couldn't stand my job. Irregular hours, broken plans. She started in on me for being unreliable, demanding I find a regular job."

She drew an audible breath. "She called a police officer unreliable? Really?"

"In all fairness, from her perspective I probably was. I lost count of the times I missed dinner or a movie date with her. She wanted a very different kind of life, and I wanted to remain in law enforcement. So then it got truly ugly. No reason to rake it up. But I learned something."

"Yes?"

He looked up and found her blue eyes on him. "That maybe I should just avoid marrying anyone. I sure as hell was doing something wrong, something I never seemed able to fix unless I gave up part of myself."

Now it was her turn to look away toward the mountains. Whatever she was thinking, Flash sensed something and stirred a bit, raising his gaze to her face. Almost instinctively, she petted him.

"I never got that close to anyone," she said after a minute or two. "I couldn't tell you whether either or both of you were at fault."

"I'm not asking for that," he said quickly. "But since we're probably going to be seeing each other quite a bit because of Flash, I thought…"

"We could be friends," she finished for him. She

turned her face toward him. "I don't make friends, Cadell. Except for Betty. She's the lone exception." She closed her eyes briefly, then snapped them open. "I'm incapable of real trust. Even years of therapy didn't help with that. So...consider me broken, which I guess I am."

Then she rose to her feet. Flash stood, too.

Cadell gave up on trying to reach her. He'd issued the warning he'd wanted to, but evidently she didn't need it.

Closed up, walled in, all because of something she saw as a child. He wished he could say that surprised him.

He stood, too. "Want to take Flash home with you today?"

"Betty's cats might object."

"I thought you were moving?"

"I almost decided to, then changed my mind. Tomorrow, when the internet is installed."

Everything settled, returning to normal. Back to business. "Okay," he said. "I'll keep him for you and bring him over tomorrow."

Flash wanted to go with her when she started toward her car, but she told him to stay. Looking forlorn, he settled on his belly and put his snout between his paws.

Dory didn't miss the expression. "Tomorrow, Flash. I promise."

Cadell watched her drive away, forgetting himself and standing too close to the penned ostriches. He ducked just in time and stepped away.

"Dang birds," he said, but his mind was elsewhere. He'd just learned a lot about Dory Lake, and far from putting him off, it made him hurt for her.

Damn her brother. If that guy showed up in this county, Cadell was going to feed him to the birds. The big birds.

Chapter 3

The next morning, Betty insisted on helping Dory move many of her belongings. Most of it was computer equipment, some very heavy, but Betty brought the clothes and lighter items for the kitchen.

The house was partially furnished, which made Dory's life easier, and already contained the items she'd had shipped here, mostly work related office furniture, including the extra battered old chair that tipped back farther than the new one. She loved to sit in it sometimes just to think. Eventually she could spiff the house or her office up if she wanted, but with most of her attention on her job, on creating graphics with her team, she was seldom more than half-aware of her surroundings.

The pile of clothes on her bed amused Betty, however. Jeans. T-shirts. More jeans. Sweatshirts. "Lord, girl, don't you ever dress up?"

"I don't have any need." But Dory laughed, too. It did look odd, all together like that. Add the plain undies and the three pairs of jogging shoes and she was sure she would appall most women.

"We have to do something about your fashion sense," Betty remarked.

"Why?" Dory asked. And that really *was* the question. She worked long days, she had no desire to socialize and the one man who'd managed to pierce her desire for isolation had told her he wasn't interested because he'd had a bad marriage. She didn't need a neon sign.

Betty followed her into her office and watched as Dory unpacked the real center of her life. "You know I love you," she said as Dory pulled out the first of six monitors.

"I know." She braced herself for what she was certain was coming.

"You need more of a life than your job. Won't you at least meet one or two people I think you'd like?"

"I met Cadell," she reminded Betty. "Nice guy. Also seriously burned by life."

Betty sighed, then said a bit sarcastically, "Well, at least you're a pair, then."

"Nope," said Dory. "Nice and all that, great dog trainer…"

"And gorgeous as hell," Betty said bluntly. "At least tell me you're not blind."

Dory paused, a power cord in her hand. "Betty? Please tell me you're not going to keep pushing me this way. Because if that's your goal, I'll stop unpacking right now."

The room nearly turned to ice as Betty stared at her. Then almost as quickly as it came, the ice thawed. "No, that's not my goal. I just worry about you. None of my business, I guess."

Betty turned and went to get some more items from the car. Dory stared after her, realizing she had just hurt her only friend in the world.

Well, take that as a warning, she told herself. All she brought was pain. Whatever lay at her core, it was locked away forever. And that hurt other people.

She returned to setting up her office, glad to know that soon she'd been in touch with her team, the nerds who were fun and smart and never demanded she get personal about anything. A meeting of minds. Who needed a meeting of hearts?

As she turned back to her desk and began to connect more cables, she felt herself easing back into her comfortable world where she could control everything she needed to. Even her desk, shipped from her old home, seemed like a warm greeting, encouraging a new life.

Her life. Then she thought of Flash. Okay, so maybe there was more to it than the digital world she lived in.

Betty returned, her voice announcing her. She was speaking with someone, and Dory instinctively stiffened. She pivoted quickly to see Betty enter the office space with a woman wearing a tool belt.

"Dory, this is Rhonda, your cable man."

Rhonda laughed. "I'm your cable tech person."

Dory couldn't help grinning. "You get that, too?"

"All the time. Say, I hear you're into graphics design?"

Dory nodded.

"Then I'll make sure you have the best connection this company can offer. I'm a gamer. So what graphics cards do you use?"

Betty rolled her eyes. "I'll go get the last few things, then make some coffee. I can see what's coming."

Dory and Rhonda both laughed but soon were involved in the nuts and bolts of computing and bandwidth and a whole range of technical subjects. While they gabbed, Rhonda busied herself putting the connectors in the wall, testing them and then adding the routers. "The best we have," she said, placing the two routers on the desk. "Betty kind of rattled some bars, you know? So you'll have two broadband connections. That's what you wanted, right?"

"As long as they're not piggybacking and sucking up the bandwidth from each other."

"I'll take care of that at the junction outside. It's wonderful how far we're coming. A federal grant is making it possible, you know. High-speed connections in rural areas. You wouldn't have been able to stand it here a few years ago. We were still with the dinosaurs and dial-up."

"Oh, man, dial-up was a nightmare."

Rhonda finished quickly, considering all she had to do inside, including hooking up Dory's TV and converter box, and that was just the beginning. A lot more to do outside. But she took time for a quick cup of coffee with Dory and Betty before getting to it.

"Hope to see you again," she said cheerfully to Dory before she zipped out the door.

"Nice woman," Dory remarked and went back screwing, snapping, plugging and otherwise turning a collection of expensive hardware into two expensive, smoothly running workstations. Everything top-of-the-line. The max.

At last, though, she was able to turn everything on

and test it. All good. She sent an email blast letting her team know she was back on the grid. Almost immediately her computer pinged with the arrival of emails.

She was home.

Cadell left for work a couple of hours early, carting two dogs with him, Flash and Dasher. Dasher was eager to get to work, recognizing the backseat cage of the sheriff's department SUV as the beginning of adventure. Flash didn't see it that way, but he was glad to take a car ride.

He hoped he didn't unnerve Dory, dressed as he was in his khaki uniform, gun belt and tan Stetson. Not the guy she was used to seeing in shirts with rolled-up sleeves and jeans.

He pulled into Dory's driveway, behind a blue Honda sedan that had seen better years. The house was small and old in the way of many in this part of town, but it had been recently painted white. The driveway was two wheel paths of concrete, the sidewalk cracked but not heaving yet, and the porch from a time when porches were inviting.

Not that Dory would probably care about that. Betty had mentioned that Dory wasn't very sociable, and that she worried about her being too deeply mired in her work.

Being mired in work was something Cadell understood perfectly, so he didn't hold that against her. Given the woman's background, he wasn't even surprised that she had told him she couldn't trust. He figured Flash would be the best therapy he could offer her. Dogs had a way of getting past defenses.

He left Dasher in the car with the engine running so

the air conditioning would keep him cool and walked Flash on a leash to the front door.

"Your new home, Flash. You take good care of it."

He knocked. There was a doorbell, but cops never used them and the habit was impossible to break. At least he didn't use the heel of his fist or his big flashlight to resound through the house. A normal type of knock that shouldn't startle her.

A couple of minutes passed while he looked around the neighborhood and wondered if she had decided to take a walk. Clearly her car was here.

Then the door opened, and Dory was blinking at him. "Oh! You look so different in uniform, I almost didn't recognize you. I'm sorry, I forgot you were coming this afternoon."

He smiled. "Not a problem. If you want to take Flash's leash, I'll go get his supplies. Can't stay— my dog's in the car, and while it's specially built with heavy-duty air-conditioning to keep him cool...well, I never trust it too far."

He hesitated, holding the leash out to her. She bit her lower lip, then blurted, "Can you bring Dasher inside, too?"

He glanced at his watch and saw that he still had plenty of time to grab a bite at Maude's Diner and get to the station. "Sure. It might help Flash feel a little more at home."

She smiled then, a faint smile, but it reached her eyes as she accepted the leash. "These dogs are practically people to you," she remarked.

He had turned and now looked over his shoulder. "Nah. They're nicer than a lot of people."

That made her laugh quietly, and the sound followed

him as he went to turn off his vehicle and get Dasher. He liked her, he realized. It wasn't just that she was beautiful. Oh, hell, he didn't need the trouble.

But he brought Dasher inside anyway and left him with Dory while he returned to the back of his car. Two bowls, a large padded bed, several tennis balls, chew toys and forty pounds of dry dog food later, he was sitting at her rickety kitchen table, watching her search her fridge for a soft drink to give him.

"So it's true computer types drink a lot of soda?" he asked casually.

"As long as it has caffeine. I can do a good job with a pot of coffee, as well. Orange, cola or lime?"

"Orange," he decided. "Cheetos?"

"Now that's a stereotype too far," she said with humor as she passed him the bottle of soda. Evidently it didn't come with a glass in her world. "Although," she said as she slid into the one other chair, "I did have a friend in college who loved to eat them sometimes, but she didn't like the grit on her keyboard. So she ate them with chopsticks."

The image drew a hearty laugh from him, and her smile deepened.

She spoke again. "Thanks for bringing all the doggy stuff. You never said, but how much do I owe you? You're giving me a well-trained guard dog that you must have spent a lot of time on."

He shook his head slowly. "I'm kinda thinking of Flash as an extension of my oath to serve and protect. He's a gift, Dory, if that won't offend you."

Her eyes widened. "But, Cadell…"

"No *but*s. You can be my advertising around town, how's that?"

Both dogs, trailing their leads, were sniffing their way around the house, checking out everything. Dory watched them for several minutes, the faint smile still on her face. After a bit she said, "I've never received a better gift."

"I hope you'll never need his finer skills."

"Me, too."

Silence fell. He glanced at his watch and saw he had a little longer. Somehow it didn't feel right to just walk out.

Then Dory surprised him by asking, "What else do you teach the dogs to do? There must be a lot involved in police work."

"Apart from what we taught Flash to do? Plenty. A dog has a wonderful nose, hundreds of times more sensitive than ours. It can follow scents that are weeks old, and even those that are high in the air. That's an extremely useful tool in searching, particularly search and rescue."

"Do you do a lot of search and rescue?"

"Around here? In the mountains, quite enough. Hikers, mainly. Then there are elderly people who sometimes ramble and forget where they are. Earlier this summer we had to hunt for an autistic girl. She'd wandered off, become frightened and hid in a culvert out of sight."

"Her parents must have been terrified. My word, *she* must have been terrified!"

He smiled. "She didn't trust us, but she trusted the dog."

He watched her smile again. For a woman who had come here to escape a possible threat, and who, according to Betty, suffered from a lot of nightmares, she smiled easily. Props to her, he thought.

"Anyway," he continued, "it's possible to train the dogs to hunt only for specific scents, too. Like explosives. Or drugs. Or cadavers."

Her smile faded. "Dead tissue?"

"We train them to distinguish human tissue from animal tissue, and their success rate is about ninety-five percent. They can find buried bodies a century old. And they can smell them down to at least fifteen feet, and some say up to thirty."

Her eyes had grown wider. "So they don't get confused?"

"No." But he didn't want to get into the details. Some things just didn't need to be talked about.

She looked down, then lifted her head and drank from her own bottle of orange soda. "How do they learn all this stuff? I mean, isn't it hard to teach them?"

"A little patience and they pick it up pretty quickly. They're remarkable, and they're eager to please." Dasher came over and laid his head on Cadell's thigh. "I think he's ready to go to work."

Dory popped to her feet immediately. "I'm sorry, I've been holding you up."

"Actually, no. I allowed some extra time." He reached into his breast pocket and pulled out a folded slip of paper. "Feeding directions and all that. If you have any questions, call me. And if you don't mind, I'll drop by every day or so to see how you two are getting on."

Holding the paper, she looked at him. "I'll never be able to thank you enough, Cadell."

He chuckled. "Tell me that again when you have fur

all over the place. He doesn't shed a lot, but he's going to shed. See you tomorrow afternoon."

He headed for the door with Dasher and heard Dory behind him telling Flash to stay. The dog needed to learn his new home. He figured Dory was going to make it easy on him.

As he climbed into his vehicle with Dasher in the cage behind him, he realized something. Betty unintentionally had painted Dory unfairly. She might not be prepared to trust people and allow them within her circle; she might be scared to death of her brother's imminent release from prison; she might be haunted by terrible nightmares.

But Dory had grit. Real inner strength.

He liked her. He respected her. And he needed to watch his step, because he sure as hell didn't ever want to make another woman miserable.

Dory and Flash regarded each other in the kitchen. She'd removed his leash, but he sat there staring up at her as if he were pleading.

She tapped the piece of paper Cadell had given her. "It says here you don't get supper for another two hours."

Flash lowered his head a bit.

Feeling like the wicked witch, Dory scanned the paper again. "But you can have your dental chew. What the heck is that?"

She looked at the heap of supplies in one corner of her kitchen, then rose to look through it. She discovered a plastic bag behind the huge bag of food. In it was a nubby nylon or plastic bone of some kind. Unzipping the bag, she pulled it out and turned to hold it out to Flash. "Is this what you want?"

He stared at it and licked his lips.

There could be a minor problem with a dog so well trained, she thought. Was he just going to sit there like a statue or let her know what he wanted? "Take it, Flash," she said finally in desperation.

He apparently understood that. In one leap he reached the bone and took it from her hand with amazing delicacy before settling down to gnaw on it.

"Well, cool," she said. "We have communication!"

Flash barely glanced at her. Almost grinning, she sat down at the table to read the directions from Cadell more carefully. From the other room she heard her email dinging, but she ignored it. Flash was more important.

She nearly giggled when she read what Cadell had typed at the top of the page: *The care and feeding of your personal K-9.* She wondered if he gave that to all his trainees.

Flash looked up at her, forgetting his bone for a few seconds as he wagged his tail at her. He seemed so happy right now, it was impossible not to feel the same.

Later, after she had caught up on email and reopened her participation in the project, she felt a nose gently prod her thigh. A glance at the clock told her it was after eleven…and she hadn't walked Flash since he arrived.

She put her conference on hold, explaining she needed to walk her dog. Hoping she didn't get the slew of jokes she half expected, she found Flash's leash. The dog gave one joyful bark, then stood perfectly still while she hooked it to his collar.

That was when it struck her how late it was. Ordinarily she worked well into the night, but before she hadn't been afraid of anything. Now she was afraid. Her brother might already be out of prison. They'd given her the exact date, but she'd run the letter through the shredder as soon as the shock had passed. She wanted nothing with his name on it.

So today. Maybe tomorrow, but most probably today. Betty knew for sure because Dory had told her, but it was too late to call and verify it.

Point was…she was suddenly frightened of the night and its secrets, a fear she hadn't felt in a long time.

She looked at Flash and saw him watching her, not a muscle twitching. He must have felt her abrupt burst of dread.

"I shouldn't be silly about this," she said aloud, not entirely believing herself. "I have you, after all."

The slightest wag of Flash's tail. God, the dog seemed to be reading her like an open book. Could he do that?

"I promised to take good care of you. I'm sorry I didn't walk you sooner, but do you think you could manage with just a short trip to the backyard?"

He looked agreeable, but he probably didn't understand a word of her prattle. God, she had grown so completely unnerved for no good reason. George, even if he wanted to find her, couldn't have located her yet. She hadn't even needed to leave a forwarding address, because she paid all her bills online and the rest was junk. She'd established no real connections here yet except the broadband and that didn't have her full name on it. She was truly off the grid as far as the world was concerned.

She would be very hard to find, she assured herself as she began to walk toward the back door. "Flash, heel," she said quietly, and he walked right beside her.

Besides, she had a guard dog. Flash would make George's life hell. So she was safe, yeah?

She just wished she could believe it.

The night beyond the door felt pregnant with threat. But it was the same backyard that had been there when she rented the place. With a locked six-foot wooden privacy fence around it. She'd know if anybody tried to get past that.

And there was Flash, of course. Oddly, however, as impressed as she was by the dog, she didn't know if she was prepared to put her life in his paws.

God, she was losing it. Stiffening her back, she pulled the door open and let herself out with the dog. Should she unleash him?

But Flash seemed to be reading the situation well. As soon as they reached grass near a shrub, he did his business, then turned around to face the house again. He sensed she wanted to get back behind locked doors.

Tonight she was in no mood to disagree, or to even try to reason through her probably unreasonable fear. Just get back inside and give Flash a treat. Tomorrow in the daylight she could give him a longer walk, even work with him.

But not tonight. She felt as if evil lurked out there, and she didn't want to find out if she was right.

George needed money to travel. Everything else was on hold until he had more than the pittance he'd received at his release late that afternoon, fourteen hours earlier than he'd expected. But then, he'd been a model prisoner, and he noticed they'd dated the paperwork for the next morning.

But he didn't have enough money to travel on or eat while he figured out exactly how he was going to deal with Dory. The bus ticket they'd given him was nonrefundable, meant only to take him back to the place where he'd originally lived—a small suburb of Saint Louis.

He'd been given the address of a halfway house, so he went there, arriving late at night, and resigned himself to spending some time figuring out how to get his hands on some money quickly. He sure as hell didn't intend to work any of the low-paying menial jobs they probably would point him to. He had bigger things to hunt.

Even though it was late, with his release papers he got inside the door. They showed him to a bedroom and didn't seem particularly worried that he asked to use a computer. The residents had one in a public room downstairs. Help himself.

So he did. He was too keyed up to just go to sleep. He'd dozed on the bus anyway. The only thing about this that shocked him was his surprising discomfort at not being surrounded by walls when he'd walked from the bus to this place. Not having his every movement watched or directed.

He'd never imagined the world could feel so big, and he suspected that once tomorrow began and life resumed out there, it was going to overwhelm him with chaos. He wasn't used to chaos anymore. The order of his days had become deeply embedded over twenty-five years.

But so had sitting at a computer and hunting for information about his sister. She had vanished from the town where she had grown up. She was reputed to be a partner in a graphics business that had no address other than a web URL and email. The godparents who had raised her were dead.

He needed to know more about her than this, but he suspected if he called people around here in their old hometown he'd meet a brick wall. Well, unless he could somehow convince them he was someone else. Not likely. He feared too many local people might remember him. Maybe not young people, but the older ones who had probably devoured all the lurid details in the newspaper and on the evening news.

With that thought in mind, he headed upstairs to his room, where his bed was ready to be made. His own room. It had been a while. Not big, but bigger than a cell, without a cell mate.

For a little while the space bothered him, but then he settled down. Room was a good thing. If he thought back very hard to his early days in the slammer, he remembered how claustrophobic he had felt. No more of that.

Now there was infinite freedom.

He needed to remember how to enjoy it. To use it.

Chapter 4

Dan Casey dropped by Cadell's place in the morning. Dan had recently married a woman with a young daughter and was now expecting an addition to the family. Fellow deputies, he and Cadell had built a good friendship.

"So," said Dan, pausing near the ostrich pen. The birds had been let out into the larger corral but didn't seem interested in taking advantage of the space. They regarded Dan with the same glare they gave Cadell. Dan shook his head.

"So?" Cadell asked.

"Krys wants to come out and see the birds," Dan remarked, referring to his five-year-old stepdaughter.

"Krys would be snack-sized for those demons," Cadell said with a wink. "Bring her anytime I'm home."

"And then there's the puppy she wants."

"Ah. Come on in, if you have time. Is she thinking young puppy? The vet has plenty for adoption."

"I know." Dan shrugged. "She likes the police dogs."

A chuckle escaped Cadell. "You're in for it. And I don't mean from the dog."

"I didn't figure."

They walked into the house together. The morning's coffee had just finished brewing, so Cadell poured a couple of cups and they settled at his trestle table, left over from the days when hired hands ate with the family.

Cadell asked, "So what's happening with Krys and what does her mother think?"

"Well, that's the other question. Vicki has mixed feelings. She thinks a dog would teach Krys some responsibility but that in the end the two of us would be taking care of most of it. The idea of a puppy is irresistible, but every time Vicki mentions it, Krys gets a very mulish look and says she wants a police dog."

Cadell nodded slowly. "Her birth father was a cop, wasn't he?"

"Yeah, and Vicki's wondering how much that has to do with this. It's hard to tell, but maybe Krys has some lingering fears because of her father's death."

Cadell pondered that as he sipped his first cup of coffee for the day. A lot more would probably follow. "Well, I can give her a well-trained dog that would protect her and obey her. But you or Vicki are going to have to keep the training fresh or you'll wind up with just another dog. Which might be okay."

Dan sighed and rapped his fingers on the table. "The problem is, Krys isn't being very clear about exactly what she means by a police dog. Does she just want to know it's a police dog? Does she want it to be able to do certain things? One thing for sure, I am not giving that child a dog that will attack on command."

Cadell had to laugh. "I wouldn't dream of it. A kid that young? One temper tantrum…"

"Exactly." Dan grinned. "I don't think she'd tell the dog to hold us at bay, but by the time she's a teen that could change."

Both men laughed then.

Cadell spoke as his laughter faded. "I can make sure the dog recognizes certain people as friends, no problem. And I can train it to protect her without an attack command." He paused and lifted one brow. "You *do* understand that if the dog perceives a threat to her, he *will* attack without a command?"

Dan frowned. "Depends on what kind of threat. I mean, the mailman holding out an envelope…"

Cadell shook his head. "No, more like a stranger takes her by her arm or hand. Or tries to get her in a car. Come on, Dan, you've worked with these dogs before. You must have some idea of how well they can discriminate."

"Most of the ones I've worked with haven't been that finely tuned. I didn't know if they could be. So, okay. I'll leave it to you."

Cadell hesitated. "Wait a sec. I have an idea. I just gave a guard dog to a new friend in town."

"Dory Lake? I heard about her from Betty, I think it was." Dan was suddenly all cop. "What's the problem?"

"Her older brother killed their parents. He just finished a twenty-five-year sentence, and Dory is naturally nervous about him being on the loose again." He didn't offer anything more than that. Not his place. Dan could look up the same files, if he wanted to.

Dan frowned. "She might have a reason to be worried." Then he returned to the subject at hand. "So what's your idea?"

"I just thought that with Dory's permission maybe you and Vicki and I could bring Krys to see Dory's dog, Flash. He's a youngster, just two, and trained only to protect. Krys might discover she wants something very different."

"I like that idea," Dan agreed. "It might settle Vicki some, too. I think she's concerned about putting a potentially lethal K-9 in the hands of a five-year-old."

"I wouldn't do that," Cadell said. "I hope you know that. But I'd really like to meet Krys again and talk about it. See if we can find out what's going on in the child's head."

"I'd love to know that, too. It's not like her dad was a K-9 handler. I don't know where this came from. But," Dan said with a shrug, "I often don't know where Krys gets some of her ideas. She's a mystery at times."

Around two that afternoon, Dory stretched and turned off her computer monitors, allowing her recent construct for the graphics scene to render into a high-definition, nearly realistic image. It wouldn't take long, given the power and number of graphics cards she had, but it did remind her that she needed to take Flash on a longer walk than just around her backyard. She'd also promised to work with him to keep him fresh.

Perfect time to do her part by the dog and grab something to eat, maybe a sandwich. She and Betty had stocked her freezer with easy-to-prepare foods, although Betty had tsked quite a bit and said Dory had to promise to come over every Sunday for a decent meal.

Amused, shaking her head, she said aloud, "Flash, walk."

She heard the scrabble of his claws on the wood floor in the hall, and by the time she reached the front door he was standing there with his leash in his mouth.

Smart dog, she thought. Also probably desperate by now. She was sure he was used to a whole lot more activity.

"I guess nobody warned you that I forget time when I work," she said to Flash as she bent to connect his leash. "Sorry about that, boy." She ruffled his fur and scratched between his ears, but there was no mistaking his eagerness. He moved from paw to paw as if he could barely contain his excitement.

Maybe she should set an alarm to remind her that she needed to make dog time now. She stuffed a plastic bag in her pocket for cleaning up after him.

"Ready?" she asked. Stupid question. The dog was overready. "Flash, heel."

They stepped out the front door together in time to see Cadell pull into her driveway. Once again the official vehicle and the uniform. Dory had never been keen on uniforms, but this guy...well, he filled that khaki uniform exceptionally well.

She waved, and he waved back as he climbed out. "Going somewhere?" he called.

"Flash and I are taking a walk."

"I'll bring Dasher along, too, if you don't mind some company."

Dory didn't even hesitate. For once she was glad of company. The world around her seemed to be growing more threatening by the day, and no amount of internal argument could change the feeling. George was on the streets again. George blamed her for his conviction. She'd heard that clear enough, even though she hadn't testified and had still been in a state of utter shock. "Great. You can tell me if I'm doing it right."

They reached the corner without either of them speaking. Dasher and Flash were completely well behaved, waiting patiently to learn which direction they were supposed to take.

"Any preference about where you want to walk?" Cadell asked.

"Honestly, I've been out jogging nearly every day, but I'm totally unaware of my surroundings. My head is on my projects, and everything else goes away when I run."

Cadell hesitated, then said, "Right now that's not wise, Dory. Yes, you'll have Flash with you, but you need to be aware of your surroundings. Not to mention learning your way around."

She flushed faintly, knowing he was right. Scared as she was of her brother, she couldn't afford to be off in her own world when she was outside. But running cut her free, let her mind wander in ways that could be extremely useful and creative.

She frowned down at the pavement, trying to figure out how to balance this. Just how afraid was she of George? Afraid enough to pay attention? To relinquish some of her best thinking time?

She lifted her head and looked around the quiet neighborhood. It seemed so benign, her fears so out of place. Yet the neighborhood she had lived in as a child hadn't been much different. Quiet. Benign. And then a monster had emerged in her own house.

"Okay," she said finally. "You're right. I don't like it, but you're absolutely right."

"You don't have to be hyperalert," he said. "You *will* have Flash keeping an eye out. But you at least have to know where you are and develop a sense for when something isn't right. For your own peace of mind, really."

He had a point. She'd skipped jogging yesterday because of George, all the while telling herself how ridiculous she was being. Even if George knew where she was—highly doubtful—it would take him at least some time to get here.

She turned to the right, and they resumed walking. Soon she admitted something that was hard to say out loud. "I think I've endowed my brother with some of the qualities of a supervillain."

"How so?"

"Oh, you know. Finding me. Getting here in an instant, walking through walls... I don't know, exactly. Even if he knew I was here, it would take time for him to arrive. Yet yesterday I skipped my run."

"I'm sorry you skipped your run. But I understand the rest."

She glanced up at him. "How could you possibly understand that kind of insanity?"

"Because I've seen what a truly horrible experience can do to the human mind and heart. The impossible has become possible. Why not all the rest, as well? That's not insanity."

"Maybe not." She couldn't believe she had just revealed that to him. But Cadell seemed like an honestly nice guy, and he'd been understanding of her fears from the outset. Maybe she needed more than one person to talk to. Betty had heard most of it more than once. Maybe all she wanted was a fresh perspective.

"So," he said two blocks later, during which she had tried to pay attention to everything around her, "do you think you might do me a favor?"

Everything inside her tensed. That would depend, she thought, although she stopped herself from saying it out loud. Heavens, the man had given her a beautiful guard dog. She owed him...if she was capable of providing what he wanted.

"What's that?" she asked cautiously.

"One of my friends—also a deputy, by the way— has a five-year-old stepdaughter, almost six. Her dad was a cop who was killed. Anyway, he says she's lately become determined to get a police dog. Neither of us is sure why or what she really wants. So...could I bring her over to see Flash? He hasn't got the kind of training that would make her parents nervous, but he might be exactly what she needs. I don't know. How could I?" He laughed quietly. "I'm not sure where this demand is coming from, but she's adamant. Not a puppy, but a police dog."

Dory felt torn. A little girl who'd lost her dad. She identified with that. But she didn't want to sink social roots in this town. She didn't want to socialize at all. Life was so much clearer when she kept to herself and simply worked. Trust never became an issue.

But a little girl? One not so very different than Dory herself had been once. Some string in her heart began to knit a connection of some kind, like it or not.

"All right," she said. She was sure she didn't sound enthusiastic.

"If it's too much trouble..."

She whirled then. Flash stopped walking and came to stand right beside her, but she hardly noticed. "It's not a matter of trouble. It's a matter of me. I'd rather be a hermit, if you haven't heard. Bring the child over. At least I can trust *her*."

She resumed her walk with Flash, leaving Cadell and Dasher behind. Well, that was a lunatic sort of thing to have said, she thought irritably. People around here were evidently going to insist on pushing into her life. She needed that to stop.

But then she remembered the gift of the dog trotting beside her and felt like an absolute ingrate. A sleaze. Couldn't she at least put a pleasant veneer over her scarred personality?

Abruptly she halted and pivoted on one foot. Cadell was right there behind her, his face revealing nothing.

"I'm sorry," she said.

"You're under a lot of stress," he replied. "I guess I'm adding to it."

Aw, heck, she thought as they resumed their walk. Now she was making *him* feel like a problem when all he had done was be incredibly kind and understanding. Flash scooted over onto some grass to do his business, and she pulled the plastic bag out of her pocket, picking up the mess, then knotting off the bag.

"You're not adding to anything," she said after a bit. "You've been great to me. The problems are all my own. I'm not usually like this, but..."

"Well, you've moved, your brother is out of prison,

you're having problems with that… I'd say that's not usual by any means."

"I don't deserve excuses. I need to learn to handle all this. It's the way life is, now."

And this version of life evidently didn't include her hiding out with her computers and her projects except when she had to emerge to buy groceries. Nope. Now there was Betty nearby, and Cadell, who seemed determined to keep an eye on her, and some little girl who'd lost her daddy.

The idea of the little girl wormed past her defenses, and she felt an ache in her heart. Their stories might be different, but she understood the loss that child must feel, and for the girl it was relatively recent.

"What's your friend's daughter's name?"

"Krystal. Everyone calls her Krys."

"How long ago did she lose her father?"

"Two years now. About anyway."

"How sad." Dory sighed. "Sorry for my outburst. By all means, bring her over to meet Flash. Just call and let me know first."

Cadell spent a little time in the backyard with Dory and Flash, refreshing him, but Dory didn't show her usual joy in the exercise. She looked pensive, and he hoped he wasn't responsible for that.

So she wanted to be a hermit. Well, some people were built that way. Completely introverted. The thing was, Dory didn't act introverted. Avoidance was something else altogether. And he gathered from what Betty said that she worked with a team online, chatting with them around the clock.

Now that might not be face time, but it was still a

group of relationships she'd built. Did she feel safer because of the distance? Because if there was one thing he'd noted, it was that people could become very close online and could be seriously hurt by people they never set eyes on.

So Dory's fortress might not be as safe as she believed.

But he shoved that aside, thinking of her fears about her brother and how they must be pushing her right now. She'd come here to hide out, and by now she might very much want a hole to disappear into.

Instead he was bringing some new people into her life, one of them a little girl he was sure wouldn't allow her to remain detached. He sensed that Dory was identifying with Krys already.

Now he had to wonder if he'd made a huge mistake by trying to help a friend. But the simple fact was he didn't want Krys to become attached to one of his nearly trained police dogs. They were already assigned. Which left Flash as an example of the dog he could train for her. Even as young as Krys was, she would certainly understand that Flash was Dory's dog, something not as easy to explain at his kennels, where he had a number of dogs and worked individually with their handlers most of the time. Out there it might not be clear that a dog wasn't adoptable.

So that left Dory. And maybe a bit of him trying to get in deeper than he should. He had this little niggle that Krys might be able to pierce Dory's barriers in a way no one else could.

He didn't bother asking why he should care. He just did. Which, he reminded himself, ought to be a huge warning. Klaxons ought to be going off in his head. Time to turn around and walk away.

But he didn't. He was, however, disappointed when she said all too soon, "I've got to get back to work. I have a team waiting on me. They know I went out with the dog, but they're probably wondering if I got kidnapped."

He managed a faint smile. "Do they know about your brother?"

Her face closed instantly. "No."

She headed toward her house, leaving him to find his way out of the fenced backyard. "I'll call before I bring Krys over," he said.

She barely glanced back. "Thanks. Thanks for everything, Cadell."

Thanks for what? he wondered as he let himself and Dasher out the gate and walked to his car. He hadn't done anything. Well, except for giving her a dog she desperately needed.

Shaking his head a little as he put Dasher in the backseat, he wondered at himself. He'd probably way overstepped himself by asking her to let Krys come over. Because it wouldn't just be Krys, and she knew it. It would be Krys and at least one parent.

People she evidently didn't care to meet. Interrupting the life she'd worked long and hard to build for herself.

He snorted at his own folly as he backed out of her driveway. He was acting like a stupid moth, coming back to the flame again and again. But she wasn't a flame. The sight of her might ignite his own fires, but he'd seen enough to know that Dory might singe him with cold. Bitter cold.

* * *

Dory slipped back into her chair at her desk and soon forgot everything else as she dived into working on her part of the animation they were creating, and chatting with the other members of her team. Mostly they talked business, tools, ways to solve problems and new ideas. Once in a while they became more personal, but she hid herself well. She doubted any of them guessed that D. K. Lake was a woman. Given the harassment of women online, she wanted to keep it that way. Not that any of her colleagues would dump on her, but if word got out that one of Major Animation's creative team was a woman? No, thanks.

After a couple of hours, concentration escaped her and she realized that her thoughts were drifting to other things. God, she been nearly rude to Cadell, if not outright rude.

No, she wasn't thrilled about meeting this little girl, because caring was such a dangerous thing. But a five-year-old? Yeah, she'd have to meet at least one of the parents, but that didn't have to go beyond a half hour or so. The kid wanted a dog. Cadell had thought one trained like Flash, rather than his other dogs, would be best.

Would it kill her to be helpful? Being helpful didn't mean she had to become involved.

Except for Betty, only her godparents had gotten inside the walls erected by one horrific night in her family kitchen. Of course she knew people. She'd made friends all the way through high school and college. But she'd never let those people close. They never met the real Dory Lake, because she never let them. She skimmed the surface with them while holding herself apart.

She'd had enough therapy to know exactly what she was doing, and she had absolutely no desire to change that about herself. That shell she kept around her innermost being was all that protected her. She'd learned that the hard way.

As Flash rested his head on her thigh, and she looked down at him, she realized her wall might have been penetrated. Just a little bit.

Sighing, she patted the dog and returned to work.

Chapter 5

More than a week later, on a Saturday morning, Cadell joined Dan and little Krystal at Dory's house. Last night he'd checked up on George Lake and had found some disturbing news. He didn't know whether to share it or not, but this morning he was determined to let no shadow hover over Krys's meeting with Flash and her desire for a police dog. Maybe later, he'd tell Dory what he'd learned.

She greeted both him and Dan pleasantly at the door, but he noticed circles under her eyes. She wore a burgundy sweatshirt labeled Heidelberg, as if she were chilled on this summer morning, and jeans. Her feet were covered with socks. Beside her, alert, stood Flash, his head cocked inquiringly.

"Come on in," she said, swinging the door wide. "I was just about to put my shoes on."

Once inside her small foyer, introductions were made. She shook hands with Dan, giving him a pleasant smile, then squatted down until she was at eye level with Krys. "I heard about you, Krys. So you want a police dog?"

Krys nodded quickly. "Dan says you have one. Is that him?"

"That's Flash. He's beautiful, isn't he?"

"He's big," came the response. "Can I touch him?"

"Sure. Flash, sit. Shake." That was her own addition to Flash's repertoire, surprisingly easy to teach to this very bright dog. Flash obediently sat and extended his right front paw.

Krys giggled and reached for it. "I like him!"

Flash apparently liked her, too. If dogs could grin, he was grinning now.

"But is he a *real* police dog?" Krys asked. Apparently, she wasn't about to be snowed. Cadell caught the smile on Dory's face as she stood up. She looked at him.

"I trained him," said Cadell. "He's a good guard."

Krys looked up at him. "No biting?"

"No biting." Not exactly true but true enough. "He only bites if you tell him to."

"Mommy says I can't have a dog that bites."

Cadell looked at Dan. Dan half shrugged, then said, "I don't think she meant a dog that wouldn't bite a bad man. Does that worry you, Krys?"

"Not if it's only bad men." Her face grew serious. "There are bad men. One killed my daddy. I wish he had a dog."

Three adults exchanged looks, but as soon as the

cloud appeared, it blew away, and Krys asked, "Can I play with him, too?"

"Of course you can," Dan said. He looked at Dory and Cadell. Dory smiled and waved toward the back door. "You guys take him out. I need to finish up something."

But instead of returning to her computers, Dory wound up standing at the back window of her bedroom, watching the two men and the little girl play with Flash.

God, Krys tugged at her heart. Another child's life forever scarred by someone murderous. She could easily imagine some of what that little girl was living with.

The window was open a few inches to let the summery breeze in, and she heard some of the conversation.

"Flash won't let you tell him what to do," Cadell was explaining. "He only listens to me and Dory. So your dog would only listen to you and your parents, okay? That's part of what makes a police dog different."

So Cadell was going to give that little girl a version of Flash. Dory wondered if the child was haunted by nightmares, or by fears she didn't know how to express.

None of her business, she told herself. Not a thing she could do about it. Returning to her office, she buried her head in her work. Work was her salvation. Creating artificial worlds made her happy.

Little else did.

A half hour later, she heard Krys's piping voice go out the front door and assumed she was once again alone. She wished she knew how to reach out better, especially to that little girl. Everything inside her seemed to freeze up, though, leaving her basically useless. God, it would be easy to hate herself.

She heard Flash trotting toward her, and soon his head rested on her thigh. She reached out automatically to scratch his neck while she watched her latest animation unfold on her screen.

Water was rushing into the ground floor of a building, sweeping furniture and other debris before it. As she watched, she was keeping an eye out for ways to improve it.

"That's cool," said a voice behind her.

She nearly jumped out of her skin. Whirling around, she saw Cadell standing in the doorway of her office. Her heart had nearly climbed into her throat, making it impossible for her to speak.

"Very cool," he repeated. "Did you make that?"

She gave a stiff nod.

"I'm impressed. Sorry I startled you—I thought you heard me heading this way. I wanted to thank you for letting Dan and Krys see Flash."

"No problem," she mumbled, waiting for her heartbeat to slow. "Krys can come again, if she wants."

"That's generous of you. I could tell you were uneasy about it. And the way you looked at Krys… At least she didn't see anything, Dory. She was at home in bed when her father was killed."

"Does it matter?" she asked stiffly.

"Sorry?"

It was as if a wrench turned inside her, loosening a huge bolt. Before she knew what she was going to do, she started talking.

"There was this little girl," she said, looking down at her lap. Flash had settled at her feet. "She was just seven years old. She thought her big brother was the best person in the whole world. She worshipped him."

Glancing up, she saw Cadell nodding, his expression utterly grave.

"Her big brother used to play games with her," she continued. "Read her stories. Carry her around on his shoulders. He made her laugh a lot. Their parents were strict, but he made it seem not so bad. Sometimes he said he'd done something when the little girl had really done it so she didn't get punished. And when the little girl couldn't sleep at night because of the fighting, he sometimes came into her room in the dark and told her stories. Safe stories. Stories without people arguing."

"I'm listening," Cadell said quietly.

"Their parents didn't fight a lot. It wasn't often. But then they started fighting with her big brother, and the little girl was bothered. She knew her big brother was staying out too late, and that her parents thought he was doing things he shouldn't, but she thought her big brother was a good guy."

She drew a shaky breath. "She loved her big brother. Until one night. The fighting was loud, bad, scary. They were fighting with her brother. She knew she wasn't supposed to go downstairs, but she was worried about him. So she crept down the stairs and…" Her voice broke. She panted the last words, struggling for the breath to get them out. "She discovered her brother had turned into a monster."

Cadell didn't move for long moments. His chest felt as if steel bands had wrapped around it and were tightening with every breath. For the first time in his life, he absolutely did not know what to do.

Touching her, even to offer comfort, might send her into flight. This was the woman who wanted to be a hermit. Part of him was amazed that she'd told him her story in such an intimate way. Another part of him was alarmed that she was so vulnerable now—a wrong word or movement could lock her down forever.

Something about Krys had drawn this out of Dory, because he was sure he'd done nothing to make it possible for her to drop her guard this way. To open up. Hesitantly, he finally said, "What about Krys?"

At that she seemed to snap into focus and looked at him. Whatever emotions had been rising out of her depths suddenly backed off—swallowed, he thought, by her cultured distance. "Krys? So what if she didn't see anything bad? She went to bed one night and woke up in the morning to learn that her dad was never coming home again. That's hard to deal with."

"I'm sure." He took a tentative step toward her, wishing the tension would leave her face. "So you think the dog will help her?"

"Flash helps *me*."

Well, that sure as hell made him feel good. Finally he reached her and squatted right in front of her chair. The news he'd learned that morning was going to have to wait.

"Can you get away?" he asked.

"Get away?"

"Out of here for a while. For a drive, a walk, whatever."

Perplexity awoke on her face, dispelling some of the tension. "You're in uniform. Don't you have to work?"

"I need to stop by the ranger station for a few minutes. They want some K-9s, too, but it won't take long to sort out. You might enjoy meeting Desi Jenks. She's a pistol. Anyway, can you take some time?"

He watched her hesitate, turning her head to the loop of flooding waters that was repeating on her monitor, almost like she wanted to dive into it. Then he watched a shudder pass through her, as if she were releasing tension. "Okay," she said finally. "I guess I do need to get out for a little while. It'd do me some good. Give me a minute to let my team know I'll be back later."

"What?" he said lightly. "You mean you don't carry them with you on a cell phone?"

At that her demeanor changed entirely, and she smiled faintly. "I've noticed there are a few dead zones around this town."

"We all have that problem. It's getting better but not perfect." He straightened and turned toward her door. "I'll be out front, but I need to get to Desi over her lunch hour." He glanced at his watch. "Which is very soon."

"Okay," she said briskly, once again all business. She turned to her computer, and he watched words popping up on one of the screens not displaying the flood or grids of some kind. "How long should we be?"

"Not long for Desi, probably, but if you want to see a little of the area, give us a couple of hours."

"Okay." She tapped away, chuckled quietly and then faced him again. "Let me get my shoes. Is Flash coming?"

"I hope you don't consider going anywhere without Flash."

"The supermarket might object," she said lightly.

"Then I'll get him a vest. Get your shoes."

* * *

Dory felt odd, and she acknowledged it as she went to get her jogging shoes. First that unexpected dump about what had happened to her as a child. She wasn't sure what had brought that on, but she had a feeling it very much had to do with Krys. Identification. A need to make it clear to at least one person that losing a parent left wounds behind, no matter whether you saw any part of it.

But she'd never told her story quite that way to anyone. She also hadn't finished it. She wondered if she should. She gave Cadell marks for not reacting as if there was anything he could do. Her experience was in the past, beyond changing, beyond reaching. Long ago she'd grown tired of those who upon hearing about her past wanted to make it better with a hug or trite phrases. She understood everyone had meant well, but it had all been useless. Her soul had been twisted and hammered into a different shape by what she had seen, and nothing was ever going to wrench it back into shape.

At last she left the house, locking it up behind her although she'd once asked Betty why she never locked her house.

Betty had laughed. "Around here? Nobody does."

But not everyone had the kind of expensive computer equipment Dory used. Hers might look just slightly larger than usual towers, but she had several four-thousand-dollar graphics cards in there, not to mention all the add-ons. If she had to replace much of that stuff—never mind her work—she could easily spend twenty thousand dollars or more. So she locked the door and kept the curtains closed all the time to conceal what was inside. Betty might say theft was rare around here, but why hang the temptation out for all to see?

She and Flash climbed into the car with Cadell. Dasher was in the backseat and woofed a greeting. Flash answered.

Dory felt relieved when her sense of humor began to awaken. "They're like best buddies."

"They'll probably have a great conversation with their noses back there. By the time we get to the station, they'll know all about what each has been doing since their last meeting."

Dory smiled, thinking it was very likely possible. "So we're going to meet a ranger?"

"Well, not a ranger, per se. She's the local senior game warden, otherwise known as a redshirt."

"Why redshirt? Or is that obvious?"

He laughed. "Obvious. They all wear red shirts. Mostly with jeans, boots and cowboy hats, although ball caps are creeping in. Very laid-back approach to uniforms."

She thought it would seem that way to him. His khakis were pressed and even had military creases in the shirt. "Well, with shirts that distinctive, they probably don't have to worry about the rest."

"Nope. They're pretty readily identified."

"I've never met a game warden before."

"You'll like Desi. No nonsense and damn good at what she does. She broke up a ring of unlicensed outfitters last fall. Pretty risky business. But then, her job has its own set of risks. I'm not the one heading out into the woods during hunting season when everyone is armed."

That drew a laugh from her. It felt good to be out, she realized. Sunshine, warm air blowing through the window. She spent too much time in her cave. Seasons could go by almost unnoticed. She averted her head, looking out the window at the small houses they passed, then the open areas. The drive to the station wasn't long, but long enough for her to start wondering if she was in love with her work or if she was hiding in it.

The question made her uncomfortable, and she shoved it aside. George was out of prison. Soul-searching was going to have to wait until she was sure he wanted nothing to do with her.

No reason he should. The words had become almost a mantra inside her head: *No reason George should want to find her.*

Now all she needed to do was believe it.

George found his sister in remarkably short order. Yeah, it took a few days, but she was a presence on the web because of her design work, no matter how hard she tried to hide behind her initials. Besides, he'd found out about her job years ago.

As for the money he needed…well, that was easy enough to pick up. No rotten job necessary. He'd sweet-talked a woman in her fifties, giving her a sob story that made her invite him to stay with her. It wasn't long before she'd given him all the money he needed, and he was quite sure she'd be too ashamed to tell the cops what had happened.

So he was able to vanish from the halfway house. He told them he'd found a job in another town. None of their concern, since he was a free man and the halfway house was only supposed to be temporary.

He hung around for another week, treating the woman like a queen, feeling sickened every time he made her titter like a girl. At her age. Really.

After that he left for a "job interview" and never went back. Even if she decided to call the cops, she didn't know his real name, she'd never taken a photo of him and he'd been very careful about what he touched...except her. Wiping up after himself had been nearly automatic.

Then he discovered he hadn't found Dory at all. Her old address had been abandoned a few weeks ago, and her neighbors hardly knew her. No one could say where she'd gone. From the looks on most of the faces of the people he talked to, he gathered they hardly cared about her disappearance and that they really didn't have any idea where she was now.

He cussed and spent some time at the local library using their computers. She had to have left a trail of some kind. She was still working. The only thing was, he'd learned from hard experience that her company didn't release detailed information about the where-abouts of the people who worked for it. The most they gave on their lead designers was a geographic region. Over the phone it became apparent they didn't answer questions about one of their team and they'd never met her. They thought she was a guy.

That amused him a bit. So she was living a pre-tense. Gutless.

Sighing, needing to put more miles between him and the woman he'd just conned—he couldn't be *pos-*

itive she'd be too embarrassed to report him—he left the library and headed down the road.

He'd find her. He knew enough about her from keeping tabs over the years to know her head would poke up eventually. Once she reappeared in one of the chat rooms she had used in the past, he'd be able to find her. Amazing how many details those social sites kept on people even after a decade or more.

When he was in prison, he'd watched plenty of his fellow inmates go to those same rooms because they wanted company. Mostly they wanted some girl to get sweet on them.

He'd avoided all of that. Leaving online traces could be a big mistake. Anyway, as long as he kept moving now and created different email addresses or log-ins at each new location, nobody would be able to track *him*.

But Dory… Dory might be smart about some things, but she probably thought she was safe behind the wall of her company and her alias. No reason for her to imagine, either, that George could find her online. After all, he'd been in prison, and she probably had absolutely no idea just how much you could learn about computers and the internet in prison.

He savored the fact that she probably thought she was perfectly safe where she was now.

She was in for a shock.

Dory forgot her fears for a little while as she met Desi Jenks, a lovely woman with a nimbus of dark curls and a very strong personality. She was clearly in charge, at least as involved her job, and both crisp and clear about what she hoped for in a couple of dogs from Cadell.

"Basically police dogs," she told him. "We'll probably be using them mostly for search and rescue, but I also need them to be able to find shells and bullets so we can triangulate a scene, sniff for drugs..." She paused and laughed. "You know all of this, don't you, Cadell? What I want isn't so very different from the dogs you train for the sheriff."

"Not really, no," he answered with a smile. "You might make a few additional demands. We'll have to see as we work through it. Will you have vests for them?"

"Orange," she answered properly. "Already on their way."

"At night, hook some glow sticks to them, okay?"

She nodded. "I don't want them mistaken for game, either. You can count on it."

"How many are you thinking?"

"Two for now. Any more and I'll bust my budget."

Cadell's eyes crinkled at the corners. "We'll see what we can do about that."

Then Desi turned to Dory, who was standing silently to the side. "So you're a graphics designer? What kind, exactly?"

"I make animations for films and ads."

Desi's eyes widened. "You mean like that stuff I see in the movies?"

"Some of it. The bigger animation studios do the work on the major films, but we get some thrown our way, and we work on independent productions."

"If I ever find time to get away from here, would you show me something?"

Dory hesitated almost imperceptibly. "Sure."

"Not that I have much free time," Desi said drily.

"Kell and I are still trying to find time to get married and fit in a honeymoon."

"Elope," Cadell suggested. "Call in sick and run away."

Desi laughed loudly. "Sure. As it is we hardly see each other."

Such normal concerns, Dory thought, watching the two of them laugh and chat easily. Maybe hiding in her work all the time was depriving her of something.

But to be that relaxed with other people...it would require more trust than she seemed capable of giving. No, she was better off staying within the world she had created for herself. Just because Betty had turned out to be special didn't mean anyone else would.

"So what breed of dogs do you want?" Cadell asked Desi a few minutes later.

"Whatever works. I'm not particular, and I wouldn't usually need my dogs to be frightening. Most of the time I need them to track. Whatever you can give me that will be willing to traipse through the woods."

Cadell nodded. "I got it. I'll call next week and tell you what kind of selection I can come up with. When I've got a few, you can come out and see what you think."

Cadell seemed lost in thought as they drove away with the dogs in the seat behind them. "I guess I need to let those two take a walk," he said eventually.

"Probably."

He looked over at her. "You okay, Dory?"

"I'm fine. Why?"

He paused. "Well, you said you wanted to be a hermit, and I've been dragging people into your life all day. Not very considerate of me."

"You asked first," she answered. Yeah, it was fatiguing when she wasn't used to being around new people, but she could have said no. However, she wouldn't have missed meeting Krys for anything. That little girl had something special about her and Dory wished she'd been able to escape her own internal frost to spend more time with her. And Desi was nice enough and hadn't pressed Dory in any way that made her uncomfortable.

"I know I asked. I'm just wondering if you felt you couldn't say no."

She was oddly touched by his concern. Most people wouldn't even have thought of that.

They stopped somewhere along a dirt road on a turnout near what appeared to be a stock gate, and Cadell let both dogs off leash to race around and work off energy.

He had a lot of confidence in them, Dory realized. More than she had in Flash. She never walked out the front door with him unless he was leashed.

The dogs were clearly in heaven. Cut loose with no orders to follow, they raced through the grasses like the waves of a sea.

"I know some guys who are going to need a bath when we get home," Cadell remarked. All of a sudden, he barked, "Flash! Dasher! No digging."

Whether they knew that particular command, both dogs immediately raised their heads and stopped working at the ground.

"Come," he said.

With tongues lolling happily, both of them came trotting back. Cadell went to the rear of his SUV and lifted up the tailgate, pulling out a gallon bottle of water and a large metal dog bowl. He set it down while the dogs sat and waited politely. When he'd filled it with water, he said, "Go ahead, guys."

They didn't need further permission. Dory felt another bubble of amusement. "These fellows understand a whole lot more than you told me."

He smiled, still holding the plastic bottle while he waited to see if the dogs wanted more. "There's some disagreement about how much verbal language dogs understand. Some say about a hundred words, some say closer to six hundred. They're also very acutely aware of other signals. Think about it, Dory. They talk to each other with sounds, postures, tails, ears…but clearly they understand some verbal commands, so they must have language centers. Given that, they probably understand a whole lot more than we think."

"I'm seeing that right now."

"Maybe." He laughed. "Or maybe you're seeing the fact that we've done this before and they know the drill."

She nodded, watching the dogs splash water everywhere with their tongues. "That would make it hard to figure out."

"Very. But one thing I'm sure of—they're a lot smarter than we give them credit for."

When they were back in the truck, Cadell said, "Let's take them to my place to clean them up. I've got a doggy shower, a whole lot easier than you trying to deal with it in a bathtub. Although I'm sure you could."

She twisted and looked back at two very happy dogs, now flopped on the backseat. "I'm more concerned about the burs than the mud."

"Burs are always fun. And I'll show you how to check them for ticks."

Ticks? Oh, man, she hadn't even thought of that. The notion made her squeamish. "Do I have to?" she asked finally.

That made Cadell laugh. "Well, if you want I can come over and do a tick check every day."

In an instant she realized that she wouldn't at all mind him dropping by every day. Something else to worry about? Because she found it almost impossible to build real connections with other people. The last thing she wanted to do was make Cadell feel bad when he'd been so good to her.

She squared her shoulders and told herself that she *would* learn how to deal with the ticks. She hoped.

"Let's go by my place," he said. "I'll wash the boys up, we can grab a small bite and then I'll take you home."

"Thanks." Then with effort, "How are the ostriches doing?"

"As usual. They're worth a lot of money, as Betty keeps saying, but I can't sell them. Some inheritance, huh? They hate me, they're expensive to maintain and they drive me nuts. I wish my dad had given me some clue as to what he was thinking when he got them. But none of his friends seem to know, either."

"That's strange."

He shrugged. "My dad was an interesting guy. He would get big ideas of one kind or another, then nothing would happen. Like the time he traded a shortwave radio for a telescope mirror. Admittedly he didn't use the radio, but he never used the mirror, either. It's still sitting on his workbench."

After a minute he said, "I wonder if I could trade two ostriches for a couple of horses."

A giggle bubbled out of Dory. "The horses might be friendlier."

"Oh, there's no question of that."

They drove through miles of open rangeland on the way to Cadell's ranch. The land rolled gently, hinting at the mountains that rose to one side like a huge, distant wall. Herds of deer or antelope grazed alongside cattle, and she wondered if the ranchers minded.

But slowly, ever so slowly, the bigness of the space around her planted uneasiness inside her. Out here there was no place to hide. You could run forever and still be visible.

Why was she having these thoughts? George. But George had no idea where she was. She tried to shake the creeping sense of unease but was failing miserably. She needed the protection of small spaces, walls, locked doors and windows. She needed to keep the bogeyman out.

That drew her up short. The bogeyman? Her brother was no bogeyman. He was a murderer, yes, but for all that he was human. She had no idea why he'd killed their parents, whether it had been born of a rage that caused him to lose control or if he was a seriously broken man. But either way, he wasn't some mythical beast. Just a man.

But the uneasiness wouldn't leave her. The skin on the back of her neck crawled, although there was no reason for it. She had enough scars, she scolded herself. Was she going to live in terror for the rest of her life because George was out of prison? That didn't impress her as a great way to spend the next forty or fifty years.

She was relieved when they reached Cadell's ranch. He had buildings she could run into. Lots of dogs that were being trained to be protective. And two ostriches that would probably love to peck George's eyes out.

That last thought at last made her laugh as tension seeped away.

"What?" asked Cadell.

"I was imagining your ostriches pecking out George's eyes."

As he switched off the engine and set the brake, he gave her one of those smiles that crinkled the corners of his eyes. "Feeling bloodthirsty?" he asked lightly.

"I guess. Better than feeling afraid."

His expression sobered instantly, but he didn't reply directly. "You can go inside if you want and hunt through my fridge for something. The thing is full of leftovers, and there are some soft drinks. I'll just take the dogs to the shower."

"You were going to show me how to check for ticks."

"Actually not difficult if you pet your dog a lot. But yeah, come along and I'll show you."

He *did* have a doggy shower, a concrete room with a sprayer attached to a long hose. Both dogs appeared to be used to the drill and didn't put up a fuss. One by one they stepped in to be shampooed and rinsed. Cadell ran his hands over them as he washed and told her she needed to pay attention to any little bump.

Even as he spoke, a tick fell off Dasher and disappeared down the drain. "Not attached yet," he remarked.

"What do I do if they've already burrowed in?"

"I like nail polish."

Her voice broke on a surprised laugh. "You like what?"

"Nail polish. Once their heads are buried, they have to breathe out the back end. You cover that with polish, and they'll back out real fast. I also don't want to chance leaving a head embedded by pulling on them. It could get infected. So a dab of nail polish, they back out, I grab with tweezers and dump them down the nearest drain or toilet."

"Seems like a good idea to me. I've heard of using something hot."

"Well, you can do that, too. But I figure why risk burning the dogs? Just be careful not to get the polish all over their coats. It only takes the thinnest smear to conquer a tick."

When he finished rinsing Dasher, he said, "Stand back."

She soon learned why. The dog began to shake out his coat, and water flew everywhere. Then he dashed out of the shower and up and down the run, shaking himself again at every kennel he passed.

"He's sharing the shower," Cadell remarked. "Flash, get in."

Dory would have almost sworn that Flash sighed, but he did as he was told, standing perfectly still. This time Cadell handed her the shampoo and spray. "He needs to know you can do this, too."

Well, she couldn't argue with that, and anyway, it was better than thinking about creepy things that could watch her across the open miles out there. Not for the first time she wondered if she were losing her mind.

Flash proved mercifully tick-free, and he seemed to like the warm water rinse the best of all. Then she got to watch him shake out and run up and down as if full of excitement.

Cadell spoke. "I've never been able to decide if they do that because they're so glad to be done with the shower, or if they're just happy."

"They look happy to me." And they did. For a few minutes, Dory forgot everything else. Flash did that for her. Even if he never did another thing, he released her inside, if only for a short while.

"I love that dog," she announced.

"I believe the feeling is mutual."

She looked at Cadell then, daring to meet his gaze directly without sliding quickly away. His gaze was warm, inviting, suggesting delights she could barely imagine. Yet he remained a perfect gentleman with her. He was getting past her guard, little by little. Just as Betty had. She tried to tell herself that wasn't a bad thing. A man who'd give her a dog like Flash had to be special. All the hours of training…she'd bet he didn't do that for free very often. Yet, he'd insisted Flash was merely an extension of his job as a lawman.

Um, wow?

An electric shock seemed to zing between them. Something invisible was trying to push her closer to him. Was he magnetic or something?

But then he broke their gaze and turned. "Wanna come inside and rummage through my fridge before I take you back?" He glanced at his watch. "I go on duty in a couple of hours."

The moment broken, she tried to find steady ground in the practical. "After the shower I think you're going to need a fresh uniform."

He looked down at himself and laughed. "What's a little water?"

Yup, in addition to sexual attraction she was learning to like him a whole lot. Sexual attraction she could deal with. She'd sent more than one guy away over the years, because she wasn't going to get that close to anyone.

But liking? That could be even more of a risk. Sex she could refuse, because she didn't want to be vulnerable and couldn't trust a guy that much. But liking... well, it grew of its own accord, and she had no idea how to prevent it. Nor did she know if she should. She didn't have to let him that far inside.

Although telling him part of her story earlier, reaching back to the little girl who had been terrorized for life by what she'd seen...well, that had involved trust, hadn't it? Trust that he wouldn't minimize it or tell her to get over it. No, he'd accepted her confidence in silence, not judging at all.

Maybe she was more afraid of judgment than trust. After all, her brother had done something inexplicable. Maybe she thought others judged her to be as bad. Or maybe it was herself she couldn't trust.

Hell. It was a mess, and she didn't want to think about it now. She needed to get back to work. Flash made her feel safe. Just leave it all at that.

They passed the ostrich pen on their way to the house. For once the ostriches didn't even look at them. Instead they stared out over the open fields, away from the mountains. Longing to run free?

But as she was about to cross the threshold behind Cadell, something stopped her. She pivoted sharply and looked out over the endless grasslands. The back of her neck prickled. No reason. Nothing out there.

Maybe she was just reacting to the ostriches' behavior. Or to her own fears.

Shrugging, she followed Cadell inside. Leftovers were beginning to sound good.

Before leaving on his patrol, Cadell checked to see if he'd gotten any pings on the whereabouts of George Lake. Nothing. After a bit of internal argument earlier, he'd decided not to tell Dory that her brother had left the halfway house. It was probably meaningless; the guy wasn't required to stay there since he'd finished his sentence. It might only mean he'd gotten a job offer in another town.

Odd, though, that nobody at the house had any idea where he'd gone or why. All they could tell him about George was that he'd spent a lot of time on their computer when he first arrived.

That made Cadell uneasy, but he'd need a warrant to get a cop out there to look at the computer and find out what George had been so interested in. Unfortunately, uneasiness was not a valid reason to get a warrant. He was lucky the people at the halfway house had told him as much as they had.

No one else in town was likely to know anything anyway. Dory had moved from there with her godparents before she reached middle school, so she had no connections in that town at all. After twenty-five years, there probably weren't even many people who remembered those long-ago murders, or would care that George Lake was hanging around town briefly.

Dead end. So it was good he hadn't said anything

to Dory about George's whereabouts. All he'd do was make Dory even more anxious, and she was already anxious enough.

Being a cop had made him acutely aware of people's unspoken reactions. He'd detected her uneasiness in the open spaces. He'd even picked up on the sudden fright that had made her turn around on his doorstep and look out over empty fields.

He wished he could ease her mind, but all he could do was try to pinpoint one man among millions. Not likely unless the guy crossed the law somehow.

Well, if this was all he could do, he'd do it. And he'd keep an eye on her, too, as unobtrusively as possible.

Because he truly didn't think her fears were unfounded. Not with that inheritance hanging out there.

Chapter 6

George didn't especially want to be found—not yet, at least—but he faced a conundrum anyway. Yeah, he'd taken that woman for quite a bit of money he could get by on, but it was difficult to get by anywhere when you didn't have identification.

He'd been told to take his release papers and his prisoner ID to a Social Security office to try to obtain a Social Security card. He wondered if anyone in the prison system had looked lately at how many proofs of identity were required to achieve that. He hadn't had a driver's license in twenty-five years and didn't think anyone would just hand him one. Getting a birth certificate turned into another set of hurdles.

Not that he wanted to put himself back on the map just yet, but although he had the cash to do it, he couldn't even buy a beater of a car without some ID.

That meant he'd have to steal one and hope he didn't get stopped on a road somewhere.

In all his dreaming about what he was going to do to Dory and how rich he was going to be once he got his rightful inheritance, he'd never once considered that even though he was outside the gates, he might as well still be inside. Every avenue seemed blocked— except committing crimes.

There was an irony that he was far from appreciating.

It fueled an old rage in him, but that wasn't helping anything. Not one bit. There was only one crime he wanted to commit, and he sure as hell didn't want to leave a trail of smaller crimes over a wide swath of the country. That would draw as much attention as getting himself a valid ID.

He knew of a guy who made fake IDs, but he wasn't cheap. George hadn't soaked the woman for enough to cover that *and* still be able to travel. Hell, he should have thought all this through better.

But he did have one breakthrough. He noticed a fresh change at the website of the animation business Dory worked for. One of the designers was now listed as living in Conard County, Wyoming. Seemed a stupid thing to put up, but the feeling he got was that the group was trying to make it clear they could work from all over the country. How that was helpful, he had no idea. He knew how it helped him, though. Well, sort of. A county was a big place.

He was sure it was Dory, though. The timing of the change was too close to his release. Evidently she never wanted to see him again, but that was fine by him. Now that he knew where to look, he just had to get there and scope the situation.

Then he spent some time enjoying daydreams. Did she guess he was coming? Did she even remotely understand that he needed her dead or why? How surprised she was going to look when she saw him.

He remembered the kid sister, the one he had read to and played with, but that kid, the one who had loved him, had died the night she'd run screaming from the house before he could clean up, make it look like someone had broken in. It was her fault he'd gone to prison.

He wondered if she remembered that.

Dory erupted on the conference. All caps got attention, and she was typing them to her cohort.

WHO THE HELL PUT MY WHEREABOUTS ON THE WEBSITE?

We always do.

THE VICINITY OF KANSAS CITY IS A WHOLE LOT DIFFERENT THAN WHAT YOU'VE PUT UP THERE.

But it's a whole county.

IT'S A COUNTY WITH HARDLY ANY PEOPLE!

The team leader stepped in. Do we need to take this to Skype?

Dory drew deep breaths, steadying herself. Did she want her team members to know she was a woman?

Did she want them to see her face? How many people might they tell?

No, she typed, forcing herself to be calmer. Please take that information down immediately. My brother's a murderer. He just got out of prison. I don't want him to find me.

Consider it done, the team leader typed back. I just removed it. We didn't know. I'm sorry, D.K.

She refreshed the webpage and saw that Reggie was as good as his word. It was gone already. She just hoped it hadn't been there for long. And why the hell had she even told them where she going? Because she'd had to explain why it would take her so long to get back on the grid? Because at the time it had seemed innocent enough? Because she hadn't been paying attention to what they put on the webpage?

Because in her panic she hadn't been thinking clearly enough. There was no other reason. She'd let slip some information because she'd been too afraid to realize that it might be unsafe to share with her coworkers. Because all she'd been concerned about was getting away from her last known address as Dory Lake.

Brilliant. She wanted to kick her own butt.

A whimper drew her attention, and she looked down. Flash was lying right beside her, but as he stared up at her without lifting his head, she got the distinct impression he was unhappy. He must be picking up on her anxiety.

He needed something to do, she decided, some purpose. She'd given him little enough, and right now she was in no mood to take a walk or a jog. Heck, right now she didn't even want to step out her front door.

Because she couldn't escape the feeling that George

might have found out who she worked for. It wasn't exactly the biggest secret on the planet. And if he knew that, what if he'd found that change on the webpage? She had no idea at all how long that change had been up.

God!

She looked into Flash's soulful eyes and took pity on him. He needed something to do, and she needed something from him. "Flash, guard."

At once he was on his feet, tail wagging. Then, as if he understood, he left her side to check out the other rooms in the tiny house. When he returned a short while later, he lay down with his back to her, head erect, ears alert. He was definitely on duty.

That should have made her feel better. After all, she *had* seen what he could do. But a dog as her only protection?

How was she to continue? Bad things could happen no matter what. She knew that indelibly. But nobody could live in the constant expectation that something bad waited around every corner. Her therapist had tried to hammer that home.

But that was also a kind of trust that Dory found difficult to gain. Trust that nothing bad would happen? Yeah, right.

A ping drew her attention back to one of her monitors. It was Reggie on private chat. You dropped out. Everything okay?

Yeah. Just taking some time to cool off.

She was grateful that he let it go. So how's that flood simulation going?

I'll have the roughed-out version ready for you in a few days.

Great. Ping me if you need anything.

Work, she told herself. *Just get to work.* She could bury herself in the intricacies of bringing a writer's idea to vivid full-dimensional life. An endlessly fascinating process, and no matter how much of it she did, there was still more to learn.

She started up the flood sequence again, looking for any points that would give it away as animation. Animations of human beings were nearly impossible to make so real that you couldn't tell it was an animation. But the stuff like this? It could fool just about anyone if she did it right.

She turned her viewing angle around slowly, seeking any hitches in the way the water moved. Just as she thought she might have found a problem, the doorbell rang.

Part of her wanted to ignore it, but then she noticed Flash had risen to his feet and was wagging his tail excitedly. He glanced back over his shoulder as if to say, "Hurry up!"

So it was someone he knew. She could guess who that was. Much as she wasn't eager to admit it, she wanted to see Cadell again. It had been over a week. Betty had only popped in once. For a hermit, she was starting to feel a bit lonely.

She was right. She opened the door to find Cadell standing there holding a big brown bag, dressed casually in jeans and a black T-shirt. "Hey," he said. "I brought dinner if you have time."

Flash was sitting obediently beside her, but his hind-quarters were twitching as if he wanted to jump up on Cadell.

Trying to shake away the fog in her head, she stepped back. "You'd better come in and pet Flash before he decides to jump on you. I guess he's been missing you." Then she remembered her last command to Flash had been to guard. Quickly she squatted down, catching his head in both hands and rubbing him. "It's okay. Playtime."

Happily he danced away, following Cadell into the kitchen. "I guess you've taught him a new command," Cadell remarked as he began to remove foam containers from the bag. "Maude's finest," he added as he put things on her shaky table. "I'm assuming you're a carnivore?"

"Absolutely."

"Thank goodness. If you'd said you were vegan, I'd be looking through here trying to find something you can eat. I'm not even sure the salad would be safe. I think Maude puts blue cheese in it."

She wished she could laugh, when he was trying so hard to be lighthearted, but laughter felt far away.

"I hope I didn't disturb your work."

"No." Truthful as far as it went. Concentration seemed to have escaped her since the shock earlier of finding her whereabouts on the website. She vaguely knew they listed her general vicinity but hadn't really paid it much attention. Why the heck hadn't she thought to tell them not to change it, or just not tell them exactly where she was going?

They were seated across from one another at the table when he spoke again. He pushed a tall coffee her way, then popped open the boxes for her to choose. "I'm not fancy. Just dig into whatever looks good." He passed her plastic utensils.

She should get out some of her few dishes, she thought. Not that she had many. She'd never needed more than one person could use.

But then Cadell rattled her. "What's wrong?" he asked bluntly.

"Wrong?" she repeated. She hadn't said anything.

"It was written all over your face when you opened the door. You had Flash on guard, I could tell. What's going on?"

She forgot the delicious-looking spread in front of her, any possible appetite disappearing. "Probably nothing." God, she hated being always afraid, and most likely afraid of an eventuality that would never happen. How many times did she have to ask herself why in the world George would ever want to find her? Was there something wrong with her?

Cadell surprised her with a sudden change in tack. "Did you testify against your brother?"

She drew a sharp breath, her vision narrowing until she was looking down a long, dark tunnel. All of a sudden she was standing in that street again, screaming, screaming and not really knowing why, just knowing in her child's heart that everything in her world was broken forever.

"Dory? Dory!" A hand gripped her upper arm gently. Cadell's voice reached her through the darkness. "Tell me," he said. A quiet command.

"Red paint," she said. "Red paint." She sagged into him, dimly feeling his arms close around her. It all came back, every bit of it, worse than the nightmares. Then everything went black.

There was a rickety couch in the front room, and Cadell carried Dory there, settling her on his lap.

What had he said? What had he done? He'd sent this woman into flight deep within herself, so deep it might be worse than a faint. All he'd asked was if she'd testified against her brother. If she had, she might have some real reasons to be afraid. She might not have even considered that her inheritance could be a threat. He'd found during his law enforcement career that most people didn't have naturally suspicious minds. They didn't think like criminals. Those kinds of ideas just didn't occur to them.

He hadn't even told her that her brother had disappeared from the halfway house after only two days. He had every right to move on, and leaving a place like that was understandable, especially if you hooked up with someone who could help you get on your feet. Lots of prisoners had contacts on the outside, some cultivated in prison. How else did they manage? Family, friends, a few agencies...

He felt a shudder pass through Dory. Looking down, he saw her eyes, as blue and deep as a cloudless sky, open. A Botticelli angel.

Only this angel was feeling like no angel. She squirmed, struggling to get off his lap. He refused to let her go. "Easy, Dory. Easy. It's just me."

It was then he saw Flash. Staring at him. His lip slightly curled. Ready to attack to protect her, but unsure because it was Cadell.

"Dory, snap out of it before your dog rips off half my face."

That reached her. Those amazing eyes abruptly focused. She looked up at him, then over at the dog. "Flash, stay." Then back to Cadell. "I don't know what happened, but you'd better let go of me."

Wow, talk about feeling as if he'd been slapped in the face. He released her immediately, ignoring his body's natural response to her wriggling off his lap. "I was worried about you," he muttered. "You all but fell out of your chair."

An eternity passed before she spoke. Flash, at least, settled at her feet, but he kept eyes on Cadell. "I'm sorry," she said finally.

"You don't have to be. I just don't understand what happened. I asked a simple question, then you said something like 'red paint,' and you were gone. Collapsing. Like you'd fainted."

When she didn't speak, he asked, "Do you need some water or something?"

"Water, please. My mouth feels like cotton."

He rose, went to the kitchen and found one of her two glasses in a cupboard beside the sink. He filled it with water and returned, saying lightly, "You could use a few more dishes."

She nodded but didn't look at him. At least she didn't object when he sat beside her. She took the glass and drained it, leaving little droplets of water on her lip that he'd have loved to lick away. Then he caught himself. Damn, was he losing his mind? This was neither the time nor the place, and most likely not the right woman. Besides, having been badly burned once, he wasn't about to volunteer for another round.

"I'm sorry," she said again.

"Dory…" He gave up. She wouldn't even look at him now, and he'd already told her she didn't need to apologize.

"Red paint." She spoke in a voice so tight it sounded as if it were ready to snap. "I never told you. I don't know if I ever even told Betty. But for a time after the…murder, I was blind and couldn't speak except for two words. *Red paint*. I thought all that blood was red paint."

A seven-year-old girl? Of course she would have no other way to explain it. It also gave him a very clear idea of just how much blood she'd seen. Man, he ached for her. For the child who had been exposed to such horror.

"Anyway," she said, her voice a little steadier, "they said it was a conversion disorder. Someone explained it to me years later. I couldn't handle what I'd seen, so I shut down. My vision came back after a couple of months, but for a year I could speak only two words."

"Red paint."

"Exactly." She let go of a long breath. "All of a sudden, when you asked me if I'd testified against George, I was back there. On that street, screaming. I don't know how long I screamed. I vaguely remember the neighbors running up, the cop cars, the lady police officer who took me away. After that, I don't remember much except my godparents taking me home with them. I was terrified because I couldn't see. As for talking… I never really wanted to talk again."

Taking a risk, Cadell reached out and covered her small hand with one of his much bigger ones. He was relieved when she didn't pull away. He felt the faintest of tremors in her hand.

"Anyway," she said eventually, "I have nightmares about that night. They'd almost stopped, but they've come back big-time since I heard George was being released. Why did he get only twenty-five years? I've never understood that."

"Lots of things play into charging and sentencing," he said carefully. "You could talk to our local judge, Wyatt Carter, if you want. I'm sure he could give you an in-depth answer. All I can tell you is from my own experience. First-degree murder is very hard to prove, for one thing. Intent isn't always easy to prove in a courtroom, and that's the only way he would have gotten a life sentence unless there were aggravating circumstances. If you want my guess…"

"Yes, please."

"An argument with your parents. Tension for some time, from what you said. Your brother lost his temper and saw red. A crime of passion, without premeditation. That weighs into the charges a prosecutor thinks she can sell to the jury. It would certainly play into his defense. Basically, I guess what I'm saying is your brother's sentence wasn't unusual given the circumstances and his youth, being only fifteen at the time. I know that doesn't make you feel any better…"

"No, it doesn't," she interrupted. "Not at all. He butchered them, Cadell. *Butchered* them."

He dared to squeeze her hand and was relieved when she turned hers over and wrapped her slender fingers around his.

"So," she asked on a shaky breath, "how likely is he to do something like that again?"

He couldn't answer that truthfully. A quarter century in prison could straighten out a man's head, or twist it more. "I don't know," he admitted.

"No one can know," she said quietly. "No one." Then she switched course. "That dinner you brought is getting ruined and I'm suddenly hungry."

He watched her stand and leave the room, Flash at her side.

Each new thing he learned about Dory filled him with more respect for her. She'd built a life for herself on some very brutal ashes. He knew well enough that kids all over the world had to survive as she'd survived because of war and natural disaster, but that didn't make her any less remarkable.

Before he followed her, he allowed himself to reflect on his marriage, on the woman whose unceasing demands had left them both so unhappy. What a difference. Somehow he didn't think Brenda could have survived half of what Dory had been through, or at least not with as much grace.

"Cadell? Are you coming?"

He rose and went to join the angel who hadn't fully spread her wings for a quarter century.

The food wasn't that cold. Neither of them opted to microwave the steak sandwiches.

"I like cold beef," Dory announced. "Cold roast beef sandwiches are at the top of my list."

"Mine, too. Although the way I live, I seldom cook at home, so no roast beef."

"I should make one," she said. "We can share it. The only reason I don't do it more often is that to get a well-cooked roast, you need more than I could ever eat by myself. And I don't like it as much if I freeze it for later."

"Well, that's one job you can expect my help with. Let me buy the roast. You cook, I'll carve."

She laughed, a small one, but enough to ease his heart a bit. She was looking forward again, at least for now. It wouldn't last forever. In fact he'd probably have to be the one who shattered her hard-won peace.

While they were putting the leftovers away, he said, "You looked upset when I got here. You never said why."

She shook her head a little, drying her hands on a dish towel. "I was furious because my company put my whereabouts on their webpage. They thought it was vague enough. I had to explain that Conard County is underpopulated."

"Wait," he said almost sharply. "Back up. Why do they include anything about where you live?"

"I guess it's felt that since we don't have a central office we might make an advantage out of being scattered all over the country but still working together. Major Animation has three teams like mine. And we *are* scattered all over."

"Okay. I suppose I can get that. Centralized without being located in one place. So how detailed are the locations?" His heart had sped up a bit. He didn't like the way he was feeling right now. Worry had begun to gnaw at him like a hungry rat.

"Well, for example, they used to have me listed as being in the vicinity of Kansas City. There are a lot of people there, and nobody could have found me easily. But I screwed up. I guess I wasn't thinking clearly. Anyway, I told someone on my team where I was moving, and today I saw it on the webpage. Conard County, Wyoming. They thought listing an entire county was vague enough."

"Not if it's this county," he agreed. "So what then?"

"They took it down. I doubt anyone noticed it."

He wished he was sure of that. "Does it have your full name?"

She shook her head. "I go by D. K. Lake. It's not even my real middle initial."

Good enough, he thought sourly, even with a wrong middle initial. If he'd discovered somehow that she was working for this company, he'd have no trouble finding her now no matter how common the last name Lake was—and it was. "So nobody's thinking about personal security for you guys?" He found that hard to stomach.

"We're just a bunch of graphics designers. Most of the people we deal with are ad companies, indie film-makers…it's not like we're putting our life stories out there." She looked down. "Except today. I raised Cain. I had to tell them about my brother."

He took a step closer. "And you didn't like that."

"Of course I didn't!" She rubbed her arms from shoulder to wrists, one after the other as of trying to push something away. "It's like an invisible stain. My brother is a murderer. Worse, he killed our parents. What does that say about him, about me, about our family?"

Oh, God, he was going to be wishing he had a grad-uate degree in psychology before much longer. Open-ing and closing his hands, he tried to find something to say, something that might actually comfort her.

The only thing that occurred to him was a question.

"Do you really believe that, Dory? Do you think you could ever have done what your brother did?"

Her entire face froze, grew still and motionless. For a few seconds, he feared he'd pushed her back into the horror, but then she shook her head. "No," she said. "I don't think I could have, ever. But who can know that, Cadell? Perfectly ordinary people go over the edge all the time."

"I'm a cop," he reminded her. He nudged her back to one of the chairs at the table and brought her one of those orange soft drinks she seemed to like so much. He unscrewed the cap before he put it on the table.

"So?" she said. "You're a cop. What's that mean?"

"I like this town because it's pretty peaceful most of the time. But I've worked in much bigger towns. What you saw your brother do? I've seen that and a helluva lot more. There's no limit to what human beings are capable of."

She tilted her head, looking up at him. "And that's comforting why?"

"I'm not sure it's comforting. But I can tell you something—there were warning signs in every one of those cases. Something askew. Maybe nobody noticed it in time, but those signs were there. Tensions building. Things being said or hinted at. A withdrawal, maybe. But by the time an investigation was complete, we almost invariably had a profile of someone who'd been sending out warnings like invisible flares for months, maybe years. Very, very few cases erupted out of nowhere, and when they did drugs were often involved."

She nodded slowly. He slid into the other chair across from her. "The thing is," he continued, "the vast majority of people never kill, and even fewer of them kill in the way your brother did. He's in a very small group. There's no reason to even wonder if you could do what he did. To feel like it's a taint of some kind. Your parents weren't murderers, were they? Have *you* ever wanted to do something like that?"

"God, no!" She shuddered as her eyes widened.

"You have no reason to be ashamed because your brother went off the rails. One of the cops I used to work with back in Seattle had a brother who was a con man. You couldn't ask for two more different guys, and they came out of the same genetic stock into the same environment. Ralph hated it, though. He was frustrated, he couldn't talk sense to his brother, and occasionally we'd arrest the guy and put him away for a few years. Ralph took some ribbing, but if ever anyone had an excuse to want to kill someone it was Ralph. His brother was good at preying on people, but as angry as it made Ralph feel, he'd put his brother in handcuffs and bring him in. He never tried to hurt him."

"Wow," she said quietly. "That's awful."

"It sure was for Ralph. He was convinced it was holding him back in his career. I don't know if it was. I mean, the higher you go, the harder it is to move up because there are fewer slots. But Ralph believed the department never quite trusted him. I know all us guys who worked with him trusted him completely."

Deciding he'd said enough for now, and feeling thirsty himself, he helped himself to a soft drink from her fridge, choosing cola.

When he came back to the table and sat, Dory had reached for a paper napkin and was creasing it absently. "I've always felt that something must be wrong with me," she admitted. Then she raised her head and smiled faintly. "Well, obviously there are some things wrong with me by other people's estimation. I'm mostly a hermit, I don't trust people much at all…but I'm talking about something else."

"I know you are."

She compressed her lips and nodded. "When something like that happens so close to you, especially in your own family, maybe you always feel different."

"Maybe." He tilted the bottle to his lips and drank deeply, figuring he'd said as much as he could or should. From what she'd mentioned, he gathered she'd had plenty of therapy. He had no business mucking around with whatever peace she'd managed to make.

"I'm sorry if I'm interrupting your work," he said. It suddenly occurred to him that he'd come over uninvited, meaning only to stay about a half hour, but with what had happened he'd been here much longer.

"Not really," she said. "I put in most of a day before I erupted at my team about the website."

"Well, I'd still better go." He glanced at his watch and realized it was getting late. Flash dozed near Dory, but he'd wake at the slightest sound. She was in good paws, he decided. He also decided not to tell her about George yet.

She'd been through hell tonight, all because of his question.

Dory sighed and went back into her office. He and Flash followed her, and as soon as she sat Dory seemed to be watching her simulation intently, was probably at least halfway back into her work. Time to go. Cadell opened his mouth to say good-night.

But then she spoke, surprising him. "So your wife couldn't handle being married to a cop?"

Astonished, he didn't answer immediately, but then tried for lightness. "Please be sure to include the *ex* part when calling her my wife. And her name was Brenda."

She turned from her screen, her hand still on her mouse, and her eyes danced a bit. In that instant she looked positively edible. "Kinda bitter?"

"That isn't the word I'd use. Not anymore anyway. I was certainly angry, back then. I felt as if she'd been lying to me from the moment we met, although that probably wasn't a fair feeling. She just had no concept of what she was getting into, and once she got there she didn't like it. A longer engagement might have been wise. In that case it probably would have helped." He shrugged. "But you never know. It only lasted two years, but that was plenty for both of us. I'm just glad we didn't have kids, because that would have made it a tragedy."

"It would indeed," she said quietly, her face shadowing. Well, of course. He'd reminded her of what it was like to lose parents.

For a half minute he actually contemplated just keeping his mouth shut around her. Then he realized that walking on eggshells would be unsettling for both of them. He decided to offer her another nugget of truth before he left.

"With Brenda," he said, "I learned something. At the time I just wanted to be with her, and I didn't think about giving her the wrong idea. I switched quite a few of my shifts with my buddies so Brenda and I could have a night out, do something she wanted to do, whatever. So if she expected that to continue, it was my fault and nobody else's."

She nodded slowly, her face smoothing again. Dang,

she was beautiful. Hard to believe that so much ugliness resided in her memory and haunted her life.

"So it couldn't continue?" she asked.

"Nope. My buddies were great, but eventually it became a problem. The brass started objecting, I got a few sarcastic comments about why I didn't just tell them when I'd be available to work..."

"Ouch." She winced, then smiled. "That would do it."

"It sure did. So I have to take a measure of responsibility for Brenda's disappointment." It had a taken him a while to face that, but it was a lesson well learned, and one good reason not to tiptoe around Dory. Only honesty could build her trust. If she ever built any real trust in him.

He stirred. "Anyway, I've taken up your entire evening, and that wasn't my intention. I'll be off now."

Something in the way her blue eyes looked at him seemed almost like an appeal. But what kind of appeal? He couldn't imagine what she might want from him. This was a woman who'd told him at least twice that she preferred to be a hermit.

Suddenly, moved by an impulse that even to him seemed to come out of nowhere, he squatted before her, not touching her. "You're beautiful, you know," he murmured. "You remind me of a Botticelli angel."

She blinked, looking uncertain. Enough, he thought. He could kick his behind when he got home. Straightening, he turned toward the door.

"Cadell?"

He half turned. "Yeah?"

"You're a hunk."

Startled, he looked directly at her, then began to

laugh. "Imagine the painting that would come out of that." Then he resumed his exit, pausing only to say good-night to Flash.

Dory laughed quietly. The painting that would come out of that? An angel and a cop? Or a cowboy? It was humorous, all right.

But gradually her humor faded. The night had closed in around the house, and she felt it as an almost physical pressure. "Flash, guard."

He obeyed, sitting beside her, alert.

Alone but not alone. Who would have thought she'd be so grateful for a dog? And what had happened just now with Cadell? She'd revealed things to him during her flashback that she was sure she'd never told anyone but her therapist. She could hear her own voice as she told the story of that night in third person, as if she were removed from it, yet still sounding a bit childlike.

He'd handled it well. Why not? He was a cop—he'd probably seen it all. Part of her was surprised that when all that had burst out the triggers of memory had made her turn to him, a near stranger. She didn't *do* that.

She tried to lose herself in work, but her mind refused to cooperate. The door to the past had opened tonight, and she felt it was as fresh as yesterday.

Damn.

Then, turning to her other computer, she brought up an image she had constructed of that terrible night. She didn't know why she had felt compelled to render it with near photo realism, but she had done it a few years ago. There it sat, just as she had seen it as a child.

What good did that do? What earthly use could it have? What part of her mind needed it? Did she think that by looking at it over and over again that she'd become desensitized?

Did she really want to become desensitized to such horrific violence?

No.

But she sat staring at it as if mesmerized. Her brother, they had said later when she could understand such things, had evidently been a drug user. Cocaine could wreck the mind and turn some people violent. Blame it on cocaine?

Hitting a key, she made the image vanish and considered just erasing it. It held no answers for her. There could be no real answer to what had happened that night. No satisfactory explanation for that kind of act.

She heard a ping and turned to see that Reggie, the team leader, had reentered the chat. Looking for her.

D. K. You there?

She hesitated then typed her answer. Yeah.

I'm really sorry about the mess up on the website. I just want to be sure you're okay.

Yeah, she replied. Like she was ever really okay.

The webmaster fixed your location. You're back to where you used to be.

Thanks, Reggie.

No problem. Countable seconds passed before he typed something else. Look, we're all worried about you. You need anything at all, ping me or Skype me. I'm usually within a few feet of this damn machine.

Me, too. Played any good games lately? Anything to get off this subject.

Nothing new, he admitted. I'm still trying to beat the goblin at the gate so I can get to the reward. Damn smart goblin.

Her spirits lifted more as they chatted about the game they sometimes played together, although she wasn't really into spending hours gaming the way some were. The advanced games that might hold her attention involved teaming up, and that made her as uneasy on the computer as it did in real life.

After a few more minutes, she signed off the chat claiming fatigue, but she didn't feel fatigued at all.

She didn't want to go to sleep. She didn't want another nightmare.

Closing her eyes, she thought about Cadell, surprised that she'd told him he was a hunk. Even more surprised that he thought she looked like an angel.

Forget Cadell, she told herself. How could she be sure he wouldn't rip her heart to shreds the way George had? Maybe not with violence, but in some other way.

She sighed, rested her chin in her hand and tried to study her scene. It sat there frozen, waiting for her attention to the misplaced vortex. There were a lot of items she needed to add, all of them listed in a file she'd received from Reggie. Every one of them had to be constructed. They weren't, unfortunately, items that the team had in its library from previous builds.

De novo. From scratch. She usually loved the challenge. Tonight she wasn't loving much of anything.

Flash stood, stretched and shook himself out before

resuming his position at her side. Life with her must be boring for that poor dog, she thought.

Time to take him into the backyard for a walk. Maybe she should bring his tennis ball and let him chase it a few times. It'd sure make him feel better. Maybe it would even help her shake off the cobwebs of horror, grief and fear that kept brushing her soul and making her want to shiver.

As soon as she picked up the ball, Flash leaped to his feet, wagging his tail like mad. Oh, yeah, he knew what was coming, and the sight of his eagerness made her smile.

"Let's go," she said and headed for the back door. It was nearing midnight, but Flash was good about not barking, so running around for ten minutes or so wouldn't disturb the neighbors.

It was not until she reached the back door and opened it that she realized something had changed tonight. She could not make herself cross the threshold. The night seemed like a huge, solid wall, holding her back.

Panic attack, her mind registered. God, it had been a while. What the hell was going on with her this evening? It was as if whatever progress she had made over time had been stripped from her.

Then Flash, right beside her, growled into the darkness.

Chapter 7

Cadell heard the call come in when he was halfway home. He turned his vehicle around immediately, lit the roof lights and hit unsafe speeds.

When he pulled up near Dory's house, there were two other cars, lights swirling around the neighborhood. They were collecting a crowd on the surrounding porches. He ignored them, only one thought on his mind.

They let him through and into the house. Dory sat rigidly on her couch, Flash on guard in front of her, holding two city cops and a deputy at bay. No one was going to get near her as far as Flash was concerned.

"Hey, Cadell," said Dan Casey, the deputy. "Ms. Lake said her dog growled at something in the backyard. We didn't find any sign of intrusion."

"Dory. Dory!"

She looked at him, and a shudder ran through her. "Tell Flash to play. We're here."

She nodded jerkily. "Flash. Play."

At once the dog eased up but remained watchful. Damn, that one had been well trained, Cadell thought. Thoroughly attached to Dory, too.

As Flash relaxed, so did the other officers. They all had a healthy respect for a trained guard dog.

"So what happened?" he asked Dory.

"I don't know. I was taking Flash out back. I figured he needed a walk and a little play. Almost as soon as I opened the back door, he started growling. I figured I shouldn't ignore him."

"Good decision," Cadell agreed.

"But I didn't mean to cause so much trouble."

"No trouble at all," said one of the city cops, Matt Hamilton. "That's what we're here for. Besides, I agree with Deputy Marcus here. Never ignore your watch-dog."

A short while later, the others left, promising to take another turn around the backyard and the alley behind before they left.

Cadell remained. Dory looked at him. "I'm sorry," she said again. "You must have been nearly home."

"Doesn't matter." There was an ancient wood rocker across from the dubious sofa, and he decided to sit in it.

"Would Flash have reacted that way to an animal? Maybe a cat or another dog?"

"He shouldn't, but I could test it for you tomorrow if you want."

She shook her head. "I'm sure you have a life to take care of, and not just me. You've been wonderful, but…"

"But what?" he said. "I don't get to choose how I

spend my time? Or are you telling me to get lost, that I'm bothering you?"

She gasped. "I didn't mean that at all."

He smiled. "Good, because I'm going to look around out back myself, then I'm camping here tonight. Got an extra blanket?"

He watched her struggle before she answered, and he guessed she was struggling with herself.

"Kind of an overreaction?" she said finally.

"I don't think so." Unfortunately, he figured he was going to have to tell her about George before long. Problem was, how much did it mean that one convict had dropped off the radar? He was quite sure it happened all the time. The fact that he couldn't get tabs on George's whereabouts didn't mean he was headed this way.

But tonight…tonight he was feeling that a little more honesty was needed from him. She had a right to know what he knew and what he suspected. She'd already set off the red alert when Flash growled, and he was quite sure Flash hadn't growled without a damn good reason.

That was what was getting to him. He looked at Flash, a dog he knew intimately and had been training for a while. The dog's growl wasn't meaningless, and he didn't ever want Dory to think it was, no matter what it signified.

"Lock the front door," he said finally. "I'm going to get my flashlight and look around."

"But the other police already did that."

"I'm sure they did." He pulled up one corner of his mouth in a half smile. "I'm also sure they did a good job. They're all fine officers. This is for me, okay?"

He guessed she got it, because she nodded and

locked the front door behind him when he went out to his car. For now he didn't pull it into her driveway, just got his flashlight and other gear.

Because something had disturbed Flash.

Flash hadn't been the only one disturbed by something out back. Dory still felt the way the night had seemed like an almost physical wall when she'd tried to walk him. How she froze on the threshold and couldn't move.

She wondered if Flash had been reacting to her and her swift change of mood. Maybe her apprehension had leaped to him. He seemed amazingly sensitive to her moods.

She looked at him now as she sat on the couch waiting, and he wagged his tail lazily, just once. He appeared relaxed.

"Maybe I imagined it," she said to him. "It was the weirdest thing I've ever felt. I wish you could tell me why you growled."

But he couldn't talk to her, although his gaze never wandered from her and his ears were at attention, twitching this way and that as if he were gauging every sound. Probably even sounds she couldn't hear. How could he look so relaxed yet still be so alert?

"You spooked me as much as that crazy feeling," she told him. He didn't seem the least abashed.

She sighed and leaned back on the sofa. Okay, so something had troubled him, too, but it probably wasn't that weird feeling she'd had. Cadell might believe he wouldn't react that way to another dog or a cat, but what about a coyote? They probably came into town sometimes. Or even a rabbit or snake.

As for her, she'd probably smelled something. A faint odor she'd noticed only subconsciously. Something that put her off. A whiff on the breeze. Maybe Flash had smelled the same thing.

Regardless, she was fairly certain that Cadell wasn't going to find anything amiss any more than the earlier cops had. She wondered if she were losing her marbles at last, then realized the dog had backed up her experience.

Okay, she wasn't crazy. So what the hell had happened?

A car pulled into her driveway, and Flash stood. Apparently he didn't need to be told to guard constantly. Except when he was chasing his ball or playing tug with her, he seemed to be on duty all the time. Quietly, but always alert for trouble.

Which, she guessed, was probably why people had taken up with dogs in the first place.

The knock on her front door brought her to her feet. She twitched the curtain back a bit and saw Cadell, so she unlocked the door and opened it.

He stepped inside, his big flashlight still in hand. He just shook his head as he closed the door behind him and locked it.

"Nothing?" she asked.

"Nothing anyone needs to worry about." He looked at Flash. "I'd be happier if I knew what made him growl, though."

She hesitated, fearful of the response she might get. For so long after her parents had been killed, people had regarded her with pity and had openly talked about how she wasn't right and might never be right again. Even at that age, they were talking about her mind. Her mental state. Unfortunately that had lingered with her as another fear, making her distrust *herself.*

"Let's go get something to drink," she said. "Maybe leftovers if you're hungry. If you plan to spend the night, I may do some talking."

She was surprised to see the warm smile spread over his face. "I'd like to listen."

As simple as that. She just wondered if she'd have the guts to speak.

Thank goodness for microwaves, Dory thought as she began reheating the leftovers from the dinner he'd brought. She'd probably have starved without one as often as she forgot to prepare a meal for herself. Sometimes weeks went by while she lived on raw veggies and frozen egg rolls. Some diet. Maybe Betty was right to be concerned about her.

Cadell put the remains of the two salads together on the inside top of a foam container. It could have been embarrassing to expose how little she actually had—a couple of plates, a few mugs, two glasses, cheap flatware—but Cadell didn't seem the least disturbed.

Maybe he'd roughed it when he was younger, she thought. But she had no excuse for this except disinterest. She made enough money, she had plenty socked away…she didn't have to live like someone who was just starting out. But she really didn't care most of the time. She wanted only what she truly needed.

Her extravagance, and it was a big one, was technology. Yes, she needed most of it for work, but not all of it. Some of it was purely for fun, or to satisfy her interest in the technology. Which, she supposed, made her a geek or nerd or whatever the current name was.

They sat at the table, and Dory started out by avoiding the things she'd been thinking about. Her usual style. Even she recognized her misdirection for what it was. Cadell probably did, too. He'd certainly proved to be very savvy so far.

"So how are the ostriches doing?" she asked.

"They're fine. I'm beginning to think they're indestructible."

She glanced up from her plate, forgetting that she was almost afraid to look at him because of the strong response he evoked in her. Longings, feminine longings buried for most of her life, stirred around him with increasing pressure. "Why?"

He shrugged. "Because they're an exotic species I know next to nothing about. Sure, the vet gave me some instructions, but they're even out of the usual for him. It's amazing that my ignorance doesn't seemed to have harmed them any."

"So they're tough."

"Like you."

The words caught her between one breath and the next, and for a few seconds she simply could not inhale. Tough? "I'm not tough," she insisted when she could find her voice. "I'm a wimp. I'm so scared you and Betty decided I needed a guard dog so I could sleep at night. And there's probably no good reason for me to feel this way."

He stabbed his fork into a cherry tomato but didn't say a word. Giving her time to find her own way, pressuring her not at all. His hands looked so powerful, like all the rest of him. She hated to imagine what he must really think of her. He was a kind enough person to try to help her out, but he probably figured her for a nut. And maybe she was.

Taking what was left of her courage in her hands, she blurted, "It wasn't only Flash's growl."

His head snapped up, his dark gaze fixing on her with total attention. "What do you mean?"

"It's crazy."

"Everything about this, all the way back to the murder of your parents, is crazy. I'm not dismissing anything. What happened?"

"Me," she admitted. "I may be the reason Flash growled. I mean…" God, how could she explain this? Words didn't seem to fit it right. "I couldn't make myself go out that door. I was taking Flash out to do his business, maybe run around the backyard a bit, and I froze. It was like…like…" The words at last forced themselves past her resistance, past the tightness in her throat. "Like the night turned solid. Into a wall. I couldn't move."

His gaze narrowed slightly. "Did you hear something? See something?"

"Not that I was aware of. It was just as if this force held me back. Then before I could fight it or push past it, Flash growled. I turned tail and called the police. But maybe he growled because of me. Maybe my crazy fear reached him."

She swallowed hard. There, she'd said it. If he suggested a butterfly net, she wouldn't blame him. She studied her plate, unwilling to read his reaction in his face.

"Has the night scared you before?" he asked calmly.

"Occasionally. Sometimes it seems threatening, but not all the time. Because running out into the night was what saved me back then. It's not like the night itself was ever a source of my terror. At least not enough to worry me or anyone else."

He pushed the salad aside and reached for his drink. "The night frightens lots of people. Understandably. We're vulnerable then. Atavistic response that probably goes back to our cave days, if not earlier. As a species, we're not night dwellers."

"You make it sound so ordinary," she protested. She didn't feel what had happened at the door was ordinary. As a measure of her mental state, it was probably a big red flag.

"I'm just saying that all by itself, fear of the dark is common, and it can become very strong sometimes. We might not even realize what triggers it. But it's not crazy."

"Maybe not," she answered, hearing the flatness of her own voice. She wondered why she was fighting his kindness. Did she *want* someone to tell her she was nuts?

"When you were really little, did you ever wonder if there might be something under your bed?"

She sighed, thinking it wasn't the same thing at all. "Of course."

"I'm pretty sure there was something under *my* bed."

His choice of words startled her. "You still think that?"

He smiled faintly, and she glimpsed it when she darted a quick look his way. "Not anymore. But for a long time, I jumped out of my bed. Far enough away that nothing could grab me. Now, just because there wasn't anything there in the daylight doesn't mean there wasn't in the dark. Reason doesn't work on that one, because we're programmed to have a sensible fear of the night."

"But this was different!" she protested.

"I believe you." He sighed and shook his head. "I guess I'm not being clear. I used to *jump* out of my bed so nothing could grab me. Nothing on earth could have convinced me to put my foot on the floor right beside my bed. It was *real*. What you felt when you tried to go out the back door was real. I don't know what triggered it, but something did, since this isn't common for you. Maybe it's being in a new place. Maybe it's knowing George is out there free now. I can't tell you, but I *believe* you and what you felt."

She swallowed again, then reached for her soda to wet her dry mouth. Her tongue and lips kept sticking. Then she came back to the important question. "Could my fear have made Flash growl?"

"It's possible. Not likely, but possible. Sensing your fear should have put him on high alert, and he should have remained quiet. No, something else bothered him, but it's anyone's guess."

She faced the grim possibility yet again. "So something out there disturbed us both."

"Evidently." He rose and began to gather up the remains of the meal. "Do you want to save any of this?"

It had been pretty well picked over. She shook her head and watched him cross the small kitchen to her wastebasket as he dumped in everything that was left. Then he rinsed their plates and flatware she had brought out for the leftovers, placing them beside the sink.

Drying his hands on the towel she kept hanging from the oven door handle, he leaned back against the small counter. "I'd suggest you move your equipment to my place, but that would only isolate you more if something worries you. I can hardly say you won't be alone there, can I? But I can put my bedroll here and be around when I'm not on duty. There are always the neighbors to help out here."

She knew the offer was meant kindly, but she stiffened anyway. "I've been living on my own since college."

"I'm sure. But George was in prison then. Things have changed a bit. I wish there was some way I could assure you that he's on his way to Brazil or some desert island, but I can't. So you're going to be worrying for a while."

"But it's so *stupid*!" she said vehemently. "*Stupid!* There's no reason for him to look for me. I know that. All these years he never tried to get in touch with me. Not even a letter from prison. Why would that change now? My fears are irrational. Even I know that."

"I don't know about that." He tossed the towel on the counter, then pulled his chair around the table so he could sit closer and take her hand. His grip was gentle, holding hers on his denim-clad thigh. "You saw your brother in the midst of an act so heinous that most people can't even adequately imagine it. You found the monster—it wasn't under your bed, and it wasn't your imagination. Why wouldn't you be frightened of him? You know what he's capable of."

She shook her head a little, although she wasn't disagreeing. His grip felt so reassuring, like a warm, strong lifeline. She'd like to bury herself in that grip.

"Then top it off with finding your whereabouts on

your company's website today… That was hardly re-assuring."

It was true. Seeing that had not only infuriated her, but it had frightened her. She'd come here to hide from George, not to have him directed practically to her doorstep. "Maybe I should leave. It's probably too easy to find someone around here."

But as soon as the words escaped her, she felt craven. Run? Again? She'd run once, but she still had as many fears, as many nightmares. She couldn't run from herself. She needed to face down the monster that had been pursuing her in her dreams for a quarter century.

Cadell hadn't spoken a word, but she squeezed his hand tightly and hung on. "I'm not running again. It won't do a damn bit of good. I'm carrying my brother around inside me. No escape."

"I don't have any idea how you get that monkey off your back," he said. Gently, he squeezed her hand in return. "But I agree about not running again. And we may be a small town and a sparsely populated county, but people notice strangers. People have noticed your arrival, but it was clear you're a friend of Betty's. He wouldn't have that going for him if he shows up here."

She looked at him, sinking into his dark eyes. They offered something warm and reassuring, welcoming. He made her feel as if he cared about her. Which she guessed he did, since he'd been talking about spreading his bedroll here indefinitely. "If you stay here, won't that cause talk?"

"Nothing that worries me. If it worries you…"

She quickly shook her head. "No. I was actually thinking about you, not myself for a change."

That made his eyes dance a bit. "Just keep your dog

in line, lady. I really think he'd have gone for me earlier if you had resisted me holding you in any way."

She blinked, surprised. "But you trained him!"

"Which may be the only reason he didn't spring.
He was certainly thinking about it." He nodded toward Flash, who appeared to be snoozing across the
kitchen doorway. "He knows he's yours now. Pretty
happy about it, too, from what I see."

Then he turned back toward her and astonished her
into complete stillness by leaning into her and brushing a kiss on her lips. "More where that came from,
if you ever want it," he murmured as he pulled back.

The maelstrom that had been whipping her about
was nothing compared to what he unleashed in her with
that butterfly touch of his lips. All her life, because she
couldn't trust, she'd refused to let anyone get close to
her. When an attraction began to grow in her, she had
squelched it mercilessly.

"Cadell," she breathed. God, she wanted more, a
whole lot more.

He shook his head slowly. "Not now. Not when
you've been feeling like a punching bag. Besides, I
want you to be sure it's what *you* really want. I don't
think you know right now."

She could have felt rejected, but she didn't. Much as
she wished it otherwise, he was taking care of her yet
again. Remembering what he'd said about his marriage,
she guessed he had some trust issues, too. What a pair.

He thought waiting was better. Given her current
state of mind, she couldn't disagree. She really did
feel all mixed up inside. Strong as her desire for him
seemed to be, she couldn't be sure it wasn't just part of

the tangled mess she'd become since she'd heard that George was going to be released.

"I'll hold you to that," she said, feeling spunky for the first time since she'd seen the website and read the riot act to her fellow team members.

He smiled. "I'm counting on it."

She did have an extra pillow and a couple of blankets, and she gave them to Cadell, although she couldn't imagine how he would sleep comfortably even on the rag rug on the living room floor. He seemed dubious about using the couch, and she didn't blame him. Every time she sat on it she was aware of how it creaked.

"You know," she said, "I'm going to stay up and work tonight. You could use my bed."

"Nope. I'll be just fine, and you might actually want to sleep at some point."

She should have been exhausted after the emotional turmoil of this day, but she felt keyed up, almost antsy. Maybe she wasn't really sure the monster hadn't been in her backyard. Although he couldn't possibly have gotten here this soon, could he?

She paused as she started to leave the living room on her way to her office. Cadell was spreading a folded blanket on the floor for his mattress. Dimly aware that despite the food she had just eaten, she was growing light-headed, she ignored that for a moment. More important things concerned her than her routine low blood pressure.

"Cadell?"

"Yeah?"

"How fast could George get here?"

He finished laying out the blanket, then straightened, standing with his hands on his narrow hips. "Depends."

"On what?"

"Well, when a prisoner is released, he's got nothing. And by nothing, I mean *nothing.* They give him a bus ticket to get back to the town where he was arrested. It's nonrefundable. If he has any ID at all, it's his inmate ID. They may give him the address of a halfway house, but basically…" He hesitated. "Unless a prisoner has a friend or family member on the outside, he's going to find life pretty hard for a while. A few bucks in his pocket, maybe a place to lay his head, and no real way to get a job or help. Hell, they can't even get temporary assistance without ID of some kind."

She faced him, leaning against the doorjamb. "That sounds brutal."

"It can be. Those who don't have someone to turn to often wind up sleeping under bridges or at a shelter. If they're lucky, someone will be willing to help them get all the paperwork together to get a new Social Security card, a state ID. Only then can they really start to look for work."

"That sounds like a great recipe for recidivism."

"It is, for long-term inmates. You go in for two years, you might well have access to all that stuff. But after twenty-five…it's hard. Most of them weren't arrested with a Social Security card to begin with. It's gone. Driver's license? It expires, and these days thanks to the new Homeland Security rules, to get it replaced or renewed, you need a birth certificate, proof of residence, Social Security card…you get the idea. It's definitely not easy."

Part of her was seriously disturbed by that news, in

a general sense, but when she thought of her brother, she was glad it wouldn't be easy for him to get going. "So it might take George a while before he can even buy another bus ticket?"

"Maybe. Like I said, I don't know his resources. Maybe he made a friend or two on the inside who are willing to help him right now. Or he might find another way to get his hands on money."

From the way he said it, she suspected it wouldn't be legal. And she needed to get to a chair soon. She gripped the doorjamb.

"I'm sorry I can't offer more reassurance," he said after a few beats. "If he's resourceful, he'll manage somehow."

"But there's still no reason he would want to find me."

She saw him hesitate visibly. "Dory?"

"Yeah?"

"Have you considered that half of your inheritance would have been his if he hadn't been convicted?"

"Of course I have," she nearly snapped. "My godparents put it in a trust. They set aside everything but the proceeds of the house, which were used for me to go to college. They told me the rest was my retirement fund, or for help if I ever got disabled. They set me up well for the future, but I can't touch it."

"But does he know that?"

"He should. My godparents told his lawyer when they did it. I think they thought it might protect me from constant pleas for money from him. If he thinks he'll get his hands on a dime, he's in for a shock. Even if I die, he can't have it."

"Maybe he thinks he can make you change that."

And that, she thought, would indeed be enough for him to hunt her down. It was her last cogent thought. Too much, too weary, too light-headed, and the last flare of anger did her in.

When she came to, she was lying on her bed, Cadell hovering over her. Flash had jumped up to lie right beside her. Tentatively he licked her cheek.

"Welcome back," Cadell remarked. "Are you eating enough? Should you see a doctor?"

She shook her head a little. "I've always had low blood pressure. Good for my health, but I can pass out easily."

"Well, that was scary," he said frankly. "I almost didn't catch you in time. Pet your damn dog, please. He's worried."

He sounded aggravated, but she didn't feel it was directed at her as much as the whole situation. Cadell struck her as a protector by nature, and right now he must be feeling next to useless.

The inheritance. She'd believed she was protected by the trust, but in an instant she realized that could be a reason for George to want to find her. What if he thought he could make her change it? To demand his share. She rolled over, wrapping her arms around Flash. "Cadell? Is there some way I could just send him money?"

"Yeah, if anyone had any idea where on earth he's gone. And what if it's not enough?"

Her mouth turned even drier and she closed her eyes, holding onto Flash for dear life. She didn't need Cadell to spell it out, but she said it anyway. "He probably thinks he's my legal heir."

"Unless you did something to change that."

"He isn't. The way the trust is set up, he can never have a dime. But what if he doesn't realize that?" Fear seized her then, running across every nerve in her body like a horde of stinging ants. She'd never know why George had killed her parents, but now she knew why he might want to kill her.

The monster was coming for her. There was no longer any doubt in her mind.

Any hope of sleep had fled. Her blood pressure had returned to normal. Dory tried to push herself into working, but instead she remained on the bed, Flash stapled to her. Across Flash, on the other side of the bed, Cadell had stretched out. Flash kept himself firmly between them, as if he'd made up his mind. Cadell had even had to negotiate permission to lie down.

But now here the three of them were: man, woman and dog, the humans staring at the ceiling, the dog watching everything. His eyes roved restlessly, remaining on duty although there was no need.

Dory rubbed his neck. "Sleep, Flash. No point in you staying up worrying with me."

Not that he seemed to understand. If he did, he didn't care. She sighed, letting the evening sink in the rest of the way. So George *did* have a reason to seek her out. Given what he'd done to their parents, it didn't require much imagination to think what he could do to her if he thought he could get money.

"He used to love me," Dory said quietly, little more than a murmur.

"George?" Cadell asked.

"Yes. He always took such good care of me. Unlike

many older brothers, he never treated me like a pest. When he was out for the evening, he'd come back and sneak into my bedroom to leave some little treat on my pillow. Sometimes I'd wake and see him and he'd smile and put his finger over his lips. No noise."

Closing her eyes, she could see that so clearly, and the memory tore at her heart. She'd loved him so much, as much as a seven-year-old could. What had gone wrong?

"Why no noise?" Cadell asked when she didn't speak for a while.

"Our parents were strict. At the time I assumed he didn't want me to get into trouble for making noise when I was supposed to be sleeping. But maybe he was protecting himself, too. I don't know. I wasn't supposed to come downstairs after I was sent to bed. But that night... God, I wish I hadn't broken the rule!"

"Me, too," he said. "I wish you'd never seen that."

She felt the bed move, and the next thing she knew he'd reached across Flash to lay one of his large hands on her upper arm.

"This dog may be good at his job, but right now he's an impediment," Cadell remarked, a tremor of amusement in his voice, surprising her. "So consider this the best hug I can give you."

"He's hugging me, too," she answered, feeling a slight lift to her spirits. A lot of hugs, something she'd been missing in her life since her godparents had died. Almost immediately, her mood sank again.

"Do you really think he'd come after me for the inheritance? Even though his lawyer should have told him it was in trust? That when I die it goes to a charity?" she asked, figuring that, like it or not, she needed to address the possibility directly. Hiding from it wouldn't help anything, and she'd been hiding from a lot for a long time.

"I don't know what he knows," he said honestly. "It's possible he thinks you can change the trust. Or that he'd be the heir anyway. It's mostly still there from what you said."

"Even if I could access the trust I wouldn't. Another way I'm weird, I guess. I didn't want to…"

"Profit from the murder of your parents. I get it."

She sighed. "Like I said, weird. They had insurance policies to make sure their kids were taken care of if anything happened. Would I feel the same if it had been a car accident?"

"I don't know," he answered honestly. "That's a question for you, but I don't know how you could answer it. That isn't what happened."

She turned onto her side, throwing her arm across the dog, too, and her hand landed on his waist. "Flash sandwich," she remarked. Not that the dog seemed to mind a bit. "You're a cop," she said a little later, her mind flea-hopping around from one item to the next. No rhyme or reason that she could determine yet.

"It's been rumored."

"You know something about people like George."

His answer was clearly cautious. "Something."

"I don't expect you to explain what he did to our parents. I'm just wondering…what did all those years in prison do to him? Could he be worse now? More dangerous?"

"I don't know," he answered frankly. "That long in prison… I can't say. I *do* know that as men get older, they're less likely to commit crimes. Less recidivism among men who are past their midthirties. On the other hand…" He just let it trail there.

"He could have gotten angrier," she said, feeling as if a stone were settling into her heart. "Meaner. It could have made him worse."

He didn't reply.

She spoke again after a minute. "You don't have any idea how much time I've spent trying to figure that night out, to understand what made George do that. It wasn't the George I thought I knew, but I was so little. I knew he was fighting with our parents, but my mother told me once that it was just his age, and he'd grow out of it."

"Often true," he said quietly.

"So what made him so different?" The question seemed to erupt from her very soul. Sitting up slowly, testing whether she'd get light-headed again, she found her feet and headed for her office, Flash right on her heels. Cadell wasn't far behind.

Then she did something she'd never done before: she shared her 3-D rendering of the murder scene that night.

"My God," Cadell whispered.

"This is what I saw. The thing is, once I put all this stuff in, I can turn it around. I can see it from different angles. It doesn't help me to understand anything, but I keep looking for answers. There aren't any. What do I expect? That some ugly demon will suddenly appear in my rendering and I can tell myself that my brother was possessed?"

She closed the image and swiveled the chair to look up at him. "I need to learn to let it go. I thought I had, until word came about George's release. It's like someone opened the floodgates on a dam. It's all coming back as if it were yesterday." She twisted her hands together. "The brother I used to love is gone. I need to face that. I need to face the fact that if he could do that once, he could do it again."

"Dory…"

She shook her head. "My brother is a murderer. I have no reason to think he's not the same person who stabbed our parents. Who cut my mother's throat. And you're right, if he thinks I still have some of that inheritance, he'll want his share. Because if there's one other thing I remember clearly about him, it's how frequently he snuck into Mom's purse or Dad's wallet and took money. Probably for drugs, I don't know. But he was never above stealing. I didn't like to think about it then, and I guess I lost that in the detritus of what came later. He was a thief. Never to be trusted to begin with."

She shook her head as if trying to wake herself up. "I've been trying to connect two pieces of a different puzzle. Trying to fit parts together that never fit to begin with. I don't know why he was often so kind to me when I was little, but that was only a piece of him."

Cadell cleared his throat. "Would you have tattled about his thievery if you hadn't liked him so much?"

She drew a sharp, long breath that seemed to carry ice all the way to her soul. "Maybe. I knew it was wrong."

He didn't say any more, but he didn't need to. Suddenly those pieces snapped into place, and it was painful. Those cherished memories of the before time, as she thought of it, turned black and drifted away like dead leaves.

In an instant it all became painfully clear. She *did* have a reason to be afraid. Her brother was capable of using her and God knew what else if he didn't get what he wanted.

Her breathing broke, and scalding tears filled her eyes, trickling down her cheeks. "Years ago," she said brokenly, "my therapist tried to tell me that he was a manipulative psychopath. I refused to believe it. I should have. I should have!"

When Cadell's arms closed around her, she grabbed his shirt with her hands and hung on for dear life. Adrift in a sea of ugly discovery, she needed an anchor in the storm.

Cadell held Dory for a long time. While he'd been suspicious that she might have valid reasons to be afraid, he hadn't expected anything like this to emerge. For her to suddenly see her childhood in a very different light had to be wrenching in the extreme. He'd heard the love in her voice when she'd spoken of how George had treated her before the murders. That had just blown up in her face.

How much can one woman take? he wondered. He also wondered if she needed a lot more help than he could provide. Maybe he should call Betty in the morning, get Dory to talk to her.

Damn, Dory was isolated. He understood it was by choice. She was a self-proclaimed hermit. But it remained there were times in life when you needed someone else, someone to lean on and talk to. He had buddies he could share almost anything with, but this woman had no one except Betty. Maybe that was enough, but after tonight he wasn't at all sure.

She had warned him she didn't trust, but she had trusted him with an amazing amount of information about herself and her brother. Because he was a cop and might understand?

Being a cop didn't make the horrors understandable. All it did was build necessary walls of self-protection.

But another question seriously troubled him, and when her tears quieted and began to dry, he kept his arms tight around her, as if he expected her to try to escape. Maybe he did. But he had to ask.

"Why'd you make that graphic of the murder scene?"

At once she stiffened against him. As he'd suspected, she pressed a hand against his chest, trying to push him away.

"Do you think I'm sick?" she asked, her voice raw. "Is that what you think?"

"I just want to understand." Not exactly true. He'd heard her say she studied it trying to find some answer, but it was frankly macabre, and he needed to know the reason behind it. It would tell him so much about Dory.

She breathed rapidly but stopped pushing against him. "Why? Because my psychologist taught me to do it."

"What?" He was startled.

"You heard me." Her thickened voice managed to grow angry and a bit sharp. "I couldn't talk, remember? So she had me draw pictures. Any kind of pictures. I drew that night over and over again. It seemed to help. So she encouraged me to keep doing it as long as I felt a need."

"Apparently you're still feeling a need."

He felt her shudder, and her hand, flattened against his chest from pushing at him, fisted and grabbed his shirt. "It's a different kind of need now. And I don't keep redrawing it. I finished that rendering over five years ago. It's a snapshot of what's stamped in my mind forever. When I was a kid, it was a way to express. You have no idea how many sheets of drawing paper got torn by crayons as I expressed my feelings from anger to terror to sorrow. It was a violent expression for a while."

He rocked a little, wishing she weren't still in her chair. The floor was hard beneath his knees, and this certainly wasn't the world's most comfortable hug. He wasn't ready to let go yet, though. Something was happening tonight. Something inside Dory had opened up. He damn well wasn't going to make any move that might shut her down.

"Police wish they had such good renderings of what a person saw at a crime scene," he remarked after a while.

"It's what I saw. What I *think* I saw." She relaxed a bit against him, tension easing out of her. "Who knows how accurate it is. I don't. Even though I think I couldn't possibly have forgotten or changed a single detail, I probably did. Memory is a funny thing."

"Yeah," he said quietly. Five witnesses could tell five different stories and believe them, even when disputed.

"Anyway," she went on, "until recently I hardly ever looked at it anymore. Then there I was beating my head on the question that didn't have an answer. Looking into my memory for some clue by looking at the image. I don't think I need it anymore."

"Really?" That startled him, and inadvertently he loosened his grip on her. At once she pivoted away from him, facing the computer where just a few minutes ago bloody horror had been displayed. She brought up a list that looked like file names, highlighted a few then hit a key. Another key, confirming the deletion, and they were gone.

"I don't need it anymore," she said quietly. "Problem solved. The psychologist was right. He's a manipulative psychopath. He manipulated me when I was a kid, and given that psychopaths don't outgrow it, he probably hasn't changed for the better. Maybe he got smoother, but nobody could supply him with empathy. It's impossible."

He stood, wincing as his knees shouted at him, then pulled the other, more battered, desk chair over from the corner so he could sit beside her. He didn't know whether all this was a good sign or a bad one for her. Her psychologist had diagnosed George as a psychopath, but had her psychologist ever interviewed George? Was the diagnosis simply based on the things Dory told her? What if it was wrong?

But cautious as he might be about things like that, it remained they couldn't afford to assume George wasn't exactly that: a manipulative psychopath. He'd met plenty of them in the course of his career, people who were simply incapable of any genuine feeling for another human being. Some were good at pretending. Quite a few never got in trouble with the law and were very successful because they were also very smart.

Then there were the others. The stone-cold rip-off artists and killers. Oh, so charming, but dead inside.

She turned her head toward him and said abruptly, "How did you know about my inheritance?"

He stiffened, watching the matchsticks of the bridge

of trust they had just started building waver and maybe begin to tumble. "I looked up the murder after I gave you Flash."

"Why didn't you mention it before tonight?"

Yup, he thought, he'd blown it. So he might as well light the final fuse. "I also checked on George's whereabouts. He vanished from the halfway house two nights after he arrived there, and his whereabouts are currently unknown."

"And you didn't think I should know that?"

"Honestly," he said, rising, "I wasn't sure you needed to know. Why add to your fear unless it became necessary?"

"Then what changed your mind? Why should I trust you enough to let you sleep in my house?"

He'd shattered their fragile trust, but he didn't want to add to it by getting into a fight about it. Time to go. "What you told me about him. Good night, Dory. I'll keep watch from my car out front. You know where to find me."

With every step away, he kept hoping to hear her call him back. She didn't.

A psychopath. As suspicious as Cadell was of long-distance diagnoses, the more he thought about it, the more he thought that psychologist had been right. As Dory had said, it brought the puzzle pieces together, matching at last.

If George was indeed a psychopath, then trouble was on its way. Standing on her front porch, he considered what he and the rest of law enforcement around here might be able to do. Sure, strangers stuck out. But George might be smart enough to stay in the shadows once he saw how small this place was. Heck, he could probably figure it out by looking up this area online.

Being a psychopath, he had no limits on what he would do. He'd proved that once before. Now, if he felt Dory had taken his inheritance, he'd do anything necessary to get it back. Coming out of prison with nothing might have exacerbated an old resentment, a feeling he'd been robbed. While Dory wasn't responsible for that, she still held his entitlement. What if he believed her death would leave it all to him, trust or no trust?

If they were lucky, he'd call and demand his share. But Cadell's neck itched with a certainty that he wouldn't do that. Whatever he'd been denied by his parents that had brought him to the point of a vicious murder, he had showed his stripes. If murder was the easy way, he'd take it.

Wishing vainly that he could locate George was a waste of time. The guy had finished his sentence. Nobody now had a reason to keep tabs on him, so unless he crossed paths with law enforcement because of a misdeed, he might never pop up on the radar again.

Damn it! What the hell had he been thinking? Sure, he wanted Dory to feel safe. She desperately needed it, and that's why he'd given her Flash. The woman had been terrified, and while at the time he'd thought she'd never really need Flash, the dog would be a comforting presence and protector to have around.

Now here he was standing in the ruins of a budding relationship with a woman who'd quite frankly told him she couldn't trust and preferred to be a hermit.

Well, he'd pushed himself into her life, and now it was time to back out. Let her be. She had Flash to look out for her.

Forgetting Dory for the moment, he sat on the top step, wished he hadn't quit smoking ten years ago, and thought about everything he knew.

The image on her computer was stamped into his brain now, like a piece of evidence, and he wasn't particularly concerned about whether her memory had been faulty. It still told him things.

So, George had been stealing from their parents and subtly manipulating Dory to keep her quiet about it. He might have taken more than money out of a purse or wallet, leading to the fights Dory had mentioned. Creating tension.

But that scene in the kitchen, the wounds Cadell had read about...that was no impulsive murder. The heat-of-passion argument had been enough to prevent a life sentence, but Cadell was no longer buying it.

Rising, he climbed the step and rapped on Dory's door. "Dory, it's me." Then he opened the door and stepped in.

Flash came charging at him.

Chapter 8

"Flash, no," Dory snapped just before the dog reached Cadell. She hadn't put him on guard, but she honestly wasn't sure if he was attacking or greeting. "Stay."

Flash immediately halted, and only then did she note that his tail was wagging happily. Then she looked at Cadell, part of her still burning angrily and part of her honestly glad to see him.

She was annoyed that he hadn't told her he knew something about George that she didn't, but on the other hand…well, Cadell was obviously protective.

"I thought you'd gone," she said.

"I didn't get all the way off your porch. The cop kicked in. Is there any chance you can recover that image of the murder? Because I'd like to look at it."

She hesitated. She'd had the sense that he'd been

horrified that she'd drawn such an image in so much detail. "What changed?"

"Like I said, the cop kicked in. Some things struck me, so I'd really like to study it."

She nodded slowly. "I can recover it." She paused, then asked, "Want a soda?"

"Any chance of coffee?"

The faintest of smiles lightened her face. "Of course. Just let me start the recovery and then I'll make it."

When she reached the kitchen, she had to grip the edge of the counter and lean on it. Her knees felt weak, and she was shaking from head to toe. Had it mattered so much to her that he'd walked out? That he'd come back? Hadn't she been mad at him?

But all of that had vanished in the contradictory realization that he hadn't left. Now he wanted to see her rendering of the murder scene. Maybe she'd been wrong in thinking that she had repelled him with it.

Drawing several deep breaths, telling herself she was overreacting, whether to Cadell's return or the idea that there was a good reason for George to seek her out, she didn't know. Too much. She'd lived with too much for a long time.

The coffee didn't take long. She seemed to remember that he took it black, so she carried a mug to him. She didn't want any herself. She was already wound up and simply relieved to have stopped shaking.

The picture once again filled the screen, every detail clear.

"You can turn it?" he asked, then thanked her for the coffee.

"Yeah, but you have to understand I couldn't see

it from any other direction, so you get the reverse of what you see here, plus the other side of the kitchen as I recall it."

"Every little bit helps. Can I rotate it myself?"

"Not easily." She pulled a chair over, and he scooted to one side while she called up a menu. She highlighted a box from the graphics software. "The problem with this is you're not really moving the picture, you're moving cameras around it. It can get awkward."

He nodded and picked up the mug, drinking, his gaze intent on the screen. "Turn it ninety degrees, if you can."

Well, that was easy enough. She hated this view, though, looking straight at her brother as he stood over their parents. It didn't look like him, of course. He was a morph, but she knew exactly who it was—an unrealistic face didn't change that.

He spoke. "The kitchen behind him. That's what you remember should have been there?"

"Yes."

"Okay, give me another ninety in the same direction."

She did. There was the dining table, the doorway, the little girl standing at the foot of the stairs. Her brother partially blocked the view, though.

"Do you have a drawing of the kitchen without him in it?"

"Of course. That's where I had to start."

"Can I see it?"

At least the shakes were gone, she thought as she reached for the mouse and switched to another image. The kitchen. Empty. The way it should have been that night at that hour.

"A back door," he muttered. "A knife block all the way over there, with the table in between."

"In between what?" she asked. Her heart was accelerating as she wondered if he'd seen something there that she hadn't.

He rubbed his chin and leaned back in the chair. It creaked, but he said nothing as he continued to stare. Finally he stabbed his finger at the screen, pointing out the knife block. "All the knives are there."

"Well, of course," she said. "Until he used one."

"I want you to look at this whole picture, Dory. The whole thing. For now just use your imagination to put the figures in it."

"Okay." That wasn't hard to do, considering that she'd looked at it until she hardly needed it anymore.

Her parents lying on the floor between the table and a wall of dish cabinets. George standing over them.

"The police report said he killed them with a ten-inch chef's knife," he said.

"Yes," she whispered, then opened her eyes in spite of his instructions.

"From that butcher's block."

"Yes."

He swiveled, and suddenly she was fixed by his gaze. "This was premeditated."

It had turned into a night of shocking revelations. She didn't even want to know how he'd reached that conclusion, not at first. Giving up all thought of sleep and peace, she headed for the kitchen and got herself a cup of coffee. Cadell wasn't far behind, refreshing his own mug.

"I'm sorry, Dory. But the more we know about him…"

"I get it," she interrupted, not caring if she was rude. "I get it."

Oh, yeah, she got it. He was saying that her brother hadn't been overcome by a blind rage, driven to an act he might never otherwise have committed. He was saying George had intended to kill them. That he'd planned it. Who knew how long he might have been planning it? Subtly bribing her and making her love him, then reinforcing their parents' dictum that she mustn't come downstairs after she was sent to bed.

Considering how many rules he'd broken, it was weird that he hadn't wanted her to break any.

"God," she whispered.

"Maybe you should sit down. I don't want you to faint again."

"I don't know if I can, and anyway I think my blood pressure is through the roof right now. Cadell, how can you be sure?"

He nudged her over to the table until she was sitting. "If you can stand to, think about that kitchen. How likely is it that he could have taken both your parents by surprise if he'd gone to get a knife? He'd have had to round the table, go to the knife block and come back around that table… Don't you think at least one of them would have run at that point? Getting the knife was a deadly threat, not some innocent act like getting a glass. The fact that they're lying beside one another… He was already armed. He took them utterly by surprise, and he knew exactly how he was going to do it."

Somehow she had moved past feeling shocked. In place of all her fears was the feeling that she was receiving repeated blows yet again, anger surging in her. Fury at George. Fury at what he had done and the scars and terrors he had left her with.

She closed her eyes, clenched her fists and wished he was there to scream at, to pound, to tell him once and for all that he'd killed part of her, too.

But George didn't care. He'd never cared. *Manipulative psychopath.* The brother who'd been so sweet to her had merely been using her. Then a strange calm came over her, leaving her feeling as if she were standing outside herself, observing from miles away.

"I have my answers now," she whispered.

"So it seems." He was quiet a moment, then said, "I guess I should leave. I've given you enough shocks and bad news for one night. You're going to hate the very sight of me."

Her eyes snapped open. Her voice emerged tonelessly. "I'm going to have nightmares if I sleep. I'm going to wake up screaming."

He stood there, his face creased with concern, his hands opening and closing as if he didn't know what to do. "Do you do that often?"

"A lot since I heard about George's release. I can feel it coming, almost like I'm already half-asleep. He's going to stalk my dreams."

"God," he muttered.

She looked down as she felt something on her thigh. Flash. He'd rested his head on her, his eyes peering up at her.

"Cadell?"

"Yeah?"

"I can't stand to be alone in the dark when I wake up screaming."

He shifted, then slid into the chair he'd pulled closer earlier. "I'll stay. I told you I'd stay tonight. I just figured after what's happened, you might want me gone. Being the bearer of bad news and all."

Still feeling oddly detached, she lifted her gaze and studied his face. "You didn't tell me anything new. Not really. Well, I *did* get angry when I found out you hadn't told me those things. Then you left."

"Not exactly," he admitted. "Didn't make it three steps. But I reckoned you felt betrayed, and for someone who says she can't trust... I figured all the bridges between us had been burned."

She shook her head slowly. "For a minute or two... Well, I'm glad you came back. And I'm glad to know for sure now about George. No questions left. You answered them. All the time I stared at my representation of that awful scene, I felt like there was an answer there somewhere. You found it."

"I'm sure that's thrilling you," he said tautly. "Good old Cadell, bringer of more bad news. I'm a great one for making people feel worse."

Her head jerked up at that. A sliver of feeling pierced the cold detachment that had overtaken her. "Brenda?"

"What?"

"Did your ex make you feel that way?"

She watched him consider it for a few minutes. "Yeah, in part. But being a cop brings a lot of that on, too. How many times have I had good news to deliver? Not many."

"I never thought about that," she confessed. "Never thought about what it could do to you and other police officers. My memory of the police is all warm and good. They took such good care of me back then. All of them. I've never forgotten it."

"I'm glad you feel that way."

Impulsively, surprising herself, she reached out for his hand and wrapped hers around it. "You're a good man. I keep thinking about how awful all this has been for me, but tonight can't have been fun for you, either. I'm surprised you came back after the way I reacted earlier."

He shrugged slightly. "Like I said, the cop kicked in. You told me you'd been looking for answers in that graphic, and while I was out on the porch doing a decent job of beating myself up for sacrificing your trust, I thought about what you'd said about seeking answers in that picture. You have an artist's eye, but I have a set of cop's eyes, and a thought occurred to me. I'm sorry it was so bad."

"The whole thing was bad." Some of her detachment was easing, and she wished she could hang on to it. She doubted she was ready to start feeling anything yet. Unfortunately, she knew she would. She always did. That night had been haunting her for over a quarter century. If she could have become ice, she certainly would have done it by now.

"Look," he said after a moment, "you really need some sleep. For that matter, so do I. It's awfully late."

So much had happened since he'd arrived with dinner that time had flown. Looking at the clock, she started. "Wow. Don't you have to work in the morning?"

"I'm off tomorrow. Maybe, if you can find time, you and Flash could come out and check on the ostriches with me. I'm certainly going to need a shower and a change."

The smallest of smiles cracked her frozen face. "Sure. Why haven't you named them?"

"The birds? Because I don't want to get attached. I'm trying to get rid of their ornery butts, remember?"

He turned his hand over and tugged her gently. "Bed. Flash will keep me in line. If you have a bad dream, I'll be right there."

At last, she nodded and felt the tension that had been building for hours let go. She wouldn't be alone. And while she was sure Flash would protect her, he wasn't the same as having someone right there she could talk to. During the time with Betty, she had learned how much that could mean. Since moving into this house, she had realized how much she missed having someone there.

Then his words struck her. "Why should Flash have to keep you in line?"

He just laughed. She felt a few more cracks in the ice that was encasing her, because she understood that laugh.

For the first time in a long time, she hugged something special close to her heart.

George cussed himself for a fool. He'd gotten all the money he needed off that woman, and she hadn't slowed him down much. It was everything else that was slowing him down.

Things had changed since he'd gone to prison. He'd been shocked to discover that he couldn't even buy a bus ticket without ID. The last thing he wanted was a record of where he'd been. The bus company might have accepted his prison ID—they had when the prison sent him home—but even if they would, he didn't want anyone to be able to trace his movements. Not with what he had in mind.

Of course, that gave him an idea. Walking boldly into the bus station, he asked for a ticket to Miami, and while the clerk hesitated a moment when seeing his prison ID, she didn't hesitate long. He walked out with a ticket to Miami, a false trail already started.

Now he just had to figure out how to get to that place in Wyoming. Once again, he walked to a different town. The outdoors still felt too big to him. He wondered if he'd get past that. Anyway, he felt better when surrounded by houses and trees. They cut the sight lines to something more reasonable. But from what he knew of Wyoming, he was going to have to get used to wide-open spaces quickly.

The next town had a small library, but that didn't mean they were without computers or the internet. He made his way to one of them without having to show a card or other ID and set to work. If they didn't want people to walk in and just use the machines, if they hassled him…well, they had books, and he was pretty sure they didn't have a problem with people browsing the books.

But no one harassed him the least little bit, and he began to do his research on Conard County.

An hour later he was wondering what had drawn Dory to a place like that. It was the ends of the earth. Hardly any people, nothing to do, really. The main town, Conrad City, was a cow town, if that. The plus was that she'd stick out and be easy to find. The minus was that so would he.

Leaning back as far as the chair would let him, keeping his hand on the mouse, he tabbed between pages. One gave him the stats about the place. Another gave him a reasonable map, although he was sure plenty of minor roads probably didn't show up. The third gave him photos. Beautiful mountains, a worn-out town and plenty of wide-open spaces.

He had no way to know if Dory had moved there on her own or if some guy had drawn her there. Her personal life was a closed book to him. Crap, she didn't even have a social media account under any possible name he could cobble together for her.

It hadn't always been like that. That was how he'd learned she'd become a graphic artist and worked for some company. Then everything had shut down ten years ago. As if she'd gone underground and wanted to stay there.

It didn't make any sense. What was she afraid of? He'd still been in prison, and anyway, he'd given her absolutely no reason to fear him.

If only she hadn't come downstairs that night. She'd loved him back then. He'd made sure of it. Made sure that she worshipped him more than their parents, that she was his ally and kept his secrets. Then she'd broken the rule and come downstairs.

Even so, she had no reason to fear *him*. No reason to think that her loving brother would come after her with murder in his heart. He'd *always* been good to her.

It did seem suspicious that her location had changed on the company's website right around the time he was released. But it had changed back. What if it was just a mistake? Because why the hell would she go so far out of the way?

"Sir?"

George looked up. A middle-aged woman smiled at him. "I'm sorry, but you've been using that computer for over an hour, and we have other people waiting."

He smiled, calling on every bit of charm and sexiness he owned. No point in making himself memorable. "I'm sorry. Let me just shut down my search."

"Oh, take a few more minutes," she said, smiling in answer. Her cheeks even flushed a little. "I'll explain you're almost done."

As she walked away, he wondered if he should chat her up a bit, maybe spend the night with her. Then his memory flashed the image of the wedding ring she wore.

Nope. He'd have to find a different flophouse.

He closed out his search, erased the search history and rose, heading for the door. He gave the librarian another smile before he stepped out into the sunny morning. The library was on a wide boulevard, and for a moment he froze, overwhelmed by the space. Then he gathered himself and began to stroll down the sidewalk, glancing in shop windows, a handsome man just past forty. He liked seeing his reflection.

All the while his mind kept ticking things over. The change of address, changed back. Too coincidental. Why the middle of nowhere? Because she was afraid, after all?

When he'd seen her standing in the kitchen, he'd tried to reassure her, telling her he'd gotten rid of the bad man. Had she believed him? She should have, but a lot of years had passed, and he'd spent them in prison. Maybe she believed his conviction more than she had believed him. Certainly something in her had snapped.

He'd never forget the way she ran from him and stood in the street screaming her fool head off. The sound had frozen him, had thrown all his plans into a mixer, and in the end he hadn't had the time he had planned on to clean himself up, get rid of the weapon and lay a false trail.

If she'd just stayed in bed... She'd never told their parents that he was stealing from them, even though she'd seen it. In the end she'd never told anyone anything about that night, as far as he could tell. Hell, she'd stopped talking entirely. His lawyer had been good about keeping him informed. The freaking lawyer thought he was worried about his sister. Idiot.

He'd kept tabs through that guy, loosely, of course. The years she spent with her godparents, a couple he'd never cared for. The trip to college when briefly he'd been able to follow her on social media. But then, for no apparent reason, she'd dropped out. Gone. Canceled her accounts.

He still wondered what the hell had brought that on. Maybe someone had been bothering her. Anyway, she'd apparently never picked it up again. She was almost as far off the radar as he was.

The idea made George smile. Maybe he could just make her disappear. Who'd be worried about it? Her coworkers? If she had friends, he hadn't been able to find out. Not even that damn lawyer could tell him, and finally the guy had gotten impatient, reminding George that he was not on retainer and while he'd been doing favors out of kindness all these years, he was through.

Bastard. George sometimes thought he'd take care of that lawyer once he'd settled matters with Dory.

With a start, he understood he'd reached the end of

town. He hesitated only a minute before deciding to just keep going, heading west. He'd been warned that hitchhiking was illegal, but that didn't mean someone wouldn't pick him up. He looked innocuous enough, clean, not too big, carrying a backpack over his shoulder. No one would guess that a slender guy like him could be trouble.

Which was just how he wanted it. He'd used his exercise periods to stay lean. Fit, but lean. Bulking up like so many of the guys did only made a man look like potential trouble. George didn't want to frighten anyone.

For now the only weapons he needed were his good looks, his smile and his tongue.

Even though it was late, the morning sunlight almost hurt Dory's eyes as she opened them. She needed to get some curtains in here.

Then she realized she was alone. At once she turned over and saw that both Flash and Cadell were absent. Reaching out, she touched the covers and felt warmth. They hadn't been gone long. Then she heard sounds from the backyard and saw that Cadell was running Flash through his paces.

She sat up and stretched until joints popped. No nightmares. None. Not even a hint. She'd just had the best sleep she'd had in weeks, maybe a month.

Feeling better than she had in quite a while, she slipped out of bed and headed for a shower that would make her feel even better.

When she emerged freshly dressed in a light T-shirt and jeans with a towel around her blond hair, she stepped outside to watch Cadell and Flash. They'd passed the work stage and were now at the play stage.

She smiled as she watched the dog jump for joy each time Cadell threw the ball. To be so happy...

Before her thoughts could take a downward spiral, Cadell called Flash to heel and came toward her. "You slept well?"

"Like a rock. It was amazing. That hasn't happened in a while."

"Good news, then. When you're ready, we'll go out to my place. I *do* have something there besides two ostriches and a dog kennel."

Her smile started to widen, then hitched. "Who's taking care of the dogs?"

"They are," he said simply. "I never know when I might have to be away for an extended period, so I have a very modern kennel. It feeds and waters them."

"And the ostriches?"

He laughed. "I hope they got all the insects out of the corral."

His cheer was contagious, and she liked it. Before long they were heading out to his ranch with Flash in the cage in back. He seemed excited, as if he knew he was going to visit his dog friends.

Dory wondered what was happening inside her. After last night's shocks, shouldn't she be more upset? Instead she felt as if she had been freed in some way. Maybe Cadell had given her some of the answers she'd been looking for. Maybe now she felt she knew what she was facing, rather than wondering.

But she was sick of her own fears this morning, and she shoved them aside. George's release didn't mean she couldn't still have an enjoyable day. In fact, now that she thought about it, she was appalled at how much power she'd given her brother over her. She'd allowed him to haunt her for years. Allowed him to terrorize her sleep and dreams. He didn't deserve that right.

Lifting her head, she looked to her left and drank in the mountains. At midday they looked a little hazy, the greens very dark except for lighter patches here and there. She wondered if she was looking at different trees or if that was the dappling of sunlight.

"Cadell?"

"Yeah?"

"After your divorce...did you find it hard to trust?"

He snorted. "Oh, yeah. I got distrustful of women, and I got distrustful of myself."

"Why yourself?"

"Because before that I thought was a fairly decent judge of character. Afterward, not so much. Which was probably a good thing for a cop."

She turned a little in her seat so she could look at the side of his face. "How so?"

He paused as he steered them into his rutted driveway. The truck began to jolt. "Because it's not possible to really judge a book by its cover. In my line of work, making that mistake can be deadly. I guess I figured out that before you can trust someone, you need to get to know them. You need to see them in stressful situations, not just dates where everything is fine. If I ever marry again, I'll want to know how a woman reacts when the toilet overflows."

The quiver began deep inside Dory, and seconds later emerged as the heartiest belly laugh she'd had in ages. "The toilet?" she gasped finally, wiping an errant tear from laughing so hard.

"Well, it could be something else," he allowed. "But I think you get my drift."

She did indeed, but it was still funny, and she couldn't stop grinning. She imagined him with a clipboard ticking off boxes as a harried woman worked on a toilet.

"Are you keeping a checklist?" she asked.

"Not consciously. But that's the best way I can explain it. People change under stress. I kind of think it's important to know how they change. Every life has problems that have to be dealt with. I'd prefer someone who can deal."

Which ruled her out, Dory thought, wondering why it should matter. He'd seen her under stress, and she didn't think she was getting any gold stars from him. Afraid of nightmares, of being alone? Afraid of her brother? Turning herself into a hermit because she trusted no one easily? How was that truly coping with anything? She was a mass of defense mechanisms.

She sighed, imagining him filling out his checklist when it came to her, or worse, writing "Failed" across the sheet.

Oh, well. She might not pass his tests, but that didn't mean she couldn't enjoy the day. Even if George were somewhere close, he'd never find her out here.

Chapter 9

Cadell had left the ostriches in the corral, which was also electrically fenced. They'd done a good job of scratching up the place looking for food. Leaving Dory to get out of his vehicle in her own time, he headed for the pen. The two birds came running.

"Yeah, you guys know who feeds you," he said. Before he let them in, though, he had to dump feed in their trough. No way was he going to let them get close. He'd learned his lesson.

He opened the gate into the pen and stepped back as the two birds entered. He didn't know if he wanted to confine them again just yet, so he left the gate open.

Dory had joined him, Flash at her side. "Man," she said. "They moved fast!"

"They didn't even get up to full speed. Quite amazing birds…at a distance."

He was pleased when she laughed again. He'd gotten the feeling just before they finished the drive that something had darkened her mood. Well, not really darkened. Not that bad. Just a kind of sadness, he guessed.

Which under the circumstances needed no explanation. He was pretty impressed with how well she'd handled last night's revelations, especially the one about the murder being premeditated. She probably had been fighting that thought for years, unwilling to believe that her beloved brother was capable of it. Much easier to believe he'd lost his temper in a big way than to imagine him plotting the entire thing.

He led her along the fence. "See the wire fencing inside the wooden corral? Courtesy of my father and the ostriches."

"What was your dad like?"

"An honest, decent, hardworking, churchgoing man. Respected by his neighbors. A good example for any kid."

She looked toward him. "Why'd you leave?"

"Youthful wanderlust, I guess." He sighed and shook his head a little. "I didn't think I was cut out to be a rancher. It about wore my dad to a nub. Same thing every day and worries that never quit." He shook his head a bit, leaned his arms on the fence and lifted one booted foot to the lower railing.

"It's hard to remember what I was thinking back then," he said. "I'm sure it made perfect sense to me. I tried staying for a couple of years, but my dad didn't stop me when I took off. He was already winding down the operation here. Cattle are expensive to raise, and he wasn't getting enough when he sold them. I sometimes wonder if he didn't think I'd be better off doing something else."

"Maybe he did," she said quietly. The breeze was blowing, tossing her hair, caressing her skin gently. A beautiful day. "Then you come home to the ostriches."

He laughed easily. "Yup. And don't think I don't wonder if he planned that. He knew me well. I wouldn't leave animals uncared for, and he probably knew just how much difficulty I'd have getting rid of this pair. What a way to get me back to my roots, but he some-times had a strange sense of humor."

"They're quite a joke," she remarked, watching the two strange-looking birds eat ravenously. "I know they're birds, but..."

"Too big," he agreed. "Dinosaurs."

"I've heard people can ride them."

He laughed again. "No, thanks."

He studied her for a few minutes before turning his attention back to the mountains that loomed over one side of his ranch. She seemed tentative. After starting the day in a mood so good it surprised him, she had retreated a little.

"I wish I could have met your father," she said.

"Why?" It occurred to him that she'd never really had a chance to know her own father or mother. After all, a child of that age would have only a few memories and very little knowledge about the adults in her life.

"Because the person you are tells me something about him." She astonished him with a small smile. "I'm sure he was every bit as good a man as you said."

Quite a compliment coming from a woman who'd frankly told him she didn't trust easily. Although say-ing something like that was hardly a matter of trust.

A bark from the kennel area drew his attention.

"Flash!" Dory said and then laughed. "He must be feeling forgotten. He wants to play with his buddies."

"Let's go let them out, then." He paused only to lock the ostriches in their pen.

The summer-baked ground was hard beneath their feet, the remaining grasses dry and crackly. Out back where the kennels resided, however, the ground softened and greened because of how often he had to spray down the concrete. Each kennel opened onto a small, individual outdoor space so the dogs didn't start feeling too cooped up, but right now they were all at the front, watching Flash, who was prancing right up the middle of the dog run.

"I could almost swear he's taunting them," Cadell remarked.

"That dog is capable of more expressions and feelings than I would have believed," she answered. "You have a lot more cages than dogs. How come?"

"It varies, actually. I don't just train police dogs. I work with service dogs and even family pets. But mainly my job is being the lead K-9 officer and trainer. Anyway, every now and then I might have eight or ten dogs here."

"That'd keep you busy."

"It sure does. Some training is far more intensive and time-consuming that other types." He walked down the row, opening the kennels and letting the dogs free. At once they entered a joyous chase all over the unfenced acreage, to the ramshackle barn and back. Their joy was infectious, and both Cadell and Dory smiled as they watched.

"So," he said, risking it, "who took care of you afterward?"

He watched her suck her lip between her teeth, and he regretted spoiling the mood. Still, he needed to know her better. Wanted to know her better. He had not the least doubt there was more to this woman than the graphics designer and the frightened little girl.

"My godparents," she said after a moment. "They'd been good friends of my parents for a long time, and I knew them somewhat. Better than foster care, I imagine."

"The only judge is you. Did you feel loved?"

"They tried. I can't have been easy. Like I said, I didn't talk for over a year. They took me to therapists and doctors. But even when I started speaking again... well, I told you I don't trust people. All the way back then, I lost my trust. It had to be hard on them. They gave me so much, and when I look back I realize I gave them very little in return."

"I doubt they were doing it for what they could get out of it, Dory. I'm sure it was more about what they could do for you. Anyway, Betty became your friend. How did that happen?"

Dory's face lightened. Relief flooded him. He hadn't ruined today for her. Enough that he'd ruined last night.

"She was my English teacher my sophomore year of high school. How well do you know Betty?"

"In passing. We're not tight, but we talk from time to time. Why?"

"I just wondered if you had any idea of how persistent she can be."

At that he laughed. "I've heard about it."

Dory's smile grew. "She was persistent with me.

I don't know why, but for some reason she wouldn't let go. She kept working on me, talking to me in odd moments. Finally she started inviting me and my godparents to have dinner at her house, and then they reciprocated and... Well, she never gave up on me. Even after I went to college, she'd drive over on a Saturday and take me out to lunch. Like water dripping on stone, I guess." She gave a little laugh, and her gaze met his. "I don't know when or how it happened, but she became my friend. My only friend. After my godparents died, Betty was the only person I had left."

He nodded. He was beginning to get a real clue about how truly alone this woman was. "What happened to them? Your godparents?"

"A tornado," she said simply, then directed her attention back to the mountains.

God, he thought. She'd been through a hell of a lot. The murder of her parents, the betrayal by her brother, then the loss of her godparents in an extreme act of nature? Without giving it a thought, he stretched out an arm, wrapped it around her shoulders and drew her to his side.

He wanted to find a way to express how bad he felt for her, but he suspected she wouldn't want that. She had made peace with most of her life, as far as he could tell. With everything except her brother. Anyway, sympathy didn't make up for the losses. So he offered what comfort he could with his touch.

After a couple of minutes, she surprised him by turning toward him and resting her cheek on his chest. "I'm such a mess," she said. "I don't know why anyone puts up with me."

"I don't think you're a mess."

She shifted a little against him. "How can you say that? I told you I can't trust. I'm afraid so much of the time…"

"I don't blame you for either. What your brother did would make it hard for anyone to trust again. As for being afraid… Well, he's a coldhearted murderer, isn't he? I wouldn't want to run into him any more than you do."

A thin laugh escaped her. "No machismo?"

"I'm not going to promise you something I have no right to promise," he said firmly. "I'm here for you, but that doesn't mean I can guarantee anything about your brother or your safety. All I can promise is that I'll do my damnedest."

Slowly her arms wrapped around his waist. He had to close his eyes against the sudden surge of passion. It had been simmering since he'd met her, and he'd been dumping cold water on it because that was probably the last thing she needed or wanted. Some problems were too big to be answered with a roll in the hay.

"Thank you," she said. "Thank you."

"For what?" He couldn't imagine.

"For being honest with me. Last night you told me things you knew I didn't want to hear, and now today you're not making wild promises. Not that I'd believe them."

The dogs were beginning to tire from their romp but weren't quite ready to quit yet. He stood there with one of the most beautiful women he'd ever met and wondered if he were capable of letting his own guard down enough. She freely said she found it hard to trust. Well, he did, too.

They made quite a pair. A hopeless one.

* * *

The surprise he had promised her came in the form of Betty. She arrived midafternoon while Cadell was still checking the dogs for ticks.

"I need some help," she announced.

"Betty!" A smile bubbled up in Dory. "What's wrong?"

"Nothing. I just have a car full of food this young man asked me to buy, and I'm danged if I'm going to carry it all myself."

"One more dog," said Cadell, looking up. "What did you do? Shop for an army?"

Betty put a hand on her hip. "Clearly you don't shop for groceries here often. Shopping for two or three is impossible. So I hope you have some freezer space."

Dory felt a spark of curiosity. "Why is it hard to shop for small numbers?"

"Because an awful lot of people hereabouts have large families or shop for a couple of weeks at a time so they don't have to drive into town."

"Then what do you do?"

Betty's eyes twinkled. "I flirt with the butcher. He'll give me a single steak or chicken breast when that's all I want. However, he wasn't there today, so I had to get what's available. We could feed six or eight easily."

"I've got the freezer space," was all that Cadell said.

For a second, Dory had feared one of them would suggest inviting others over. She knew Betty wanted her to meet people, but not right now. Please, not right now. She was still feeling too stirred up.

"I'll help you," she said, ready to follow Betty to her car. She could at least do that much.

"I'll be along in just a minute," Cadell said. "Just

go ahead and put everything on the table. You know your way, Betty, right?"

"That house isn't so big I could get lost," Betty answered drily. "Yes, I've been here before, that time you had that barbecue." She eyed Dory. "The man is popular. I think a couple of hundred people showed up for that one. He had to send runners to the store for more burgers."

Cadell's laugh followed them. "It was the free barbecue," he called.

"More like the ostriches," Betty commented as she led the way around to the trunk. "They're the talk of the whole damn county."

"I've been missing you," Dory said truthfully as she helped Betty pulled the reusable bags from the trunk.

"You'd miss me a whole lot less if you weren't always working," Betty retorted. "Those times I dropped in, I felt like I was interrupting."

"You probably were, but that doesn't mean I minded."

Betty laughed. "I'll keep that in mind." They climbed the front steps together. The house had a wide porch, and the front door was unlocked. "How are you and that dog making out?"

"I love him," Dory said simply. "I hardly have to tell him what to do. He seems to know."

"Cadell's a great dog trainer, from all I've heard." Betty turned left into the kitchen. She'd been right: the house wasn't big enough to get lost in. They put the bags on the kitchen table—much bigger and sturdier than Dory's—and began unpacking.

"You sure went to town," Dory remarked as she began to stack items. "You could feed an army!"

"Hardly," Betty said. "But I figured you could take some of this home with you. What have you got in your refrigerator? Soda. In your cupboard? Popcorn. Really, Dory."

"Hey, it's not as bad as all that."

"Right," Betty drawled.

Cadell joined them and separated out the three steaks, the potato salad and the bag of frozen broccoli. "For our meal?" he asked.

"Yeah," said Betty. "Then I'm thinking Dory can take home most of the rest. I just don't want it to spoil in the meantime. Have you seen her refrigerator?"

Cadell grinned at her. "An awful lot of raw vegetables. And soda pop."

"Ha."

Dory smiled. "What is this, a conspiracy to feed me?"

"Somebody has to. You'd forget to go to sleep if you could."

Being here with the two of them made Dory feel even better than she had upon awakening that morning. The not knowing must have been making her feel worse than knowing. Cadell had certainly answered one of her most pressing questions about the murder, and that was a relief, too. The whole thing had been so horrific. Facing her brother's capacity for such acts removed all the doubt that had plagued her over the years.

He'd never loved her. He'd used her. And he'd use her again if he could. Strange as it seemed, that made her feel stronger. Made her feel that she could face the moment when he came for her. If he came for her.

Or maybe it had simply taken love out of the equation, relieving her of the torment of wanting to understand because she still remembered loving George. Her unwillingness to face what he really was in the hope that he wasn't that bad. Yet terrified of him at the same time.

A royal emotional mess, she thought as she helped make dinner. Clarity, after all that, was welcome.

Not that it killed her fears. She suspected they'd always be there if George was on the loose. But at least she didn't have to feel guilty and confused because he'd loved her as a child. He'd never loved her at all.

After a delicious dinner, they settled on the front porch with cups of coffee to enjoy the late-afternoon breeze.

"So," Betty asked after a while, "any news on George?"

"Not exactly," Cadell answered when Dory remained silent. He looked at her, not Betty, as he spoke, hoping he wouldn't see shadows chasing across her face again. So far her face remained untroubled. "He went to a halfway house in his hometown, then vanished from it after only two days. There's been no trace of him since. I'm keeping my ears and eyes on it, though."

"Good," said Betty. "Although if that man has a lick of sense, he'll stay far away from her."

Dory turned her head. "Why do you say that?"

"Because you're the one person he can reasonably be expected to contact. Does he think no one would be watching out for you?"

Betty had a point, Cadell thought, but she was reckoning without knowledge of the inheritance. George had been willing to steal to get what he wanted, to lie to keep it secret. And to kill when something went wrong. Right now he was out there with nothing. Why would he pass up a chance to go for all that money if he thought there was any way to get it? Cadell seriously doubted he would just show up and ask for it. After all, Dory knew who had murdered their parents. Why would she turn all that money over to him?

If he'd been keeping tabs on Dory, he probably knew she hadn't married and didn't have children. But even if he hadn't, he wasn't above taking out her whole family to get what he wanted. Of that Cadell had not the least doubt. He'd seen it in that graphic Dory had made. Clear as crystal.

Dory spoke, surprising him. "Cadell says the murder was premeditated."

Betty drew a shocked breath. "How can he know that?"

"Because I made a three-dimensional graphic of the kitchen and murder scene."

"Oh, my God," Betty breathed. "Why? Didn't it just make everything worse?"

"No. I was using it to try to understand. My therapist taught me to draw things I couldn't cope with. It just continued. So I had this graphic."

"Amazing," Cadell intervened smoothly. "She wanted her answers, and it was right there in her drawing or whatever it's called. Clear as day if you knew what to look for. The man's a psychopath, Betty. And yes, as a cop, I would call the murder impossible unless it was premeditated."

Betty leaned over and seized Dory's hand. "How are you coping with this? Are you okay?"

"I'm fine, actually. Knowing is better than not

knowing. Especially now that I don't have to wonder any longer if George loved me. He never did. He used me. I can't tell you why, but that makes this easier somehow."

"But you're still afraid?"

"Of course." Dory regarded her from eyes that suddenly looked hollow. "At least there's nothing left to muddy the waters if he shows up, but I think I'll be living with fear for a long, long time."

Cadell ached for the woman. He hadn't thought her good mood could survive the day, not as last night's blows began to sink in. But he *did* understand what she meant about it being easier knowing George had plotted the murder and had used her. It gave her permission to throw out her last lingering hopes about her brother. It gave her permission to hate him if she needed to.

It gave her permission to do whatever was necessary to protect herself.

He stared out over the rolling plain, the dry summer grasses, the tumbleweed caught on his neighbor's fence, feeling the weight of the mountains behind almost like a physical force. An energy. If they had lived and breathed, he wouldn't have been surprised.

Part of him hoped George Lake would show up here. Part of him wanted to wring the man's neck for all the suffering he had caused Dory.

Another, more sensible part of him hoped George was next seen somewhere in South America.

He didn't feel a lot of hope.

A little while later, Betty stood up. "I've got to get home. Dory, do you want to come with me?"

"I'll take her," Cadell said. "Her dog is here, too."

"Well, don't forget the food. I mean it, girl, you need to eat better. You're too thin already."

Dory gave a little laugh. "That's a matter of opinion."

Betty simply shook her head. "I don't know how anyone can stay that thin sitting at a desk all day and evening. Which means you're not eating enough. I'll say no more...until next time. So it's okay if I drop in?"

"Absolutely."

A short while later, Cadell watched the dust cloud rise behind Betty's small sport utility vehicle. It sat high enough to get over the rough roads around here but was just big enough to carry her, one passenger and her groceries. Putting Flash in there would have been ridiculous. A seventy-five-pound dog wasn't exactly small.

"It'll start getting dark soon," Cadell remarked.

"The mountains really suck the light out of the afternoon."

"I kinda like it. Anyway, let me know when you want to head home. You seemed to enjoy the day."

"I did." She gave him the full force of her lovely smile. "I really did. I didn't expect to, but...well, it was a relief. I suppose it won't last long."

"You never know. You could move your stuff out here if you think you'd feel more comfortable. The thing that bothers me, though, is that you'd be really isolated out here when I'm at work. In town, you can always get help."

All of a sudden, maybe because of the words *in town*, she slammed back to the little girl standing in the street screaming. She'd gotten plenty of help. Out here, no one would hear her scream.

"Thanks, but I'll stay where I am. Generous offer, though."

"Not entirely without ulterior motive," he admitted.

Startled, her eyes widened and she uttered a totally uncharacteristic "Huh?"

He chuckled quietly. "You know I'm attracted to you. Admit it. I've even let you know. From the first moment I saw you, I thought you were the most beautiful woman I'd ever seen."

He could see her cheeks redden. "Don't exaggerate."

"I'm not. It's my personal opinion. You're absolutely beautiful. But it's more than that. The better I get to know you, the more I want you."

He paused, watching a rapid play of emotions run across her face, too quickly to read.

"Anyway," he said, rising. "I don't want to scare you more. Let's pack up the groceries and the dog and get you home. You can decide if you want me around tonight."

"I'd like you to stay with me," she said.

Well, his heart leaped a little at that. *Down, boy*, he said to himself, as if he were one of his dogs. "Okay. Let me pack what I need for tomorrow, check the dogs one last time and then we'll load up."

Dory wondered why she'd asked him to stay. Flash was a great protector, but for some reason she felt safer with Cadell around. Crazy, since the last people in her life to make her feel at all safe had been her godparents, and it had taken them years.

Cadell brought out his uniform in plastic from a dry cleaner, neatly pressed on a hanger. His gun belt and all those accoutrements went in the back end with what looked like a whole bunch of other law enforcement stuff.

She peered in. "I never saw what was in a policeman's trunk before." About the only thing she recognized was the body armor.

"Not nearly as much as I used to cart in Seattle. There's actually room for the groceries."

He brought Dasher as well as Flash, probably because he needed his dog for work the next day. He'd also brought a sleeping bag.

She couldn't have begun to say why that made her feel cheated. She wanted no involvements, she didn't trust anyone except Betty and she was just beginning to trust Cadell.

No, it was best this way. Having him there would make her feel safer. Any more than that was a risk she didn't yet dare take.

Even if she felt the constant irritant of desire when he was around.

Over the next days, Dory and Cadell settled into a routine of sorts. She began working a little less during the daylight hours, instead driving herself out to spend time with him at his ranch as he trained dogs and tended the ostriches.

She thought he'd die of laughter when she told him she'd named the birds Itsy and Bitsy. Well, she was smiling more, too.

Except when she looked out over the wide-open spaces. Deep in her bones, she felt George was coming, that her fear was no figment of her imagination. Not since Cadell had mentioned her inheritance. People had killed for a lot less money.

A nugget of real anger had begun to burn in her, however. That man had destroyed her childhood, had blighted her life, and now he wanted to steal more. She was sure of it. If he'd cared about her at all, he'd have left instead of killing their parents. He wouldn't have taken them from her.

Ergo, he didn't care. Not at all. It was all about George.

The anger felt empowering, reducing her fear bit by bit. She knew the terror would return; it always had. But for now anger was a great reprieve. When she was out at the ranch with Cadell, she channeled that energy into working with the dogs, helping where she could. Daily she grew increasingly impressed with how much labor and patience went into training the dogs. Cadell wouldn't settle for half measures. These dogs would be walking with someone carrying a badge, and no one could afford the least miscalculation or misbehavior.

Most of the dogs were simply eager to please and did what was required of them. They were happy knowing their good behavior would be rewarded by playtime.

But one, a week later, failed the course.

"It's killing me," he told her as they watched a Malinois dash around the backyard. "He's going to have to go."

"Why? Are you going to put him down?" A new kind of horror filled her. She had grown attached to all these dogs.

"Of course I'm not going to put him down." He spoke almost sharply, then softened his tone. "No, nothing like that. But I can't curb his energy sufficiently. He's stubborn, and while all the things I teach these dogs should be fun for them, he keeps rewriting the rules. I'll wind him down a bit, and then he'll be suitable for a pet."

Considering she had been consistently amazed by how hard these dogs tried to please, she was surprised that any of them would fail the course. But when she thought about it, it made sense. One of the other things she'd learned from working beside Cadell was that the dogs had their own quite distinct personalities.

Cadell touched her arm, and a ribbon of pleasure ran through her. "It's okay, Dory. Not every dog is cut out for police work. Or rescue work. Just like some aren't cut out to be service dogs."

That sparked interest in her. "Do you teach service dogs, too?"

"Sometimes. That's a really special skill, though, so I don't do it often."

"I don't get it."

"It's simple. Service dogs need a lot of in-depth special training, and they have to be individually trained to serve a particular kind of companion. It's better to have someone familiar with all that do the job. But service dogs are expensive. Not everybody can afford one, and not everyone can be supplied by a charity. So occasionally, I do it. It's a hell of a lot bigger job than what I usually do. In many cases it's a matter of teaching dogs to do things they don't normally do. Whereas a police or rescue dog…the talent is pretty much innate for that kind of work. It's mostly a matter of directing it."

She laughed then. "And making sure they listen."

He winked and looked back at the corral. The dog was still running around, chasing and tossing the tennis ball for his own amusement. Itsy and Bitsy watched from their pen, their huge dark eyes intent.

"Now watch," Cadell said. "This is part of the problem." He whistled and called the dog's name. The animal looked at him, then went back to the tennis ball. "See? Two months and I still can't get him to come reliably. He'll make a couple of kids happy, but I can't send him out with an officer. *Most of the time* just won't work for them."

Later he persuaded her to stop at the diner for supper, although she wasn't entirely comfortable with being out in public. Dang, she thought, this man was pulling her out of her comfortable hidey-hole whether she wanted it or not.

But she felt safe going with Cadell, which worried her. Was she turning him into another bubble around herself, a safe place that held everything else at bay?

Troubled, she hardly said anything throughout the meal. She put down a hamburger and fries and didn't taste a thing.

She was a psychological mess. Nothing had ever completely sorted her out, but so far she'd managed not to hurt anyone else with it.

After dinner, he insisted on paying the bill, then surprised her again. "Let's go over to the sheriff's office."

She balked on the sidewalk. "Why?"

"You don't think I'm the only one trying to track down your brother, do you? I've asked for some help. I don't know about you, but I'd feel a whole lot better if we could pinpoint his location. Come on, nobody bites, and everyone would like to be sure you're safe."

Her temper flared. "Who gave you the right to discuss me with anyone?"

He put his hands on his hips, tilted his head and simply looked at her. God, he looked good in that blue shirt, jeans snug on his narrow hips, a cowboy hat shadowing his head. So good. Why the hell was she trying to start a fight?

But she hadn't given him permission to make her problems public, and it troubled her that other people knew. Even police officers.

"If you want me to apologize for protecting you," he said, "then I will. But I won't mean it, and you'll know it. So what's the point, Dory?"

"It's having so many people know about me! I don't like it."

"They're cops," he said, an edge of frustration creeping into his voice. "They know how to keep things secret. Not a one of them is going to gossip about you or your brother. Not here, not ever. Unlike the rest of this town, they know how to zip their lips about matters like this."

She couldn't speak, the turmoil inside her was so great. She felt as if she'd been left exposed in plain sight, tied out like a goat.

"Dory, you can't face this alone. You don't need to."

She'd had enough. She never should have come to this benighted town. Letting Betty talk her into coming here had been a huge mistake. Painful layers had been stripped from her once again. Her privacy. Her small sense of security. Even her coworkers had helped expose her.

George. She should have just hit the road and kept moving on a regular basis. The idea that she could now ever stay in one place seemed like insanity.

Without a word, she opened the back door of Cadell's truck and took Flash out. He'd been sitting in there in a wire cage with the windows open. Now, glad to be free, he jumped down eagerly.

"Flash, heel." She grabbed his leash and hooked it to his collar, then started walking home.

Alone.

Because alone was the safest way to be. The only way to survive.

Chapter 10

"Damn it," Cadell said under his breath. Had he really done something wrong by trying to trace her brother? Evidently she thought so. But it was the kind of thing he'd have done for anyone as a cop, and usually people were grateful for the interest and possible help.

She was one confusing woman. Life had seriously wounded her, and he wasn't sure that she was able to be truly rational when it came to George. Well, of course she wasn't. None of this was about reason. It was about gut feelings. He ought to know that.

After a moment's debate, he hopped into his vehicle and drove the half block to the sheriff's offices on the corner. A parking space awaited him, and he slid into it a little too fast. Then he walked into the station, where he was greeted by the dispatcher, a new hire who'd started only the month before over the old dispatcher's objections. He gathered that Velma, who'd been with the department longer than anyone could remember, felt she was the only one who knew how to do the job properly, which had caused a parade of new hires to quit over the years. Duty officers had often had to fill in the excess hours. Harriet, the new woman, was at least adequate, although Cadell was already wondering how long she'd last with Velma constantly carping at her.

"Gage?" he asked.

"In his office," Harriet answered. "Getting ready to leave."

Gage had an open-door policy, so Cadell didn't hesitate to walk himself back and knock. Gage looked up from the papers he was straightening, his burn-scarred face offering a crooked smile. "Hey. What's going on?"

"Apart from me stepping knee-deep into a pile of manure, nothing. I've got one less dog I'm going to train—wrong temperament. I'll have a couple more sometime next week."

Gage pointed to the chair. "And?"

"The manure, you mean?"

"Obviously."

Cadell didn't want to sit. "Dory Lake is furious with me for bringing you in on her problem, and she's walking home alone with her dog, Flash."

"The one you trained?"

"Yes."

Gage nodded. "Then she should be safe enough." But that didn't keep him from reaching for a radio. Five minutes later he had both deputies and city police officers advised to keep an unobtrusive eye on Dory Lake as she walked home. "Make sure she doesn't know."

The tension inside Cadell eased.

After a moment, Gage spoke. "She doesn't have any reason to trust us, you know. I read her case. Sure, cops took care of her after she ran out of that abattoir that had been her home, but I gather she hasn't trusted much since."

"No," Cadell admitted. "I may have blown it entirely, but I'll head over there in a little while and try to mend the fences."

Gage rocked back in his chair. "That's up to you."

"Meaning?"

"Exactly what I said. If you want to mend fences, mend them. I tried to call earlier, but you didn't answer. It seems her brother bought a bus ticket to Miami. Last week."

"So he's headed the other way."

"Uh, not yet. He never used the ticket."

Cadell closed his eyes. "Hell."

"Misdirection? Maybe. I've asked my counterpart in Florida to keep an eye out for him, but if he never went there…"

"I get it." Cadell stood up. "Thanks, Gage."

"You might not want to wait," Gage said as Cadell was walking out. "Don't give her time to raise the drawbridge over the moat."

Cadell paused and looked back. "You're troubled, too?"

"Let's just say from what I read, I wouldn't put anything past George Lake. Not even murdering his sister. She may have every reason to be terrified."

Dory didn't want to answer the knock at her door. She'd been vaguely aware that there seemed to be more than the usual number of police cars on the streets, and one corner of her mind wondered what was coming down.

But Flash's tail told her who was at the door. At the moment she wouldn't have opened it for anyone without knowing who was there. She needed to get a peephole installed, she thought vaguely, but right now there was no threat outside, simply Cadell.

She wasn't sure she wanted to see him ever again. She felt exposed, like a raw nerve ending, and it was his fault. Her past haunted her, not only within her own mind and heart, but everywhere else, it seemed. She'd had to tell her coworkers about her brother, which she'd never wanted to do, and now Cadell had broadcast it. So what if only other officers knew about it? She couldn't manage to hide from it, no matter what she did.

Flash danced a little from side to side, impatient. The slightest begging whimper escaped him. Damn it.

She opened the door at last. Flash did a little happy dance, then immediately sat, realizing he was in danger of breaking his rules. Not that Dory cared. She hadn't put him on duty yet.

Cadell looked somber, standing there with his hands at his sides. "May I come in?"

She wanted to slam the door in his face but caught herself in time. Just because the rest of the world was going insane around her didn't mean she had to, as well. Anyway, she was already crazy enough.

"Sure." She stepped back, letting him pass. Flash wiggled a bit in his seated position, hoping for a pat. He got one from Cadell as she closed the door.

She led the way to the shoddy living room and let

him have the couch. She had her doubts about the wooden rocking chair holding him for long. It barely held her.

"I ran into your neighbor out front. Marissa Tremaine. Have you met her?"

What did this have to do with anything? "Not yet." And with the urge to pack up and move on growing stronger in her, she doubted she was going to meet anyone.

"Her first husband was killed overseas a few years ago. She lives in that big house across the street with her new husband and child. It's nice to see her happy again."

Point? She wondered where he was going with all of this. So what if that woman was happy again? Happiness had eluded Dory most of her life. Oh, here and there she'd run into it, but it didn't last long. Somehow it felt disrespectful. All the therapy hadn't changed that, either.

"Look," he said, "I'm sorry I upset you, but I'm not sorry that I spoke to the sheriff about this. All he can access is public records."

Her lips tightened a bit, but she nodded. Public records? Anyone could get those if they looked.

"Anyway, it turned out to be useful. He found that your brother purchased a bus ticket last week from Saint Louis to Miami."

Tension hissed out of her like the leaking of a balloon. "He's headed away."

"We don't know that. The ticket hasn't been used."

That was all it took. Tension once again gripped her, winding around her every nerve ending. "Damn it," she muttered. "Damn him." She looked at Cadell. "He's not stupid."

"Nobody's counting on him being stupid. The sheriff has someone in Miami keeping an eye out for him, but if he uses the bus ticket, we should hear quickly."

"But he could give the ticket to anyone!"

"These days you can't travel by bus without ID. I doubt his prison ID would pass muster for anyone else unless he can find a near-identical twin. Regardless, he found the money to buy the ticket. I'm wondering what else he's been up to."

"Stealing," she snapped. "What he used to do all the time. I'm surprised he's not leaving a string of police reports in his wake. Oh, wait...he's probably being careful not to be noticed. So we really don't know anything."

"I'm afraid not."

But she saw that he didn't really believe this was nothing. No. She closed her eyes. "He tried to lay a false trail. He's coming here."

Cadell didn't immediately answer her. When he did, it was clear he was choosing his words carefully. "We can't know that based on just one thing."

Her eyes snapped open. "Tell me you don't really believe that."

His frown deepened, and he rose from the couch, pacing the small room, seeming to nearly fill it with his presence. She easily imagined that everywhere he went he made rooms feel small. "We can't know that," he repeated. "But it's suspicious enough to put me on alert. I'm sure the sheriff feels the same."

"Well, thank you for that."

He stopped and stared directly at her. "Meaning?"

She'd been extremely sarcastic, and she really hadn't meant to be. Or maybe she had. "Sometimes I feel as if people just dismiss me as crazy. I've felt that way for years. Well, I am a little crazy, I suppose. Untrusting, afraid of shadows…even when George was in prison, I didn't feel entirely safe. It just wasn't something I could explain. I guess I don't need to explain it anymore."

"Of course not. Anyway, I don't think you're crazy. What happened to you as a child was bound to have a long-term impact. I'd be amazed if it hadn't. *Then* there'd be something wrong with you."

Unexpected gratitude filled her, washing away the last of her irritation with him. "I'm sorry," she said finally.

"For what?"

"For getting so mad at you. You were right, you were only trying to protect me. I'm not used to that."

He shook his head a little. "I should have asked you first. I was high-handed, and I know it."

"The cop?" she said, allowing a little amusement to slip into her dark internal places.

He smiled faintly. "The cop," he agreed. "I have this thing about taking charge."

She rose from the rocker. There was little room to put between them, and other feelings began to niggle at her. Among them an overpowering desire for him, to put aside everything for just one night. She'd given in to that urge only a couple of times in her life and had learned how rarely it turned out well. But Cadell…since the beginning something about him had been calling to her on multiple levels. She wanted his friendship, though, and after what he'd said about his marriage, she doubted he'd be interested in anything more. Even though he'd mentioned it...

Her thoughts stuttered between one breath and the next. He'd told her he wanted her. What kind of delusion was she feeding herself now?

"I need a drink," she said and marched to the kitchen for a bottle of soda.

"I could do with something strong," he remarked, following her.

"I don't have anything. I don't like liquor."

"I meant coffee," he retorted. "I'm not much of a drinker myself. I've seen too many problems arise from alcohol. So call me an occasional one-beer man."

She screwed up her face. "No beer for me. I don't like the taste."

"Tsk," he said, but she could tell he was teasing. Someone teasing her was a relatively rare experience. Probably her own fault. After all, she was far from the easiest person to get along with. So many hot buttons, who would dare?

She started the coffee and got herself a cola. She was oranged out for the day. Settling in at the table, with Flash beside her, she sipped from the bottle and thought about her reactions that day. One minute she was enjoying Cadell's company, enjoying the dogs and—dare she admit it—amused by the ostriches, Itsy and Bitsy. Then she'd gone off like a rocket because he'd asked his colleagues to keep an eye out for developments with George.

"Why do you put up with me?" she asked bluntly. "I'm a pain."

"True." He leaned back against the corner while the coffeemaker hissed and streamed black brew. The corners of his eyes, however, were crinkled. "You don't come close to Itsy and Bitsy, however."

"What have those ostriches ever done to you?" Once again, amusement was trying to creep in. She decided to let it.

"They ate two of my favorite hats. Felt. Leather hat bands. Stretched just right to fit my head perfectly. I'm ashamed to admit that not until after they grabbed the second one did I realize it was going to be a continuing problem. I thought about getting a football helmet."

At that she cracked a helpless laugh. "Why did they want the hats?"

"Ask them." He shrugged. "Didn't take them long to shred them, though. The goats aren't nearly so bad."

She straightened. "You have *goats*?"

"Sorta, but not exactly. I pasture them farther from the house for one of my neighbors. I don't need them arguing with the birds or the dogs."

"But the dogs could hurt them, too."

He shook his head. "One of the ways I finish up training is by taking the dogs out to the goat pasture. A new distraction. If they can follow orders despite the goats, they pass."

She shook head, feeling a smile tickle the edges of her lips. "I thought you weren't ranching."

"I'm not. I've got two birds and I provide grazing for a neighbor's goats. That's not ranching. Ask anyone." The coffee had finished brewing and he snagged a cup from the cupboard to pour himself some. Then, at last, he gave her room to breathe again by coming to the table and sitting.

"The goats amuse me," he said. "Last spring I headed out there with one of my dogs. There were lots of little kids gamboling about, but one of those damn adult goats had jumped up on the roof of the hay shed. I still can't figure out how he got up there. I wonder if he was sick of all those noisy, excited kids. Or maybe he thought he was on guard duty. Anyway, I called my neighbor, asked what he wanted me to do about it."

"And?" She was loving this.

"He said, 'Damn goat got up there, he can get hisself down.' Which he did by the next day."

This was a whole part of the world she'd never been exposed to before, and it delighted her. Most of her life she'd lived in suburban or urban areas, and the last decade or so she'd pretty much become a troglodyte. Her graphics work endlessly fascinated her. It always offered a fresh challenge, and the amount of detail required kept her fully engaged.

But goats and ostriches? Her exposure had been one trip to a local zoo when she was ten, and she didn't remember any ostriches.

For the very first time, she considered the possibility of remaining here, once her problems with George were behind her. There seemed to be a whole wealth of new experiences awaiting her, something she hadn't thought about in a long time, if ever.

"You know," she said slowly, wondering how she had come to trust him this much, "I've let George deprive me of too much. Even when he was in prison, he controlled my choices in a lot of ways. Made me avoid other people. Made me distrustful." She paused then hit on the underlying truth. "It's time I realized that he hasn't been the one depriving me. I've made all the choices since he went to prison. He's no Svengali, controlling me at a distance."

She sighed and stared down at the table, at the familiar bottle of cola, and took a hard look at herself. "Plenty of people go through terrible things that leave deep and abiding scars. That doesn't mean they quit. I've quit, Cadell."

The chair creaked as he leaned forward and stretched out a hand, palm up. Uncertainly, she placed her hand in his. "You haven't given up," he said.

"What do you call it when I want to be a hermit? Betty's the only person I've let get close to me in my entire life."

"Including your godparents?"

"Including them. God, they gave me so much, and I gave almost nothing back, and now it's too late. There were people in college who tried to be my friends, but I always pushed them back until they quit trying. I've made myself a nice, safe little world, but it's far from complete."

A few beats passed before he responded. "What made you think of that?"

"Goats. Ostriches. Dogs." She shook her head and lifted her gaze to his. "It just struck me—I'm missing so many things by living in my little cave. It's not that I don't enjoy what I'm doing, because actually I do. But there's so much more out there. Maybe I ought to make a little time for it."

"You've been coming out to the ranch and working with me and the dogs," he reminded her.

"It's true. But that's a baby step. Maybe I should meet my neighbors. Talk to that Marissa you mentioned earlier. Meet other people."

"I'm not opposed to that, but I'd suggest you take it slowly."

"But why?"

"You don't want to overload yourself. You're not used to a big social life, are you?"

"I'm used to words on a screen," she admitted. "But maybe that's not enough anymore." Then she sighed. "Anyway, George."

"George?"

"All these ideas about changing my life would be easier to implement if I didn't have him hanging out there like an albatross around my neck." The part of her that had been trying to expand pinched a little. She felt it happen. "He's coming, Cadell. I think we both know that."

He didn't disagree.

"So all plans are on hold for now," she said. "I've got to deal with him somehow. If he just wants money, he can have it. If he wants me dead…well, I don't think I'm going to let that happen. So I'm going to stop hassling you about everything you do to try to help. I'm just sorry I'm taking over your life."

His hand tightened around hers. "You're not taking over anything. I'm exactly where I want to be."

She half smiled without humor. "Cop?"

"Cop," he answered. "But only partly. I also happen to like you. And yeah, you can be difficult, but who can't? I'm the take-charge guy who'll probably annoy you again. But unless you want to throw me out, this is where I'm staying."

A warm rush of gratitude filled her. "You're a nice guy, you know."

"Don't feed my ego." Then he grew serious. "I mean it, Dory. I'm here because I want to be. And I *do* like you, thorns and all."

"Why is that the sweetest thing anyone's ever said to me?"

"I can't imagine. But it's not sweet, it's just true." He paused. "I'm not one to shine people on. Never have been. If I have a problem with you, you'll know it. And if I say I like you, I mean it."

"Thank you." But even as the warmth continued to remain with her, her mind insisted on jumping around, which wasn't a usual state for her. She could summon a laser-like focus for hours when she needed it, and had long ago learned a reasonable control of her thoughts. That was what cognitive therapy was all about. Which was not to say she never slipped, and the news of George's release had caused a big-time slip. She'd come running to the first offer of a haven like a scared mouse.

But now she was glad she had, because she would have missed a lot if she hadn't.

"You're never going to believe this," she remarked, "but I like Itsy and Bitsy."

He didn't seem disturbed by her change of subject away from him liking her—a pregnant statement, full of possibilities she wasn't ready to consider. Possibilities she somehow knew she was going to hug to herself, because she liked him, too.

"I don't *dislike* them," he answered. "We have a mutually irritable relationship."

"Well, I'm not saying I want to pet either of them." She summoned a smile. "What happened to your mother? You never mentioned her."

"Where did that come from?" But he didn't wait for an answer. "She died shortly after I was born. Some kind of infection."

"I'm really sorry."

He shook his head a little. "I never knew her, never knew what it was like to have a mother. Sometimes I wished I was like other kids, but mostly I just accepted it. My father took good care of me. He worked me hard on the ranch. But he still made space for me to have a social life when I was in high school. I guess I never thought about the work he must have been doing when I wasn't there."

"But he didn't have a problem with you becoming a policeman?"

"If he did, he never let on. I may have mentioned it already, but by then he was winding the ranch down. Swore the land had more value than the livestock."

"Did it?"

"I lease a lot of it, so yeah, I guess. But then I look at those dang ostriches and wonder if they weren't a plot on his part to keep me rooted here. He was a great believer in roots. So am I, I guess. No regrets at all about coming back here."

"Roots." She spoke the word, feeling around it in her mind. "I'm not sure I really had any. Even when I was with my godparents. Uncle Bill, as I called him, was always being transferred. Sometimes we went with him if it was going to be a long stay, and sometimes Auntie Jane and I remained where we were. They did more of that when I was in high school. I guess they thought that was important."

"Wasn't it?"

She shrugged. "I don't know. Like I said, I don't make friends. Well, except for Betty. I met her in the high school in Saint Louis."

"Well, I'm your friend now, so live with it."

He was teasing her again, and she liked it. There was something so normal about it, a normalcy she'd avoided for years. Now that she was trying it on, a piece at a time, she was discovering that it was good.

She was acutely aware that these feelings were just a house of cards that would tumble the instant George arrived, but she couldn't give up these moments.

"He stole too much from me," she announced. Then, with a boldness she exhibited in her work, she rose and came to his side. "You busy tonight, Deputy?"

He looked up at her, his eyes narrowing. "I was planning on being here."

"That's not what I meant." Then she opened the dam she'd built to avoid thinking about what she truly wanted and let the needs pour through her for the first time. She was done holding them at bay. Good experience or bad experience, she didn't care. She was damn well going to have the experience.

"Come to bed with me," she murmured. "Now."

Chapter 11

Cadell froze, conflicting emotions welling up in him. He wanted this woman, no secret there, but he was also afraid of hurting her in some way. He wasn't even sure why she was asking so boldly. Every time he'd thought he glimpsed heat in her gaze, she'd concealed it quickly. Even so, just a short time ago she'd been furious with him, and now this? What had brought it on?

Rising, he slipped his arms around her waist and felt a tremor pass through her. There was only one way to know. "Why?"

She closed her eyes and shook her head a little but didn't draw away. "Is this the time for analysis?"

"I'm not asking for analysis. I want a reason. I'd like to know that you don't want to use me to make you forget. I need to be more than that."

"Nothing can make me forget," she whispered. "But

I've missed a whole hell of a lot because of that. I want you. I've wanted you for a while, but I kept coming up with reasons to tell myself no. I tried to bury it." Her blue eyes opened and met his straightly. "I can't bury it, Cadell."

He supposed that was honest enough. And from the tightness of her whispered words, he sensed this honesty wasn't easy for her. Why should it be? People talked easily about a lot of things, but sex seemed to be different. He'd also gathered that it was never easy for her to admit her own desires and needs, whatever they were.

Living in a cave hadn't helped her to blossom in many ways. She was a flower in desperate need of some sunshine.

He leaned closer and brushed his lips against hers. "You should know I want you, too. I've mentioned it more than once. But it has to be good, Dory. Are you sure this is the right time for you?"

"There'll never be a right time if I think about it too much. Cadell…"

These could be the tenderest moments between two human beings or they could become an ugly mistake. He wanted her more than he could say, but he needed to protect her, too.

So do that and quit being a jerk. See where it leads. Satisfy her in every way.

And to hell with his qualms. If regret were coming, it was going to have to wait a few hours.

He kissed her again, pushing his tongue a little past her lips until it met the gate of her teeth. Another shiver passed through her, then she let her head fall back and her mouth open. She hadn't changed her mind.

For right now, that was all he needed.

Flash stood up as Cadell swept Dory up into his arms. "Darlin', could you tell your watchdog to stay?"

Dory quickly clasped her arms around Cadell's neck and spoke thickly. "Flash, stay. Guard."

"You could sound like you mean it," Cadell remarked as he easily carried Dory the short distance to her bedroom.

"He better not get in the way," Dory mumbled. "You'd think he'd understand he doesn't need to guard against you."

"He does." He'd made sure of that over the past week. He just hadn't wanted the dog in here, where he might misinterpret something as play to join.

He set Dory down slowly, sliding her along the entire length of his body. She inhaled sharply as she felt him hard against her. No secret about his desire anymore. The pressure even through his jeans made him want to groan. He reminded himself to take his time, to make sure she could savor every sensation. Then thought started to slip from his grasp as she reached down and touched him through the denim.

"Mmm," she murmured.

He had this thing in his head, where he undressed a woman, then himself. Where it had come from, he had no idea, but it now completely vanished. She reached for the snaps on the front of his shirt and ripped them open ruthlessly. Then her soft, small hands began to explore his chest, sending shafts of pleasure through him with each stroke, each caress, even each pause as she learned his contours.

When she brushed over his small nipples, he was unable to repress a shudder.

"You, too?" she murmured. Before he could respond in any way, she'd leaned forward and taken him into her mouth, licking and sucking until the drumbeat in his head grew deafening.

Not only was this woman an angel, she was also a witch. A very talented witch with her tongue. Then she gave him a gentle nip, and he jerked.

He looked down at her, and there was no mistaking that pleased, sleepy smile. "Happy with yourself, huh?" he asked, his voice low. He was now sure he wasn't dealing with a totally inexperienced woman, which removed his last inhibition.

Oh, this was going to be good.

Reaching out, he grabbed the bottom of her T-shirt and pulled it over her head. Amazement grabbed him as he discovered a lacy bra, not at all what he would have expected. Delightfully, it pushed up the globes of her breasts invitingly.

Bending his head, he kissed the top of each breast, then ran his tongue lightly over her skin. A soft moan escaped her. Then, with a twist of his hand, he found the back clasp and released it.

At once the bra gave up its control, but before he could slide it away, Dory did so. She stood before him in the dim light from the hallway, making no attempt to conceal herself from his gaze. Instead she took his hands and pressed them to her breasts, then leaned in again to suck on his small nipples.

As he massaged her breasts, trying to judge her response by her soft moans, he felt her hands reach for the snap on his jeans. So that was how it was going to be?

Thrilled, he reached for her jeans, too. With almost surprising speed, underwear and denim fell to the floor.

Now the damn shoes. He pushed her down so that she sat on the edge of the bed, then squatted to remove her tennis shoes, her socks and the last of her jeans.

A giggle escaped her, surprising him.

"What?" he asked, looking up before attending to his own problem.

"Is there any graceful way to do this?" she asked.

"Yeah. Robes. Negligees. Nudity." But a smile creased his face as he sat beside her on the bed and fought his way out of his work boots and all the rest. He even remembered to grab a condom and roll it on. "Kind of a punctuation mark."

But then she stole his breath by reaching out to close her hand around his erection. "Dory..." Her name escaped him on a choked breath.

"You're a beautiful hunk," she murmured, her own breath beginning to come rapidly. "Can we..."

"Anything," he promised, caught in a consuming fire.

"Hurry," she gasped. "Rerun later."

He couldn't pass that up. All the finesse he'd been planning ceased to matter as the firestorm took over. As soon as she lay back, he slid over her, her delicious curves melding with his angles in all the best ways possible.

For an instant he couldn't even move because it felt so good. Catching her face between his hands, he looked down into her blue eyes. Botticelli angel. His for now.

Then he slid himself into her, feeling her rise up to meet him. Her legs twined around his hips, holding him as close as she could, and her body arched in response to his every thrust.

Almost too soon, she stiffened and cried out, a shudder running through her from head to foot. He couldn't contain himself another minute and joined her, erupting into her as if he were turning inside out.

When he collapsed on her, her hands settled lightly on his shoulders. A welcome. The most beautiful welcome of all.

George finally hitched a long ride on a big rig headed in the right direction. This one had pulled up alongside him as he'd been walking down the shoulder in the dark, unwilling to risk sticking his thumb out for fear the law would take an interest.

But this guy seemed bored with his long haul and wanted someone to chat with. The radio was unusually quiet. Well, George was a good talker, able to readily make up entertaining tales, and it was a small price to pay for getting to the truck stop just outside Conard City.

He cast himself in the role of a down-on-his-luck bartender who was heading home to see his sick mother. That one always brought sympathy his way. But he didn't linger over those details, instead coming up with amusing stories about things he'd supposedly experienced while tending bar. Soon enough, the driver was chuckling, and with the laughter the guy decided he liked George. George knew how to read people, and this one was in his pocket. Now he was assured the guy wouldn't drop him off at a crossroads in the middle of nowhere.

Eventually the driver asked him about being out of work. "I thought a bartender could always get a job."

"I will eventually, after I look in on my mother. But I was stupid, man. This woman looked thirty years old at least, and I served her without asking for ID. Bitch got me canned because she was working for the state. Trying to catch ordinary joes like me."

"That stinks," the truck driver said.

"Ah, my fault," George said. "It's getting harder and harder to tell how old a person is by looking. Always check the ID."

The driver snorted. "She must have been pretty."

George laughed. "Believe it. But I was still stupid."

"I make it a rule never to pick up riders," the driver remarked. "But I picked you up. I figured, what's the harm? I dumped my load in Omaha, couldn't find a return load anywhere, so I'm driving an empty trailer and burning gas. I ain't got nothin' to steal."

"What about your truck?" George asked.

"Not likely. This baby is old. She keeps going because I hold her together. Besides, she's got LoJack. I don't get home on time, my wife will be calling the cops."

"Tight rein, huh?" George asked. "No time for a little fun on the road?"

The driver laughed again. "Not for me."

Satisfied he had the driver exactly where he wanted him, George began to consider his plans for the days ahead. This guy would leave him at the truck stop, but he had no idea where Dory was in relation to that. She might have settled into a log cabin in the middle of nowhere.

Naw, probably not, he decided. He gathered from

what little he knew of her work that she must need a great internet connection. Those generally didn't reach isolated cabins.

So she'd be somewhere in or near one of the towns. There were a bunch of really small ones, then the big one where he'd be dropped off.

He rubbed his chin, feeling the beard he'd begun growing almost as soon as he'd been freed. Right now he didn't look a whole lot like himself, which was exactly what he wanted. The gray streaks in it helped, too, making him look a lot older.

But this town he was going to wasn't that big. It might be best to lie low as much as possible. Maybe people minded their own business, and maybe they didn't. He couldn't risk the latter, couldn't risk people commenting on a stranger who didn't have a job and didn't seem to be passing through. The last thing he wanted was anyone's attention.

The truck stop would probably be a reasonably safe place to hang on and off, with a constant turnover of clientele. But apart from that?

He needed to keep low.

Which multiplied the problem of locating Dory.

Around five in the morning, he gave up his comfortable ride with the trucker, asking to be let out in a larger town, away from his destination. A town that would give him the freedom to plan and the tools he might need.

And that sign about Rodeo Days meant there'd be a lot of strangers around. Good. Not a soul would notice him unless he wanted it.

He waved goodbye to the trucker as he stood beside the road. He'd long ago learned not to do anything that might make someone remember him, so he was always polite and friendly but not too much so.

Smiling, he started to whistle. He was on his way, getting it together.

Limp with pleasure and fatigue, Dory could hardly move. She lay on the bed waiting for Cadell to return and felt Flash lick her hand. The air was filled with the musky aroma of their lovemaking, delicious to her.

"Down," she said, barely able to muster the energy for that one word. She had forgotten that she could feel so good, so sated, so complete…if she ever had before. She felt the corners of her mouth curve, as if she couldn't stop smiling. Heck, her whole body was smiling.

She just hoped her impatience hadn't turned off Cadell. Well, she didn't know how to be a lady. She was a woman, and nothing in her life had made her feel she needed to take a backseat, although she'd learned online that there were plenty of men out there who wanted just that. Hence her secrecy about her identity.

Well, that and George. She knew he was coming. She could feel it. Somehow she would have to face him down, get him to move on and leave her alone. Money. With him it had always been about money. She'd gladly give him her last dime if he'd move to another continent.

The bed dipped as Cadell returned. She was surprised she'd delved so deeply into her thoughts that she hadn't heard him coming. The light was still dim, coming from the bathroom, but she could see he was smiling. She reached up a hand and cupped his cheek.

"I'm limp," she told him.

His smile widened. "You're not the only one. And we're not done."

Her heart leaped. "We're not?"

"Oh, no. I hardly got to explore you. That needs a bit of correction." He stretched out and propped his head on his hand, still smiling. "Close your eyes. Just *feel*."

Excitement was already galloping through her veins, though just a minute ago she would have thought it impossible. She obliged, closing her eyes, nearly holding her breath in anticipation.

First came the featherlight touch of his fingertips, tracing the shell of her ear, the line of her jaw. Passing sweetly over her lips until they parted and she drew a long, quivering breath. With each moment, every nerve in her body felt as if it were growing more sensitive.

Then his touch trailed lower, remaining light, offering no pressure. Across her shoulders, her collarbones, down to her fingertips and then back up the inside of her arm. Now a helpless shiver raced through her.

"Easy," he murmured. "Just enjoy."

Oh, man, was she enjoying. When he found her breasts at last, she bit her lip, hoping...and his fingertips moved on. She could have cried out.

He trailed his hand down, tracing the most fragile of ribbons across her midriff, then lower, making circles around her navel, moving side to side but taking ever so long to dip lower.

Just as she thought he would, his hand slipped down her thigh, stroking the outside first, then the inside, but coming no nearer to her most sensitive places.

He was driving her out of her mind with an impatient excitement like none she had ever known. Then her other leg, down the outside then up until he returned to her belly.

Now! Please, now! Her thoughts had turned into a stew of boiling need and even some fear that he might leave her like this, hungry but unsated. She felt as if she were vibrating from head to toe, like a stringed instrument that he was playing skillfully.

Oh, so skillfully.

Then, causing her to suck air between her teeth, his fingers slid downward and found her moist cleft. She could no longer hold still but arched upward against his touch, needing so much more.

For a little while, he indulged her, stroking her with gentle fingers, but then it stopped.

She couldn't even open her eyes, she couldn't stand it. "Cadell…"

"Easy."

She felt him part her legs, felt him settle between them, then the most exquisite sensation in the world, almost painful in its intense pleasure. With his tongue, he drove her upward until she mindlessly dug her fingers into the sheets and hung on for dear life.

When at last she reached the pinnacle and shattered into a million flaming pieces, all that was left of her was woman, flying free among stars.

Cadell's arms wrapped her in warmth and strength. He'd pulled the blanket up over them and held her close, close enough that she could feel his hard contours, the slightest movement as he breathed. The whisper of his breath on her hair. Her own arm lay over his waist, feeling more of his warmth, more of his skin.

The intimacy of the moment pierced her. She'd taken

a couple of lovers before, never for more than a single night or two, but those experiences had been nothing like this. She'd walked away from both of them thinking she was really not missing much by avoiding men.

All that had changed in an earthquake named Cadell. The intimacy. The closeness. Again, the understanding floated through her. She had never felt this close to anyone, at least not since her childhood.

She should have run from it. Where had love and trust gotten her the last time? But she could not quell it. It filled her, altering her, changing her, and she didn't want to fight it.

Come what may, she thought sleepily, she was going to be a different person. Maybe a better person. Now if only they could get rid of the threat.

Then, safe in the arms of a man who had taken it on himself to protect her, she drifted off into the happiest dreams she had enjoyed for years.

Cadell awoke first in the morning. Slipping carefully out of bed, he pulled on his jeans and boots, then took Flash for a run in the backyard. When they came back in, he started a pot of coffee for himself and began looking for something to use to make a breakfast for the two of them.

After last night, he had the appetite of a lumberjack.

Then he paused, realization setting in almost hard enough to knock the wind from him. The woman who had warned him that she didn't trust anyone had trusted *him*.

And not just last night. Little by little she'd been opening herself, sharing herself, talking about herself, her feelings, her thoughts. No longer was it all about

George. No, it was sometimes about the changes in her, her personal growth.

She'd shared herself in so many ways over the last couple of weeks. Even announced she was thinking about meeting other people.

Dory had come a long way.

And so had he. He sat abruptly, waiting for the coffee, waiting for the changes inside him to settle. He'd tried to help a woman who had good reason to be afraid. He'd thought at the outset he'd give her the dog, maybe check up on her from time to time. Instead his days had steadily become more and more entwined with hers. Especially since the moment when she had shared her graphic of the murder with him. He'd looked into a small child's heart and seen how it had affected the woman she'd become.

With that, all distance on his part had vanished. All thoughts of forever avoiding another debacle like Brenda went away. He'd crossed his own personal barriers with Dory, and he wasn't at all sure he wanted to put them back in place.

What he did know was he wanted more than a one-night stand with her. Whether it grew into anything more than casual, only time could tell, but for the first time since Brenda, he was willing to give it a chance.

Besides, he was growing very fond of Dory. As she emerged from her shell, he saw more than a Botticelli angel who took his breath away. He saw a rose blossoming into fullness, no longer a cramped bud hiding in work and her computers. She was showing strength. Fortitude. Determination. She was no longer talking of running.

For his part, he felt truly alive in every way this morning. He kind of hoped the feeling would last.

He'd rediscovered the man he used to be. What could be wrong with that? It felt good.

Smiling, he went back to trying to devise a breakfast from the slim pickings in her fridge. He guessed he was going to have to be the cook as long as they stayed together.

"I thought I smelled coffee," Dory said from the kitchen doorway. She wore a blue robe and slippers.

He looked over his shoulder and smiled at her. "It's there if you want some. I hope you don't mind, but I was looking through your fridge and cupboards trying to find something to make for breakfast."

She arched a brow at him. "You don't eat cereal?"

"Not often. Most of what you have in there is too sweet."

A slow smile spread across her face. "Try it at 3:00 a.m. after working for ten hours. It's the absolute greatest energizer." She started to move past him, but he snagged her around her waist and drew her down onto his lap. At once she wrapped her arms around his neck.

He smiled into those blue, blue eyes of hers. "Good morning, darlin'." Then he kissed her soundly, feeling his body stir in response. This, he thought dimly, was not likely to lead to breakfast.

He pulled his head back reluctantly, enjoying the way her eyes had closed, the way her mouth looked slightly swollen. Beautiful. "But this won't feed us," he said gruffly.

"Depends," she answered pertly, her eyes opening. Then with a little laugh, she slid off his lap. "You're too distracting. So no cereal, huh?"

Then she pulled a can of soup out of the cupboard. "Will you eat lunch for breakfast? Because I can make a mean grilled cheese sandwich, and with a little tomato soup, I think we can top the tanks."

Why hadn't he thought of that? Dang, was he getting too mired in his routine?

What made the breakfast wonderful, however, was the woman sitting across from him, smiling and chatting as if she hadn't a care in the world.

He knew that wouldn't last. It couldn't.

"I need to go in to work for a couple of hours today," he told her as he ate his second sandwich. "But then, if you can spare the time, we can go out to my place. Doc Windwalker is bringing me a young dog he thinks might be perfect to train as a companion for a little autistic boy."

"I thought you didn't do that kind of thing."

"I don't do it often. I can call on help if I need it, but this has landed in my lap. The family can't afford to go elsewhere, so…" He shrugged. "We'll see what we can do."

The smile she gave him then made him feel about ten feet tall.

By the time Dory showered, dressed and went to her computers, she found a raft of messages awaiting her. The team was discussing a potential new project and whether they could accomplish what the client wanted in the time allotted. Dory read the specs, such as they were, and the comments from the rest of the team. It was clear everyone wanted to do it, but it was going to be a huge challenge, something they'd never done before. Almost like going back to the very beginning of graphics design. It intrigued her, too, as she thought about it.

Then a private message popped up from Reggie.

Where you been?

Busy. Sorry. Life.

Yeah, I know about the whole life thing. Was getting worried because of your brother.

I'm fine. Pretty protected, too, by a trained guard dog. She didn't want to mention Cadell. Not their business.

Well, good. But I needed to let you know something. We had a hack attempt from a library in Nebraska a few days ago. Our webmaster didn't think a whole lot about it, just put it in his report. Anyway, I'm telling you because the hacker was trying to get into our personnel files. He failed, but…

Thanks, Dory typed back quickly, even as her heart slammed into high gear. How many days ago?

There was a pause and she could imagine Reggie switching to another file. Then came the answer.

Five days.

Five days was long enough to get here from Nebraska. Plenty long enough. All of a sudden the day didn't seem as beautiful as it had just a few minutes ago.

Then another ping. Reggie typing more.

If there's anything at all we can do, just ask. Nobody's happy about this.

Thanks, she typed again. I really appreciate it.

Now about that new project...

She was glad to think about the project. Work had been her salvation for a long time, and it was again that morning. The less room she made in her thoughts for her brother, the better she felt.

Heck, she hadn't even had a nightmare last night. That made her smile even though she felt as if a dark cloud were steadily moving her way.

But then it occurred to her that she needed to let Cadell know about this. It might be nothing. Or it might be George.

Dory's phone call blew up Cadell's plan for the day. Or at least delayed things a bit. He called Mike Windwalker and asked him to postpone bringing the family and the dog to his place for a couple of hours. Mike thought he could manage that, but if not what about tomorrow?

"Tomorrow would be fine, too, but I'm pretty sure I can look over the situation this afternoon. I'm just sorry about the holdup."

"I know all about that," Mike responded drily. "I'm a veterinarian, remember?"

A vet with a wife and a daughter in a wheelchair. He probably hated it when he couldn't get home on time.

Then he headed for Gage's office. The sheriff looked up expectantly.

"I'm not sure this means anything," Cadell began, "but I think we need to check it out. Dory's coworker told her that someone attempted to hack the company's personnel files from a library in Nebraska."

"Maybe nothing," Gage said, but as he straightened, it was clear he didn't believe it. "Can we find out which library?"

"I'll call Dory right now."

It took Dory a few minutes to realize how many times her cell phone rang. Persistent, whoever it was. She surfaced from her study of the new program specs and reached for it. Cadell? And for once she felt as if her heart smiled.

"Hey," he said warmly. "Got a question for you."

"Sure."

"Is there any way to find out which library that hack attempt came from?"

"Hang on while I message Reggie. It might take a few if he's busy. Would it be better if I called you back?"

"I'll wait." There was no mistaking the resolve in Cadell's voice. The hack attempt, which she had been trying so hard to forget, surged back to the foreground, and with it her level of anxiety. Clearly Cadell didn't think it was innocent.

"God, what next," she muttered as she typed rapidly to Reggie.

Cadell answered her. "Next I'm going to come over and get you, and we're going to meet a family with an autistic child and try to make him happy. In the meantime…"

In the meantime. Yeah. She drummed her fingers

impatiently, waiting for Reggie. When nearly five minutes had passed, she got his familiar Yo.

I need to know which library that hack attempt came from.

What I got is an IP.

Give it to me, I'll look it up.

K.

Another pause, then a string of numbers, three at a time with a decimal between them.

Thanks, she typed. I'm liking the project, btw.

Great!

Then she picked up her cell. "I've got the IP address. For nongeeks, that means it can lead you right to the computer that was used, as long as he didn't use an anonymous server."

"I'll take it."

"I can also look it up for you."

He gave a quiet laugh. "Maybe you should do that. We could use a more advanced IT department here, but who has the funds?"

"I hear a lot of police departments have that problem and hence still use fax machines."

"You'd be right."

"So last century," she remarked, trying to sound light when she didn't feel good about this at all. It could be a random hacker, though. It always amazed her how many brains wasted themselves on trying to disrupt other people's computers just for kicks.

It didn't take long to trace the IP. The internet was decent about keeping track of itself, or it would have blown up and become useless from the start. "Okay," she said to Cadell. "It's one of four computers assigned to a library in Landoun, Nebraska. Small, like Conard City."

"So maybe the librarian will remember someone. Okay, thanks. I'll get back to you shortly."

She wondered if she would survive waiting even a few minutes. Then, with determination, she pushed all thoughts of George aside. Focus on her job. She was good at burying everything else.

Soon she was lost in a world of storyboards the team had begun to build, offering a few opinions, making some changes that would be a little less difficult to carry out.

But then her phone rang, and all hope of distraction fled. It was Cadell.

"Okay," he said. "The librarian didn't recognize George's inmate photo when we emailed it to her. But she did say a few days ago a man she didn't know used the computer for several hours. He had a thick beard, though. So I'm sending George's inmate photo to the state to have them put a beard on it. Just in case. I'll pass it by the librarian and see if we come up with someone who resembles her unknown man."

Dory sagged in her chair. "Thank you," she answered. "I have the software to put a beard on him, too, if it would save time." She needed to know. Even as she sagged, a vise had gripped her heart. She was sure it was George. Who else would be trying to penetrate Animation's personnel files?

"Dory? You know this is slim."

"Then why am I having so much trouble believing it?" she snapped.

He paused. "So you've got software that can do this? I'll be right over with his faxed photo."

She disconnected, staring at her screen, knowing full well that she wasn't going to be able to focus until she'd dealt with the photograph. It was as if everything had moved out of the realm of possibility and into the realm of reality.

She felt a poke on her leg and saw Flash nudging her and looking up at her. Almost automatically she reached out to pet him. "Can you hold it until Cadell gets here?"

Because all of sudden she didn't even want to walk into her backyard alone.

George heisted a pickup and switched the plates with a similar vehicle before pulling it out of the dirt parking lot from among a great many others. Rodeo Days must be a big thing around here. Once he was safely out of town, he hit the state highway, and at the first opportunity in the middle of nowhere, he pulled onto the shoulder and began to check what was in the truck. Registration and insurance. Good, but he still had no license. He'd better not get stopped.

And a gun? That might be useful. Although guns made a mess, and he wanted Dory's death to look accidental. In the back of the truck, which was dirty enough to convince him it was used for some serious work, he found other items that could be useful, from rope to barbed wire, regular tools and then something he couldn't at first identify.

Curious, he pulled out the three-foot-long rod by its handle, then noticed the two tines on the end. It looked like a Taser. An awfully big Taser. He pressed the button and saw the spark with satisfaction. A cattle prod. He smiled. That could be useful. He just wished it were smaller in size so it could be more easily hidden.

He climbed back into the cab and drove toward Conard City. Not much longer now. He had plenty of tools in this truck that could be useful. Now all he had to do was find his sister without being seen himself.

There was a battered, misshapen cowboy hat on the seat beside him, looking like someone's castoff. He put it on, pulling it low over his brow. Beard or no beard, the less anyone could see of his face, the better. He whistled tunelessly, thinking that it was a beautiful day. The wide-open spaces didn't even bother him as much anymore.

Life was finally going his way.

Chapter 12

The photo Cadell brought Dory was from a fax machine. Not the highest resolution, but she put it through her scanner and some software to enhance the clarity. Then she plugged it into the software that would add a beard.

"Did the librarian say what kind of beard?"

"Full. Not terribly long."

"Okay. This is going to take a while, though."

"How long do you think?"

"A few hours."

"Then let's go see an autistic child about a dog."

"Sounds good to me." The last thing she wanted to do was hang around here wondering and worrying. Keeping busy had always been her salvation. But then she found she couldn't stand up.

"Oh, God," she whispered.

"What?"

"I just looked at my brother for the first time in a quarter century. He could be a stranger, Cadell. I barely recognize him."

"Let's hope he has the same problem with you." He squatted. "You going to be all right?"

"I always am," she said irritably. But her legs still felt like noodles, and she reached for the fax again, staring at a face that had changed an awful lot but still belonged to the brother she had once loved.

"It's a shame," she said presently.

"What is?"

"That he was never the person I thought he was. That person could have done wonderful things with his life. Instead…" She didn't finish. She tossed the photo to one side.

He straightened and touched her shoulder. "Put George on the back burner while your software works. And remember, if he really is looking for you, he has to find you first."

"Maybe I need a wig and some big sunglasses."

He looked at her, then his eyes twinkled.

On the ride out to Cadell's place, she once again drank in the countryside. At first it had been so different from anything she'd known before that it had looked dry and scrubby to her, not especially attractive except for the mountains.

But time had taught her to see differently. All that space, dotted occasionally with copses of trees, a lot of scrub and the tumbleweeds, fascinated her. She loved to see the wind catch a tumbleweed and carry it along.

"Every place has its charms," she remarked. "It took me a while to see them here."

Cadell tossed her a grin before returning his attention to the roads. "I was overwhelmed when I first moved to Seattle. All the green seemed suffocating—there were no long lines of sight. Kinda claustrophobic at first. But it didn't take long before I began to see it differently. Anyway, when I came home here to visit, *this* place looked bad to me. I used to run up into the mountains just to see the forest. So yeah, I get what you mean."

"Well, I'm beginning to appreciate it. Mostly I love the mountains, though."

"One of these days soon I'll take you up there. Some great vistas overlooking the valley. And lots of trees."

She laughed, feeling the last remnants of her concern about George slip away. He could wait, at least for a few hours. Being with Cadell was more important.

And certainly a whole lot more pleasant.

Cadell had just enough time to make some coffee to offer to Mike when the vet arrived in his fully equipped van. The man had to be ready at a moment's notice to provide care to livestock almost anywhere around here, and he had half a clinic in the back of his vehicle.

A tall Cheyenne with black hair he refused to cut short, Mike was a great guy. Over the last couple of years his practice had grown by leaps and bounds. So had his kennels and the number of dogs and cats he had for adoption.

He greeted Cadell warmly, asking after the ostriches.

"Itsy and Bitsy are doing fine, as far as I can tell."

"Itsy and Bitsy?" Mike's eyes widened.

"Blame her," Cadell said with a grin, indicating

Dory with his thumb. Then he introduced the two of them. "So now, what kind of dog did you bring me?"

"A good one, I think," Mike said, walking around to the back of the van. "He's a mutt, already neutered. Near as I can tell he's got some golden Lab in him and something much smaller. Regardless, he's just about two, so he's lost some of the puppy energy, he's smart and he listens. So we'll see."

Mike opened the carrier in the back of his van, grabbed a lead already attached to the dog's collar, then let the animal jump down.

Cadell thought he looked like a somewhat miniaturized golden Lab, good-looking but probably not big enough to intimidate a child of about six. "Great choice," he said. "Listen, you know where the coffee is. Go on in and help yourself. I want to run him around the corral and get to know him. Does he have a name?"

"I've been trying to avoid that."

Cadell arched a brow. "So what have you been calling him?"

"Dog."

"Ha!" Cadell laughed, and Dory joined in.

"But why avoid a name?" she asked Mike.

"Because I'll get attached. Because whoever adopts my animals is going to want to name them. I realize that's ridiculous, because I've found you can change a dog's name a dozen times and he'll still answer. But…" He shrugged. "Okay, I don't want to get attached. Sooner or later I've got to let them go."

At that moment, Flash, who'd been allowed his freedom in the kennels and fenced yard, came dashing up to sit beside Dory. He regarded the new dog inquisitively, tilting his head a little to one side, his tail sweeping the ground in a friendly manner.

"Test one," remarked Cadell. The small golden came trotting over and began to sniff Flash from top to bottom. Flash lay down as if to make it easier, and soon the golden was lying right beside him. Friends, it seemed.

"Okay, no dog aggression," remarked Cadell. "Dory, keep Flash beside you while I take Dog into the corral."

Dory noticed as she and Mike walked to the back of the house that the ostriches leaned over their pen's fence as if they wanted a better look.

"I don't think they've forgotten me," Mike remarked. "Or the injections I gave them. I'm not a popular person with them."

"Is anyone?" Dory asked.

Mike chuckled. "They're really not so bad, usually. They'd rather run than fight. But getting into a fight with one…well, I wouldn't recommend it. They may not have teeth, but they can peck with a lot of force. Then, while the nail on their single clawed toe on each foot isn't the sharpest, they pack a hell of a kick. Bones could break. If they're trapped and feel threatened, a human might not survive it."

Good to know, Dory thought. Not that she ever intended to get into the pen with them.

Cadell was already at work with Dog, and from his face and posture, Dory thought he was pleased. In almost no time at all, the dog was following commands to sit and stay. When Cadell saw Mike and Dory approach the corral fence, he called out, "Good one. Smart and eager to please. That's what we want, right? A companion."

"As far as I know, they don't have any other needs for their son. Just that he be perfectly safe with the animal because…well, I guess the child can get rough and loud sometimes."

"What child can't?" Cadell asked rhetorically. Then he turned his head. "I guess that's them."

Dory peered in the direction he was looking and saw a dust cloud just beginning to come up the long drive.

Soon a family of three, one of whom was a thin boy of about six, were coming around the house to the back. The boy was incredibly silent, Dory thought. Sadly so. He walked past the kennels of dogs, looking at them but not making a sound.

His parents were young, dressed like a hardworking ranch couple, in jeans and somewhat faded shirts. Neither of them held the boy's hand.

"Brad doesn't like to be touched," the woman said. "I'm Letty Embrow, and this is my husband, Jase." She looked at Mike. "What do you think?"

"I picked the one I think is best. Cadell's pleased with him."

Her eyes trailed to Cadell. She seemed like a pleasant woman, but right now there was a deep tension riding her. Because she didn't know how her son was going to react? Or was she afraid the dog might do something?

They walked together, with the Embrows in the rear, until they reached the gate into the training yard. Cadell looked at the parents. "Can I talk to him, or do you need to do that?"

"Let's see what happens," Letty answered.

So Cadell squatted and looked at the child from about five feet away. "I hear you want a dog."

Dory thought the boy's gaze fixated for the first time since he'd arrived. His attention was fastened to Cadell.

"I have one I think you'll like, Brad. But you and I have to go inside the fence to meet him. If you like him, I'll get him ready to go home with you."

Cadell glanced up. "I may need a couple of days to be sure he's well trained, but I'd like you to bring Brad every afternoon to work with him. Doable?"

Both parents nodded, and Cadell returned his attention to the boy. "Want to come through the fence and meet the dog, Brad?"

For the first time, the boy became animated. He bobbed his head in the affirmative. Dog was waiting on the other side of the fence a few feet away. The instant Cadell opened it wide enough, the little boy slipped through and ran right up to the dog.

Dory heard everyone's breath catch. Then Brad threw his arms around Dog's neck and crowed, "Doggy! Doggy!"

And Dog didn't seem to mind it one bit.

Magic, thought Dory. There was still magic in the world.

The long summer twilight covered the world when Cadell and Dory got back to her house. They'd taken time to care for the animals, cleaning kennels, letting the ostriches into the larger corral so they could clean up their small pen, then putting them back in the pen and feeding them again.

They stopped at Maude's on the way back for carry-out, because Dory was concerned about her work. "I keep taking time off," she told Cadell frankly. "I've got to make up for at least some of it."

"Yeah, for me working with the canines is the largest part of my job. I appreciate all your help, though."

"I've enjoyed doing it. I never really had the chance to find out before, but I like animals. Someday I want to meet the goats."

"That's easy enough."

They pulled into the driveway behind her car, then climbed out with the bags and started for the front door.

The evening suddenly changed for Dory. "God," she whispered.

Cadell stopped and faced her. "What?"

"I feel watched. That's ridiculous." She tried to brush it away, but the feeling was an icy one, just awful.

Cadell set the bags on the rickety porch bench. "Unlock the door, but stay here. I'm going to make sure no one got into your house."

"Why would…"

"I'm just going to make sure. Meanwhile, you look around and see if something has changed right around the house, something minor that troubled you, okay?"

So she stood there with Flash sitting at her side. Foolish as it felt, the feeling would not go away, and she put him on guard. The dog missed little, but when she ordered Flash to guard her, his attention grew more intense.

She studied the house as Cadell had told her to but didn't see anything amiss. Not that she'd paid that much attention. The house had never been intended to be more than a way station for her.

Although maybe… But she pushed the thought

aside. She and Cadell might be having sex now, but that didn't necessarily mean anything about next week.

She watched as lights turned on inside the house. He was going room by room. Like someone could hide in her very few rooms. She might have been amused if the itchy feeling of being watched hadn't persisted.

She studied the street, looking for another human being, but most humans were probably indoors eating dinner, or maybe in their backyards having a picnic. The street was as silent as it was empty.

She heard an engine start way down toward the edge of town. A battered old red pickup appeared eventually, and she watched it approach. Before it got near, however, Cadell opened the door.

"All clear inside. Did you note anything?"

"Nope." She stepped in beside him, hardly noticing as the pickup rolled by behind her. "I guess I was just feeling too good most of the day. God forbid I should forget George for too long."

His eyes crinkled as he smiled, but she didn't miss the way he locked the door behind them.

"Do you want to check your computer for the image of that guy first, or do you want to eat? I'd hate for the food to get cold. Maude's a master with steak."

"Let's eat." Honestly, right now she didn't want to see her brother's face again, bearded or not.

Cadell carried the bags into the kitchen. Flash followed along hopefully, but he got dry food and a fresh bowl of water. Dory wondered what Cadell would think if she fed the dog people food. Sometimes she was tempted.

They sat facing each other, Cadell with a tall coffee from Maude's, she with another one of her inevitable soft drinks. The sandwiches were perfect, the steak tender enough to melt in the mouth, and still warm. He'd been right not to wait.

"I'm surprised you didn't dismiss my feeling," she said when her appetite settled into more reasonable proportions. She had no idea what had made her so hungry. Must have been all that fresh air, because it wasn't unusual for her to miss lunch.

"I never discount the feeling of being watched. Plenty of people get it sometimes, and the amazing thing is that plenty of people are right. It's not always important, of course, but when you're a cop and you get the feeling someone is focused on you? You don't ignore it."

"I just want you to know I appreciated it. It's not a sensation I've had very often. Besides, there was no reason to be afraid of it with you right there."

Again that smile danced in his dark eyes. "I'm no superhero, but thanks for the vote of confidence."

He really was a nice guy, she thought as she continued eating. She'd have grown impatient with herself long ago. Amorphous fears about a brother who might never want to see her again. She wished she could just erase him from her memory.

But erasure had proved impossible, and Cadell wasn't about to dismiss the possibility that George might feel he had business with her. Money business. Well, that wouldn't surprise her.

She shifted a little in her chair. "Do you have any idea how much I inherited?"

He swallowed and took a drink of coffee. "Not really. The news articles from back then suggested a million-dollar insurance policy."

She snorted. "So much more sensational, huh? No, actually it was about half of that, including what my godparents got for me from the sale of the house. That's a lot of money—it might have grown over the years sitting in CDs and bank accounts, but I don't know. You see, I have a vice."

His brows rose. "Tell me it's not cocaine."

If she'd felt more comfortable, she would have laughed. "No. I can't touch it, I told you. But when I turned twenty-one I made just one change to the trust with my godparents' permission... I started donating half the interest."

"That's a *vice*?"

She shrugged faintly. "Some financial advisers think so, but not me. They handle the trust and apparently keep it growing. Anyway, the interest goes to various causes, mostly those helping children. Which brings me around to today. Brad couldn't have afforded a companion dog without you and Mike Windwalker stepping up, right?"

"I don't believe so."

She nodded. "Maybe that'll be my next charity. Kids like Brad who need companion animals. They shouldn't be out of anyone's reach."

A warm smile spread across his face. "I like the way you think, Dory Lake."

"George wouldn't agree. When my godparents set up the trust they made it clear that they wanted me to save it for the future. I didn't have any reason to disagree, but when I turned twenty-one, ownership passed to me. I left everything the way they'd made it except the use of the interest. And that's when I made it irrevocable. If George had ever tried to contact me for money, I wouldn't have responded. Not by then."

"Theoretically he didn't know where you were to contact you."

"Probably not. My godparents moved a lot because of Uncle Bill's job." She sighed and pushed her dinner to one side. "I'm tired of every discussion coming back to him. I want him gone. Out of my life. Not constantly hanging over my head." She closed her eyes briefly, then opened them so she could see his face. "The thing is, I think I create that threat myself more than anything. He might be headed to the opposite end of the country. He might not want to see me any more than I want to see him."

"It's possible."

She didn't miss the doubt in his tone. He believed George was going to show up. Her biggest fear was going to materialize. And Cadell intended to be at her side as much as he could. Gratitude filled her.

She looked down at Flash. "He'll take care of George."

"He'll certainly try."

The word hovered in the air along with her fears. Flash would try. No guarantees.

"Will you stay tonight?" she asked, trying to sound casual.

"I wouldn't be anywhere else in the world."

George never would have dreamed it would finally be so easy to find his sister. Changing license plates on the truck had made him think of something that hadn't occurred to him before: she had a car, and that was information he could get for a fee from a private company online. The library in the place he thought of as "Rodeo Town" along with a prepaid debit card, had made it possible for him to find out what kind of vehicle she was driving. It still bore Kansas plates, the site claimed, which would stick out in Wyoming, even though the site wouldn't give him the plate number or VIN.

And lo and behold, when he drove through Conard City late last night, he'd seen it. There she was. The only problem was that parked behind her car was a police SUV. Sheriff's department. K-9 Unit blazoned on its side.

Curious, he'd parked up the street and waited until it was evident that cop wasn't going anywhere else.

Hell. She'd hooked up with a guy—fast work, he thought—and worse, she'd hooked up with a cop. A freaking cop.

Anger shook him to his core, and he cleared out of town before he blew his stack. Pounding on a steering wheel and cussing loudly would only have drawn unwanted attention.

It wasn't long, though, before he regained his self-control and came back to town. Rage was a tool to be used, not something he should ever let control him. He knew that.

He kept watch from a safe distance. And what he'd seen had both given him ideas and frustrated him more.

The cop never left her side. When they came out of her house in the late morning, it was together and with a dog. Probably the cop's K-9, although he had to wonder why Dory was holding the leash.

He also had to admire his sister. She'd been a cute kid, everyone said so, but she'd grown into a stunning woman. Too bad he had to get rid of her. If he'd thought he could have talked her into working with him, she'd have been a great asset. But from everything he could tell about her—which wasn't a whole lot—she had chosen to live on the right side of the law.

What a waste.

He watched them drive out of town toward the mountains and hung a safe distance back. If he lost them…well, there was always tomorrow.

He trailed behind, but not so far he didn't see them turn in to a ranch. He kept going for another couple of miles and then headed back. In the distance, near a two-story white house, the cop's vehicle was still parked. It must be his place.

Ideas were beginning to swim again. Once he was sure the two of them were safely tucked in for the night at her place, he was going to come back out here and see what kind of opportunity he could create.

Because opportunities were always there, just waiting for a clear enough eye to see them.

He'd waited a long time to put an end to Dory and get what he truly deserved. He could wait a little longer.

"I've got work in the morning," Cadell told her later that night. Lovemaking had once again left her feeling limp and good all over. She wondered if she had been missing something all these years or if she had been missing Cadell.

She rolled lazily toward him. "No one's ever made me feel this wonderful."

He turned his head on the pillow and gave her a smile. "Now that's a great thing to hear."

"Truth."

He stirred until he was on his side, too, and draped his arm over her waist. He lifted it briefly to brush a strand of her blond hair back from her face. "Truth," he agreed. "You make me feel wonderful, too."

She sighed happily and buried her face in his shoulder.

"Work in the morning," he said again.

"I heard," she mumbled.

"Are you going to be okay?"

"I've got my work, too."

"You know I wasn't referring to that."

She did, but she didn't want to think about it. "Let's not ruin this by thinking about tomorrow. If I get uneasy, I'll run over to Betty's, okay? But don't forget, I have Flash. I wouldn't want to argue with him."

"He *does* have a lot of teeth," Cadell said, allowing the mood to lighten.

But she felt the concern in him and knew he was right. Until George was dealt with somehow, there *was* a threat. She sought a way to reassure him. "You know, I'm not exactly in the middle of nowhere. It'll be daytime, people are around, I'll have Flash, and if I scream for help, I think someone will call for it."

"You're right," he admitted. "Everyone around here would call for help and probably come running, too."

"So I'll be fine. But if you're worried about it, I'll go to Betty's."

After a moment he shook his head. "You have to work, too."

"What are you doing?"

"I've got patrol duty. I don't just train the dogs, you know." He tightened his hold on her, and she snuggled closer. "Four hours. I'll be back in four hours."

"Okay." But she didn't feel okay. Long after she felt his breathing deepen and steady, she stared into the dark and shared her mind and heart with a little girl who was still traumatized.

She doubted any number of years would entirely get her past that. It was better now, much better, even if George's release had awakened long-buried fears. But that little girl? Sometimes she needed attention, too.

Before Cadell left in the morning, he suggested she drive out to his place. He could meet her there shortly after noon, but he needed to check on the animals again. Maybe work with them some.

She was happy to agree. Plenty of time to work, a nice afternoon break, and then some more work this evening. Or something else, she thought with a private smile. Something else with Cadell had become the high point of her days.

Maybe a dangerous place to go, but she was going anyway. It kept hitting her that life as a hermit might provide safety, but it sure hadn't given her a lot of good times. Not good times like Cadell gave her. However long it lasted, she wanted as much as he'd give her.

She spent a little time with her eyes closed, remembering last night, remembering Cadell's smile, thinking about the way he looked striding around his ranch. Incredibly male, yet incredibly kind. She wasn't used to men who were so kind. Heck, she worked with kind men, but she didn't allow them to know she was a woman. Women weren't welcome in the men's world of computers. Although maybe she wasn't being fair to the guys she worked with.

Then she laughed. For all she knew, some of them might be women, too.

Sometime later as she was finishing up her work, she ran into a mental hitch and couldn't quite get her finger on it. Something was wrong.

Sighing, she heard an answering sigh and looked over to see Flash, his head on the floor, looking up at her as if to say, "Have you forgotten I need exercise?"

"Okay," she said. "We'll go for a run." It would clear her head about work and allow her a good excuse to let her mind wander over Cadell and all his attractive attributes. He made her body sing, true. But he was bringing long-cold parts of her back to warmth and light.

It was probably going to hurt, but right now she didn't care. She was willing to take whatever this slice of life offered her and pay the cost later.

She knew all about costs. And she knew she could survive them.

George watched her come out of the house with that dog of hers. He'd learned a little about her boyfriend last night when he'd explored the guy's ranch. Dog trainer? K-9s? Cop dogs? He looked at the dog trotting beside Dory on a leash and suspected it had been trained by that man. An extra wrinkle, but one he could deal with.

What he'd found at the ranch was the perfect way to get rid of Dory and keep himself out of it. Ostriches had a kick worse than a boxer's punch. All he had to do was get Dory in with them and then stir them up. That'd look like an accident, especially since he planned to break the lock on the pen when it was over. At worst it would look like she'd been trying to round them up after the lock failed.

But nobody would think they'd been used as a murder weapon. And thanks to the electric fencing, she wouldn't be able to climb out.

Man, sometimes his own brilliance blinded him.

Cadell spent his morning missing Dory. Not a good sign. He'd vowed a long time ago not to get into another deep relationship, and here he was violating his own oath. Dory wasn't the best bet, either. He doubted she fully trusted him, and that meant he'd be wise not to trust her completely, either.

Nor could he be sure she wouldn't just pack up and leave. She'd been avoiding real human contact for a long time and had said as much. She preferred being a hermit. This was an interlude for her, a bit of entertainment by helping him with his dogs, a change of pace. But soon she'd probably feel it was interfering with her work, and she'd want to crawl back into her safe emotional cave. Especially if they couldn't somehow put the issue of George to rest for good.

He sighed and prowled the roads, filling in for Carter Birch, whose wife had just had a baby. He hated patrolling. Yeah, he'd done thousands of miles of it over the years, but back in Seattle at least he was likely to see something or do something, even if it was only writing a traffic ticket. Out here on the prairie and the foot of the mountains, there was almost nothing to do unless he got a call.

It was important, of course. If a call came, the idea was that a patrol wouldn't be too far away. Distance could cost a life in an emergency. But he vastly preferred training the dogs and K-9 officers, and he often wondered just how he could expand his business so it would become full-time.

Again his thoughts trailed back to Dory, and he glanced at his watch. Another hour, then he could start heading toward his place to meet her. Another hour.

He pulled over to the side of the road and poured himself a cup of coffee from the thermos bottle he'd had Maude fill for him that morning. Still hot, still good.

He scanned the wide-open spaces that led up the mountains. A beautiful summer day easing slowly into autumn. The air was dry, the breeze steady.

And he wished he could ignore the sense that Dory needed him. She was fine. She had Flash, she was at work, she'd have called if she needed help and the department would have called him.

Everything was fine.

So why couldn't he believe it?

Chapter 13

Dory figured she could give Flash a good thirty-minute run before she'd need to shower and head out to Cadell's ranch. She was eagerly looking forward to seeing him again, and not all her good reasons for avoiding those feelings would get rid of that.

Oh, well, she thought as she ran down the sidewalk, her jogging shoes slapping on pavement. She passed a couple in their front yard, and they exchanged waves and smiles. Maybe getting out of her shell wasn't so bad.

Her run took her to the edge of town, where a vacant lot with a brook running through it covered several acres. Tall trees grew there, and she loved the way they dappled the light. No houses were nearby, but that was okay. She had Flash.

When she reached the end of the trees, she sometimes paused to watch the brook, but today she didn't have time. "No stops today, Flash," she told him. He didn't appear to mind. Tongue lolling, he was galloping along happily at her side.

A truck pulled up, and she barely spared it a glance until a voice called to her, chilling her to her bones.

"Dory? Get in."

Turning, ice running through her veins, she saw a gun pointed at her. Then she saw the man behind it, leaning out of a battered red truck. George. *Oh, my God, George.*

"Make that dog behave or he gets the first bullet."

Neck stiff, she looked down at Flash. He was at full attention, his gaze fixed on George and the gun. Cadell had said he would recognize a threat when he saw it.

"I'm warning you, Dory. You think I won't kill that dog?"

She never doubted it. But there was only one way to take Flash off guard. Shoving her hand into her pocket, she pulled out a tennis ball.

His entire demeanor changed. His tail wagged, and for an instant she thought he was going to get down and gnaw the ball. But instead he dropped it and lowered his head as he stared at George.

"Okay, then," George said. "Bring him a few steps closer."

"No."

"I won't shoot him unless you don't do what I say. Get him closer."

Step by agonizing step, she approached, feeling Flash start to pull at the leash. He wanted to go after George.

But when they stood a few feet away, the barrel of

that gun still leveled at her, George thrust the truck door open and stuck out a yellow pole. What the…

Then she heard the sizzle and Flash's yelp. He fell to the ground, jerking.

"More than one way to deal with you and that dog. Now get your behind into this truck."

She dropped the leash, looking down at Flash, relieved to see he was still breathing. It was the last relief she was able to feel.

Then, almost numb, past fear, she climbed into the passenger side of the truck. He kept the pistol aimed at her every second.

"I'll give you money," she said stiffly as he shoved the truck into gear.

"You bet your sweet butt you will. Now shut up or I'll use that prod on you."

Cadell got a radio call just before he was scheduled to get off duty. It was the sheriff, Gage Dalton.

"We've got Dory Lake's dog here. He's fine, but Dory's missing. Not at her house. I've put out a countywide alert."

Just as Gage finished speaking, the alert popped up on Cadell's mobile unit, along with the rendered photo of a bearded George Lake.

Cadell jammed on the brakes, closed his eyes and gripped the steering wheel so hard his hands cramped. He didn't need to know the odds against finding someone in all these hundreds of square miles of open space.

"We're doing a door to door," Gage said. "Meantime, we've started the phone tree with the ranches. Get yourself home, Cadell."

"Home? What the hell can I do there?"

"Get us a bunch of search dogs."

The old pickup rattled down roads that Dory recognized. A smidgen of hope awoke in her. Either she'd be able to talk her brother into taking money, or she'd find another way to deal with him. Because when they turned in to Cadell's ranch, it was well-known territory to her. She guessed that Cadell would be there in about an hour, as he'd planned…as long as the job didn't delay him. But she refused to consider that possibility. He'd come and he'd come on time. She just had to make it for one hour. Surely she could do that.

"I never did anything to you," she said trying to make herself sound small, almost childlike.

"You should have stayed in bed."

"I wish I had." She closed her eyes briefly. "I wish I'd never seen. But I never did anything to *you*."

"You took away my escape time. You ran screaming out onto the street. I thought you loved me."

"I did."

"Then why did you run, Dory. Why?"

She shook her head a little, watching Cadell's house grow closer. Soon she could see the ostriches. Dog pens out back. If she could manage to let the dogs out somehow…

Why was he bringing her here, of all places?

"I ran because I was terrified. George… I didn't even understand what I was seeing! For more than a year I could only speak two words, *red paint*. That's all I could compare it to."

He said nothing more. She struggled to think about how she could distract him. Thought of Flash and hoped he would be okay, because her poor dog hadn't done anything to deserve that shock.

And mile by mile, she had felt her fear of George transforming into hatred. Then she remembered what Cadell had said about George being her only heir.

Her heart slammed, and she realized for absolute certain, all the way to her very core, that she was not going to survive this. Far from weakening her, the knowledge pumped strength into her. If she was going to die, she wasn't going to make it easy.

"You know," she said, watching the house grow closer, "I didn't take the inheritance away from you. The court did. You can have it all if you want. I'll turn it over to you." A lie, but he wouldn't know that.

"A little late, don't you think? Twenty-five years in prison. I need to even the score more than that. Anyway, my lawyer told me that it's in a trust you can't break. You couldn't pay me enough to leave you alone now."

Her hands clenched. "I didn't put you in prison, George. I didn't testify. Hell, I couldn't even tell anyone what had happened. Conversion disorder, they called it. For more than a year I only spoke two words, and for over three months I was blind."

That caught his attention as the house rolled closer. "Blind, huh?"

"Blind," she said. "I didn't even understand what had happened. I couldn't. I had nightmares, though. Plenty of nightmares."

"You should have stayed in bed," he said again. But this time his voice was stony cold. Whatever charm he exerted on the rest of the world, he wasn't going to waste any on her. Not anymore.

They pulled up to one side of the house. The familiarity of the scene jarred Dory, contrasting as it did with George's abduction of her. This was a place where she'd always found peace and welcome. Just having George here seemed to shatter all that.

"Dory."

Reluctantly she looked at her brother. The gun was pointing at her again.

"Get out."

"Just shoot me here." Yeah, the anger was growing huge, and a mental voice warned her to rein it in. Now was not the time to stop thinking. But oh, the things she wanted to do to George right now would get her thrown in prison herself. Flash popped into her mind's eye, and a little crack broke through the anger. Her beloved Flash. This man had taken everything from her. Her parents. Her childhood. Her trust. Now even her dog.

Oh, yeah, she wanted him to pay. He hadn't paid nearly enough.

But she had to be smart, await her chance. Right now all she'd get for her efforts was a gunshot wound. So she climbed out of the truck, scanning the area, looking for anything she could use.

Curious, the ostriches watched them with those inscrutable dark eyes, but they had backed up in their pen, getting as far away as they could, unlike when Cadell showed up.

"Ostriches seem like a weird thing to have out here," George remarked.

Dory didn't answer, still trying to figure out what she could do. If she ran toward the kennels to let the dogs out, he'd probably put a bullet in her back before she got halfway around the house.

"I like those birds," her brother continued conversationally. "Big, beautiful and scaredy-cats."

She glanced at him, wondering how he could know that. But clearly he'd been out here before. When? Last night?

He motioned with the gun. "Let's go get a closer look at those birds. I hear their feathers are worth a fortune."

Was he going to kill the birds and steal their feathers? But then she realized he was still carrying that long yellow stick, the one that had zapped Flash. What the hell was he up to?

As they drew closer to the cage, the birds pulled back to the farthest side, then hunkered down, making themselves as small as possible. They didn't seem to like the strangers. Or at least George.

"That's how they protect themselves," George remarked. "They either try to become invisible or they run. Did you know they can run nearly forty miles an hour? Only a cheetah can catch one."

She wondered why the hell he was talking about this and taking her ever closer to the pen. Maybe he had gone crazy. This was making no sense.

"Now here's the deal," George said when they reached the pen, watched by suspicious birds. "You can either go into that pen with them, or I'll zap you with this prod and put you in there myself."

Dory's heart nearly stopped. For a few seconds, her anger drained completely, leaving her filled with terror. Her knees weakened, and the urge to run nearly overwhelmed her. A sane voice in her head shouted it would do no good to run. She needed to buy time. She stiffened inwardly, feeling a crazy rush of strength.

One thing became clear to her: if she was going to be in the pen with those birds, she didn't want to be para-lyzed for even a few minutes. No way.

She couldn't scale the wire fence because it was electrified at the top, but maybe she could soothe the birds, keep them from getting too agitated. Just be-come small and inoffensive, she told herself. Maybe they'd leave her alone.

Her mouth turned dry, but she ignored it. Her hands moistened, making it difficult to work the latch. The birds remained hunkered down, watching.

And all the while, she wondered at the point of this. Was he going to shoot her inside the pen with the birds? What good would that do? Why not just leave her corpse somewhere along the roadside?

Eventually, with fumbling fingers, she opened the latch. The gate dragged on the ground as she pulled it open then slid inside, moving very slowly. Behind her, she heard George latch it once again. Then she heard an unmistakable *snick*. He'd added a padlock. From in-side this pen, she didn't think it was possible to open the other gate into the corral. Whenever Cadell did it, he opened it with a mechanism on the outside.

She was breathing too heavily, in danger of becom-ing light-headed. She couldn't afford to faint again. Not now. So far the birds had offered no protest at her presence but stayed hunkered down.

Maybe she should imitate them. Slowly, she low-ered herself to the ground, wrapping her arms around her knees.

"What do you want, George?" she asked, keeping her voice steady, beginning to hope that the birds would remain calm. God, she knew how huge they were, and she didn't like being in here with them, with those enormous feet. They didn't have talons like ordinary birds, but they each had one toe that grew a nail so large it looked like a weapon.

Anger toward George was surging again, erasing her fear, making her scan the enclosure for just one item she could use to get out of here, or to attack George once he'd finished enjoying torturing her.

The birds, though. She just couldn't figure out why he wanted her in here with the birds.

Then he told her. "I left out one interesting fact about these birds, dear sister. They have a powerful kick. If they can't run and feel threatened, they kick with enough power to break bones."

She caught her breath. If anyone could think of something like this...her brother had. But how could he make that happen?

And then she saw. Walking around the pen, he poked his rod through the wire, and she heard the snap and sizzle. One of the birds screamed and rose to its full height.

For the first time, anger began to give way to despair. Those birds had nowhere to run. If he kept torturing them...

She closed her eyes. Cadell should be here soon, she thought. The only question was whether he'd arrive before she was kicked to death by frantic, tortured ostriches. She desperately hoped nothing would delay him.

Cadell raced so fast over the back roads that when he hit a rut, he literally went airborne, killing the suspension. He didn't care. As long as he didn't break an axle.

Dory was missing. Her worst nightmare had come true. Only now did he realize it was his own worst nightmare, as well.

He keyed his radio. "Nobody saw a thing?"

"Not a thing," answered Gage. "One of Jake's city cops saw the dog trailing its leash back toward her house. He recognized Flash immediately. That's all we know."

There was hope in that, Cadell tried to tell himself. At least George hadn't killed the dog. Maybe all he wanted from Dory was money, after all.

He wished he believed it.

Dasher whimpered from the backseat, voicing a protest at the rough ride. Cadell couldn't bring himself to slow down. The dog would be fine. His crate was belted in and not so big that that he was being thrown all over the back.

He pounded his fist against the steering wheel. How in hell were they going to find one woman who could be anywhere in these vast, open spaces? Hope a ranch hand came upon her before it was too late? Even with the phone tree operating, there was no way the folks on these huge ranches could check every acre. They'd have to catch sight of something by sheer chance.

No, all the phone tree would do was serve notice to be watching for anything unusual. Better than nothing, but not by much.

Then he heard the *whop* of helicopter blades pass over. So they'd taken to the air, as well. That might help. Maybe. But you couldn't tell who was driving a car from above.

Then, when he was ten minutes away from his place, **the radio crackled. "Cadell? You read?"**

"I read."

"There's a truck parked beside your house. An old red pickup. Anyone you know?"

"Damn it, no!" He floored the vehicle even more, hardly hearing the call for units to head toward his ranch.

Lying on the ground curled up with her arms over her head, Dory awaited the blow that might kill her. Except that things weren't going according to George's plan. The ostriches were growing increasingly frantic, but they didn't seem to regard the small ball of human at their feet as a threat. Or anything they even wanted to step on. When she dared to open her eyes, she saw those ostrich feet racing around, coming close, but never striking her.

She heard George cussing, heard the awful sound and smelled the terrible smell of singed feathers every time he prodded one of those poor ostriches. She just wished she had a gun so she could put an end to this. So she could save those birds from more terror and pain.

But she didn't have a weapon and didn't dare move.

Then, wonder of wonders, she heard helicopter rotors overhead. She desperately wanted to look but didn't chance it. She heard George start cussing even more viciously, though. Soon the rotors passed on into the distance.

The cops? Had the cops already discovered she was missing?

Oh, God, please let help come soon. Those birds couldn't take much more, and she hated feeling so helpless to put a stop to George's hatefulness.

George spoke, his voice tight with fury. "I'll get you later, *sis.*"

Then the truck engine started. Risking a kick, she lifted her head a little and saw George taking off. It must have been the cops.

She waited, hoping the birds would settle soon. As they began to quiet, she eased herself into a sitting position and looked at them. Each was pecking at its own feathers, as if to remove the singed ones. And neither of them showed the least interest in her.

Cadell wheeled into his driveway, nearly losing his traction on the gravel and headed straight up it. One lane, a ditch to either side, invisible beneath the cut grasses. No place for anyone to go.

Then he saw the red truck bearing down on him. It, too, appeared to be moving at top speed. Cadell gripped the wheel tighter, his mind made up. He was not going into the ditch. Either that so-and-so would swerve or they were going to meet head-on. He had not the least difficulty imagining who would get the worst of a head-on, and it wasn't going to be his official vehicle with the heavy-duty front bumper, strengthened frame and roll bar.

He had one moment when hesitation pierced him. One moment when terror rose as he realized that Dory could be in that truck. But as it came closer, he could see only one head.

His heart and chest tightened. She might already be dead. Well, if so, she was about to get some company, because for the first time in his life Cadell wanted to commit murder. It was an ugly feeling; he hated it even as it rose in him. But he didn't let go of it.

George had already hurt Dory in ways she'd never recover from. If he'd killed her… Well, he was going to join her. He wasn't fit to share the air with another living soul.

George came charging on, sure the cop would swerve. But he didn't. There was no place to go except to drive around him. It was mowed flat on either side of the road, dry grasses waving. At the last second, he wrenched the wheel, expecting to bypass the oncoming vehicle.

Except those evenly mowed grasses concealed a ditch.

He jolted to a stop so hard his face hit the steering wheel. Searing pain erupted in his chest, but he ignored it. He pushed the door of the truck open and slid out, scrambling up the ditch and heading for the distant trees. He'd always been a fast runner. He could outrun some cop who lived on doughnuts and coffee.

"Police dog," shouted a male voice. "Stop or he'll bite you."

He kept running, ignoring the command, then he heard a word that made no sense.

"Foos!"

He didn't dare look back. He fixed his gaze on those trees and kept pumping his legs and arms, ignoring the pain in his chest.

Cadell watched Dasher take off after the guy. Off lead, as fast as he could run. Cadell paused to look into the red truck. No Dory.

He stared toward the dog chasing the man and knew

he had to go after them. The guy might shoot the dog. His partner. Some things a cop couldn't do.

But he called the news in as he began to run and was assured cops were converging at his place, with a chopper standing by if needed. They'd find Dory. He had to finish his job.

The sirens blared behind him. Then, to his great pleasure, other K-9s on the hunt fell into line behind Dasher. That meant not far behind them came their handlers.

George didn't stand a chance.

Back at the ranch, however, perplexity had set in. Several deputies stood around the ostrich pen, and they might as well have scratched their heads.

"I'm fine," Dory said, now sitting upright, legs tucked. "They didn't hurt me. But they're scared because that guy kept poking them with an electric prod. Just back away. Cadell will know what to do when he gets here."

"It might be a while, ma'am," answered one. "He was last seen running with his K-9 after the guy who abandoned the red truck."

For the first time since early morning, Dory felt like smiling. "He is, is he? I hope Dasher shreds my brother. What about my dog, Flash? He got shocked, too."

"The one that was found in town?"

"Probably."

At that the deputy smiled. "He's fine. The vet's going to look him over, but other than refusing to leave your house, he's okay."

Dory breathed a huge sigh of relief, then felt a warmth in her heart. For Flash. For Cadell. Imagine the dog not wanting to leave her house. "Couldn't coax him away?"

"Not from what I heard. He snapped at anyone who tried."

"He's had a tough morning."

"Seems like he's not the only one," the deputy answered.

No, she thought, letting her head fall back against the ground. No, indeed. All she knew was Cadell had better come back here safe and sound, or she was going to do something she might regret for the rest of her life.

George didn't get far into the woods. Dasher bit him on the forearm and hung on, even after George collapsed. Cadell caught up to find his dog holding George's arm like a stuffed toy, which he wouldn't release until Cadell told him to. Cadell pulled his service pistol, took a bead on George and told Dasher to release him. Not that George had much fight left in him. He was having trouble breathing, panting hard.

So instead of the pleasure of putting him in handcuffs, Cadell had to settle for allowing medevac to take him to the hospital. "Cuff him to the gurney," he told the medics. They promised, accepting a set of flex cuffs from him.

Then he and Dasher headed the rest of the way up his private road and found an almost fantastical scene. Under other circumstances he might have laughed.

But there was only one thing he wanted to know. He trotted up to the pen. "Dory? Are you okay?"

She smiled up at him from where she sat inside the ostrich pen. "I'm fine, but my new friends are going to need to see the doc. I don't know how many times George shocked them."

Then, to his utter amazement, one of those orncry birds craned its neck downward and nuzzled Dory gently.

Well, at least one of them had good taste.

"So," she asked, "do you think you can get me out of here?"

He got her out of the pen with surprisingly little trouble. The birds settled down in their hiding positions, which made him worry. Usually they seemed to take great delight in regarding him balefully from above. He hoped George hadn't hurt them beyond repair.

Though Dory claimed she was quite all right, the paramedics insisted on examining her for shock. When she seemed okay, they warned Cadell to keep an eye on her.

"It could hit at any time," Jess McGregor said. "If it does, bring her in to the clinic or the ER." Then he limped on his artificial leg around to the front of the truck.

Dory didn't want to leave until Mike Windwalker arrived to check the ostriches. Cadell didn't argue with her, although the thing he most wanted to do was get her home and check her out from head to foot. He couldn't believe she had come through this unscathed.

But for the moment all she wanted to talk about was the ostriches, how they'd avoided hurting her even when George was torturing them. She took clear delight in the fact that Dasher had locked onto George's arm and that her brother had been taken cuffed to the hospital. "I hope he has more than a bite," she said.

Cadell almost smiled. "I'm sure he has more. He crashed his truck in the ditch, and when I got to him he was having trouble breathing. I'm betting broken ribs."

"Good. I hear those hurt."

"Like hell," he agreed.

He watched her with appreciation and amazement. The woman he'd first met had seemed pinched, locked inside herself, stalked by fear. Gradually she'd been emerging from her inner prison, at least with him, but right now she seemed to have busted the doors wide-open. The closest she'd ever come to this much happy animation had been in bed with him. Now she was showering the world with it.

He hoped, for her sake, it lasted. It could begin a whole new chapter in her life.

As he drove her home finally, she grew a bit quieter. He could sense her eagerness to see Flash. Mike Windwalker had said he had a bit of singed fur but no burns. She was still on edge about it, though, which he could understand.

But he was growing increasingly edgy himself. This morning, as he'd raced heedlessly over dangerous roads at unsafe speeds, he'd realized he wanted Dory Lake in his life from now on.

All the flags he'd planted after Brenda—warning flags telling him to avoid long-term relationships with women—had become meaningless. Just like that. Unfortunately, you could waste years trying to avoid getting kicked in the gut until you awoke one morning and found yourself utterly vulnerable.

So he was about to get gut punched again. Because

now that George would be going to prison for a good long time again, she could pick up the threads of her old life, and he couldn't imagine why in the world she might want to stay here.

If she was emerging from her private hermitage, surely she'd want to test her wings, taste the world she'd been avoiding. Hell, she hadn't even really dated, from what he could tell. Wouldn't she want to do some sampling? Look for a life in a city with more action? Dang, she'd been in prison as long as her brother had.

And she'd only come here because she thought she could hide and she knew Betty. She'd be crazy not to look for something better.

The signs were all around anyway. She'd set up her office, but she was still using a rickety dining table in her kitchen. She hadn't prettied up even a single corner of the place by hanging a picture. Leaving almost no mark that she had been there.

So, she was planning to move on quickly. Nothing was permanent, not even the high-speed internet she'd had installed, and that was a cord that could be severed with a phone call.

Of course, he had only himself to blame. The flags had been there from the beginning. He should have known better than to break his own rule. Women couldn't be trusted to stay. Brenda had proved that.

When they got to her house, Flash was still on the porch waiting. Someone had put a bowl of water out for him, but he was concerned about only one thing.

When Dory climbed out of the SUV, Flash dashed toward her, forgot all his training and jumped up on her, knocking her to the patchy front lawn.

Cadell listened to her giggle as Flash licked her

face, and he smiled faintly, poised to leave. She didn't need him anymore.

But then she freed herself from Flash's attentions and jumped to her feet. "Come on in," she said to Cadell. "I don't know about you, but I could really use some coffee."

He hesitated. "I was just about to go."

She froze. "Why?"

"You must have stuff you want to do."

"Stuff?" She tilted her head. "Okay, then. You're on my list of stuff. Come inside."

He took his usual place at the rickety kitchen table while she fed Flash, then started the coffee.

Then she faced him. "So tell me something, Deputy Marcus. Was I just a job to you?"

He felt almost sickened by the question. "What?" He didn't want to believe she'd just said that.

"All the nights you spent here. Was that just protection, like Flash? You said you were a protector. Was that all I was? A job?"

Her words punched him. "No," he said hoarsely.

"Then why are you in such a hurry to leave?"

His self-control was usually pretty good, but after the stressors of that day, it had frayed. The words burst from him, almost angrily. "Because you're getting ready to leave now that George is no longer a threat."

She frowned. "Did I say that? I don't remember ever saying that."

"Well, why the hell would you want to stay here?"

Her face changed, and he thought he detected a flicker of the fear that had once been there so often. When she spoke, her voice was small. "You?"

Astonishment gripped him. Before he could respond, she'd turned her back to him, reaching for mugs.

"I realize," she said, "that you don't want another woman in your life. I get it. Brenda must have been the witch of all witches. Anyway, maybe you're done with me. Maybe I was just a job to you. Regardless, I'm not leaving. I don't want to leave. I want joint custody."

Now he was confused. "Joint custody of what?"

"Itsy and Bitsy."

That did it. Circuitous as she was being, he got it. Being willfully dense would serve nothing. He shoved the chair back so hard it tipped over.

She whirled, startled by the sound, and he was amazed to see tears rolling down her cheeks.

"Those ostriches," he said firmly, "don't come without *me.*"

She wiped the tears away with her sleeve, but her smile still hadn't appeared. "You'd better mean that."

"I never meant anything more in my life. We're a package, me and those birds. Take it or leave it."

The smile began to peek out. "I'll take it," she said quietly.

He grabbed her then, forgetting finesse, drawing her into a hug so tight she squeaked. "You take it, you can't leave it."

"I couldn't possibly leave those birds," she said shakily.

He closed his eyes, pressed his lips to her hair and muttered, "So I have to keep them?"

"If you want me."

"I guess I'm stuck with them. Because I love you."

She threw her arms around his neck, and he felt his uniform shirt dampen with her warm tears. "I love

you, too, Cadell. I want you, the dogs, the ostriches…
I want it all."

"Babies?"

Her head tipped back. "Babies," she agreed firmly.
"But you get joint custody."

Finally he laughed. It was the most joyous sound
that had escaped him in a long time. "I'll help with
it all."

She pressed her lips to his, giving him a salty kiss.
"Forever."

"Forever," he repeated. "Forever."

* * * * *

Jen Delaney loved Bent, Wyoming, the town she'd been born in, grown up in. She was a respected member of the community, in part because she ran the only store that sold groceries and other essentials within a twenty-mile radius of town.

From her position crouched on the linoleum while she stocked shelves, she looked around the small store she'd taken over at the ripe age of eighteen. For the past ten years it had been her baby, with its narrow aisles and hodgepodge of necessities.

She'd always known she'd spend the entirety of her life happily ensconced in Bent and her store, no matter what happened around her.

The reappearance of Ty Carson didn't change that knowledge so much as make it…annoying. No, annoying would have been just his being in town again. The fact their families had somehow intermingled in the last year was…a catastrophe.

Her sister, Laurel, marrying Ty's cousin Grady had been a shock, very close to a betrayal, though it was hard to hold it against Laurel when Grady was so head over heels for her it was comical. They both glowed with love and happiness and impending parenthood.

Jen tried not to hate them for it.

She could forgive Cam, her eldest brother, for his serious relationship with Hilly. Hilly was biologically a Carson, but she'd only just found that out. Besides, Hilly wasn't like other Carsons. She was so sweet and earnest.

But Dylan and Vanessa… Her business-minded, sophisticated older brother *impregnating* and marrying snarky bad girl Vanessa Carson… *That* was a nightmare.

And none of it was fair. Jen was now, out of nowhere, surrounded by Carsons and Delaneys intermingling—which went against everything Bent had ever stood for. Carsons and Delaneys hated each other. They didn't fall in love and get married and have *babies*.

And still, she could have handled all that in a certain amount of stride if it weren't for *Ty* Carson. Everywhere she turned he seemed to be right there, his stoic gaze always locked on *her*, reminding her of a past she'd spent a lot of time trying to bury and forget.

When she'd been seventeen and the stupidest girl alive, she would have done anything for Ty Carson. Risked the Delaney-Carson curse that, even with all these Carson-Delaney marriages, Bent still had their heart set on. She would have risked her father's wrath over daring to connect herself with a *Carson*. She would have given up anything and everything for Ty.

Instead he'd made promises to love her forever, then disappeared to join the army—which she'd found out only a good month after the fact. He hadn't just broken her heart—he'd crushed it to bits.

But Ty was a blip of her past she'd been able to forget about, mostly, for the past ten years. She'd accepted his choices and moved on with her life. For a decade she had grown into the adult who didn't care at all about Ty Carson.

Then Ty had come home for good, and all she'd convinced herself of faded away.

She was half convinced he'd returned simply to make her miserable.

"You look angry. Must be thinking about me."

Don't miss
Wyoming Cowboy Ranger *by Nicole Helm,*
available June 2019 wherever
Harlequin® Intrigue books and ebooks are sold.

www.Harlequin.com

HIEXP0519

Eva Kendall slowed her pace as she approached the
training facility where she worked training guide dogs.

Using her key, she entered the training center, thinking
about the male chocolate Lab named Cocoa that she would
work with this morning. Cocoa was a ten-week-old puppy
born to Stella, a gift from the Czech Republic to the NYC
K-9 Command Unit located in Queens. Most of Stella's
pups were being trained as police dogs, but not Cocoa.
In less than a month after basic puppy training, Cocoa
would be able to go home with Eva to be fostered during
his initial first-year training to become a full-fledged guide
dog. Once that year passed, guide dogs like Cocoa would
return to the center to train with their new owners.

A few steps into the building, Eva frowned at the loud
thumps interspersed between a cacophony of barking. The
raucous noise from the various canines contained a level
of panic and fear rather than excitement.

Concerned, she moved quickly through the dimly lit training center to the back hallway, where the kennels were located. Normally she was the first one in every morning, but maybe one of the other trainers had gotten an early start.

Rounding the corner, she paused in the doorway when she saw a tall, heavyset stranger scooping Cocoa out of his kennel. Panic squeezed her chest. "Hey! What are you doing?"

The ferocious barking increased in volume, echoing off the walls and ceiling. The stranger must have heard her. He turned to look at her, then roughly tucked Cocoa under his arm like a football.

"No! Stop!" Panicked, Eva charged toward the man, desperately wishing she had a weapon of some sort.

"Get out of my way," he said in a guttural voice.

"No. Put that puppy down right now!" Eva stopped and stood her ground.

"Last chance," he taunted, coming closer.

Don't miss
Blind Trust *by Laura Scott,*
available June 2019 wherever
Love Inspired® *Suspense books and ebooks are sold.*

www.LoveInspired.com